D0920980

WYATT EARP
FRONTIER MARSHAL

Stuart N. Lake

POCKET BOOKS

New York   London   Toronto   Sydney   Tokyo   Singapore

In acknowledgment to
WYATT BERRY STAPP EARP
who lived and relived
this book

 POCKET BOOKS, a division of Simon & Schuster Inc.
1230 Avenue of the Americas, New York, NY 10020

Copyright © 1931 by Stuart N. Lake
Introduction copyright © 1994 by Loren D. Estleman

Published by arrangement with Houghton Mifflin.

ISBN: 0-671-88537-5

First Pocket Books printing July 1994

10 9 8 7 6

POCKET and colophon are registered trademarks of
Simon & Schuster Inc.

Cover art by Electronic Photo-Imaging

Printed in the U.S.A.

CONTENTS

Contents

FOREWORD

Wyatt Earp was a man of action. He was born, reared, and lived in an environment which held words and theories of small account, in which sheer survival often, and eminence invariably, might be achieved through deeds alone. Withal, Wyatt Earp was a thinking man, whose mental processes were as quick, as direct, as unflustered by circumstance and as effective as the actions they inspired.

The man won from contemporaries who were his most competent judges—from intimates, from acquaintances, and from enemies, alike—frontier-wide recognition as the most proficient peace officer, the greatest gunfighting marshal that the Old West knew. He attained this eminence through the only method his time and place might comprehend. Wherefore, this narrative of Wyatt Earp's career, this account of his rise to forty-five-caliber dominance over cowtown and mining camp in the Red Decade of the Southwest, is set forth largely in terms of what Wyatt Earp did.

To the lover of swift and decisive action, Wyatt Earp's achievements surely must be of interest in themselves. His taming of Mannen Clements and fifty cowboy killers in the streets of Wichita; his play against Clay Allison of the Washita in the Plaza at Dodge City; his protection of insignificant Johnny-Behind-the-Deuce against a Tombstone mob; the sanguinary battle of the O. K. Corral, possibly the most celebrated gunfight in frontier history; or his sawed-off shotgun duel with Curly Bill—tales of these exploits could not fail, even were they meaningless, to stir a reader's blood. Through them Wyatt Earp moves steadily, surely, sagaciously, implacably on, guided by a philosophy fitted to his surroundings, to which he gave fullest expression in admonishment of Ike Clanton, braggart outlaw, cow thief, and murderer.

"Go on home, Ike," Wyatt suggested in the face of Clanton's threats to gun the marshal; "you talk too much for a fighting man."

In themselves these things that Wyatt Earp did made him a myth of his own era, a legend while he lived, in the mouth-to-mouth sagas of the West. But the judgment of the years has awarded a higher honor to the man. He no longer stands simply an unbelievably courageous figure distinguished by fabulous feats of arms and an extraordinary domination over men. In true perspective he is recognized as something more, as an epitomizing symbol of a powerful factor—an economic factor, if you will—all-important in the history of the Western United States of America. The Old West cannot be understood unless Wyatt Earp also is understood. More than any other man of record in his time, possibly, he represents the exact combination of breeding and human experience which laid the foundations of Western empire. His genius is less an accident than an inevitable expression; Wyatt Earp is less an effect than a cause.

Since Wyatt Earp has so long been a myth to lovers of the Old West, it is no more than fair to state definitely that this biography is in no part a mythic tale. It would be less than fair to subject and to reader if any least resource of effort had been spared in seeking the utmost accuracy of fact. Scores of eyewitnesses to the scenes portrayed have been interviewed to verify circumstantial details; thousands of miles have been traveled to unearth substantiating material;

hundreds of time-worn documents and files of frontier newspapers have been examined for pertinent content; literally thousands of letters have been exchanged with competent old-timers in developing this work.

The book had inception in an observation by Bat Masterson, more than twenty years ago.

"The real story of the Old West can never be told," Bat said, "unless Wyatt Earp will tell what he knows; and Wyatt will not talk."

Happily, time and circumstance combined to bring Masterson's foreboding to naught, and Wyatt Earp was persuaded to devote the closing months of his long life to the narration of his full story, to a firsthand and a factual account of his career. It is upon this account that the succeeding pages are entirely based.

I make these statements, not in a spirit of pride, but in memory of that retiring, world-weary old gentleman with whom so many hours devoted to the work of compilation were spent. In view of the responsibility to him and to the reader which our association involves—a responsibility, I should add, which never was absent from his mind—my own feeling in offering the life-story of Wyatt Earp, Frontier Marshal, is one of notable inadequacy in the presence of the material of which this book is made.

STUART N. LAKE

STUART LAKE:
FRONTIER MYTHMAKER
by
Loren D. Estleman
Author of *Bloody Season,*
a novel of Tombstone

Stuart N. Lake's *Wyatt Earp: Frontier Marshal* is a pivotal work in the uniquely American process by which the common straw of history is spun into legendary gold.

The book has been scorned repeatedly by historians of the revisionist type, who in their fanatical pursuit of Truth often gallop straight past the facts. If, for example, Lake's undisguised admiration for his subject compels him to paint an impossible picture of Wyatt Earp as saint, Frank Waters's personal grudge against Earp's widow moves him just as surely, in *The Earp Brothers of Tombstone,* to cast the lawman-entrepreneur in the equally untenable role of antichrist.

The reality lies outside both extremes

But first, a few words about how this book came to exist

Wyatt Berry Stapp Earp, the third of five sons born to

Nicholas and Virginia Earp, originally of Illinois, was thirty-three years old when the incident that would make him immortal took place. In October 1881, while serving as a deputy city marshal under his older brother Virgil, Wyatt, younger brother Morgan, and John Henry Holliday, a family friend, sided Virgil in an attempt to disarm a party of belligerent cowboys who were flouting the local anti-firearms ordinance near the O. K. Corral in Tombstone, Arizona Territory. In the ensuing firefight, which began and ended in less than a minute, three cowboys lost their lives and three officers were wounded.

The incident was one of many in the young life of a particularly obstreperous mining boomtown, and might have been forgotten with the rest except for the politics involved.

Wyatt, then running for the lucrative position of county sheriff, had the endorsement of John Clum, Tombstone's mayor and editor of the daily *Epitaph*. His opponent, incumbent Sheriff John Behan, owned and published the rival *Nugget*. Behan counted friends and supporters among the brothers Clanton and McLaury, big losers in the gun battle. The journalistic duel that followed, with each newspaper trumpeting the righteousness of its favorites against the wickedness on the other side, raged on for months, igniting a controversy that continues to this day.

The Lake biography enjoys a distinction claimed by no other: the cooperation of its subject. When Lake first made contact with Wyatt Earp around Christmas 1927, Wyatt had given up hope of placing his "autobiography" with a publisher. Even the influence of silent-screen cowboy actor William S. Hart, then at the apex of his fame, had failed to push family friend John Flood's turgid jumble of half-heard anecdotes into print, and Wyatt was eager to get in his innings before Billy Breakenridge, an old enemy and a former deputy sheriff under John Behan, could publish his libelous *Helldorado* and blacken the Earp name forever. With Flood's manuscript at hand and through numerous personal interviews with Wyatt, Lake had by the time of his famous collaborator's death in January 1929 hammered out what might have been a fairly authentic personal history of an adventurous life on the frontier.

How much we know of what happened next is largely conjecture.

Latter-day revisionists maintain that in the absence of his subject, Lake sensationalized his story with numerous inventions intended to make the book more salable. Certainly this was the belief of Wyatt's widow, Josephine Sarah Marcus Earp, who sought to prevent its publication with a tearful personal appeal to Lake's editors at Houghton Mifflin. She succeeded only in changing the subtitle, originally *Gunfighter. Frontier Marshal* was as much as she could countenance.

Vindictively, and somewhat puritanically, some historians suggest that Josephine's motives were selfish, concerned more with obscuring certain details of her flamboyant past than with setting the record straight about her late husband's experiences. We do know that the rancor between the Earps and Sheriff Behan was, in addition to a matter of political differences, an *affair du coeur;* Josephine lived openly with Behan as his common-law wife before Wyatt replaced him in her affections. However, since no mention of the earlier relationship occurs in Lake's book, and no evidence exists to suggest that any part of the manuscript was deleted as a result of her entreaties, the charge appears unfounded. We may therefore award Josephine the benefit of the doubt and assume she acted out of loyalty to Wyatt's memory. More than anything else, he was a man who inspired loyalty.

The accusations of sensationalism on Lake's part are more difficult to deny. Although on at least one occasion Wyatt credited John Henry Holliday with having saved his life prior to the Tombstone episode, nothing on record indicates that the gunslinging dentist helped face down and apprehend a gang of rowdy cowboys in Dodge City, and the very existence of the "Buntline Special" with which Lake insists the famous dime novelist presented Wyatt has been disputed convincingly. Like today's Hollywood, the publishing industry of Lake's day seldom allowed facts to get in the way of a healthy bottom line.

Still, *Wyatt Earp: Frontier Marshal* compares favorably to

all other accounts of the period in which it was written. Breakenridge's *Helldorado: Bringing the Law to the Mesquite,* while a more balanced view, is rather too much the reminiscences of a quaint old character to be considered more than a curiosity. Walter Noble Burns's *Tombstone: An Iliad of the Southwest* is indistinguishable from the more openly fictional works of contemporary novelists Zane Grey and Rex Beach. And a recent edition of the Flood "autobiography," privately printed by an Earp historian of some renown, vindicates that narrative's early rejections. No more need be said of it than that it equips the Tombstone city marshal's office with a working telephone.

Wyatt Berry Stapp Earp is a conundrum. Neither the sobriquet *lawman* nor the epithets *gunman* and *badman* serve to explain all his actions. Frank Waters's clumsy attempt to reverse the negative by making the Earps the villains and the Clantons and McLaurys the heroes of his morality play is unsupported by Wyatt's lifelong friendship with the peace-loving John Clum. Similarly, Lake's stalwart *Frontier Marshal* is scarcely the man variously accused of horse-thieving and whoremongering and run out of the saloonkeeping business in Alaska during the gold rush for his reported role in sundry swindles. For the key to the puzzle of his character, one need examine the whole of his activities, from his gambling, timber, and mineral interests in and around Tombstone to his horse-breeding efforts in California; or, more simply, to pay heed to Wyatt's own oft-repeated answer to queries about his occupation: "I am a businessman."

In the Old West, a boomtown did not make noise for long before local authority drafted an ordinance prohibiting the carriage of firearms within the city limits. But in a climate that encouraged expansion far beyond the confines of organized law enforcement, a businessman's interests required protection at gunpoint. The brothers Earp, who considered themselves robber barons of the Vanderbilt stamp, made haste upon entering a raw commercial center to wrangle themselves badges in order to justify carrying guns to defend their businesses. Chief among these was gambling, with an occasional foray into procurement for purposes of prostitution: pimping. In the territories these activities were quite legal, and in view of the paucity of women and amusements, as respectable after their fashion as banking. In the cow capital of Dodge City, the circle spread to encompass cattle speculation; mining claims and timber rights in the silver-rich, lumber-starved settlement of Tombstone. With men the likes of bushwhackers Ike, Phin, and Billy Clanton and gun sharps Frank and Tom McLaury abroad, no cash transaction was safe unless conducted within convenient reach of a sidearm. Thus was born the legend of the "fighting Earps," in particular the steel-eyed determination with which the most notorious member of the clan employed the manly arts of fisticuffs and shooting. There is none so brave as he who stands in front of what belongs to him.

Why, then, the choice of posterity—as directed by Stuart N. Lake—of Wyatt Earp as champion of justice? The process of elimination offers one answer. Ike Clanton and his brothers were illiterate rustlers and bandits, clearly implicated in the 1879 ambush-slaughter of a large party of Mexican mule-skinners for the silver in their possession. Any defense of the McLaurys as honest cowpokes fades further with each spring rain that washes up hundreds of brass shells from the soil of their old ranch, attesting to prodigious bouts of target-shooting hardly in keeping with the above-board cattle trade. The Earps and Holliday, with their superior education, better tailoring, and peace-officer status, clean up better.

Whatever their limitations, they were men of courage. The evidence of a precarious foothold in a community fed up with violence bears out the claim that Virgil and Wyatt hoped for a peaceful solution to the situation near the O. K. Corral. Yet when that hope dissolved into gunplay, both men displayed cool heads and steady hands and turned an unwanted confrontation into a decisive victory. Ike ran. Tom McLaury ran. Behan bowed out.

One hundred twelve years later, the fight continues. In Tombstone and elsewhere, but especially in Tombstone, the mere mention of Wyatt Earp's name is sufficient to start a fistfight. Specialist historians, for whom the color and consistency of the lint in Morgan Earp's pocket carries greater significance than the moral and political climate of

America's most volatile era, squander their scholarship on poison-pen letters to obscure publications whenever a writer unknown to them trespasses upon their staked-out territory. For them—indeed, for all of us—Wyatt Earp stands forever in that dusty lot, tall and terrible, wreathed in gray smoke, six-shooter in hand.

We have Stuart Lake to thank for this image. It is forgotten and then rediscovered by each new generation. A dim recollection at the time of his death, Wyatt was catapulted into legend when the book appeared in 1931. Children born since the run of a popular 1950s television series starring Hugh O'Brian as Wyatt were unaware of him until the resurgence in the 1990s of the Hollywood western, which has yielded not one but *two* current major motion pictures about the gunfight at the O. K. Corral. Like Tombstone, Earp has proven himself too tough to die.

Wyatt Earp: Frontier Marshal is exceedingly well written and contains a vast amount of authentic information braided in among the tall tales. Its account of Wyatt's early life has seldom been questioned, and it fills the gap plausibly where no witnesses have come forward to dispute the version attributed to Wyatt. Serious writers determined to respect the greater truth of a time and its people have turned to Lake again and again when more fastidious researchers have been found wanting. It is a distinction he shares with Thomas Mallory and Homer. One could do far worse than to spend a rainy afternoon with any of them.

Whitmore Lake, Michigan
December 23, 1993

1

The Mold of a Man

The frontier breeds men. Good or evil, law-abiding or lawless, the pick of the strain are fighting men.

For two sanguinary centuries in which North American civilization battled westward, Earps were in the vanguard of those hardy, self-reliant pioneers who led the course of empire across the wilderness. To an Earp, intrepid confidence in his own strength, his own sagacity, his own courage, became a birthright; utter loyalty to the clan and a firm belief in the native dignity of his manhood, hereditary complements.

Wyatt Earp, of the sixth American-born generation of his family, was destined to a time and territory of which it was written that there was no law west of Kansas City and, west of Fort Scott, no God. Environment was fated to test the fullest worth of his heritage.

Wyatt Earp's paternal ancestors were Scotch. James Earp, first of the blood to reach American soil, settled in Fairfax County, Virginia, in the latter half of the seventeenth century. During the French and Indian Wars and the War of

1

Independence, a half-dozen Earps fought in the Colonial armies. As early as 1760, their adventurous sons had visited the Ohio Valley, and soon after the Revolution, Wyatt Earp's great-grandfather sold his Fairfax County holding, to settle near the later site of Wheeling, West Virginia, on land received for military services. Wyatt's grandfather, Walter Earp, was then a boy. Later, Walter Earp was sent to the Atlantic seaboard to study law. He returned to the frontier, opened a law office in the village of Wheeling, began to work farm property nearby, and married the daughter of a neighboring Scotch family. To this union Wyatt Earp's father, Nicholas Porter Earp, was born in 1813.

Now, Walter Earp moved west again, to Hartford, Kentucky, where he acquired another large landholding and resumed the practice of law. At Hartford, Nicholas Earp married for the first time, his wife dying soon after the birth of Newton Earp, her only child. On July 30, 1840, at Hartford, Nicholas Earp married Virginia Anne Cooksey, as his second wife. The Cookseys, an English family, had settled in Eastern Virginia, in the early eighteenth century, and later had moved to an Ohio Valley land grant, where Virginia Anne was born in 1823.

Nicholas and Virginia Earp purchased a plantation near Hartford, on which their eldest sons were born, James in 1841 and Virgil in 1843. Nicholas Earp read law with his father and appeared occasionally at the Kentucky bar, but his interest and abilities were naturally with the development of land. He worked his father's farm with his own until the influx of settlers to Kentucky in the boom of 1843 brought cash buyers for the land at a handsome profit for father and son.

Lorenzo Earp, Nicholas's brother, who had pressed on to the West, sent back glowing word of the richness of Illinois soil. Walter and Nicholas Earp responded to his urging, and once more took their places in the van of the pioneers. They reached Monmouth, Illinois, in the summer of '43. Father and son each took a section of virgin prairie near the village;

2

Nicholas began to develop both properties while his father opened a law office in the little town.

Western Illinois, in 1843, was raw frontier, overrun by border ruffians, renegades, and stock thieves who made life hazardous for the peaceably inclined. Insistence that Warren County could rid itself of undesirables, if the law-and-order faction would show as much spirit as the outlaws, was speedily exemplified by Walter and Nicholas Earp in protecting their own property, and in a fashion which led neighbors to dependence upon them in matters of the kind. Walter Earp was elected judge of the Illinois Circuit Court; Nicholas was commissioned a deputy sheriff to serve without pay. It has been recorded that Nicholas Earp as a volunteer peace officer established a precedent for fearless efficiency which might well have motivated his more famous son.

In 1845, a daughter, Martha, was born to Nicholas and Virginia Earp. By this time Nicholas had brought his raw land to a highly productive state. When the United States declared war on Mexico in the spring of 1846, he sold the farm readily, moved his family into Monmouth, and joined a cavalry regiment. He was invalided home from Mexico in 1847.

Colonel Wyatt Berry Stapp had been Captain Earp's commanding officer during his military adventure, and when a third son was born to Nicholas and Virginia Earp at Monmouth on March 19, 1848, he was christened Wyatt Berry Stapp Earp.

When Wyatt was two years old, his parents moved across the Mississippi River to Pella, Iowa, where two sons and a daughter were born to them: Morgan, in 1851; Warren, in 1855; Adelia, in 1861. For a time Nicholas Earp found contentment here; again he was plowing virgin soil.

While the influence of Nicholas Earp was the more apparent in his children's lives, Virginia Anne Cooksey unquestionably contributed no small portion of that high courage for which her sons were famed. Certainly, in one outstanding test of the qualities through which pioneer men

3

and women might survive, her fearless initiative in the face of a greater danger than any man may know equaled that displayed by any one of forty frontiersmen in her company at the time.

All of which is not to exclude from his rightful consideration the half-brother, Newton Earp, who set up no mean record for valiant conduct on his own account, but who never was associated with the full-brothers in the various enterprises which took them the length and breadth of the frontier. For that matter, the identities of Nicholas Earp's six sons have been so thoroughly jumbled in the legendary accounts of their joint and separate careers that it may be advisable to fix them definitely before taking up the thread of their family life.

The famous fighting triumvirate of the clan which, under Wyatt's leadership, won frontier-wide acclaim as "The Fearless Earps," was composed of Wyatt, Virgil, and Morgan Earp. James Earp was barred from later affrays of major caliber by a wound received during the Civil War; Warren was kept from the more sanguinary encounters by his youth and his brothers' intent.

The extent to which Wyatt, Virgil, and Morgan Earp shared their common heritage as they carried the Earp tradition to its high place in the history of the West may be surmised from the purely physical likeness which in their young manhood often led casual acquaintances to error. When, for example, the first council of Tombstone, Arizona, wished to appoint Virgil Earp as town marshal, the messenger summoned an Earp to whom the badge of office had been handed before the recipient revealed that he was Wyatt. On another occasion, E. B. Gage, a Tombstone mine-owner, gave a saddle-horse to Morgan Earp in the belief that he was transferring ownership to Wyatt, who in an earlier conversation had sought to purchase the animal.

"As the result of our resemblance at the time we went to Tombstone," Wyatt once recalled, "Virg, Morg, and I were the subjects of some betting. To settle the argument, we were weighed and measured. Boots off, there wasn't a quarter-inch difference in our heights; each was just over the six-foot mark. There wasn't three pounds difference in our weights, and not one of us scaled above a hundred and fifty-eight. Virg was the heaviest, Morg a shade heavier than I. When you add that each of us had wavy, light-brown hair, blue eyes, and a mustache of the sweeping variety then in Western fashion, you may understand why our comings and goings often were reported inaccurately and why certain persons in Arizona ascribed supernatural qualities to the Earps."

Wyatt's earliest recollections were of a family reared to the belief that ownership of land constitutes man's most desirable lot, a creed that was tempered by what he called the curse of the itching foot.

"Father's love for the soil and for making things grow was fanatical," he said. "Even when he made our home in town, he would have forty, eighty, or one hundred and sixty acres under cultivation somewhere outside. He never rented, always owned; and he never sold a farm that was not greatly improved over the condition in which it had been acquired.

"One reason for his success with farms was a belief that he was under personal obligation to every living, growing thing. To this he added practical experience and as much theory as he could get from farm papers of the day. He was particularly fond of animals and as forward-looking with them as he was with land. Neighbors who poked fun at his ideas were, a few years later, following methods he had adopted earlier through studying his job. He developed and sold farm lands steadily throughout my boyhood and that he acquired a competence in the process is some evidence of his ability as a pioneer.

"This love for land, and for animals, seems to have been an Earp trait for generations, always offset by the itch to get to some place that was new. With all the roaming my brothers and I did, we were forever acquiring real estate—farms, cattle ranches, mining claims, and town lots.

"Father's regard for the land was equaled by his respect for the law and his detestation for the lawless element so prevalent in the West. I have heard him say many times that, while the law might not be entirely just, it generally ex

5

pressed the will of the decent folks who were trying to build up the country, and that until someone could offer a better safeguard for a man's rights, enforcement of the law was the duty of every man who asked for its protection in any way.

"My grandfather and he were in accord on that matter, as well as in the belief that the Western country could never amount to much until the lawless element had been put down. They had greater contempt for those who lacked the courage to enforce the law than for the outlaws themselves, and expressed it freely. We boys had their opinions literally drummed into us. It doesn't seem farfetched to assume that they had lasting effect."

Nicholas Earp likewise held certain convictions concerning the value of education. His children took what village schools could offer and were required to follow more advanced studies at home. Wyatt, until he was sixteen, was looked upon as the family's successor to the grandfather's legal practice and was coached with this career in view until a taste of frontier adventure blasted parental hopes.

In the matter of religion, Nicholas and Virginia Earp appear to have been unusually tolerant for their time and place. They were members of a Protestant congregation and with their children attended services regularly, but Wyatt remembered clearly the greater freedom which the Earp youngsters enjoyed, as against that of playmates with more devout parents.

"As we grew older," Wyatt recollected, "we were given to understand that it was our conduct toward others which really counted, were thoroughly grounded in this practical creed, and left to our own devices as far as religion was concerned.

"'Religion,' my father once said to me in later years, 'is a matter which every man must settle for himself. Your mother and I tried to make you children understand your responsibilities, to yourselves and to others; beyond that we did not expect to accomplish much.'

"That," Wyatt observed, "is as typical of my parents as anything I can recall."

In the early fifties, Nicholas Earp responded again to the

urge of pioneering blood and went overland to California in search of a new home. He took no part in the frenzied hunt for gold, but pinned his hopes for the future to agricultural land with an ample water supply. He decided to settle in San Bernardino County and returned to Iowa to move his wife and children westward. Protracted illness, which ended in the death of Wyatt's sister, Martha, first postponed the Earp migration to California. Then, the spring of '61 brought the Civil War.

Although Southern born and raised, Nicholas Earp was stoutly opposed to secession and he entered the service of the Union, with his old rank of captain and as provost marshal of Marion County. In this capacity he recruited and drilled three companies of troops for Federal service, and sent his three oldest sons to the front.

Newton joined the Fourth Iowa Cavalry; James and Virgil Earp returned to Illinois to enlist. Newton and Virgil served with the Union forces until the spring of '65, but James, after receiving a severe wound at Fredericktown, Missouri, was sent home as permanently disabled in the summer of '63.

"While my brothers were at war," Wyatt said, "I gained my lifelong sympathy for the man with a hoe. We were living in town, but Father had an eighty-acre piece just outside the village which he planted to corn upon the declaration of war, and for which he made me responsible. I was barely thirteen, but I was warned that if I didn't bring that corn crop through, my brothers in the army might go hungry. Father was too busy recruiting and drilling troops to do anything about the cornfield. So, with Morgan, who was ten, and Warren, who was six, as helpers, I cultivated and harvested that eighty acres of corn.

"According to the standards by which he had been raised, there was nothing a son of Nicholas Earp could do to preserve the family's repute in Pella but bring that corn crop through, and we had as fine a yield that year as any man in our district."

With the second spring of the war, Wyatt was hoeing the same eighty acres for another crop of corn. One morning while his father was absent, as the boy thought, in the western part of the county, Wyatt ran away from the job, heading for Ottumwa and an army recruiting office. Greatly to his surprise and chagrin, about the first person he met in Ottumwa was his father, and Wyatt was taken back to his cornfield. And there, the boy worked out another summer, after giving his word not to attempt enlistment without his mother's consent.

The year 1863 found Nicholas Earp still firmly opposed to secession, but unable actively to support the Northern determination to free the slaves in those states in which slavery was a century-old institution. He was opposed to the spread of slave-holding territory, but he was the product of communities which based their very existence on slaves as property. He had been a slave owner himself, and he knew of the dependence which his Virginia and Kentucky relatives placed upon their human chattels; he could not believe that they should be ruthlessly deprived of their slaves any more than of other property which had been lawfully acquired.

It was wholly characteristic of Nicholas Earp that, when it became evident to him that the Emancipation Proclamation was to be perpetuated by Constitutional Amendment in the event that the Union armies were victorious and that the fighting was now solely to that end, he should resign from army service and resume arrangements for moving to California in the spring of 1864.

The Earp brothers in the army disagreed with their father's views and told him so. Whereupon, Nicholas Earp was at some pains to assure them that in view of their opinions it was their duty to continue in the Union army until the question of slave ownership had been fought out, and that they were no sons of his who did not thus serve to the full measure of ability. When James came home from battle, an invalid, his father and he had one discussion of the issue; until the war was over, the subject was not dwelled upon again in the family circle.

Several households of Southern antecedents among the

Earp acquaintances in the neighborhoods of Pella and Monmouth had similar opinions of the war as it now had turned, and joined Nicholas Earp in his plans for the California move. The train they formed was destined, incidentally, to provide the West and the United States with some of its foremost citizens, noted jurists, famous surgeons, great educators, and at least two United States cabinet officers. Among those in the expedition were the Curtis, Rousseau, Hamilton, Ellis, and Hayes families. Nicholas Earp was elected captain of the train, which numbered forty wagons and about one hundred and fifty emigrants.

For the conveyance of his wife and himself, Captain Earp purchased a buckboard with four Morgan horses. To transport his children and the family possessions, he fitted out two covered wagons, each hauled by eight oxen. Because of Jim's continued disability, Wyatt, although barely sixteen, took charge of the Earp wagons and stock. He drove the key oxteam of the train, first in line behind his father's buckboard, carrying as passengers his baby sister, Adelia, and his brother, Warren. The second Earp wagon was driven by Charles Copeley, hired to make the trip. With him, Jim and Morgan rode. At the rear of the train were the extra oxen, saddle- and workhorses, and some cattle, about forty head of Earp stock, and something more than five hundred head in all. Taylor, a cream-colored thoroughbred colt which Mrs. Earp had gentled to saddle and harness for her own use, was led at the rear of the buckboard.

Before the Earps left Pella, Nicholas Earp gave to his son, Wyatt, the first firearm which the boy ever had to call his own.

"It was a cumbersome weapon," Wyatt recollected, "but I thought more of it than any other I owned in later years. It was an 'under-and-over,' a combination rifle and shotgun with one barrel underneath the other. On top was the rifle, about forty-caliber; underneath, the scatter-gun, both muzzle-loaders. The range of the rifle was not much greater than that of the shotgun; one hundred yards was certainly its limit for accurate work. But I was proud of that gun, and with it I was to keep a group of twenty persons in fresh meat all the way to California.

"I had hunted prairie chickens, rabbits, squirrels, and deer around home from the time I was seven or eight, but always with guns that really belonged to Father or the older boys. It is no conceit for me to say that I was the best shot in the family. Accuracy with firearms came naturally to me, I guess. As far back as I can remember, I had that direction-sense which makes good shooting more a matter of instinct than of training. Father and his friends knew this, so I drew the hunter's job."

Units of the Earp emigrant train mobilized at Council Bluffs, Iowa, and Nicholas Earp led the caravan across the Missouri River into Omaha, Nebraska, on May 12, 1864.

2

Covered Wagon Days

On the frontier, a lad of fourteen, fifteen, or sixteen, might be at one moment a mere boy; in the next, he must be a man. Responsibility usually brought the transition, often with a suddenness which simply cut adolescence short.

Wyatt Earp, at sixteen, has been recalled by those in his father's wagon train as a fine specimen of youthful pioneer stock. He was nearly six feet tall, weighed possibly one hundred forty pounds, and gave the impression of wiry, symmetrically muscled strength rather than lankiness, with his long legs and arms; a handsome youngster with lean, clear-cut features, light brown hair, the straight nose and generous mouth of Earp tradition, above the family's indomitable jaw. His inherent steadiness of mind and habit already was indicated by the habitually earnest expression of his well-set, large blue eyes.

That this recollection is in no wise overdrawn as a portrait of the boy is attested by an old photograph of Virgil Earp, at eighteen, taken when he enlisted in the army. It has often been remarked that in their youth Virgil and Wyatt Earp, bore such co-natural resemblance that, as soon as Wyatt caught up with Virgil in the matter of inches, they might readily have passed as twins. Granting the accuracy of such remembrance, the photograph of Virgil may be accepted as a likeness of Wyatt as he neared the same stage of life; which, it may be added, it has been by more than one person who knew the brothers well.

In Pella, Wyatt Earp had enjoyed no recognition beyond that accorded to the average boy, but the manner in which he filled his place in the emigrant train soon changed his elders' attitude.

"We had not been long on the Overland Trail," one of Nicholas Earp's friends wrote, "before we realized that Wyatt had a head on his shoulders, a most dependable one at that. We accepted him in his full worth as a man; he proved his right to the confidence in him we learned to share with his father, in every emergency that arose."

Wyatt's introduction to that form of gunplay which contributed so largely to keeping the Old West wild came with his first day on trans-Missouri soil. Back in Iowa he had heard and read of pistol methods employed to settle human differences which prevailed on the frontier; in the streets of Omaha, he witnessed the first gunfight of many he was to see.

Omaha, in the spring of '64, was a flimsy settlement sprawling in the mud, with a handful of permanent residents and a floating population of several thousand, shifting from day to day as emigrants converged from the East upon the Overland Trail, crossed the Missouri from Council Bluffs, camped overnight, then started across the plains. After the Earp party had made camp at the edge of the town on the afternoon of May 12, Wyatt and Copeley were sent to purchase supplies.

There were more saloons in the Omaha of '64 than other commercial establishments combined, and from a bar, as Wyatt and Copeley passed the door, two men with drawn pistols stepped into the middle of the road.

"It was a cold-blooded affair," Wyatt recalled. "Neither man spoke. Copeley and I were too startled, I guess, to look for shelter. The men faced each other, possibly thirty feet apart; one fired twice and the other three times, and both dropped in the mud.

"I don't know what I thought. I know I did not join Copeley in the group around the bodies. I heard someone say one man was dead and the other dying. Then, I was suddenly sick at my stomach and I got away as quickly as I could.

"That night I told my father about the fight. He did his best to explain conditions which made possible such affairs as I had witnessed that afternoon, to make me understand why no one had attempted to stop the fight, and to make it very plain that from that time on my own safety and my own life might at any moment hang entirely on my readiness and my ability to defend them for myself. It was years before I appreciated fully what my father tried to accomplish by that talk. He laid down for me, as man to man, and to the best of his ability, what might be called the code of the frontier. It had little to do with the law as, boylike, I had imagined it must be; it consisted largely of distinctions to be drawn between men who used their weapons in self-defense or on the side of law and order, and killers who made gunplay on the least excuse. The line was hard to draw, and while I can't recall Father's exact words, I can give the gist of them, which was something to this effect:

"'Always give every man the full benefit of every possible doubt; you'll have to stretch many a point to allow for the free-and-easy life of these Western camps. But, whenever you're certain that you're dealing with downright viciousness, the complete disregard for human rights and decency, remember that such lawlessness is the greatest enemy of mankind. Any man who is honestly combating such lawlessness is justified in going to any lengths to which lawlessness forces the fight.

"'When you know you have a fight with viciousness on your hands, hit first, if you can, and when you do hit, hit to kill.'

"As anyone who knew him could tell you, that was my father in so many words."

13

From Omaha, the Earp emigrant train plodded westward along the North Platte at a pace varying from ten to fifteen miles a day. Water was plentiful, feed good, and game in abundance was on every side. Prairie chickens could be flushed by the thousands from their dust baths in the trail ahead of Captain Earp's buckboard, or Wyatt could ride off to either side of the route and within an hour have all the antelope meat his pony could pack in. The twenty persons for whose larders the boy was responsible ate antelope or prairie chicken three times a day for weeks on end.

Just after the Earp wagons passed Fort Laramie, Wyoming, Indians took their first toll. A hunter named Chapman who had gone out on foot after antelope sighted a band of Sioux warriors when about five hundred yards from the train. Chapman turned to run.

"My father," Wyatt said, "had told me time and again, as he had the others, that if I was set upon by Indians while hunting I was to drop prone in the best cover available, even if that was no more than grass, and shoot to kill at the first Indian who came into rifle range. The Indians would then circle around me, probably, but I might hold them beyond arrow shot with my rifle, which I was to reload at once, saving my shotgun charge and my pistol for closer action. As we hunters were never out of sound range, and seldom out of sight of the train, I would stand a chance of holding my own until a rescue party could reach me.

"Chapman had heard this advice repeatedly, but when the Sioux rode at him, he lost his head. Men in the train sighted the Indians, but before they could get into action the Sioux had killed Chapman, scalped him, stolen his rifle, pistol, and ammunition, and ridden away, all within our view. We buried Chapman beside the Platte, assigned one of the older boys to look after his outfit and family, and went on. I think I began to realize about that time that any advice my father gave was apt to be sound."

The confidence in Wyatt which had led Nicholas Earp to place the boy in a man's role for the overland trip was amply justified in the next Indian attack on the train, and the same crisis revealed something of the qualities with which Virginia Cooksey Earp endowed her sons. The attack took place about forty miles west of Fort Laramie, the second day after Chapman's death.

While emigrant breakfasts were cooking, the horses, with picket ropes dragging, were grazing at a short distance from the fires. Wyatt and Morgan Earp were watching their father's animals, with men from other wagons doing like duty with their stock. Taylor, Mrs. Earp's thoroughbred, was feeding between the main bunch of Earp horses and the camp.

About forty Sioux horsemen suddenly burst into view from behind a butte and headed full tilt for the herds, whooping and yelling to stampede the grazing animals in a dash around the wagon corral, and shooting at the herders as they rode. Twenty men with rifles blazed away at the Indians from behind the wagons, while most of the horse-guards ran for cover.

Wyatt's job was to protect his father's stock. The animals were bunched and the boy had been among the first to discover the charging Sioux.

"Grab the picket ropes, Morg!" Wyatt shouted, and fell to carrying out the order himself.

Although but thirteen, Morgan was every inch an Earp; for when the raid ended, as suddenly as it began, the brothers stood together with their father's bunch of horses intact, the picket ropes held fast. Others had lost twenty head of stock.

Between the boys and the wagon circle, in the space across which the Sioux had galloped, stood Mrs. Earp at Taylor's head. She had run from her breakfast fire at the first alarm, seized her colt's picket rope and held it fast, despite the fact that she had been directly in the path of the raid, and might readily have been carried off by any Indian who swooped past.

A second Sioux raid on the wagon train was made about a week after the first, when the Earp caravan was about halfway between Fort Laramie and the later site of Fort

Fetterman. Again the hour was daybreak, and on this occasion Wyatt and Copeley, his father's hired hand, were out with the cattle and horses.

Grass was scarce on the trail bank of the Platte, so the animals had been forded to a mesa reached from the crossing by a sharp defile and for some distance in either direction bordering the river in fifty-foot bluffs. Two mounted men were posted downriver to prevent straying; two were on the flat beyond the herd; Wyatt and Copeley were on the edge of the bluff, upstream from the ford.

Wyatt heard a splashing below. Peering over the bluff, Copeley and he counted twelve Sioux riding single-file down the stream, and hidden from casual view by the riverbanks. Wyatt drew his weapon to his shoulder, but Copeley pulled him back.

"They'll kill us if you shoot at them," the man whispered.

With his chance to pick off the Sioux leader ruined, Wyatt's next thought was for the animals. He sensed that the Indians were riding for the trail leading up from the ford to get between the camp and the herd, and that once in that strategic position they would whoop up the declivity to stampede horses, mules, and oxen into the buttes.

Shaking off Copeley's arm, Wyatt fired his shotgun barrel to warn the men in camp. As the Sioux recognized discovery by taking full speed for the trail, the boy put his pony on the run for the animals grazing farthest from the ford. He rounded the edge of the herd, yelling and waving his hat, not reassured at all by the sight of more Sioux in the distance, ready to join their fellow raiders when they might start up the herd.

A pair of mules were the first animals to stampede before Wyatt's commotion. Following their leadership, he got the others—five hundred mules, horses, and lumbering oxen—headed for the crossing. He had them charging wildly for the defile as the Indians topped the rise.

The Sioux had small choice. To save themselves from the hoofs and horns of the frenzied herd they scattered from the narrow trail. Still whooping and yelling, Wyatt drove the stock full tilt across the river, Copeley and the other guards now helping him. With the animals safe, the herders turned to join the pursuit of the Indians.

In this chase, Wyatt shot at a human being for the first time in his life, aiming, he judged, at a chief. To his chagrin, his rifle was not equal to the range. One Sioux was wounded in the fusillade, however, and the raiders drew off.

Following the North Platte to the fork of the Sweetwater, the emigrant train made its way through the South Pass to Fort Bridger. There, while the oxteams rested in anticipation of the trip to Salt Lake, Wyatt had the experience which ever after provided his most vivid recollections of the Overland Trail.

Nearly every day, for more than two weeks, Wyatt went fishing with Jim Bridger, famous scout and mountain man, possibly the most proficient frontiersman that this country has known.

Nicholas Earp had met Bridger on his earlier trip to California, and the old scout came to the emigrant camp from his mountain fortress to renew the acquaintance. When Wyatt decided to provide a change in the family diet with trout, Bridger offered to show him several likely holes. The noted trapper and Indian fighter was then nearly sixty years old, but he and his youthful admirer fished together until the other Earps insisted upon reversion to antelope. Between catches Jim Bridger regaled his companion with tales of adventure and lore of the frontier.

From Fort Bridger the Earp train made an uneventful journey to Salt Lake, and started the hazardous seven-hundred-mile haul across the Mojave Desert, the last lap of their trek. This led them down the route established by Mormon settlers, up through Cajon Pass and into San Bernardino, trail's end, on December 19, 1864, seven months and seven days after leaving Council Bluffs.

San Bernardino in 1864 was the Anglo-Saxon metropolis of Southern California with more white residents than Los Angeles—possibly twenty-five hundred, all told. And San Berdoo, as the village was known in Western parlance, was the outfitting post for thousands of prospectors who scoured the Southwestern mountains in search of treasure, the

17

central trans-shipping point for tons of supplies hauled to the Arizona, Nevada, and Utah camps, the final jumping-off place for all hardy adventurers who dared the perils of an American hinterland as little known as the fastnesses of Tibet. The town lay in a great, fertile valley with perennial water assured from nearby mountain ranges—such a supply as at that time was unique in California south of the Tehachapi. The ranch which Nicholas Earp purchased was about twelve miles from San Berdoo along the headwaters of the Santa Ana River, a site later to be covered by the city of Redlands, and to it the Earp family moved on Christmas Day, 1864.

Nicholas Earp was to become a leader in the development of Southern California. He improved his original land purchase, acquired additional acreage, including a section on which much of a latter-day San Bernardino was built; and for years the head of the San Bernardino County Pioneers' Society, was elected to the county court and served on the bench until retirement some years before his death.

It had been anticipated that Wyatt would continue the study of law in California, but the taste of life he had enjoyed during the covered wagon journey made him loath to return to books. With the work of establishing the new home at hand, it was not difficult for Wyatt to postpone his resumption of study for a time; by spring he had set his own mind definitely against any vocation that might hold him from adventuring.

3

Desert Hauls

San Bernardino of the 1860s was rendezvous for hordes of outdoor men—prospectors, bullwhackers, mule skinners, trappers, scouts, and cattlemen—with tales of adventure on their tongues and the color of vast, unsettled country in their equipment and attire. Even at the age of seventeen and in such company, Wyatt had something of a reputation for those attributes which constituted eminence in the Old West. For his courage and initiative in the face of danger, men of his father's emigrant train bore witness; and the youngster speedily won equal footing with older hands in trials of skill with firearms. In shooting matches with rifles or the cumbersome cap-and-ball revolvers, few around the village could tie Wyatt's scores; none could beat them consistently. Still another quality which won admiration was Wyatt's uncanny way with the half-wild horses and mules which constituted the Western adventurer's major transportation problem.

Wyatt had been reared with horses and schooled in his

father's affectionate knowledge of them, and on more than one occasion the youth astounded veteran handlers of the ten- and sixteen-animal hitches by climbing to the freighter's saddle on a nigh wheeler and putting a jerkline team which was strange to him through its paces as well as might the regular driver. This ability with horseflesh, as much as any one influence, definitely ended Wyatt's school career.

In 1865, General Phineas Banning operated a stage line between San Bernardino and the pueblo of Los Angeles. The route covered sixty miles, down mountain passes, across wide stretches of desert, along streambeds which were rocky washes in summer and raging torrents in winter. Because of competition, a one-way trip over this route must be negotiated in six hours and a round-trip made each day. What with the quality of the roads when there were any, the character of the horses which General Banning deemed it economical to provide, repeated interference from bandits, and truculence of the run of passengers, stage driving on the Banning line was a job.

In the summer after Wyatt turned seventeen, Banning's regular driver broke his leg.

"Who'll take your place?" his employer asked.

"Get Nicholas Earp's boy Wyatt," the driver advised, as General Banning told the story. "You've got bad horses and bad men to handle on that run and young Wyatt Earp can do both. What's more, the animals won't be ruined when I take 'em over again."

Before morning, Wyatt Earp had a man-sized job at a man's rate of pay. He drove the six-horse coach one hundred and twenty miles a day, changing animals at hostler corrals every ten miles along the route, seven days a week for three months, straight through a half-dozen ambuscades set by highwaymen, never was late—so Phineas Banning testified —never lost a horse, a passenger, or an ounce of mail, and added to his reputation tremendously.

When the regular driver returned to the Banning box, Frank Binkley, who hauled freight from the California port of San Pedro to the Arizona settlements, hired Wyatt to drive a ten-animal team to Prescott, Arizona. At that time, few supplies reached Arizona by the Overland Trail from the East. Merchandise was shipped from Atlantic ports around the Horn and then teamed over mountains and desert at a charge of $12.50 a hundredweight between San Pedro and Prescott.

From San Pedro to San Bernardino, freighters encountered few hazards. From San Berdoo the Arizona trail led over San Gorgonio Pass and down to the wind-scoured sands of the Salton Sink, two hundred and eighty feet below sea-level, across an expanse so infernally desolate that teams were held in harness to feed and water, and kept steadily on the move for the last white-hot hundred miles to Colorado Crossing. Wagons with trailers carried one thousand pounds of freight to the animal, plus five hundred pounds of fodder for each one in the team. The schedule allowed twenty days for the journey of four hundred and fifty miles. Periodical attacks on wagon trains by Indians and renegade white bandits provided risks in addition to the desert haul.

Wyatt had now attained his full height of six feet and one quarter inch, and weighed about one hundred and forty-five pounds, but no one who knew him was deceived by his slenderness. He seems to have been born with that rare and, in his day, priceless ability to hold more than his own in any company. He was lean, but powerful, with a perfectly coordinated nervous and muscular development which he employed with a high degree of proficiency, as more than one person who questioned his physical prowess could testify.

Long after Wyatt Earp left Binkley's employ, the freighter recalled him as one of the best hands he had known on the Arizona trace. "Wyatt was a quiet, good-natured, dependable young fellow," he said, "and not afraid of work. What I remember him for, principally, is the apparent ease with which he did everything. He never wasted a move, always got his teams through on time and in fine condition. He was as careful with his animals as he was with himself."

Binkley, a noted frontier character, demanded just four qualities in a driver for each of the fifteen teams which ordinarily made up an Arizona train. First, was the ability to handle half-broken horses and mules well enough to make Prescott on schedule without injuring the animals; second, the physical strength and stamina to withstand great hardship; third, unerring skill with rifle and pistol; fourth, dauntless courage. As a rule, only drivers of seasoned maturity were hired for the Binkley trains. Wyatt Earp, at seventeen, drove two trips for him, then left him in the spring of '66 to handle a sixteen-animal outfit over the longer, even more hazardous, route from San Berdoo to Salt Lake, hiring out as a top hand to Chris Taylor, another celebrated frontier wagon master.

The Salt Lake trace traversed seven hundred miles of the most difficult desert and mountain wilderness, through a territory infested by the Paiutes, and on Wyatt's first trip for Taylor his train was attacked by Indians. The wagons were strung along the trail at the time of the raid; there was no opportunity to circle them into a protective corral, so the teamsters stuck to their saddles and fought Paiutes while keeping their mules to a steady pace. They killed two Indians whose bodies were left where they fell, and killed or wounded a number of other raiders who were carried off by their companions.

By the time Wyatt returned to San Bernardino, there seems to have been no question concerning his status among frontiersmen, for he was chosen with a select group of fighters to rescue a detachment of United States Cavalry besieged by Paiutes at the desert outpost, Camp Cadiz. Indians had killed three soldiers, wounded several others, and had the survivors penned in.

Sheriff John King, who organized the rescue party, knew that the most effective force would be small and numbering only men who could ride hard, shoot with deadly accuracy, and be relied upon for courage in any circumstance. He picked twenty such, from several hundred frontier fighting men, one Wyatt Earp, then eighteen. King and his handful drove several hundred Paiutes from Camp Cadiz into the Nevada mountains and rescued the surviving soldiers.

In the spring of '67, Charles Chrisman, Chris Taylor's principal competitor on the Salt Lake Trail, paid further recognition to Wyatt Earp's reputation by offering the young man a share in the profits if he would join his train. As the freight rate from San Pedro to the Mormon colony was sixteen cents a pound and each working team meant at least twenty-five hundred dollars in cash for the owners at the end of the haul, Wyatt threw in with Chrisman. Their journey to Utah was without incident, but there they learned that Union Pacific Railroad construction had brought Eastern merchandise to Julesburg, Colorado, upon which twenty cents a pound would be paid for delivery in Salt Lake. No one in the Mormon country seemed anxious for the hauling contract, but Chrisman took it.

Trail feed was so scanty that year as to be almost non-existent—one reason why Chrisman found no competition for the Julesburg venture—and upon Wyatt's suggestion the Chrisman wagons left Salt Lake loaded with sacked barley which during the journey eastward was cached in convenient amounts at intervals along the route. Otherwise, the eastbound wagons would have been empty, and it was entirely due to this foresight that the mule-teams survived the arduous journey back to Salt Lake at all. Thanks to the barley ration, the animals finished the westward trip in such fine physical condition that the train immediately returned to Sidney, Nebraska, to which point the railhead had meanwhile progressed, and hauled another trainload of freight into Salt Lake for a gross payment of twenty-four thousand dollars. Before snowfall blocked the passes, Wyatt left Chrisman and returned to San Berdoo.

In the spring of '68, Nicholas Earp went East to dispose of farm properties acquired before the war. His family made the trip overland by wagon to the railhead of the Union Pacific then building across Wyoming. There, Wyatt found Charles Chrisman with a railroad grading contract and need for a man to handle the string of animals required for the job. Other Earps went on; Wyatt hired to Chrisman, at wages of seventy-five dollars a month and found, to have supervision of all horses and mules in the camp and to drive a four-animal plow which turned the sod for graders a hundred miles ahead of steel.

Wyatt now embarked on his first independent business venture, the forerunner of many which were to mark him as of a type not commonly classified with gunfighters in the Old West. Although but twenty years old, and despite constant association with the notoriously thriftless frontiersmen, he had accumulated a supply of ready cash, then a rare commodity in the Western territories with men of any age. When a grader driving his own team wished to sell his mules and quit the job, Wyatt purchased the animals for ninety dollars; he was the only person in the camp of two hundred men, except Chrisman, who had that much money. As his employer agreed not to compete in the bargaining, Wyatt closed the deal on his own terms.

A driver was hired at two dollars a day, and services of man and team were let to the railroad for five dollars a day and feed for mules and driver, netting three dollars a day on the investment. Wyatt immediately decided to increase his livestock holdings. He scoured the neighboring camps for dissatisfied workers and purchased four good teams at an average cost of less than one hundred and twenty-five dollars each; each of these netted three dollars a day for the remainder of the season.

Railway construction camps in the Wyoming of 1868 were populated by rough and roistering fellows, but Wyatt Earp did not remember them as spontaneously wild or genuinely bad in comparison with cowcamps and mining towns. They were strung across the state, at approximately twenty-mile intervals, with about two hundred men in each camp. Laborers, for the greater part, were veterans of the Civil War—from both armies—earning one to two dollars a day and board. They were a hard-driven, hardworking crowd inured to the hardest living, and they found their recreation in hard drinking and hard fighting. They carried guns at their work as protection against Indian attacks, but in settling differences among themselves usually laid weapons aside and fought with fists. Possibly war had provided a sufficiency of gunplay; at any rate, Wyatt could remember but one instance in which he saw railroad workers choose pistols to settle a quarrel.

The Chrisman camps were miles beyond the mushroom centers of colorful iniquity which sprouted as fast as spikes were driven at the ever-advancing end of steel. It was at the railhead that the large majority of saloons, gambling houses, dancehalls, and tented bagnios came into overnight existence, for only at the railhead was there enough money to make such enterprises profitable. Occasionally an itinerant Cyprian found her way into a grading camp, and a few professional gamblers estimated the hardships of the advance guard as worthwhile, but whiskey merchants were the only parasites who fattened to any degree on the small sums that graders had to spend.

As plows broke sod along the right of way, saloons kept abreast of the mules in every form of housing from frame-and-canvas shacks to dugouts in the nearby buttes. Raw whiskey was the only drink. For six days and five nights of each week saloonkeepers and gamblers had their places largely to themselves; on Saturday nights and Sundays, everyone else also got drunk. With the hangers-on gunfights were not uncommon, but small attention was paid to them. Occasionally some camp foreman would buckle on a gun to run some whiskey merchant or gambler out of the neighborhood, but knock-down-and-drag-out fights had the laborers' preferences as long as they stayed ahead of steel.

The regular Sunday morning amusement for the graders was a prizefight between representatives of two camps. Each camp made up one half of a fifty-dollar purse, selected a champion to uphold its prestige, and adjourned in a body to the neutral ground outside a convenient saloon. The fights were bare-knuckled affairs, to a finish, under London Prize Ring rules—which by no means emasculated the sport—and the winner took the purse. Four or five hundred men might witness such a bout; betting was brisk, with stakes limited only by earning capacities, and fights at the ringside often outclassed the main event in intensity and bloodiness.

Wyatt Earp was a skillful boxer and, for an amateur, a keen student of a game just beginning to attract popular fancy in the West. Chrisman knew this, and upon his suggestion Wyatt was chosen to referee an important bout between two camp bullies. Among other duties, the referee was custodian of the purse and stakeholder for a hundred or more ringside bets ranging in amount from two to twenty dollars. Prizefighting took the railroad camps by storm, and Wyatt soon had his Sunday mornings mapped out for him. That such a youngster should have been chosen for such jobs by such men as were interested in the referee's capabilities offers an additional commentary on Wyatt Earp at twenty years of age.

The great event of the Wyoming season of 1868 was a professional prizefight arranged for Fourth of July in Cheyenne between Mike Donovan and John Shanssey. Donovan was the widely known professional; Shanssey, a youngster with more ambition than skill, was later to make a name for courage by carrying United States mail through Indian-infested territories, and to serve as Mayor of Yuma, Arizona, before he died.

Fourth of July fell on Saturday, and by Friday afternoon every railroad camp within one hundred miles of Cheyenne was deserted, while men from the grading camps farther west had been straggling into the town for several days. Nearly three thousand laborers, foremen, contractors, prospectors, gamblers, and other frontier characters gathered for the big fight. Among them was Wyatt Earp. Betting was brisk and the graders from the outlying camps pooled their cash for Wyatt to handle as commissioner. In this capacity he was introduced to the fighters on the night preceding their encounter. As one result of the interviews, Wyatt bet the graders' pool on Donovan.

In their Fourth-of-July battle, Mike Donovan beat John Shanssey so badly that the latter abandoned the prize ring. Wyatt was not to meet Donovan again, but some years later Shanssey was to recall the Cheyenne acquaintance in a manner which would color in striking fashion the careers of the Fighting Earps.

Late fall found Chrisman and Earp completing a contract between Hams Fork and Fort Bridger. With that done, and the Union Pacific construction nearing its end, Wyatt sold his teams. With a profit on his grading venture of about twenty-five hundred dollars added to his stake, he set out to visit his grandfather in Monmouth, Illinois.

Soon after his arrival in Illinois, Wyatt met and married the daughter of a family neighbor to his grandparents. His happiness ended tragically with the death of his girl-bride in a typhus epidemic. Memory of this short-lived romance was one that Wyatt treasured always. Few suspected the tender and abiding quality of this emotion, yet with his intimates there was the understanding that the poignancy of this experience determined Wyatt Earp's generally uncomprehended attitude toward certain accepted phases of life in the Western camps. He was loyal to the young love, in a manner and from a sentiment which few of his casual associates could have fathomed.

During his stay with his grandfather, the judge, there was one more attempt to get Wyatt at a belated study of the law. For some time the young man endeavored to adjust himself to a life in the settlements which might satisfy both his relatives and himself and, to his way of thinking, thus wasted nearly a year. The summer of '69 found him utterly discontented, his cash dwindling, and the lure of frontier freedom no longer to be denied.

Wyatt bolstered his courage to the point of announcing flatly and finally that he was through with humdrum existence in some Eastern town. To his surprise he found that the determination he had summoned for facing his parents with this pronouncement was not needed at all.

"I know that my father and mother were deeply disappointed," Wyatt said, "but they were at some pains to make it perfectly clear that they would not interfere with whatever I chose to do. I felt rather sheepish over the speech I had worked up, but they seemed to understand about that, too, and when I left, they were arranging to have Morgan read law."

It was late fall when Wyatt reached St. Louis, from which point he intended to strike overland. Where he would settle and what he would do, he had not planned, beyond his decision to throw in his lot, for good and all, with the hazards of the West.

4

Guns and Gunfighters

Indian Territory—The Nations—in 1869 was largely
unsurveyed, unexplored prairie and mountain wilderness in
which the United States had corralled a troublesome horde
of aboriginal Americans. Tribal boundaries may have existed for bureaucrats who had never seen the country, but
Indians roamed from the Arkansas to the Red River almost
at will, their only restraint an occasional cavalry detachment at one of the far-flung army posts which were supposed
to hem them in. Old Jesse Chisholm, it was true, had blazed
the trail that was to carry him into history; south of the
Canadian River and east of the Neosho, the land was fairly
well known, and there were a number of settlements. But to
the north and west, there was no white habitation from Salt
Fork to Camp Supply.

Suspicion that natural wealth inadvertently had been
handed to the Red Man under a too-hasty assumption that it
was worthless was, however, already stirring the cupidity of
the white. The State of Texas claimed a slice of the Indian
refuge and was willing to fight for it. Kansas appeared ready

to bleed some more over certain territorial prairies, and Texas, Kansas, New Mexico, and Colorado, each asserted ownership of No Man's Land, between the Texas Panhandle and the Kansas–Colorado lines. Soil of The Nations was rich, timber and water fairly plentiful, and although petroleum was an unthought-of resource, certain interests persuaded the Federal Government to have the territory surveyed by sections, which would facilitate, they hoped, land grabs without a border war.

Wyatt Earp reached Springfield, Missouri, in December 1869 to find Government surveyors preparing for invasion of The Nations with level and transit. The engineering party needed a hunter to keep them in fresh meat and as additional protection against marauding Indians and white outlaws. Wyatt got the job.

There were twelve surveyors in the party, and a cook. Their outfit consisted of two wagons, each drawn by four mules, a string of pack animals, and enough saddle ponies to provide an extra mount for each man. Wyatt's wages were thirty-five dollars, cash, a month, plus ten cents a pound for all buffalo meat the surveyors required, one dollar for each deer or antelope and one dollar and fifty cents for each wild turkey killed. In addition to the cash, he was to receive such instruction in the art of surveying as duties and inclination made him free to accept.

Early in January 1870, the surveying party left Baxter Springs, Kansas, and drove south along the Neosho to the Creek Indian Agency, across the Arkansas from Fort Gibson. There they struck into the wilderness. As his arsenal, Wyatt had a pair of forty-four-caliber pistols, a rifle of the same caliber, and a muzzle-loading shotgun, with ammunition calculated to last eighteen months.

As matters transpired, there was no serious trouble with either red men or white. The cook was pestered to distraction by Indians who begged for sugar, coffee, and tobacco, and rustlers made one or two futile attempts to run off the stock; that was all. At that, the official hunter had plenty of practice with his firearms, practice that in later years was to stand him in good stead. His party lived almost entirely on meat, and as all were performing hard, physical tasks, about five pounds of edible game a day was provided for each man.

After leaving Fort Gibson, the expedition worked south to the Red River through the heart of the Choctaw Nation, then west and north through the Chickasaw, the Seminole, the Creek, and the Cherokee countries. Wyatt did not experience a single morning during the time on this trail when he had to go farther than a few hundred yards from camp or spend more than an hour in shooting a day's supply of meat, with a choice of buffalo, venison, or turkey.

On days when he furnished buffalo meat to the surveyors' table, the hunter earned six to eight dollars. Venison was not so profitable, although the men became so finicky about the parts of animals that they would or would not eat, that a venison day meant at least three dollars in wages. Turkeys were first choice from a monetary point of view, and Wyatt fed them to his outfit until salt horse would have made a welcome change.

"At times when I have told how these Government survey parties were supplied with meat," Wyatt said, "I have aroused criticism for the waste of money in high living for the type of man who went on such expeditions, a matter which I recollect was once the subject of a bitter debate in Congress. The Congressman who attacked the Administration for authorizing large payments to game hunters wanted to know why plain, everyday surveyors could not live on bacon and other ordinary fare. As usual, the folks back in the settlements knew no more of actual conditions on the frontier than they did for decades afterward.

"Our party did buy a little bacon at Baxter Springs when we outfitted. Back in the settlements bacon was ten cents a pound. At Baxter Springs it was seventy-five cents; it had been freighted in by team. A meal of bacon for our party would cost about seven dollars, not to mention the extra equipment to pack it along. Those of us who did know conditions knew also that for any expedition into such a country as The Indian Nations the professional hunter was the most economical source of food supply."

Working northward from the Red River, the survey party reached the Kansas line in April 1871, and then turned eastward to Arkansas City, where the men were paid off. They had come through without loss of man or animal. Wyatt had acquired a fair knowledge of surveying as it then was practiced, and nearly three thousand dollars in cash.

With a comfortable sum in his belt, Wyatt decided to take another look at civilization before heading west. He headed for Kansas City, the metropolitan playground for frontiersmen who hankered for the finest and fanciest in entertainment, food, and drink, or the latest styles in weapons and accoutrement for man and horse.

In the Kansas City of '71, a young man of Wyatt Earp's leanings naturally would make for Market Square, where traders, teamsters, hunters, and cowmen made headquarters in their holidays on the edge of the encroaching East. For buffalo hunters, the square was a summer resort, when the herds which furnished them a livelihood were in poor coat and less profitable to kill. There, they lolled in the shade of stores and saloons from morning until night, spinning yarns of the hunting range, reviewing the season just closed, discussing information received and dispatched by the grapevine telegraph which could spread the news of an individual or event across the frontier in an unbelievably short time, and planning expeditions to come. Periodically, a group would move indoors for a drink, then return to loaf and yarn some more.

"When I first saw Market Square," Wyatt Earp recalled, "the spot favored by the men best known in frontier life was a bench in front of the police station where Tom Speers, then marshal of Kansas City, held forth each afternoon. Because these hunters, freighters, and cattlemen knew so much of the country and the life which held my interest at the time, I spent most of the summer on or near Tom Speers's bench. I made acquaintances that I was to renew later, all over the West, on the buffalo range, in cowtowns, mining camps, and along the trails between; some as far away as the Alaskan goldfields in '97 and '98.

"I met Wild Bill Hickok in Kansas City in 1871. Jack Gallagher, the celebrated scout, was there; and I remember Jack Martin, Billy Dixon, Jim Hanrahan, Tom O'Keefe, Cheyenne Jack, Billy Ogg, Bermuda Carlisle, Old Man Keeler, Kirk Jordan, and Andy Johnson. The names may not mean much to another century, but in my younger days each was a noted man. Much that they accomplished has been ignored by the records of their time, but every one made history. Most of them, I know, were illiterate and crude; a few were well educated and well informed; all were keenly intelligent, resourceful, and fearless—they had to be, for they made possible the settlement of the West.

"To the average Easterner, the most surprising feature about these frontier characters was their mode of dress while in Kansas City. On the plains they wore buckskin garments made by the Indians, or heavy woolen shirts, jackets, and trousers, with leather leggings. But, on a Market Square vacation, the hunters were most exacting in their demands on the local tailors and haberdashers. They stuck to boots, handmade of fine black calfskin, but white linen replaced the hunting-shirts, and black broadcloth was preferred for coats and trousers. Trouser legs were pulled down over the boot tops, and most of the coats were of the long-tailed frock variety, with velvet collars or lapel facings. Fancy vests were silk or brocade, or possibly beaded buckskin ordered from an Indian squaw especially for show. Turndown collars with black string-ties were the stylish neckwear. Wide-brimmed, black sombreros were generally worn, but a number of frontiersmen while in Kansas City actually displayed silk hats. Some of those old buffalo hunters could get on a bigger spree in a clothing store than any saloon could inspire.

"During the hot, sunshiny days the men sat around Market Square in their shirt-sleeves, with as much pride in fine spotless linen as they had for the velvet-trimmed frock coats and fancy vests which they wore later in the day. Evenings were spent at variety shows, in the dancehalls, or at the theater when a traveling dramatic company was in town. After the snow, the real sport of the day got under full steam—monte, faro, and poker. Gambling went on day and night, but big games rarely started much before midnight; they might run well into the following morning.

"There was steady drinking. Kansas City offered a change from the raw liquor of the camps. Saloons were as well stocked with beers, wines, cordials, and fine whiskeys as the choosiest drinker could require, and the best in the land was none too good for the frontiersman who could pay. Some men went on sprees which lasted for days and weeks, but for the majority one protracted session immediately after hitting town was enough; then they'd be satisfied with an occasional drink in the daytime, and a reasonable amount of sociable drinking at night.

"Conversation around Tom Speers's bench dealt with subjects in which the men were interested, chiefly buffalo hunting, the rising market for hides, and the increased demand for meat to be shipped East. Until that year, buffalo killing had been largely for supplying meat to railway construction gangs and army posts, on contracts, with small attention given to the hides. It was not until 1870 that private business concerned itself seriously with the enormous profits to be had from the great buffalo herds that roamed the plains from the Brazos to beyond the Canadian line. By 1871, buyers of hides and meat were falling over one another to pay cash to the hunter for every animal he could kill.

"My long jaunt through the Indian Nations had shown me the possibilities for a skillful buffalo hunter. In Kansas City I heard that General Crook had estimated for the Government that there were fifty million buffalo on the prairies, with ten million grazing between Fort Dodge and Camp Supply. From personal observation I was certain that, while General Crook might have overestimated things a bit in regard to his first figure, his second was not far from correct.

"There was much talk, too, of the announcement that the United States Government was encouraging the wholesale slaughter of the great herds, and that, as long as the white hunters kept away from Indian reservations, the Interior Department and War Department would do all that they could to assist them.

"In later years I heard much criticism of the part which the Government played in the extermination of the buffalo, but it always struck me as poorly informed, coming from persons who meant well, but who saw but one side of the question—preservation of wildlife.

"I have no defense for the manner in which the professional buffalohunter did his work; the result is another matter. Buffalo hunting on a commercial scale, as I took part in it, was criminal waste. The fact remains, however, that if the buffalo hunter had not performed his work in some manner, development of the West would have been impossible.

"As long as the buffalo roamed the plains, the Indians had every necessity of life ready to hand, and all the soldiers in the army could not hold them in check as long as that held true. Records will show that, as a whole, the bad Indians were subdued into good Indians almost concurrently with the slaughter of the buffalo, their one sure source of livelihood on the open range. Whether the means was justified by the end is not for me to say.

"Again, if the buffalo had not been killed off, neither the cattle business nor agriculture could have prospered in the West. There was not sufficient natural forage on the plains for buffalo and beef cattle, too. Which was more important to civilization, the buffalo or the cow? As for crops, no fence could withstand a buffalo herd, and a million hoofs in a grainfield would trample a homesteader out of existence.

"I'll admit that in 1871 no buffalo hunter of my acquaintance—myself, least of all—planned his work as a crusade for civilization; but in a sense it was that. I went into the business to make money while enjoying life that appealed to me.

"Bill Hickok told me he'd make five thousand dollars between September 1 and April 1; as it turned out, he did not hunt that season of '71 and '72. Jack Gallagher expected his earnings to run even higher. So I decided to try my hand at the game.

"Wild Bill and Gallagher were respected around Tom Speers's bench. They were accepted as authorities on buffalo killing, and their opinions settled many a Market Square argument over man-killing, as well. They knew Indians inside-out, and both had participated in or witnessed gunfights between white men that were talked of all over the West. Gallagher certainly knew more of buffalo hunting and Indian battles, but Bill Hickok was regarded as the deadliest pistol-shot alive, as well as a man of great courage. The truth of certain stories about Bill's achievements may have been open to debate, but he had earned the respect paid to him.

"As I recall them after all these years, Market Square conversations not concerned with buffalo, usually dealt with gunplay of another sort, with the sudden end to which some well-known character had come, or a stand against heavy odds by some fighter whom most of the hunters knew. Discussions naturally led to arguments over the merits of weapons and methods of getting them into play. Supporters of any theory were willing and able to demonstrate their points.

"There were few gunfights in Kansas City that summer, none between men of reputation that I recall; and, unless participants in a killing were well known, no one gave much attention to what they did. The prominent characters were not trouble-hunters, as a rule; and their relations with Tom Speers placed them under obligation to save him the embarrassment which might follow if topnotchers went to shooting. But it was a dull day when we were not entertained by exhibitions of gunplay by past masters in the art, or target matches between them.

"I was a fair hand with pistol, rifle, or shotgun, but I learned more about gunfighting from Tom Speers's cronies during the summer of '71 than I had dreamed was in the book. Those old-timers took their gunplay seriously, which was natural under conditions in which they lived. Shooting, to them, was considerably more than aiming at a mark and

35

pulling a trigger. Models of weapons, methods of wearing them, means of getting them into action and of operating them, all to the one end of combining high speed with absolute accuracy, contributed to the frontiersman's shooting skill. The sought-after degree of proficiency was that which could turn to most effective account the split-second between life and death. Hours upon hours of practice, and wide experience in actualities supported their arguments over style.

"The most important lesson I learned from those proficient gunfighters was that the winner of a gunplay usually was the man who took his time. The second was that, if I hoped to live long on the frontier, I would shun flashy trick-shooting—grandstand play—as I would poison. Later, as a peace officer, I was to fight some desperate battles against notorious gunmen of the Old West, and wonder has been expressed that I came through them all unscathed. Certain outlaws and their friends have said I wore a steel vest under my shirt. There have been times when I'd have welcomed such a garment, but I never saw one in my life outside of a museum, and I very much doubt that any other frontiersman has either. Luck was with me in my gunfights, of course; so were the lessons learned in Market Square during the summer of '71.

"Jack Gallagher's advice summed up what others had to say, to wear weapons in the handiest position—in my case as far as pistols were concerned, in open holsters, one on each hip if I was carrying two, hung rather low as my arms were long, and with the muzzles a little forward on my thighs. Some men wore their guns belted high on the waist; a few, butts forward, army style, for a cross-draw; others carried one gun directly in front of the stomach, either inside or outside the waistband, and another gun in a holster slung below the left armpit; still others wore two of these shoulder holsters. Style was a matter of individual preference.

"When mounted on a horse and 'armed to the teeth,' as the saying goes, a man's rifle was slung in a boot just ahead of his right stirrup, his shotgun carried on the left by a thong looped over the saddle-horn. With the adoption of breech-loading weapons, a rider equipped with two pistols, rifle, and shotgun customarily had one of the belts to which his pistol holsters were attached filled with pistol ammunition, the other with rifle cartridges, while a heavier, wider belt filled with shotgun shells was looped around the saddle-horn underneath the thong which held that weapon. He was a riding arsenal, but there might well be times when he would need the munitions. Bowie knives were worn largely for utility's sake in a belt sheath back of the hip; when I came on the scene, their popularity for purposes of offense was on the wane, although I have seen old-timers who carried them slung about their necks and who preferred them above all other weapons in the settlement of purely personal quarrels.

"When I say that I learned to take my time in a gunfight, I do not wish to be misunderstood, for the time to be taken was only that split fraction of a second that means the difference between deadly accuracy with a six-gun and a miss. It is hard to make this clear to a man who has never been in a gunfight. Perhaps I can best describe such time-taking as going into action with the greatest speed of which a man's muscles are capable, but mentally unflustered by an urge to hurry or the need for complicated nervous and muscular actions which trick-shooting involves. Mentally deliberate, but muscularly faster than thought, is what I mean.

"In all my life as a frontier peace officer, I did not know a really proficient gunfighter who had anything but contempt for the gun-fanner, or the man who literally shot from the hip. In later years I read a great deal about this type of gunplay, supposedly employed by men noted for skill with a forty-five.

"From personal experience and from numerous six-gun battles which I witnessed, I can only support the opinion advanced by the men who gave me my most valuable instruction in fast and accurate shooting, which was that the gun-fanner and the hip-shooter stood small chance to live against a man who, as old Jack Gallagher always put it, took his time and pulled the trigger once.

"Cocking and firing mechanisms on new revolvers were almost invariably altered by their purchasers in the interests of smoother, effortless handling, usually by filing the dog which controlled the hammer, some going so far as to remove triggers entirely or lash them against the guard, in which cases the guns were fired by thumbing the hammer. This is not to be confused with fanning, in which the triggerless gun was held in one hand while the other was brushed rapidly across the hammer fanwise to cock the gun, and firing it by the weight of the hammer itself. A skillful gun-fanner could fire five shots from a forty-five so rapidly that the individual reports were indistinguishable, but what could happen to him in a gunfight was pretty close to murder.

"I saw Jack Gallagher's theory borne out so many times in deadly operation that I was never tempted to forsake the principles of gunfighting as I had them from him and his associates.

"There was no man in the Kansas City group who was Wild Bill's equal with a six-gun. Bill's correct name, by the way, was James B. Hickok. Legend and the imaginations of certain people have exaggerated the number of men he killed in gunfights and have misrepresented the manner in which he did his killing. At that, they could not very well overdo his skill with pistols.

"Hickok knew all the fancy tricks and was as good as the best at that sort of gunplay, but when he had serious business in hand, a man to get, the acid test of marksmanship, I doubt if he employed them. At least, he told me that he did not. I have seen him in action and I never saw him fan a gun, shoot from the hip, or try to fire two pistols simultaneously. Neither have I ever heard a reliable old-timer tell of any trick-shooting employed by Hickok when fast straight-shooting meant life or death.

"That two-gun business is another matter that can stand some truth before the last of the old-time gunfighters has gone on. They wore two guns, most of six-gun–toters did, and when the time came for action went after them with both hands. But they didn't shoot them that way.

"Primarily, two guns made the threat of something in reserve; they were useful as a display of force when a lone man stacked up against a crowd. Some men could shoot equally well with either hand, and in a gunplay might alternate their fire; others exhausted the loads from the gun in the right hand, or left, as the case might be, then shifted the reserve weapon to the natural shooting hand if that was necessary and possible. Such a move—the border-shift—could be made faster than the eye could follow a top-notch gun-thrower, but if the man was as good as that, the shift seldom would be required.

"Whenever you see a picture of some two-gun man in action with both weapons held closely against his hips and both spitting smoke together, you can put it down that you are looking at the picture of a fool, or at a fake. I remember quite a few of those so-called two-gun men who tried to operate everything at once, but like the fanners, they didn't last long in proficient company.

"In the days of which I am talking, among men whom I have in mind, when a man went after his guns, he did so with a single, serious purpose. There was no such thing as a bluff; when a gunfighter reached for his forty-five, every faculty he owned was keyed to shooting as speedily and as accurately as possible, to making his first shot the last of the fight. He just had to think of his gun solely as something with which to kill another before he himself could be killed. The possibility of intimidating an antagonist was remote, although the "drop" was thoroughly respected, and few men in the West would draw against it. I have seen men so fast and so sure of themselves that they did go after their guns while men who intended to kill them had them covered, and what is more win out in the play. They were rare. It is safe to say, for all general purposes, that anything in gunfighting which smacked of show-off or bluff was left to braggarts who were ignorant or careless of their lives.

"I might add that I never knew a man who amounted to

anything to notch his guns with 'credits,' as they were called, for men he had killed. Outlaws, gunmen of the wild crew who killed for the sake of brag, followed this custom. I have worked with most of the noted peace officers—Hickok, Billy Tilghman, Pat Sughrue, Bat Masterson, Charlie Bassett, and others of like caliber—have handled their weapons many times, but never knew one of them to carry a notched gun.

"Strange how such wild tales become current. I know the start of one, about Bat Masterson's 'favorite six-gun with twenty-two notches in the butt.' Bat's sense of humor was responsible, and he didn't dream of the consequences.

"Some rapacious collector of souvenirs pestered Bat half to death with demands for a six-gun that Bat had used on the frontier. This collector called on Bat in his New York office and so insistently that Bat decided to give him a gun to get rid of him. Bat did not want to part with one he had used, so he went to a pawnshop and bought an old Colt's forty-five which he took to his office in anticipation of the collector's return. With the gun lying on the desk, Bat was struck with the idea that while he was providing a souvenir, he might as well give one worth the trouble it had caused, so he took out his penknife and then and there cut twenty-two 'credits' in the pawnshop gun. When the collector called for his souvenir and Bat handed it to him, he managed to gasp a question as to whether Bat had killed twenty-two men with it.

"'I didn't tell him yes, and I didn't tell him no,' Bat said, 'and I didn't exactly lie to him. I simply said I hadn't counted either Mexicans or Indians, and he went away tickled to death.'

"It wasn't long, however, before tales of the Old West with stories about Bat Masterson's notched gun and the twenty-two men he had killed began to creep into print. The case may offer a fair example of how other yarns started.

"There are two other points about the old-time method of using six-guns most effectively that do not seem to be generally known. One is that the gun was not cocked with the ball of the thumb. As his gun was jerked into action, the old-timer closed the whole joint of his thumb over the hammer and the gun was cocked in that fashion. The soft flesh of the thumb ball might slip if a man's hands were moist, and a slip was not to be chanced if humanly avoidable. This thumb-joint method was employed whether or not a man used the trigger for firing.

"On the second point, I have often been asked why five shots without reloading were all a top-notch gunfighter ever fired, when his guns were chambered for six cartridges. The answer is, merely, safety. To ensure against accidental discharge of the gun while in the holster, due to hair-trigger adjustment, the hammer rested upon an empty chamber. As widely as this was known and practiced, the number of cartridges a man carried in his six-gun may be taken as one indication of a man's rank with the gunfighters of the old school. Practiced gun-wielders had too much respect for their weapons to take unnecessary chances with them; it was only with tyros and would-bes that you heard of accidental discharges or didn't-know-it-was-loaded injuries in the country where carrying a Colt's was a man's prerogative.

"But let me go back to Bill Hickok's marksmanship. That summer in Kansas City he performed a feat of pistol-shooting which often has been cited as one of the most remarkable on record. It was all of that, but widely circulated accounts give the impression that Wild Bill did his shooting from the hip. What actually happened may be of interest.

"Hickok was showing a pair of ivory-handled six-guns which Senator Wilson had given him in appreciation of his services as guide on a tour of the West. Tom Speers knew, as we all did, Bill's two favorite exhibitions of marksmanship; one, driving a cork through the neck of a bottle with a bullet; the other, splitting a bullet against the edge of a dime; both at about twenty paces. So when Tom asked Bill what he could do with the new guns, he added that he did not mean at close range, but at a distance that would be a test.

"Diagonally across Market Square, possibly one hundred yards away, was a saloon, and on the side-wall toward the police station a sign that carried a capital letter O. The sign ran off at an angle from Hickok's line of sight, yet, before anyone guessed what his target was, Wild Bill had fired five shots from the gun in his right hand, shifted weapons, and fired five more shots. Then he told Tom to send someone over to look at the O. All ten of Bill's slugs were found inside the ring of the letter.

"That was shooting. I am not belittling Wild Bill when I bear witness that while he was shooting at the O, he held his gun as almost every man skilled in such matters preferred to hold one when in action, with a half-bent elbow that brought the gun slightly in front of his body at about, or slightly above, the level of the waist.

"It may surprise some to know that a man of Hickok's skill could make a six-gun effective up to four hundred yards. A rifle, of course, was preferred for shooting over such a distance, but in a pinch the old-fashioned single-action forty-five-caliber revolver could be made to do the work. Luck figured largely in such shooting, and a man had to know his gun to score, but I have known them to kill at that range.

"Soon after his shooting exhibition, Bill Hickok was called back to Abilene, Kansas. Bear River Tom Smith, whom I had known in Wyoming, where he was the hero of the Bear River troubles, and who was one of the most courageous men who fought for law and order on the old frontier, had been marshal of Abilene. Texas men from the cattle trail had been standing the town on end, and two of them had killed Tom. After a long hunt for an able citizen to take the marshal's place, Abilene sent for Bill. Hickok tamed the Texas men in short order, although he had to kill two or three in the process.

"I had definitely decided to hunt buffalo, and late in August I left Kansas City for Stone's Store, a trading post that was to be Caldwell, Kansas, to purchase an outfit of wagons, animals, and supplies. I wanted to get to the range early in September."

5

The Buffalo Range

Wyatt Earp's venture as a buffalo hunter undoubtedly gave first rise to legends which picture him as invariably playing a lone hand. He ignored established hunting practices and avoided the populous camps, whereupon other hunters ascribed to him a habitual aloofness which the man never possessed. Wyatt simply followed that independence of thought and action which repeatedly set him apart from his contemporaries, and by which, unquestionably, he won his ultimate rank on the frontier.

With Kansas City associates and other buffalo hunters assembled at Caldwell, Wyatt discovered that success of a season's hunt was measured solely by animals killed and cash received for hides and meat. Only gross sums paid for their hazardous labors entered the calculations of the adventurers, and figures were reached when the hunt was done; expenditures for horses, wagons, supplies, and skinners' wages had small place in their accounting scheme. Any hunter could boast of the money in his pockets at the end of a season; not many could say accurately how much was gain.

Wyatt Earp weighed accepted methods of hunting buffalo on a commercial scale against possibilities which he analyzed with equal care. His months in the Indian Nations furnished working knowledge of buffalo peculiarities in habit and disposition, second to none, upon which he based hunting plans characteristically his own. Wyatt's first calculation was the cost of a season's hunt; his next, a conservative estimate of the number of animals he could shoot and skin, and the cash to come for their hides and meat. As he had also developed certain theories concerning methods of killing, he then set a course of action which he followed as long as he hunted buffalo.

Again and again in the folklore of the Old West, a similar attitude on Wyatt Earp's part toward problems of action where men instead of buffaloes were involved has been cited as proof of cold-bloodedness. Actually, it was merely the application of his intelligence to any matter in hand. That his mentality functioned in the flash of a six-gun as effectively as with opportunity for deliberation made it only more incomprehensible to casual acquaintances.

With each buffalo hunter who set out for the range in the fall of '71 and who held himself in any esteem, there were customarily four or five four-horse wagons, with one driver, the stocktender, camp watchman, and cook; the others to skin the kill. The hunter provided horses, wagons, and supplies for several months. Money received for hides and meat would be divided into two equal parts; one went to the hunter, and from his share he paid all expenses; the second was again split into as many shares as there were drivers and skinners and a share paid to each helper as his seasonal wage. Thus, the titular head of the party paid through the nose for adherence to the camp convention which held that no really top-notch buffalo hunter would stoop to skinning the animals he shot. Caste devoured profit.

The first flaw which Wyatt Earp saw was that the average hunter outfitted in expectation of killing one hundred buffalo a day, and selling each animal's hide and meat for two to five dollars, depending upon size and quality. While one good hunter and four skinners could handle one hundred buffalo a day, few outfits did so at any time, none consistently. Traits of the game and methods of hunting combined to hold the average daily kill well below fifty.

In place of four or five wagons and twenty-odd horses, Wyatt purchased one wagon, four sound animals for harness and one to ride. He engaged an experienced skinner in a straight profit-sharing scheme. Wyatt was to finance the hunt and shoot; the helper would drive and cook; and, greatly to the disgust of older hands, Wyatt was to assist in skinning and butchering. At the end of the hunt, Wyatt was to keep the team and wagons, deduct all other expenses from the gross receipts, and share any net equally with his skinner.

Veteran hunters at Caldwell attempted to dissuade Wyatt from violation of the conventions by pointing out that the best he might hope for under his system would be a kill of twenty-five buffalo a day; two men could not handle a greater number and care for their camp. The well-meaning advisers were told that an average daily kill of twenty formed the basis of the young man's plans, and, furthermore, that he intended to hunt at some distance from established camps. Whereupon, they turned to warning him that neither he nor his skinner would live long enough to cash in on their hides, as they would certainly fall victim to the Indians who periodically raided the range. When informed that in place of the unwieldy Sharps "Fifty" rifle, which was the buffalo hunter's standby, Wyatt intended to kill buffalo with a shotgun, the old-timers abandoned argument.

One thing for which the veterans failed to give Wyatt Earp credit was a carefully considered reason for every move he made. There would be several thousand hunters on the plains, he knew; the majority operating from closely adjoining camps. Their activity would keep the buffalo herds migrating steadily and so waste time for the hunters, who had to move camp in keeping pace. It would also interfere seriously with the individual hunter's opportunities to shoot from a "stand," the one certain means to profitable skinhunting. He estimated, moreover, that a greater net profit was to be gained from skinning twenty to twenty-five buffalo a day, with expenses for two men deducted from sixty to seventy-five dollars received for the work, than from an average kill of fifty animals which brought about one hundred and fifty dollars, but with expenses for five or six men and the initial outlay for horses and wagons to be met from the hunter's share.

The Indian hazard offered no greater deterrent to a man of Wyatt's temperament than the possibility that he might be caught by the hoofs or horns of a stampeding buffalo herd. Face to face with either danger, he would do what he might. Beyond that realization, he gave such matters no thought.

The problem of firearms Wyatt settled within his own experience. The heavy Sharps—some of these rifles weighed more than twenty pounds—which all right-minded buffalo hunters carried, was usually overloaded to fire a slug of lead two inches in length, a half-inch in diameter, weighing approximately eight to the pound. The complement to the piece was a shooting rest, two sticks tied together, X-fashion, set in the ground to support the rifle while the marksman aimed and fired. The Sharps was unquestionably the best weapon then obtainable for long-range buffalo-shooting, but notable among its drawbacks were the cost of ammunition and the fact that the rifle's accuracy was seriously affected by continued rapid fire. The wise user of a Sharps, under conditions imposed by buffalo hunting with profit in view, ran a water-soaked rag through the barrel after every second or third shot and let the metal cool, to keep the rifle from distortion.

In common with all who knew buffalo from contact with the herds, Wyatt was well acquainted with their idiosyncrasy of stampeding at sight or scent of a man on horseback, but generally ignoring one on foot. He intended to make use of this in reaching shotgun range of the herds. He purchased a breech-loading gun, with apparatus for reloading shells, and this, with a supply of powder, lead, and caps, was to constitute his hunting arsenal. He loaded a single one-and-one-half-ounce slug to the shell, and reverted to earlier experiences for conviction that at any range under one hundred yards he could score as accurately with his shotgun as any rifleman.

Wyatt waited in Caldwell until the large parties of hunters were well on their way to intercept the herds then migrating southward across the prairies. When he did leave, he kept south of the Arkansas River and west to the Medicine Lodge to avoid the expeditions which by their size and activity kept the buffalo constantly on the move. Fortune vindicated his reasoning.

"To understand why I outfitted as I did and why I held away from the beaten track," Wyatt explained, "it is necessary to know something of buffalo peculiarities and methods employed in killing them.

"Early white hunters had followed the Indian practice of shooting buffalo from the back of a horse galloping full tilt at the edge of a stampeding herd. In skin hunting this did not pay. Shooting from horseback could not be as accurate as from a stand, and the animals killed during a run would be strung for miles across the prairie, making a lot of travel for the skinners, with the added certainty that many hides would be missed. Also, every buffalo left alive would be stampeded clear out of the country in a day's hunt, and the killers would have to move camp or wait for another herd.

"In 1871, a strip of country about five hundred miles wide and fifteen hundred miles long, running from the Colorado River in Texas well into Canada, was a solid carpet of buffalo grass. Over it the herds grazed year in and year out, as the seasons changed; the strip was cut repeatedly by rivers and creeks with an ample water supply.

"Buffalo grass is not much to look at, green or cured. At best, the grass is seldom more than six inches tall. It spreads over the ground like a vine and with its closely curled leaf looks something like moss. Its growing season starts with earliest spring, it cures on the stalk, and is actually sweeter and more nutritious in the fall and winter than at any other time. The buffalo knew this long before the cattleman. But its most remarkable quality is that, despite continuous grazing and the pounding from millions of hoofs, it comes up just the same, year after year.

"Each spring as grass-growing weather moved northward with the sun, the largest buffalo herds followed to spend the summer in the Dakotas, Montana, and Canada. With the approach of snow to the northern plains, they turned south again to winter in the valleys of the Republican, the Smoky Hill, the Solomon, the Arkansas, the Cimarron, the Canadian, the Brazos, and the Colorado Rivers. On this southward migration they came into winter coats, and were more valuable to the hide hunters from September to March than at other times.

"The majority of hunters outfitting in the Kansas settlements headed north in late summer to intercept the southbound buffalo in Nebraska and follow them into the Texas Panhandle, killing as they went. By the time a few thousand hunters had shot at them for a few weeks, the buffalo herds would be skittish enough to stampede without encouragement.

"I knew that thousands of buffalo, out of touch with the main groups, stayed the year around in the valleys at the northern edge of the Indian Nations and decided to get into that country before the big herds came down from the North. There might not be as many buffalo to shoot at, but it would be easier to keep within gunshot of what there were.

"In recent years I have realized that not much is known of the way buffalo hunters operated or of what they accomplished. The prevailing ideas of what went on during the extermination of the herds may have been drawn from Buffalo Bill Cody's widely advertised shooting match against Buffalo Bill Comstock for a doubtful title and an entirely mythical championship. Their match was merely an excuse for a railway excursion to the Wyoming country where it was staged; there were five hundred buffalo hunters on the plains more successful at the business than either Cody or Comstock ever was. Cody killed sixty-nine buffalo in a horseback run, as I recall, and a few hundred excursionists saw him do it. Then his show was organized, with Cody billed as champion buffalo hunter of all time. Possibly he was that, under the conditions of his match with Comstock. That contest demonstrated nothing more than ability to

48

shoot from the back of a running horse and was meaningless to a real buffalo hunter. Yet, ever after, it was held to be the true picture of the buffalo hunter in action.

"In stories about Cody and other Western characters who went into the circus business, I've read of a single horseman holding a bunch of buffalo stock-still by riding around and around them for hours and shooting as he rode. That was an impossibility. Two minutes after the horseman started his riding and shooting, there would not have been a buffalo within rifle range. Buffalo would stampede instantly at sight or smell of a man on horseback; they would ignore a man on foot, or eye him in curiosity. That was why hide hunters shot from a stand.

"Buffalo did not graze in the closely packed herds numbering thousands of head; they scattered in small bands, twenty to two hundred in a bunch, with ten, twenty, or one hundred yards between bunches. Strictly speaking, all animals on a twenty-mile range of prairie might belong to the same herd.

"A hunter would drag his Sharps to a rise of ground giving a good view of the herd, pick a bunch of animals, set his rest-sticks and start shooting. He aimed to hit an animal on the edge of the bunch, the leader if possible, just back of the foreleg and about one third of the way up the body. If the slug went true, the animal would drop in his tracks or stagger a few steps and fall. Strangely enough, the buffalo paid no attention to the report of the rifle and very little, if any, to one that fell.

"A first-class hunter would kill with almost every shot, and if he was good, he could drop game until some buffalo still on his feet chanced to sniff closely at one that had fallen. Then it was up to the hunter to drop the sniffer before he could spread his excitement over the smell of blood. If he could do this, the slaughter might continue, but eventually the blood scent became so strong that several animals noticed it. They would bellow and paw, their frenzy would spread to the bunches nearby, and suddenly the whole herd was off on a wild run. The hunter could kill no more until he found conditions suitable for another stand.

"Where large parties of hunters were working the plains by such methods in fairly close quarters, the periodical scarcity of buffalo was a certainty.

"With the best of luck a single hunter might kill one hundred buffalo in a day, from several stands. That would be all that four skinners could handle. I found that the average bunch would stampede by the time thirty or forty had been killed.

"In my years on the plains the known record kill from a single stand was held by Tom Nixon, a famous shot who made headquarters at Dodge. He downed one hundred and twenty animals without moving his rest-sticks, but he ruined his Sharps rifle. I have known other hunters who boasted of more than one hundred from a stand. The best authenticated total for a season's kill was set by Billy Tilghman. He took thirty-three hundred hides between September 1 of one year and April 1 of the next; no buffalo hunter that I knew ever topped that score.

"Aside from the constant menace of Indians, the great danger in a buffalo hunter's life came when herds stampeded after a stand. No man could guess in what direction the animals would run, nor what might swerve their blind rush from the blood smell that drove them insane. As a rule, the hunter worked up on his game from downwind, and had his saddle horse picketed just back of the rise from which he shot, out of sight and scent. When the buffalo started to run, the hunter made for his horse. In the saddle he was safe. Sometimes his horse would catch the excitement and break away before the hunter could reach him. Then, if the herd headed for him, the man on foot was doomed unless some ruse could split the herd, change its direction, or get him out of its path.

"Years after I left the prairies, Lucky Baldwin—the same E. J. Baldwin who made millions in the Comstock Lode—and I were yarning about early days on the frontier. Among other things, Baldwin told me that he got his real start in life from a poker game. He was in Iowa with his wife and child and almost destitute. He was an inveterate gambler, and a good one. When he saw a soft spot in a poker game, he decided to risk a few dollars that he had just borrowed for food on the chance for a stake that would carry his family through the winter. He left the table with all the money in sight, enough to finance a move to California, where he became wealthy and well known.

"I knew that Lucky had hunted buffalo for meat years before the hide business attracted me, and he told me that he was one of the first white hunters to abandon the Indian system of running the herds in favor of the stand. He also told of his experience when caught on foot by a stampeding herd.

"As Baldwin recounted the incident, his horse broke away and left him so close to the charging, blood-crazy buffalo that he could do nothing to divert them. Like most plainsmen, he was strong and as quick as a cat. A huge bull was leading the buffalo stampede, and as this old fellow reached him, Lucky made his last desperate attempt for life. He grabbed for the old bull's horns, caught them, and drew himself to the animal's back, where he clung while the herd raced across the prairie. The buffalo headed for some cottonwoods, and as the bull led his followers into the grove, Lucky let go of the horns, seized an overhanging branch, and drew himself safely into the tree.

"As I knew of similar happenings during my time on the range—that is, instances in which other hunters had ridden out stampedes on the backs of buffalo—I had no reason to question Lucky Baldwin's yarn. It was merely another example of the resourcefulness which kept the old-timers alive.

"My system for hunting buffalo was to work my way on foot nearer to the herds than the rifle users liked to locate. The shorter range of my shotgun made this necessary, but I could fire the piece as rapidly as I wished without harming it. I planned to get within fifty yards of the buffalo before I started shooting, and at that range pick off selected animals. I would shoot until I had downed all the skinner and I could handle that day. I figured to offset the danger of a stampede by finishing my kill before the animals smelled blood and then working the herd away quietly in the direction I wanted it to go. To do this, I would stand up, wave my coat in the air, and shout. The buffalo would probably move away quietly if I got them started before they scented blood. Then the skinner and I would get to work. In practice, my idea worked out exactly as I had calculated it would.

"Some people called my method foolhardy. To me, it was simply a question of whether or not I could outguess a buffalo. The best answer is that there never was a moment during my three seasons as a buffalo hunter when I was in danger from a stampede, nor a day when I hunted that I did not have a profitable kill. My lowest score for a single stand was eighteen buffalo, the highest, twenty-seven. I shot one stand a day, which meant twenty to thirty-five dollars apiece for the skinner and myself every day we worked. That was cash in hand, not hopes.

"No wonder the average buffalo hunter was glad that the code forbade him to skin his kill; skinning was hard, dirty work.

"My helper kept out of sight with the wagon until I had finished shooting. Then he came on the job. In skinning a buffalo, we slit down the inside of each leg and along the belly from neck to tail. The legs and a strip along each side of the belly-cut were skinned out and the neck skinned all the way around. The head skin was not taken. We gathered the heavy neck hide into a bunch around which we looped a short length of rope, and a horse hitched to the other end ripped the hide off.

"In camp, we dusted the hides and the ground nearby with poison to keep off flies and bugs, and pegged out the skins, flesh-side up. In the dry prairie air, first curing took but a day or so. The hides were then turned, and, after they had cured so water would not injure them, they were stacked in piles, hair-side up, until we hauled them to a hide buyer's station, or a buyer's wagon came to our camp.

"In my first season as a buffalo hunter, many buyers made headquarters at Caldwell, which had not yet been reached by a railroad. In Caldwell, the hides were collected to fill the bull-wains which took them by the thousands to the rail-head. During a greater part of the hunting season, climatic conditions made it possible to keep buffalo meat in good condition until the buyers could prepare it for shipment to the Eastern markets, so most of them took hindquarters and tongues as well as fur.

"With all the buffalo I saw in the days when they roamed the range, I shall never forget a herd we sighted in the fall of '71. We had seen a few small bunches, but none that I stopped for, as I wanted to make camp as permanent as possible. We had crossed the Medicine Lodge when the plenticity of buffalo sign indicated that we were closing on a sizable herd. I went to a rise possibly three hundred feet above the creek bottom. The sight that greeted me as I topped the hill soon disappeared for all time.

"I stood on the highest point within miles. To the west and south, the prairie rolled in mounds and level stretches pitted with buffalo wallows as far as I could see, twenty or thirty miles. For all that distance the range was packed with grazing buffalo.

"The animals were feeding in their customary bunches, and in the foreground the open spaces were evident. In the middle distance the prairie appeared to be a solid mass of furry heads and humps, moving slowly along like a great, muddy river. Beyond the point where I could make out individual animals or groups, I remember thinking some freak might have covered the treeless plains with a dense forest of stunted shrubbery. Clear to the horizon, the herd was endless.

"I signaled my skinner to join me.

"'My God!' he said, 'there must be a million.'

"How close to correct his guess was, neither of us realized. But I was to view one more similar spectacle, in the Texas Panhandle between the Canadian River and Prairie Dog Creek. Then army officers in my company fixed the count of a herd by mathematical process and said we were looking at more than one million buffalo. The Texas herd was not as large as the one I saw near the Medicine Lodge.

"It might give a better idea of the results of buffalo hunting to jump ahead seven years to 1878, when Billy Tilghman, Bat Masterson, and I went buffalo hunting for sport. We traveled due west from Dodge City more than one hundred miles along the Arkansas River, south to the Cimarron, and east to Crooked Creek again, at the height of the best hunting season over what in 1871 had been the greatest buffalo ground in the world. Grass was as plentiful and as succulent as ever, but we never saw a buffalo. The herds were gone, wiped out.

"To go back to 1871 and my first hunting expedition, in October I made camp beyond the Medicine Lodge, and from that base I hunted until after Christmas."

The success of Wyatt Earp's venture against cherished customs was definitely established when he encountered hunters who had worked down from the north to the Salt Fork of the Arkansas. Hide butchers swarmed over the southerly range until avoiding them and the results of their slaughter was impossible. Upon checking tallies, the lone hunter found that, while some had killed greater numbers than he from given stands, or had larger seasonal totals, his daily count of hides was well above the average. Rudimentary arithmetic proved that his profits were much higher.

Wyatt now met again the men whom he had known in Kansas City, and others to become equally well known in the West. Jack Gallagher, Jack Martin, Billy Dixon, Jim Hanrahan, Tom O'Keefe, Cheyenne Jack, Billy Ogg, Bermuda Carlisle, Old Man Keeler, Kirk Jordan, Emmanuel Dubbs, and Andy Johnson were on the Salt Fork. So were Curly Walker, Mike Welch, Jack McCloskey, Dutch Henry, Hendry Brown, Jack Bridges, Billy Rivers, John W. Poe, and Billy Tilghman. These were destined to lasting fame or notoriety. Some turned outlaw; others won recognition as fearless peace officers; almost every one died in his boots.

Dutch Henry developed into the most astute cattle and horse thief on the plains in a day when stock stealing was a capital offense. Hendry Brown threw in with William Bonney, the New York street urchin who became the Western desperado, Billy the Kid. John W. Poe was to become a peace officer, and with the celebrated Pat Garrett would run this same Billy the Kid to the end of his rope and be in at his violent death. Jack Bridges was slated to be marshal of

Dodge when that frontier hamlet was battling toward law and order; also, Billy Rivers.

Hanrahan, Welch, Carlisle, Hendry, Ogg, Dixon, Keeler, Johnson, and a half-dozen more were to make history in that classic of the buffalo range, the fight at Adobe Walls when nineteen buffalo hunters stood off for two weeks the attack of a thousand Kiowa, Arapahoe, Cheyenne, and Comanche Indians under the leadership of Quanah Parker, a battle which countless Pawnees, Osages, and other non-combatant red men rode hundred of miles to witness from the nearby hills, like an audience at a pageant. The hunters rimmed this famous stand with the bodies of dead warriors.

Among the younger men on the Salt Fork with whom Wyatt's life was to be closely bound were Bill Tilghman, Charlie Bassett, Neal Brown, Frank McLean, and Bat Masterson.

6

The Genesis of Reputation

When Wyatt Earp first met Bat Masterson on the Salt Fork early in '72, Masterson was barely sixteen. And Bat has recorded that his admiration for Wyatt, which was to ripen into lifelong friendship, had inception in Wyatt's kindliness to an exceedingly homesick boy.

As one result of their relationship, it is possible to recount fully certain incidents of the buffalo camps to which Wyatt Earp attached small importance. Masterson always insisted that, before Wyatt left the Salt Fork in the spring of '72, he owned the frontier-wide reputation for fearlessness which definitely shaped his career, in support of which Bat quoted others less prejudiced than he may have been.

"Wyatt was a shy young man with few intimates," Bat said that Billy Dixon recalled. "With casual acquaintances he seldom spoke unless spoken to. When he did say anything, it was to the point, without fear or favor, which wasn't relished by some; but that never bothered Wyatt. To those who knew him well he was a genial companion. He had the most even disposition I ever saw; I never knew him to lose his temper. He was more intelligent, better educated, and far better mannered than the majority of his associates, which probably did not help them to understand him. His reserve limited his friendships, but more than one stranger, down on his luck, has had firsthand evidence of Wyatt's generosity. I think his outstanding quality was the nicety with which he gauged the effort and the time for every move. That, plus his absolute confidence in himself, gave him the edge over the run of men. Another thing I remember is that Wyatt had the best horses on the Salt Fork."

An additional Earp characteristic which did not tend to increase Wyatt's general popularity was mentioned by both Dixon and Tilghman.

"In all the years during which I was intimately associated with Wyatt, as a buffalo hunter and as a peace officer," Tilghman said, "I never knew him to take a drink of liquor." (Tilghman neither drank nor smoked.) "He never questioned another man's right to drink as he pleased, and I have been with him in more than one all-night session where whiskey was consumed as rapidly as drinks could be drawn from the barrel, but Wyatt did his tanking-up on coffee."

In the buffalo camps of '72, abstinence from the wild sprees with which the hunters periodically relieved monotony was regarded as peculiar rather than virtuous, but Wyatt Earp has agreed that Dixon and Tilghman were correct in ascribing this trait to him. Until he was well past forty, he never drank spirits; during his career in Kansas and Arizona, indulgence was limited to an occasional glass of wine or beer when these luxuries were available. Morals had nothing to do with Wyatt's aversion to potent liquors; taste governed conviviality, perhaps fortunately.

Wyatt experienced some difficulty in making his preferences tolerated, if not understood. Bat Masterson has testified that he established with his fists his right to drink as he pleased.

In the early weeks of the hunting season, while buffalo were migrating, there was scant opportunity for recreation with the killers and skinners. But in more permanent camps on the winter range came periods of comparative leisure which might be devoted to the favorite sports of drinking and gambling. What passed for whiskey was provided by itinerant vendors who hauled their barreled stock by the wagonload; preferred games of chance were poker and monte; money for all three was available as buyers picked up and paid for hides.

Some hide buyers sold whiskey as a sideline, but this traffic was generally carried on by camp followers. The whiskey wagon was drawn up at the edge of some camp, or in a spot accessible to several, and a tapped barrel rolled into position at the tailboard. Prospective drinkers filed past with cups or buckets, the vendor named his price for the quantity desired and collected the money before he drew the liquor. Purchasers might do their drinking at the tailboard or their campfires, and the tail-end bar continued business as long as money and liquor were in supply.

Buffalo hunters demanded potency in their beverages and the liquor sellers provided it. Raw alcohol colored with coffee was commonly offered in the guise of whiskey, the sting heightened by red pepper and the flavor toned with tobacco. The popularity of a whiskey wagon was determined by the mixture dispensed over its tailboard; as customers judged liquor by the "bite" it took on the way down and the speed of its stranglehold after swallowing, numerous blending recipes were concocted in the competition for patronage.

There has been to succeeding generations a fascination in nicknames conferred by the frontier upon picturesque characters, as well as speculation upon their origin. An incident of the whiskey business in the buffalo camps of 1872, which Wyatt recalled, gave to one itinerant liquor dealer a sobriquet which clung until it was carved upon his gravestone a quarter of a century later. What it did to those who drank his liquor is still an open question.

Ordinarily, empty whiskey barrels—a valuable commodity on the frontier—were hauled back to the settlements for refilling. Hunters, however, found them most desirable water-butts, and, as prices asked for empty barrels were exorbitant, preferred stealing to buying them.

A buffalo skinner named Thompson who had turned

whiskey peddler boasted that his liquor carried a potency unrivaled on the range, and enjoyed a lucrative patronage until a buffalo hunter stole one of his empty barrels and knocked in the head. The thief quickly summoned a number of his colleagues to a conference which promptly adjourned to the tailboard of Thompson's wagon. In his hand the hunter carried a half-dozen objects of disconcerting familiarity, which he had found in the barrel.

Without much regard for customers who stood by, whiskey sales were interrupted as the irate spokesman thrust his handful under Thompson's nose.

"What are these?" he demanded.

Thompson probably recognized what he saw, but it is not recalled that he answered.

"Snake heads, ain't they?" the hunter inquired. "Rattlesnake heads?"

Thompson granted the accuracy of the description.

"I found 'em in one of your whiskey barrels. Did you put 'em there?"

To prevent the loss of his entire stock in the search for additional evidence, Thompson now admitted that there were half-a-dozen rattlesnake heads in each barrel of his whiskey.

"I always put 'em in," he explained. "They give power to the liquor."

"You don't sell any more snakehead whiskey in this camp," his inquisitors decreed. "Hitch up and get going."

Thompson moved his saloon-on-wheels to another camp and resumed business. Word of his liquor formula undoubtedly reached the ears of his new customers, for the man became known the West over as Snakehead Thompson. Wyatt encountered him repeatedly for years afterward; Thompson peddled whiskey from a barrel on the frontier as long as there was one, but beyond the irate group who first exposed his trade secret, his reputation apparently cost him few customers.

When quality and quantity of liquor consumed in the buffalo camps is considered, the character and number of fights necessary to the hunters' peace of mind give small cause for wonder. The affrays generally fell into one of two classifications. There was the suddenly flaring dissension which might turn to rough-and-tumble encounter, or see two adversaries go for their guns for immediately final decision. In such cases, bystanders never intervened. Or, there was the affair which developed more gradually to a climax staged before all the camp under supervision of an umpire. This took on the aspects of a formal duel, with a code and choice of weapons. Pistols, knives, or fists might be decided upon, and in more than one instance duelists employed Sharps rifles fired at fifty paces, in which event the first shot to hit the target ended all argument.

On spree days in the camps, with two or three hundred fighting men three quarters full of raw spirits and hunting trouble, only the rankest coward or a man of great courage could dodge difficulties of a serious nature through general recognition of his status. Old buffalo hunters unanimously agreed that Wyatt Earp was one of a few men whom the trouble-seekers avoided and that with certain rare exceptions he went about his business unmolested.

Even thus early in his life, without a single gunfight in his record, Wyatt enjoyed the wholesome respect of the adventure-hardened men into whose company his calling took him. He was reputed to be speedier and surer with a pistol than was safe in an adversary; several episodes of the camps had established the quality of his courage.

Wyatt's reputation with firearms had been won at the target matches upon which the hunters bet large sums in cash or hides. Marksmanship of high degree was essential to success in these contests, and he had repeatedly demonstrated that with pistol or rifle, and shooting under any of the numerous conditions imposed to determine all-around proficiency, he had few equals. One or two affairs in which some hunter had decided to shoot out a difference of opinion with Wyatt Earp and had found himself looking into Wyatt's pistol barrel before he could get his own from the holster had been enough to satisfy the most exacting as to his speed. In these instances Wyatt would have been justified by the code of the camps in pressing his advantage to a fatal conclusion. That he did not do so, that he carried his gunplay but far enough to protect his own life and refused to take another's, struck most of the hunters as peculiar, so much so that it later was a subject of considerable comment. In other years there were other men who could not fathom this magnanimity; certain ones who owed their lives to its existence in the marshal, Wyatt Earp, lived, perversely enough, to hate him bitterly for its gesture.

Another accomplishment for which Wyatt has been remembered was his fortune as a gambler. Bat Masterson has said that Wyatt was the best poker player he ever saw in action, and that in bucking a monte or a faro game, as well as banking one, he had few equals in nerve to back his judgment, a prime factor in success at those pastimes. It was further held—and not without reason—that any game in which Wyatt Earp participated would be played on the square, that he possessed both the astuteness and the courage to keep it so.

Among camp followers who preyed upon prodigal buffalo hunters were hundreds of crooked gamblers, on the range ostensibly after hides, but in reality to fleece unwary cardplayers. Stakes ran high—protracted games might see thousands of dollars change hands—and daring operators might take heavy winnings. The crooks worked in pairs, or trios, and trimmed their victims methodically. They recruited their numbers from reputed man-killers and to them skill with guns was of even greater importance than card-dexterity. Two or three of these sure-thing artists in the same game would build up interest in the play until it suited them to introduce their trickery. From that point on, their answers to any charges were made with pistols. A hunter who objected to play which he thought questionable might be shot out of his seat for his protest; the best he could expect was enforced retirement.

To certain old-timers the most notable recollection of Wyatt Earp in the buffalo camps dealt with a Salt Fork poker game for high stakes, in which two players were notorious gunmen suspected of a partnership in crooked gambling, and by which Wyatt stood as a spectator. After the tide of fortune had definitely set in the direction of the two suspected men, Wyatt left the circle of onlookers for a time; he returned wearing his pistols.

It may be well to record here another peculiarity of habit which distinguished Wyatt from his associates: unless hunting, he seldom went armed. His camp was a half-mile from his nearest neighbors, and on visits to friends in the larger groups, it was unusual for him to wear guns. Thus, their presence at his hips upon his return to the poker game attracted the attention of those who knew him.

When a player quit, Wyatt sat into the game. He shifted his pistols to handy position, placed a roll of greenbacks on the blanket before him, and observed quietly:

"If no one objects, we'll play honest poker."

No one objected audibly, and the game continued. Eventually, with one of the sharpers dealing, came the play which Wyatt Earp had anticipated. From the betting it was apparent that every player had been dealt a strong hand and the pot was swelled until nearly all the money in sight was at the center of the blanket. The men under suspicion forced the play before the draw until Wyatt asked the one with the larger sum in front of him how much was in his pile. In a table-stake game, the man had to answer.

"All right," Wyatt said, as he counted out an equal amount, "I'll tap you."

This left the gunman with the choice of risking all his money on the hand or resigning his interest in the pot. And every other player in the game must stake a like amount, or as much as he had left toward it, on the outcome of the draw. To those who did not fathom his purpose, it appeared that Wyatt was turning the play to suit a crooked gambler. With all bets down, cards were drawn. Then Wyatt interrupted proceedings. With his cards in his left hand, his right resting on the blanket in front of him, he addressed the dealer and his accomplice by name.

"Throw down your cards and get out," he ordered. "I guess you didn't hear me when I said we'd play honest poker."

In that time and place, the accusation of cheating at cards

meant gunplay, and men who made a business of gambling went prepared for it. The two against whom Wyatt had called the turn were no exceptions; each wore two pistols. The inference needed no explanation, yet Wyatt had made no move for his weapons; he was looking steadily across the blanket at his adversaries.

"Throw down your cards," he repeated, "and don't reach for anything else."

Wyatt's left hand held his cards, his right was still empty. This was unadulterated nerve.

As if at some prearranged signal, and simultaneously, both crooks went after their weapons. Before either had a gun half-drawn from the holster, they were looking into the muzzle of a six-shooter in Wyatt Earp's right hand. Bat Masterson, who saw the play, said that Wyatt's move was faster than his eye could follow.

"Put 'em back," Wyatt cautioned, "and get out of here."

To witnesses of the episode there was something inexplicable about the whole business. They could not understand why the cardsharps had withheld immediate gunplay; it should have followed Wyatt's first challenge, instantaneously. Because of their unwonted hesitancy, the two gamblers could do nothing, and live, but get out of camp, leaving behind all the money they had staked in the poker game. The young man who had driven them away did not trouble to disarm them and apparently paid no attention to them after they left the circle of players. At this the spectators also wondered. Why, when the killers went for their guns, and Wyatt beat them in the draw, hadn't he exercised the established prerogative and shot both of them as he could have done easily? In after years Wyatt answered this latter question.

"Why should I have killed that pair?" he said. "I protected my money against their attempt to cheat me out of it, and showed them up for a couple of cowards whose bluff caved in quickly enough, once the break wasn't all on their side. That was all the occasion called for."

Some hours after the gunmen left, the poker game ended with Wyatt Earp, as he remembered well, a loser as far as cash was concerned. But he had called the turn on a pair of professional killers in a manner that was to spread the fame of his courage from the Rio Grande to Great Slave Lake. It was the forerunner of a series of similar displays of fearlessness which are still a source of apparently endless speculation.

On at least two occasions, as Bat Masterson has further testified, Wyatt found it necessary to establish his prowess in the knock-down-and-drag-out, rough-and-tumble physical encounters into which he was forced by men who had openly boasted that they would take his measure. In frontier parlance such affrays were simply fights, to distinguish them from battles in which guns or knives were employed.

Fights were all that the term implied, for in them anything went, including hitting, wrestling, kicking, gouging, and biting. The fight was a continuous affair from start to finish, usually until one combatant was dead or unconscious. More than one prominent citizen of the West has lived out his life after such an encounter with but the fragment of an ear on one side of his head, and that fragment showing plainly the teeth marks of the man who chewed off the rest of the organ.

In each of two instances which Bat Masterson recalled, a professional bully who had fought his way to championship reputation in the buffalo camps challenged Wyatt Earp in such fashion that there was no dodging the issue. Whereupon Wyatt proceeded about the defense of his person as coolly and as efficiently as he seems to have done everything else.

Wyatt had exceptional strength and was marvelously fast with his hands and feet. Also he was a skillful boxer, a rarity among frontier fighters, and knew as many tricks of wrestling as the next. He whipped both of his challengers so soundly that after the second one had been accommodated, no one else cared to press a similar issue.

Years after these encounters, Bat Masterson turned for purposes of description to that New Orleans classic which changed the trend of professional prizefighting, with its demonstration of the superiority of reasonable strength, coolly and efficiently employed, over mere bulk and ferocity.

"I can see Wyatt going against those tough, husky fellows who outweighed him by twenty or thirty pounds as plainly as though it were yesterday," Bat said. "It reminds me more of Jim Corbett battling old John L. Sullivan than any other one thing that occurs to me."

With the fact established that he avoided trouble because he disliked it and not because he feared the outcome of battle, Wyatt Earp's inclinations were apt to be respected, and thereafter in the buffalo camps he experienced no difficulty in regulating his own conduct. A score of exploits similar to his affrays with the gamblers and the professional bullies were credited to Wyatt during his buffalo-hunting days—by the time he became a peace officer he was celebrated throughout the West because of them—but beyond the three which have been noted here, all seem to be fabulous. The feature of each legendary yarn is that Wyatt allowed some killer who had forced a gunplay upon him to go unharmed after he had beaten the killer to the draw, and for that reason—not to mention numerous others—it is probable that the fabrications were built upon the one episode of the poker game.

In further consideration of the spread of Wyatt Earp legends which dealt with his gun-throwing proficiency it is pertinent to remember that the buffalo camps of the seventies were the training schools which turned loose on the frontier the most talented gunfighters and gunmen of any time or territory. From them there traveled over the West to the cowtowns and the mining camps a great majority of the outlaw killers, the gunmen who made frontier life a hazardous affair for peaceably inclined citizens long after dangers inherent to the country itself had been overcome. From them, too, came frontier marshals and sheriffs who blazed the trail for law and order with six-shooters and sawed-off shotguns.

To graduate from this school at the head of the class, with all honors conferred by fellow students who were also the faculty, and that without having fired a shot to solve any problem of life-or-death, was indeed a distinction, so unique that of itself, perhaps, it demanded legendary justification. However that may have been, it is evident, from reminiscences of those who completed the colorful course of draw-and-shoot instruction, that if Wyatt Earp's gun-toting alma mater had known of the phrase, she would have certified him to his profession *summa cum laude*.

In April 1872, Wyatt went into Caldwell, where he settled accounts with the hide buyers and found that his skinner and he each had cleared more than twenty-five hundred dollars on the winter's work. The following September found him back on the buffalo range, but forced to ride much farther west to find profitable hunting. That winter of 1872–73 brought ten thousand additional buffalo hunters and the herds suffered proportionately. The Sante Fe Railroad had pushed the end of steel into Dodge City, and from that single newly born community of two stores, five saloons, and two dancehalls, 400,000 buffalo hides were shipped before the season closed. By hunting the lessfrequented areas, Wyatt and his skinner managed to approximate their kill of the preceding year. But they foresaw the rapidly approaching end to large profits for the many in wholesale buffalo slaughter.

Already the character of the Kansas prairie settlements was changing, as, on the range, the buffalo gave way before beef cattle. The tide of the great Texas trail herds was mounting, speeding buffalo extinction and supplanting overnight the business built up by the hunters as tradingposts which had existed solely for their patronage competed for prestige as cowtowns.

In April of 1873, just after he had turned twenty-five, Wyatt settled accounts with the hide buyers and started on a tour of the newly created cattle-shipping centers. He had several thousand dollars in his possession, and in his mind was the possibility that his stake might provide an opening wedge in this cow business at which, he heard, so many were building fortunes.

7

Cowcamps and Cattle Trails

In the Red Decade of frontier history the Kansas cowtowns, Abilene, Newton, Caldwell, Ellsworth, Hunnewell, Hays, Wichita, and Dodge, were born, boomed, and broke as terminals of the Texas Trail. One was like another in their heyday of untrammeled iniquity, blatantly lawless, uproariously sinful, and boastfully bad. "Too wild to be curried, too tough to be tamed," their local braggarts yelled.

During the Civil War the United States Government had herded some three thousand Wichita, Caddo, Waco, and Anadarko Indians into a camp on the Kansas prairies near the junction of Cowskin Creek and the Arkansas River. After the war, the Government decided to move them into Indian Territory, and in 1867, contracted with Jesse Chisholm, a Cherokee half-breed, to open a trail and establish supply camps along the route the Indians were to follow.

Chisholm loaded his bull teams and rounded up a herd of one hundred Indian ponies which wranglers drove ahead of the wagon train. Quicksand was an ever-present menace in fording the treacherous Salt Fork of the Arkansas, the North and South Canadian Rivers and their tributaries, and Chisholm used his pony herd to settle these sands, driving the animals, full tilt, back and forth across the fords until the footing was packed solid, after which the teams could cross. Indians, soldiers, and livestock by the thousands followed the ruts of the Chisholm bull-wains into the Nations.

Texas cattle herds driven north immediately after the Civil War had followed the army route from Austin toward Sedalia, Missouri, turning off at the mouth of the Grand River to strike for the railroad. In 1871, cattlemen had generally abandoned this trace for the shorter Chisholm Trail, and to handle the booming beef business a score of shipping centers sprang into existence at points where they met the railroads. Wichita was among the first Kansas villages to bid actively for the cattle trade, but failure of the railroad to build into that camp on schedule took the early drives past the site of the Indian encampment. By 1873, the Chisholm Trail was a roadway several hundred yards wide, hoof-packed to concrete solidity, stretching across the wilderness from Red River Crossing to the Smoky Hill near Abilene.

Millions of beef cattle and horses which sold for hundreds of millions of dollars were to be driven to market over the Chisholm Trail and its successors with which stockmen eventually cross-hatched the Western prairies. As early as 1873, the vanguard was counted by the hundreds of thousands, and at Abilene, Hays City, and Newton, Wyatt found literally thousands of faces strange to the Northern country in the Texas men who had come up with the herds.

As long as the Texas Trail brought cattle from the South to the Northern markets, trail drivers were hailed as Texas men. Cowpunchers might come from the ranches of New Mexico, Southern Colorado, the Indian Nations, or even Arizona, but as most of them had at one time or another been residents of the Lone Star State, they did not object to the classification.

Consciously and boastfully these Texas men were the troublemakers of the frontier. Practically all were of Southern birth, either veterans of the Confederate army or sons of men who had fought for the South in the Civil War. To them the Lost Cause was a living issue, one to justify any subterfuge by which a Northern man might be discomfited in any degree, or, if Fate was particularly kind, goaded into a fight. Certain trail outfits measured success of their Kansas drives in the names of Northern settlements they had "treed," or of Northern men—peace officers preferably— they had killed, which could be chalked on the sides of a homebound chuck wagon for Texas to note and cheer.

The frontier maxim, that any horse from Texas would buck and any man from Texas would shoot, carried a considerable measure of truth. For years the Rio Grande frontier was the bloodiest in the world. Forebears of the Texas trail drivers for generations had fought Indians and Mexicans in turn. Their home country was too vast for the operation of any system of law and order other than that under which every man depended upon himself and was raised in the faith that outside the family circle the only arbitrament was a gun. In every outlying Texas home there were rifles and pistols for every male child old enough to handle them; boys were schooled in the use of arms as the prime requisite of border life. Such youngsters, grown to manhood, found conditions incident to the cattle drives merely the wild times of earlier environment prolonged, and *Texas man* became synonymous with *gunman* throughout the West. At home and at work in familiar suraroundings, the Texas man was a highly desirable citizen; on the loose in the habitat of those whom his religion held hereditary foemen, he was bad; his inevitable punishment was an uncomprehended upshot of his provincial creed.

Wyatt Earp's most vivid recollection of the early Kansas cowcamps was that in them all money was evident in far greater quantities than the frontier had ever known and that opportunities for spending it had been provided at every hand. Furthermore, with the exception of an occasional eating-house and a few general merchandise establishments, every last one of these opportunities was to be included in the category which a softer civilization refers to as vice.

Abilene, with a handful of actual residents, had twenty saloons and gambling houses to one block of street and a dancehall for every two saloons, in ratio of ten to one over all other types of business houses in the camp. Twenty-five hundred cowboys thronged these centers of attraction in a single night, each with a year's wages to spend. Bosses and herd owners had thousands of dollars to throw away. Whiskey was delivered to the cowcamp in carload lots. Monte, keno, poker, and faro games, as well as the frontier bordellos—honky-tonks or hurdy-gurdies, they were called—ran full-blast, twenty-four hours a day. Every man in town wore at least one, more often two six-shooters at his belt. Fights were hourly incidents.

Temperament plus cowtown whiskey made gunplay among Texas men such a commonplace at the shipping terminals of the Chisholm Trail that, so long as only cowmen were embroiled, it was generally ignored. Every Kansas community adopted as the first ordinance of existence a law against personal adornment with deadly weapons within its limits, but the rule was seldom observed. Cowpunchers wore six-guns into town and nothing was done about it until exuberance or turbulence moved them to damaging locally owned property too greatly, or endangering the lives of the local citizenry in too brazen fashion. Then the frontier peace officer was supposed to take a hand. In such event, the code demanded that the hand be played to a speedy and, preferably, a fatal finish. When such a play was imminent, Texas men dropped internal dissensions and stood together against the world.

That galaxy of shooting stars which reddened the cowtown firmament in the 1870s included Ben and Billy Thompson, Gyp, Joe, Jim, and Mannen Clements, Clay Allison, John Wesley Hardin, Smoky Hill Thompson, Ed King, the Catfish Kid, Curly Bill Brocius, Cal Polk, John Ringo, Bill Moore—to pick offhand but a few of the scores who won six-gun immortality. Gunfighter, or gunman—it was thus the Old West phrased distinction between good men and evil—he who held his own against such competition shot ahead of fast company.

Against the wild and lawless gun-toters, and against the gangs of rustlers, murderers, thugs, and highwaymen who fattened upon the untold riches in cattle and coin which the gunmen themselves commanded, the gunfighter—as he who shot in behalf of law and order was known—came upon the Western stage, as fearless, as reckless of his life, and as skilled with weapons as the outlaws and desperadoes he was to subdue; superior to them, in that sense of moral courage which comes to any man from the conviction that back of him is the sentiment of decent citizens. This gunfighting peace officer customarily bore the title of marshal; and he was far more than a policeman; often he was, perforce, not only the arresting officer, but witness, prosecuting attorney, jury, judge, and executioner, all in one. He filed the only record of his duties performed in the vaults of a convenient Boot Hill—as frontier wit termed a burial ground preponderantly tenanted by those who had passed on too hastily for due attention to the niceties accorded at the end of more prosaic lives.

Bear River Tom Smith, Wild Bill Hickok, William Tilghman, Mysterious Dave Mather, Shotgun Collins, Bat Masterson, Neal Brown, Frank McLean, Pat Garrett, Joshua Webb, Charlie Bassett, are but a few of the noted frontier marshals who have come down in the old-timers' folk-tales as tutelary saints of the six-shooter. The most cursory examination of frontier history reveals that in the palmy days of the Wild West any man who ranked in popular esteem with this group of colleagues was veritably a Herculean arm of forty-five-caliber law.

In any attempt to gauge the accomplishments of those frontier peace officers who dominated the cowcamps of the seventies, first consideration must be given to the single law of the old gunfighter's code, unbreakable to the man who would hold his own respect or that of friends and enemies. Assassinations were not uncommon in the Western settlements, but they were the resort of gunmen held beneath contempt, even by the most notorious outlaws. A top-notch gunfighter of Wyatt Earp's day did no shooting from cover and fired at no man's back; the object of his attentions must

71

get what the West called an even break. Least of all might the majesty of the law stoop to ignominious play. Wherefore, it was axiomatic with Western peace officers to whom distinction was accorded that no malefactor, no matter what his crime, was to be shot down without his chance to surrender or to make his fight.

"Throw 'em up!" was the warning to a potential prisoner. Then, a pause for that fraction of a second in which the challenged one decided which way to move his hands. Skyward, he was disarmed and led to the nearest calaboose; to his belt, or his armpits, and one or more combatants usually was carried to Boot Hill.

In the lore of bustling cities and humdrum villages from whose terminology "Boot Hill" has long since vanished, in the sagas of the Old West that have reached a third generation from the campfire bards who sang with first-hand authority, the figure of Wyatt Earp as the Kansas cowtowns knew him appears as the legendary type-specimen of the old-time gunfighting marshal. The validity of his eminence is attested by a hundred contemporaries who insist that in combat Wyatt Earp had no equal on the frontier, whether an encounter hung upon mere physical prowess or pure courage plus deadly skill with a Colt's forty-five, a Winchester, or a sawed-off shotgun. To this consensus Bat Masterson contributed.

"In the eighteen-seventies," Bat wrote, "that immense territory stretching from the Missouri River to the Pacific Ocean and from the Brazos River in Texas to the Red Cloud Agency in Dakota knew no braver man than Wyatt Earp. He was the one man I personally knew whom I regarded as absolutely destitute of fear.

"I have often remarked—and I am not alone in my conclusions—that what goes for courage in a man is generally the fear of what others may think of him; in other words, personal bravery is largely egotism and apprehension. Wyatt's daring and apparent recklessness, however, were wholly characteristic of himself. When everything was said and done, he valued his opinion of himself far more than the opinion of others; it was his own good report that he sought to preserve.

"No man ever saw Wyatt Earp display the white feather.

"Wyatt could scrap with his fists; I doubt if there was a man in the West who could whip him in a rough-and-tumble fight. He often took all the fight out of notorious gunmen with no other weapons than his two hands, and that not only with the bad man armed, but surrounded by gun-toting friends. In all his relations with his fellow men, however, even the bad ones, he was magnanimous in the extreme. But when he had to, he could shoot to kill, and did. No man could have a more loyal friend than Wyatt Earp might be, nor a more dangerous enemy."

Another matter of importance to comprehension of the role thrust upon the border peace officer is an understanding of the social order which he served, an order which existed almost entirely on contacts made and continued in about the only places in the frontier villages where men might foregather in some degree of comfort, the gambling houses and saloons. On one occasion, when Wyatt Earp was recalling some incident of a visit to Abilene, a younger person observed somewhat disdainfully that in all of his stories of the cowcamps all of the people he mentioned were invariably going into or coming out of gambling houses, dancehalls, or saloons.

Wyatt was his laconic self as he replied: "We had no Y.M.C.A.'s."

In the days when Wyatt first stepped into prominence upon the Western scene, gambling, for example, occupied about the same avocative position in the life of the cowcamps as later was accorded to golf, and the owner of a faro bank quite possibly enjoyed more respect as a citizen than the proprietor of a commercial bank across the street. The gambling business was generally conducted on a different basis from that which later brought it into disrepute, was as legitimate and as ethical an enterprise as the merchandising of groceries and so recognized by law—for that matter, still is in certain Western towns.

In one rough frontier settlement, for example, a man destined to prove a powerfully constructive force in the development of the West, to be chosen United States Senator repeatedly when civilization brought an electorate, and to accumulate one of the largest fortunes in America, operated a thriving faro bank in one shack and a commercial bank, not doing nearly so well, next door. He often declared that only the prosperity of the faro bank kept the commercial bank open. And Wyatt's first acquaintance with the governor-to-be of a Western state was made while the latter dealt faro in an establishment where Wyatt sometimes played.

The list of prominent Western citizens, from bank presidents and preachers on down, who in early days were gamblers and saloonkeepers is well-nigh endless. They are not mentioned thus generally, to palliate possible offense against the moral niceties; the point is, such men were the leaders of communities in which they lived by virtue of qualities they showed, and as long as they dealt fairly with their fellows no one thought less of them for their calling. They set up a government that necessarily functioned almost entirely on the executive side, and realization that their neighbors respected them as courageously active sponsors of the only government there was may provide fuller appreciation of their era.

In the summer of '73, Wyatt Earp roamed from one cowcamp to another on the Kansas plains. At Abilene, he heard that leaders of the beef industry had transferred headquarters to Ellsworth, a village some sixty-five miles west. Ellsworth was advertising herself as the coming town of the frontier, with what justification may be gleaned from the columns of a weekly journal in a rival camp, which printed under the heading, "State News":

As we go to press, Hell is still in session at Ellsworth.

Wyatt's visit to the booming cowcamp was, perhaps, the most far-reaching move of his career.

No more typical trail drivers' rendezvous existed on the

plains than Ellsworth, Kansas, in August 1873. More important cattle-shipping centers developed as the Texas trail
herds grew; but, geographically, architecturally and cultur-
ally, the settlement of three hundred residents was all that
the woolliest cowtown of the Wild West ever was reputed to
be.

The village lay depressingly flat on the bank of the Smoky
Hill River, surrounded by a thousand square miles of what
old-time cowmen regarded as the finest range at any northern terminal of the Texas Trail. To the sightseer the country
roundabout may have been a vast, slightly rolling, most
uninteresting prairie, with endless miles of grass-brown
monotony unrelieved by living green. To the cattleman's eye
that great expanse was a perennial carpet of grama grass, an
apparently inexhaustible source of fat-producing fodder for
his longhorns on which it was easy to hold the herds.

Life in Ellsworth centered on a treeless plaza, fetlock deep
with dust, or mud. Bordering one side was the new railroad,
with a shack ticket office and freight house; across the
square, and parallel to the tracks, the single business street.
Within the confines of the plaza this roadway widened to
provide hitching space for cow ponies and wagon teams on
either edge of the thoroughfare, and about the crude rectan-
gle were grouped the hastily erected frame structures which
housed commercial enterprise. Back toward the open prairie were residence shacks—one-story, two-room, sod
houses—while beyond the railroad, near the river, were
warehouses, horse corrals, dance halls, saloons, and one or
two hotels frequented by Texas cowmen. Just outside the
village and alongside the tracks were acres of whitewashed
cattle-shipping pens. All told, five hotels, a bank, a newspaper shop, a half-dozen stores, and some twenty or thirty
saloons and gambling houses faced the square.

George W. Saunders, of the Old-Time Trail-Drivers'
Association, of San Antonio, Texas, has estimated that more
than a half-million cattle driven by five thousand Texas men
reached Kansas in 1873 over the Chisholm Trail. In August
150,000 head were grazing the prairies around Ellsworth,
awaiting shipment to the East. With them were fifteen

hundred cowboys, money in their clothes and long months
of hazardous, lonesome hardship to be lived down in a rush.
In Ellsworth, the cowmen had no responsibility beyond
holding their charges on a range, which made the job
routine.

Climatic conditions of 1873 had lowered the quality and
quantity of range grass farther east in Kansas, but had not
impaired the Ellsworth grazing area. The financial panic of
1873 had affected the early cattle market, and in holding for
better prices owners of the larger herds deemed it advisable
to drive to a shipping point where cattle might fatten on free
grass while awaiting sale. This combination of circumstances and events gave Ellsworth six months of fleeting
fame as the wildest cowtown of the West.

Day and night the sweltering plaza was lined on either
side by unbroken rows of cow ponies tethered to the
hitching rails. Horse corrals overflowed. Flimsy hotels slept
six and eight cattlemen to the room. Along the plank walks
or sun-baked dirt paths from saloon to gambling house, to
dance hall, to the stores, and back to the saloons again,
roamed hundreds of Texas men, in sombreros, chaps, and
high-heeled boots, cartridge belts and six-guns, picturesque
swashbucklers hunting excitement.

If, with the herds at her gates and the cattle drivers within,
Ellsworth needed one touch to establish, beyond the carping
of Wichita, Hays, and Abilene, her supremacy as the
cowboy capital of the West, she got it when Ben Thompson
and his brother Bill reached her Grand Central Hotel. Wyatt
Earp had encountered the Thompsons before, in a casual
way; he knew them, their reputations, and their history.

Ben and Bill were Texas men who dealt a peripatetic faro
game, moving from town to town with shifts of the cattle
trade. In each cow capital where they opened their bank, the
Thompsons arrogated to themselves the rule of life in that
community. As this arrogance was predicated upon their
frontier-wide reputations as man-killers and backed by
extreme proficiency in the art of gun-throwing, it was
seldom resented openly. Furthermore, as Texans, the

Thompsons could count upon the active assistance of nearly every cowman in a camp in repelling an enforcement of Northern law and order. Life in a cowtown where Ben and Bill did business was to be lived as long as they remained there in entirely untrammeled fashion.

Ben Thompson, the elder, dominated the brotherly partnership. The two were born in England, but their parents had emigrated to Austin, Texas, where Ben at eighteen joined the Confederate army at the outbreak of the Civil War. At the close of the war, he went with Shelby to Old Mexico, for a time, but by the early seventies, he and Bill had gambled and shot their way through almost every frontier town from the Rio Grande to the Canadian line.

Both Thompsons were remarkably courageous men. Bill was the quicker to start an argument, possibly, but Ben could be counted on to finish any quarrel which either of them opened. As Bill was particularly pugnacious when drinking and always had some liquor in him, he kept his brother's love of finish-fights reasonably well satiated.

According to Bat Masterson, Ben Thompson was the most dangerous killer in the Old West. In his "Story of the Outlaw," Emerson Hough substantiates this estimate. Hough calls Ben Thompson "a very perfect exemplar of the creed of the six-shooter."

"With the six-shooter," Hough continues, "he [Thompson] was a peerless shot, an absolute genius, none in all his wide surrounding claiming to be his superior; and he had a ferocity of disposition which grew with years until he had, as one of his friends put it, 'a craving to kill people.'"

Masterson possessed over Hough the advantage of having seen Ben Thompson in gunplay, and qualified certain of the latter's statements. Bat recorded that there was one man living during Ben's time who was his equal for six-shooter speed and accuracy. That one was Wyatt Earp. But he agrees with Hough unqualifiedly in the statement that Ben Thompson during his career shot his way out of a greater number of six-gun duels than any other desperado of his era, and that his very name was enough to make the general run of gunmen or gunfighting marshals avoid him when humanly possible.

Hays, Ogallala, Baxter Springs, and Abilene saw the Thompson faro game come and go, and lived their hectic weeks under the high, wide, and handsome splurge of Thompson rule. In Abilene, the brothers operated the Bull's Head Tavern and Gambling Saloon, where Brother Ben added to his reputation by backing the redoubtable Hickok into his hole and suggesting that he pull the hole in after him, when Wild Bill, as marshal, objected to Bull's Head goings-on. No history has been more garbled than that of Western gunmen, and the Thompson careers have been no exception—the brothers have been held responsible for fifty killings; but it has been definitely established that by the time they moved to Ellsworth, they had planted at least twenty-seven denizens of various frontier Boot Hills. Of this number, Bill was known to have killed two; Ben, presumably, had disposed of the other twenty-five.

Wyatt Earp quickly learned that Ben Thompson, in local parlance, had Ellsworth treed. Earlier in the season, when it became evident that the village was to be the recreational rendezvous for some two thousand cowboys who preferred their pleasures raw and red, the Ellsworth councilmen had made precautionary moves by hiring J. W., "Brocky Jack," Norton, a famous gunfighter, as marshal, and appointing as first deputy John, "Happy Jack," Morco, with a record as an Indian fighter and authentic credit for a dozen six-gun killings against white men. Two additional deputies, Charlie Brown and Ed Crawford, also were gunfighters of repute. As a contribution to the hope for a peaceful summer, the county offered its sheriff, C. B. Whitney—a merchant rather than a peace officer, but noted for his courage—and the deputy sheriff, John Hogue, who had more than a local reputation for fearless proficiency with his forty-fives.

With this array of six-shooter talent on the side of law and order, the mayor, Jim Miller, trusted that the business of the visiting cattle-owners could be encouraged while the pleasures of their roistering retinues could be held within reason-

able bounds. Throughout May, June, and July, the editor of
the *Ellsworth Reporter,* the cowcamp's weekly newspaper,
gave the mayor his moral support by printing each Thursday
at the head of his local column:

All is quiet in Ellsworth

Other, more specific records, and news items below the
editorial dictum, show that fistfights, gunfights, and general
melees were of hourly occurrence, day and night.

Ben Thompson was leading spirit of the lawless; his
right-hand man was Brother Bill; as left bower, Ben had
George Peshaur, another Texas killer, and as additional
backing an army of cowpunchers who could be counted
upon to the limit in any gunplay against Northern men. Of
the cowboys, the ringleaders were Cad Pierce, John Good,
and Neil Kane, notorious as troublemakers in every camp
on the Texas trail.

For two months of the summer of '73, Ben Thompson,
from headquarters at the Grand Central, where he had
opened his faro bank, defied the vaunted Ellsworth marshals with impunity, and the hundreds of cowboys in town
did likewise. Citizenry, mayor, councilmen, and imported
peace officers had been treed together and apparently did
not intend to come down until the last Texas man had
started South. Such was the status of Ellsworth's hope for
law and order when Wyatt Earp reached the camp.

From the experienced cattlemen, Wyatt soon learned that
the cow business had been too thoroughly upset by the
money panic and bad range conditions to make his proposed investment advisable, so he decided to hunt buffalo
another season. Meanwhile, he witnessed numerous gunfights in the streets and saloons and noted with some
amusement the manner in which the Ellsworth constabu-
lary took cover before the Texas men.

Early in the afternoon of August 18, 1873, Wyatt had the
sun-scorched plaza almost to himself as he lounged beneath
the wooden awning which shaded Beebe's General Store
and Brennan's Saloon, next door. At intervals someone

passed on the walk, cowboys left one saloon for another, or a sweating horseman rode in from the prairie, hitched his cayuse and sought relief from the blazing heat at a favorite bar. For the most part, the dusty cowtown square was devoid of life, except the drooping horses tethered to the rails and their attendant swarms of flies. Sweltering wild and woolly Ellsworth was as peaceful as a cool green-and-white New England village.

In a saloon beyond Brennan's, Wyatt knew, an "open" poker game was in progress, with stakes of unusual size. Play was so high that the Thompsons had left their faro bank to sit in. When informed of a table rule against guns, Ben and Bill had still been sufficiently intrigued by the size of the pots to send their weapons back to the Grand Central and draw cards. Wyatt had heard that the Thompsons were forcing the play, that Bill was drinking steadily and getting mean. Whereupon he was well satisfied to be out of the game. Wyatt had small fancy for the Thompsons in any case, less for Bill at a poker table with high stakes and drunk.

From the saloon in which the Thompsons were gambling, a violent uproar was followed by the appearance of the brothers on the plaza. They came out of the door on the run, Bill cursing loudly and shouting threats over his shoulder as the pair made for the Grand Central. A moment later, they reappeared from the hotel and headed back toward the saloon, Ben carrying a double-barreled shotgun and Bill, a rifle. At the rail in front of the saloon stood a pair of horses hitched to a hay wagon and behind this rack the Thompsons took their stand, Bill shouting threats and imprecations and Ben adding profanely insulting invitations to those inside the saloon to "Come out and make your fight."

Wyatt stepped into Beebe's doorway, for cover from stray lead, as the racket of the belligerent brothers drew several hundred persons from the various establishments bordering the plaza as hopeful spectators. Sheriff Whitney hurried from his store, stopping at Beebe's doorway to ask Wyatt if he knew what had started the row. The question was answered by a bystander at the poker game who had sensed that its immediate vicinity was not the safest place in Ellsworth. He had run from the saloon by a rear door and around to the plaza to view forthcoming festivities.

"John Sterling slapped Bill Thompson's face," this on-looker volunteered. "Bill got nasty and John gave him the flat of his hand across the mouth. When Bill invited John to get a gun and meet him outside, John hit him again and knocked him out of his seat. Then Bill and Ben ran after their guns."

Sheriff Whitney was in his shirt-sleeves and palpably unarmed, yet without further hesitation he walked over to the hay wagon where the Thompsons stood with cocked weapons waiting for someone to come out of the saloon.

"You keep out of this, Sheriff," Ben warned him. "We don't want to hurt you."

"Don't be foolish, Ben," Whitney replied.

Thompson's rejoinder was a torrent of profanity directed at Sterling and his friends, whereupon the sheriff went into the saloon. He returned to the walk with word that Sterling had been forcibly prevented from coming out to fight and had been taken by friends to his camp outside the town by way of the back door.

Whitney feared that Sterling might be shot on sight by one of the Thompsons when he again came into Ellsworth, and to smooth over the quarrel, invited the Thompsons into Brennan's saloon for a drink and a talk. Cowpunchers and merchants went indoors, and as Wyatt moved back to his lounging place between Brennan's doorway and Beebe's entrance, he again had the plaza to himself. Fifteen minutes later, Whitney came out of the saloon, alone, and stopped to talk.

"They've calmed down a bit," the sheriff reported. "They're inside with a bunch of Texas men."

"Did you take their guns away from them?" Wyatt asked.

"No," Whitney replied, "they wouldn't stand for that."

Before Wyatt had time to comment on this matter, Bill Thompson appeared in Brennan's doorway with Ben's shotgun.

"I'll get a sheriff if I don't get anybody else," he declared.

Wyatt and Whitney turned to face him; Bill fired both barrels of the gun—eighteen buckshot—point-blank into the sheriff's breast, and ran back into the saloon.

Wyatt caught Whitney in his arms.

"I'm done," the sheriff gasped. "Get me home."

8

Ellsworth Sees Some Forty-Five-Caliber Law

At the roar of gunfire, saloon, hotels, and stores spouted five hundred men into the Ellsworth plaza, nine tenths of them Texas gun-toters, an unarmed minority, local citizens. Ben and Bill Thompson walked deliberately out of Brennan's to a string of saddled cow ponies at a nearby rail, Ben covering one flank with the rifle, Bill, the other with the shotgun. In front of the Grand Central, Thompson followers collected under George Peshaur, Cad Pierce, Neil Kane, and John Good, to forestall attack, and the brothers swung their gun muzzles back and forth to menace the storefronts as they argued over ensuing procedure.

Friends of Sheriff Whitney volunteered to take the dying man home and Wyatt Earp turned his attention to the Thompsons. He stepped again into Beebe's entrance, and peered around the door casing into the plaza for sight of the Ellsworth peace officers. None was in view. Beebe's door opened, and there at Wyatt's shoulder was Happy Jack Morco, Indian fighter and six-gun expert, two belts of ammunition around his waist and a forty-five Colt's at either hip. Wyatt gave way to let Morco reconnoiter.

"For God's sake, get out of town," Ben Thompson urged Bill. "You shot Sheriff Whitney."

"I know it," Bill replied. "I'd have shot him if he'd been Jesus Christ."

Happy Jack peeped cautiously around the door casing. Ben took a potshot without sighting his rifle. The bullet struck half an inch above the deputy marshal's head and he ducked for cover.

"Too high," Ben informed Bill with an oath of regret. "Get on that horse and get out of here before Whitney's friends get organized. Take this rifle and give me my shotgun. I'll cover your getaway."

Wyatt realized that the brothers were appropriating a cow pony and exchanging weapons, as the rifle would be preferable for Bill on a lone ride down the trail. Here was Happy Jack's opportunity.

"Jump out and get 'em," Wyatt suggested. "Hurry, while they're switching guns."

"Not me," Happy Jack replied. "Those fellows across the street might get me."

"You'd get both Thompsons first," Wyatt urged, but Morco refused to budge.

Wyatt restrained an impulse to boot the deputy marshal onto the open walk, and peered around the casing again. Bill was in the saddle with the Winchester in front of him; Ben, with the shotgun, backed into the road. To quote the *Ellsworth Reporter:*

> He [Bill] then rode slowly out of town, cursing and inviting a fight.

No one accepted the invitation.

As Bill Thompson rode out of shooting range, Ben, still covering the assembled citizens with his shotgun, backed over to the Grand Central. A Texas man brought out his six-guns. With these favorites buckled in place and the shotgun in the crook of his arm, Ben paraded in front of the hotel shouting taunts and threats at the town of Ellsworth in general and at her peace officers in profane particular. At his back were a hundred Texas men, half of them man-killers of record, the rest more than willing to be. Peshaur, Pierce, Good, and Kane were slightly in advance of the crowd. In groups, around the plaza, three or four hundred more Texans were distributed. Every man-jack had six-guns at his hips and a gun hand itching for play. As Ben Thompson halted his tirade momentarily, Cad Pierce sought the limelight.

"I'll give one thousand dollars to anybody who'll knock off another marshal!" he shouted.

As the cowboys yelled appreciation of this offer, Deputy Marshal Brown appeared at the far end of a railroad building. A hundred forty-five slugs screeched across the plaza, and Brown took cover. To quote *The Reporter* again:

Ben Thompson retained his arms for a full hour after this and no attempt was made to disarm him. Mayor Miller was at his residence. . . . During this long hour, where were the police? No arrest had been made and the street was full of armed men ready to defend Thompson. The police were arming themselves, and, as they claim, just ready to rally out and take alive or dead the violators of the law. They were loading their muskets [sic] just as the mayor, impatient at the delay in making arrests, came along and discharged the whole force. It would have been better to have increased the force and discharged or retained the old police after quiet had been restored. The mayor acted promptly and according to his judgment, but we certainly think it was a bad move. A poor police is better than none, and if, as they claim, they were just ready for work, they should have had a chance to redeem themselves and the honor of the city. Thus the city was left without a police, with no one but Deputy Sheriff Hogue to make arrests.

Hogue, it chanced, was absent in the country. For some reason unexplained, beyond a statement that it was "not at liberty to do so," the newspaper failed to publish later testimony before Coroner Duck and Police Judge Osborne which furnished a detailed account of events precipitated by the belated appearance of Mayor Jim Miller on the side of the plaza farthest from Ben Thompson.

Wyatt and Happy Jack were still in Beebe's doorway, and Ben Thompson was still strutting up and down before the hotel, when Mayor Miller edged around the corner to the store entrance. Brocky Jack Norton, the marshal, came through Beebe's from the rear; he, too, wore a pair of forty-five-caliber Colt's. Deputy Marshal Brown, armed with a rifle and revolvers, was somewhere behind the railroad shacks. Deputy Marshal Crawford had not made the gesture of plaza appearance. The mayor wasted ten minutes of time and breath in orders to his marshals for Ben Thompson's capture. Neither Brocky Jack nor Happy Jack relished obedience and said so.

Mayor Miller tried another tack. He shouted across the plaza to Thompson, ordering the gunman to lay down his arms and submit to arrest. Ben answered in raucous profanity, at which his followers whooped gleefully. Ellsworth was treed at the tip of the topmost limb.

After urging Happy Jack to jump out and kill the Thompsons, Wyatt had kept silent. But the mayor's pleas to the marshals and contempt for their discretion, abetted by reaction to the cold-blooded fashion in which Sheriff Whitney had been shot down, moved him to comment.

"Nice police force you've got," Wyatt said to Miller.

"Who are you?" the mayor demanded.

"Just a looker-on," Wyatt replied.

"Well, don't talk so much," Miller snapped. "You haven't even got a gun."

As Wyatt was in shirt-sleeves, it was evident that he was unarmed. He seldom carried weapons in the settlements and those he owned were in his hotel room.

"It's none of my business," Wyatt admitted, "but if it was, I'd get me a gun and arrest Ben Thompson or kill him."

Brocky Jack erred.

"Don't pay any attention to that kid, Jim," he interrupted.

But Miller was desperate.

"You're fired, Norton," he said. "You, too, Morco."

The mayor snatched the marshal's badge from Brocky Jack's shirtfront.

"As soon as I can find Brown and Crawford, I'll fire them."

He turned to Wyatt Earp.

"I'll make this your business. You're marshal of Ellsworth. Here's your badge. Go into Beebe's and get some guns. I order you to arrest Ben Thompson."

To the best of Wyatt Earp's recollection, he voiced no formal acceptance of his impromptu appointment as an Ellsworth peace officer. He turned and walked to Beebe's firearms counter and asked for a pair of second-hand forty-fives, with holsters and cartridge belts.

"New guns and holsters," he explained in after years, "might have slowed me down."

Selecting two six-shooters with trigger-dogs that some former gunwise owner had filed to split-second smoothness and a pair of well-worn holsters, Wyatt tested the weapons thoroughly, loaded five cylinders in each, spun them, filled the cartridge loops, settled the guns on his hips, and walked out to the plaza. He said nothing to Mayor Miller or the two Jacks. Not one of the three offered company or suggestion. Beebe's clerk always asserted that the trio remained huddled in the doorway while the youthful marshal, *pro tem,* walked out to face the deadliest gunman then alive.

Wyatt Earp's short journey across the Ellsworth plaza under the muzzle of Ben Thompson's shotgun established for all time his preeminence among gunfighters of the West, but the episode has been ignored in written tales. That the camp never shared popular recognition with Wichita and Dodge as a top-notch cowtown, that its glory was but a season long, may have been responsible for the oversight; in any event, narrators of Earp history seem unaware that Wyatt was marshal of Ellsworth for one portentous hour. His appointment was not entered in the records and he was never paid for the service; yet, the amazing single exploit of his brief incumbency was a word-of-mouth sensation in '73, from the Platte to the Rio Grande. From a number of onlookers, who, all uncomprehendingly, were witnesses at the dawning of a new era in the Kansas cowtowns and who later recounted what they saw, has come an authentic picture of the high moment in Ellsworth's lurid heyday, and of Wyatt Earp as he appeared.

As the young man stepped from the shelter of Beebe's door, he pulled at the brim of his black sombrero to set it firmly in place and started diagonally across the plaza toward the Grand Central. Ben Thompson squared around, shifting his shotgun to hold the weapon across his stomach, the fore-end in his left hand, his right on grip and triggers. From that position a single motion would bring it into play.

Ben Thompson was a squarely built, stocky fellow, about five feet eight inches in height. A bloated face, bushy brows above his wide blue eyes, and a sweeping mustache gave him an appearance of greater maturity than his thirty years would justify; and this, as well as his bulkiness, was accentuated as he squatted slightly for effective handling of his gun.

Old-timers have said that Wyatt Earp looked like a boy as he crossed the plaza. Six feet tall, weighing not more than one hundred and fifty-five pounds, he, too, was the owner of good blue eyes; but, in contrast to Thompson's red and puffy countenance, Wyatt's lean and muscular features were smooth-shaven and tanned brown, his slimness further set off by white shirt, black trousers, wide-brimmed black hat, and high-heeled horseman's boots. As he walked, his hands swung easily, conveniently close to his holsters, but making no overt moves.

As Wyatt reached a point possibly fifty yards from Thompson, Cad Pierce said something to which Ben snarled over his shoulder in reply. Pierce subsided, and with the other Texas men waited for Ben to call the turn.

Wyatt Earp had a definite course of action in mind as he advanced toward the hundred or more half-drunken cowboys, any and all of whom were keyed to cutting loose at him with twice that many guns for the mere satisfaction of seeing him die. He knew that to half the men in the crowd he was an utter stranger; the rest might know him by sight or name; he had no fear-inspiring record as a killer, and, so far as anyone in Ellsworth might know, had never used guns against a human adversary in all his life. He realized, too, that he was a target few men in the hundred could miss at fifty yards. That he was heeled with a pair of guns was evident to all; one false or hesitant gesture with either hand and he was fair game for the first to draw.

"I knew what I would do before the mayor pinned Brocky Jack's badge on my shirt," Wyatt said in recalling the affair. "I based my action on my knowledge of Ben Thompson's vanity and of the Texas men in his crowd.

"In the first place, I knew better than to walk out of Beebe's with a gun in my hand. If I had, I would have been filled with lead before I reached the road. But I also knew that, as long as I did not draw, the Texas men would leave it to Ben to make the play; he would have turned and shot down anyone who dared to cut loose before he opened the ball. Whatever happened must first be between him and me.

"So, all I had to do was keep my eye on Ben's shotgun; not on the muzzle, but on his right hand at the grip and trigger guard. That held my eye on the target I had picked, his stomach just back of his hand. I figured he'd wait for me to get within thirty or forty yards to make his weapon most effective and that he could not get the shotgun into action without 'telegraphing the move,' as a boxer would say, through his wrist. When I saw his wrist move to put his arm muscles into play, I'd go for my guns and I had enough confidence in myself to be certain that I could put at least one slug into his belly before he could pull a trigger.

"I realized that after I'd plugged Ben, some of his crowd might get me, and I had some idea, I suppose, of taking as many with me as I could. Beyond figuring to get Cad Pierce after I got Ben, if that was possible, I don't recall thinking much about that. All I really cared about was heading Thompson into his hole. I intended to arrest him if I could. But it was a moral certainty that he'd try to shoot. If he did, I'd kill him. I could hit a target the size of his stomach ten times out of ten shots with a forty-five at any range up to one hundred yards, and I had perfect confidence in my speed."

When Wyatt Earp was about forty yards distant, Ben Thompson called to him.

"What do you want, Wyatt?" he shouted.

"I want you, Ben," Wyatt replied, walking steadily forward.

Neither Ben Thompson nor any onlooker, and least of all Wyatt Earp, has offered a completely satisfactory explanation for what followed. Thompson made no move with his gun, and did not speak again until Wyatt was less than thirty yards away.

"I'd rather talk than fight," the killer called.

"I'll get you either way, Ben," Wyatt assured him, without halting in his stride.

"Wait a minute," said Thompson. "What do you want me to do?"

"Throw your shotgun into the road, put up your hands, and tell your friends to stay out of this play," Wyatt answered. Less than fifteen yards now separated the men.

"Will you stop and let me talk to you?" Ben asked.

Wyatt halted. He now knew positively that he could take Thompson, alive or dead, whichever way the gunman chose to turn events. He had Ben talking, which is the gravest error possible to a gun-thrower who has serious business at hand.

"What are you going to do with me?" Thompson asked.

"Kill you or take you to jail," Wyatt informed him.

"Brown's over there by the depot with a rifle," Ben objected. "The minute I give up my guns he'll cut loose at me."

"If he does," Wyatt promised, "I'll give you back your guns and we'll shoot it out with him. As long as you're my prisoner, the man that gets you will have to get me."

Thompson hesitated.

"Come on," Wyatt ordered; "throw down your gun or make your fight."

Ben Thompson grinned.

"You win," he said, tossed his shotgun into the road, and shoved both hands above his head.

Wyatt Earp's guns were still in their holsters. Now, for the first time, his hand went to his right hip.

"You fellows get back!" he ordered the Texas men. "Move!"

As they obeyed, Wyatt stepped up to Thompson and un-buckled his prisoner's gunbelts.

"Come on, Ben," he said. "We'll go over to the cala-boose."

With the famous Thompson six-guns dangling from their belts in his left hand, Wyatt marched his prisoner across the plaza to Judge V. B. Osborne's court. Until he reached the entrance, no onlookers spoke to him, or moved to follow. Once Wyatt and Ben were inside, the mayor and his erstwhile officers hurried after them. A moment later, five hundred milling men stormed at the narrow doorway, Thompson's friends leading the mob.

Deputy Sheriff Hogue, who had just ridden into town, forced a way through the crowd as a messenger from the Whitney home arrived with the shouted news that the sheriff was dead. The announcement was premature—Whitney actually lived for several hours after the Thompson hearing—but to the mob it was final.

There was talk of lynching, but Wyatt anticipated no serious trouble on that score; real danger would come with any attempt of the Texas men to rescue Ben from the law. The Thompson element dictated his next move. Peshaur, Pierce, Kane, and Good shouldered into the front rank, each with his forty-fives belted to his waist and Pierce carrying the shotgun with which Whitney had been assassi-nated and which Ben had thrown into the road. Wyatt spoke to Hogue in an undertone, then turned on the gunmen.

"Get out of here!" he ordered. "Pierce, take your crowd outside and keep 'em there. There'll be no lynching and no rescue."

Pierce looked at Thompson.

"Better go, Cad," Ben suggested. "He means what he says."

With the courtroom cleared, Thompson's arraignment proceeded.

"What's the charge?" asked Judge Osborne.

As no one else volunteered a reply, Wyatt suggested that Ben was probably an accessory to murder. The judge turned to Mayor Miller as the proper person to indicate the enormity of Thompson's offense. The mayor hesitated, possibly in embarrassment under the keen blue eye of his hastily selected peace officer, considered the economic importance of the Texas men to the community, then offered as an amendment his opinion that maybe Ben had disturbed the peace.

"Guilty," said the judge. "Twenty-five dollars fine."

Thompson grinned as he peeled the assessment from a roll of greenbacks.

"Do I get my guns?" he inquired.

"Certainly," said the judge. "You have paid your fine and the marshal will restore any property he may have taken from you."

As Thompson reached for his gunbelts, Wyatt issued his last order as an Ellsworth peace officer.

"Ben," he said, "court or no court, don't you put those on here. You carry them straight to the Grand Central, and don't so much as hesitate on the way. I'll be watching you. Keep moving until you're out of my sight. After that, what you do will be none of my business."

Wyatt stood in the courtroom door with his eye on Thompson until the gunman reached his hotel, then turned to Mayor Miller.

"Here," he said, "is your badge, and here are the guns I got at Beebe's. I don't need 'em any longer."

"Don't you want to be marshal of Ellsworth?" Miller asked.

"I do not," Wyatt replied.

"We'll pay you one hundred and twenty-five dollars a month," the mayor offered.

"Ellsworth," Wyatt answered sententiously, "figures sheriffs at twenty-five dollars a head. I don't figure the town's my size."

Some years after this Ellsworth episode, Bat Masterson asked Ben Thompson why he had so docilely submitted to arrest by Wyatt Earp. Thompson's reply is quoted for what it may be worth.

"It was just a hunch," Ben told Bat, "a hunch that Wyatt would get me if I opened up. I wasn't afraid of him, but I didn't want to die just then, and I had a hunch I was slated to if Wyatt went after his guns. But that wasn't all. It took nerve to come after me the way he did. He was just a youngster, but I could tell he'd go through with his play. He wouldn't have stood a chance to live against my crowd, even if he had knocked me off. I didn't want to see a young fellow as game as Wyatt go out with no chance for an even break. Cad Pierce wanted me to cut loose when Wyatt was about halfway across the plaza. I didn't, and I've never regretted it; if I had, I wouldn't be here telling about it, either."

When Wyatt Earp reached the buffalo range in September, he found that hunting in the winter of 1873–74 was to be far less profitable than in prior years. Game was scarce; the huge herds no longer roamed north and south; in truth, the seasonal migration of the buffalo had ended for all time. The comparatively few animals which had escaped slaughter had separated into two major groups, one remaining the seasons through in the Dakota–Wyoming–Montana country, the other in The Nations and on the Texas plains.

Wyatt Earp decided in the spring of '74 that he would not hunt buffalo commercially again, squared accounts, and sold his outfit, down to his guns. He declined an invitation from Bat Masterson, Billy Dixon, Jim Hanrahan, and others to join a summer hunt in the Texas Panhandle, and by so doing missed participation in the famous Indian fight at Adobe Walls in June of '74.

Wyatt still hankered for a go at the cattle business. He had a larger stake than he had owned a year before, and he struck for Wichita, which, after a season's depression, was reasserting its claim as the real terminal of the Chisholm Trail.

9

Wild and Woolly Wichita

Late in a May evening, Wyatt Earp crossed the Arkansas River toll bridge at the west end of Wichita's Douglas Avenue, turned his pony in at the first corral, and took a room at an adjoining hotel. The corral was owned by Doc Black, and upon this casual selection of quarters hung much of Wyatt's destiny.

Barring size—her brag was twelve hundred residents—the boom cowcamp of '74 differed little from Ellsworth of the prior year. Frame houses were rising among the "soddies" and in the commercial district brick buildings were under construction; but, in the main, Wichita sprawled in the dust and mud on her riverbank as unattractively as any Kansas settlement of the decade. Sidewalks of plank or of heel-tamped clay ran underneath the inevitable wooden awnings which stretched from the ludicrously false façades of stores and saloons to shade the loafers' benches; post was linked to post at the curb lines by cayuse-cribbed hitching-rails.

One night in town established the fact of Wichita's

restoration as the cowboy capital, as well as a certainty that
Texas trail drivers still followed habit with regard to law and
order. As Wyatt first saw her, Wichita was merely another
Kansas cowcamp, with longer streets, more stores, saloons,
gambling houses, and honky-tonks, larger crowds of cowboys, and, by these tokens, more trouble.

Wyatt's first move was to hunt out his brother Jim, who
had been in Wichita for several weeks. From him he had
warning that Ben Thompson and George Peshaur were in
town, making headquarters at the Keno House, then the
most famous gambling establishment in the prairie West, at
the corner of Main Street and Douglas Avenue, and next
door to which Jim had a job with one Pryor. Jim suggested
that, as the Texas men were running wild in Wichita, it
behooved Wyatt to watch for their attempt to even the
Ellsworth score. Ben Thompson had had little to say about
the Whitney murder and its aftermath, but George Peshaur
had boasted openly of what he would do to Wyatt Earp at
the first opportunity, which those who knew the Texan took
to mean the first time that Peshaur caught Wyatt short.

On his second morning in town, Wyatt and several other
men followed the noise of a ruction to the rear of Doc
Black's corral, where they found the burly proprietor beating a small chore boy. In the struggle of prying Black's two
hundred–odd pounds of fat and spleen away from his
victim, Doc's rage carried him out of that discretion in
matters of physical encounter for which he was noted and he
swung wildly at those who interfered with discipline; by
chance, he hit Wyatt in the face. Wyatt promptly blacked
Doc's eyes and knocked him down. Upon regaining his feet,
the corral proprietor hurried up Douglas Avenue, to return a
few moments later with a deputy marshal.

"I'm arresting you, Earp," the deputy said. "Black's
charging you with assault."

"All right," Wyatt answered. "Let's see the judge and get
it over."

Judge Ed Jewett was not in his court, the officer explained.
Temporarily, the village was using a nearby shack as a jail,
and if the prisoner would walk over to it and consider

himself locked in, he could save trouble. Wyatt complied, and the deputy sat down in the doorway while the vindictively impatient Black waddled off to find the judge.

All unwittingly, the deputy marshal had arrested Wyatt Earp at a time fixed by Texas gunmen for treeing Wichita. A few days earlier, two cowboys had run afoul of a giant Negro hod carrier, who had first drubbed the pair in a fistfight, then added insult to their injuries by dragging them before Judge Jewett, who had fined them for assault. The cowboys and their friends decided to pay off the camp with an object lesson.

Throughout the morning of the day appointed, Texas men had been drifting into town unostentatiously, and stationing themselves at strategic points, principally in saloons along Douglas Avenue. By the time of Wyatt's arrest, the earlier arrivals had absorbed enough whiskey to wax impatient, and when Doc Black, in his search for Jewett, spread word that Wyatt Earp was under arrest, a dozen agreed that, while waiting to avenge the Negro's insult, they might as well get the man who had discomfited their friends in Ellsworth.

Wyatt and his guardian in the doorway of the shack saw the Texas crowd, on foot and patently very drunk, turn off Douglas Avenue in their direction.

"I'll get some help," the deputy marshal said, and started 'cross-lots.

Wyatt slammed the flimsy door in the cowboys' faces.

"Is Wyatt Earp in there?" a Texan demanded.

"I'm Wyatt Earp. What do you want?"

"We want you."

"What for?"

"You killed a couple of our friends up in Ellsworth last summer; that's what for," someone answered.

"You're wrong," Wyatt parleyed. "I didn't kill anyone in Ellsworth, but I'll kill the first man through this door. Before you start anything, go ask Ben Thompson what happened. He'll tell you you don't want me."

The only weapon in Wyatt's possession was a stool with which he stood ready to bash in the first head that came in any rush through the doorway; he used Ben Thompson's name in the hope of diverting the maudlin gang long enough to let him reach more substantial cover. The Texans fell to arguing.

"Come on," Wyatt heard one suggest. "We'll ask Ben if he wants us to knock this fellow off. We can get him any time. Let's get another drink, anyway."

The last argument prevailed, and the dozen or fifteen cowboys moved off toward the Douglas Avenue saloons. As they left, the deputy marshal returned.

"Hell's going to pop someplace," he reported. "Every joint in town is full of Texas men."

"Are they after me?" Wyatt asked.

The deputy guessed they were, and that he'd better around up some assistance.

"You expect me to stay here to be murdered by a bunch of drunks?" Wyatt inquired.

"Well, I wouldn't want you to do that," the deputy admitted. "Haven't you got any guns?"

"I checked 'em up at Pryor's," Wyatt explained.

"Take mine," said the deputy. "I'll get another pair uptown. If that mob comes after you, maybe you can stand 'em off. I'll get someone to come down here and help us."

Wyatt buckled on the gunbelts and ran over to a stable, where he posted himself in a stall which commanded both street and rear entrance. He heard two pistol shots in the distance, followed by the pound of hoofs down Douglas Avenue. A buckskin pony on the dead run, rider low in the saddle, sped past the doorway, over the toll bridge and on across the prairie. Behind him a mob of cowboys with drawn guns backed past the barn where Wyatt was concealed, and halted at the bridgehead.

Wyatt was puzzled. The Texas men paid no attention to the shack in which he had been a prisoner, but held their eyes up Douglas Avenue. Borrowed pistols in hand, he peered around the corner of the stable doorway, and as he did so, Bill Smith, chief marshal of Wichita, sidled along the building directly in front of him.

"Get out of the way," Wyatt said. "You're right in range."

Smith jumped.

"Don't shoot," he said; then looked around. "Oh," he added with apparent relief, "you're Earp. They're not after you; they're covering Shorty's getaway."

"Who's Shorty?" Wyatt asked.

"He's the fellow who crossed the bridge in a hurry. He killed a nigger up in Main Street. The nigger and some cowboys had trouble a few days ago, and the boys picked Shorty to pay the grudge. Shorty stood about fifty feet from where the nigger was working and waited until he got to the top of a ladder with a hod of bricks. Then he cut him down. The first shot drilled the nigger clean through the head, and while he and the bricks were in the air, Shorty put another slug through his belly. That nigger was dead before the first brick hit the ground. Then Shorty rode some."

"What are you going to do," Wyatt asked, "arrest them?"

"Shorty's gone and there are too many to arrest," the marshal replied. "I'm going to see if I can keep them from hurrahing the whole town. You stay out of sight until I come for you.

"Hey," Smith called to the cowboys, "I want to talk to you."

"Come on over," one of the mob replied.

The parley ended when the Texans agreed to put up their guns if they were not to be molested for the death of the hod carrier. Wyatt waited in the barn while the marshal carried word of the compromise uptown. Twenty minutes later, Smith stuck his head in the door.

"Come on," he said, "the mayor wants to see you."

At the entrance to the mayor's office, Wyatt met the deputy who had arrested him and returned the borrowed weapons. Inside, he found Jim Hope, mayor of Wichita, and two town councilmen.

"Are you Wyatt Earp?" Hope asked.

"That's my name."

"You the fellow that run it over Ben Thompson in Ellsworth last summer?"

"I arrested him."

"How'd you like to be deputy marshal of Wichita?"

Wyatt, who thought that he was on the carpet for punching Doc Black, was momentarily taken aback by the question. In after years he recalled clearly the rapid reasoning which followed surprise and determined his answer. There was a deal of egotism involved, he admitted; it had occurred to him before that he'd like to stack up against these men who terrorized the prairie towns and to try out certain theories concerning them. Briefly, he believed he was a better man than any braggart gun-thrower who rode the cattle trail; there was considerable zest to be anticipated in this opportunity to justify that confidence.

"We pay one hundred and twenty-five dollars a month and supply guns and ammunition," Mayor Hope suggested.

"I've got seventy-five hundred dollars in my clothes," Wyatt replied, "and the wages don't interest me."

Which remark, as Wyatt once commented, was bumptious, but honest. He was young, and seventy-five hundred dollars was a large sum of money in that time and country. Moreover, the last thing he foresaw was any extended career as a peace officer.

"I was out to prove a little something," he said; "that accomplished, I'd be quitting."

In considering the manner in which the deputy's badge was tendered to Wyatt Earp, it should be recalled that in the seventies it often was difficult to obtain competent marshals for the frontier villages. The jobs were fraught with danger and applications for the positions were rarely made; in some instances the posts were filled by tempting able men with high wages; in many cases, the peace officers were youthful adventurers lured by promise of action; the roster of famous frontier peace officers reveals that a majority attained eminence well under the age of thirty.

"How far can I go in making your ordinances stick?" Wyatt asked.

"The limit," Mayor Hope answered.

"I'll take your job," Wyatt told him.

Jim Hope handed over a deputy marshal's badge.

"Pin that on your shirt," he said, "and go down to the New York Store and get yourself some guns. Charge 'em to me. Then come back here."

Fifteen minutes later, Wyatt reentered Hope's office with a single-action Colt's forty-five at his right hip and a belt of cartridges around his waist. The mayor took one look at him.

"Guns," he snapped; "not gun. You've got a two-gun job."

"Suits me," Wyatt answered, and went back to add to his arsenal.

The policy of the Hope administration was to work the deputy marshals in pairs, and Wyatt was teamed with Jimmy Cairns. Cairns in 1929 was still living in Wichita, and of Wyatt's accomplishments in the community he wrote:

"Wyatt was a wonderful officer; a gamer one never drew breath. He was the most dependable man I ever knew; a quiet, unassuming chap who never drank and in all respects a clean young fellow. He never hunted trouble, but he was ready for any that came his way. There wasn't a bad man in the whole West that Wyatt was afraid of, and some of them came pretty mean. He was always cool and collected in the face of danger and never let a threat bother him. His reputation as a dead shot and a man not to be monkeyed with soon spread and the gunmen were few and far between who chose to cross him. The chance which made him a Wichita peace officer made him one of the most spectacular figures of the early West."

Wyatt's appointment as a deputy marshal was resented by the cowboys, many of whom had witnessed the Ellsworth affair of the preceding summer, and threats of reprisal were openly employed to bring about his dismissal. Mayor Hope stood by the appointment, however, and, beyond a few arrests of routine nature, the early weeks of the cattle-shipping season passed uneventfully. The larger drives had not yet reached Wichita and the cowboys encamped on Cowskin Creek were disposed to await reinforcement before putting threats into execution. Meanwhile, Wyatt found opportunity to get acquainted in the community.

Such life in the Wichita of '74 as required the supervision of a peace officer was lived for the most part within pistol shot of the two-storied Keno House at Main Street and

Douglas Avenue, and along either one of these intersecting
thoroughfares. In this famous gambling establishment, operated by Whitey (W. W.) Rupp, the keno goose laid golden
eggs all day and night without a pause and from it at
approximately sixty-second intervals the exultant shout of
"Keno!" rang out over the cowcamp's principal four corners. Faro, monte, poker, roulette, chuck-a-luck, and other
games were as constantly in operation. Around the tables
gathered the two or three thousand transients which summer brought to Wichita—cowboys, professional gamblers,
horse thieves, land-seekers, outlaws, and cattlemen—as well
as local citizens. From the standpoint of money changing
hands, Whitey Rupp ran the most important gambling place
west of the Mississippi River.

Rupp also had "the finest bar in Wichita." Next door was
Pryor's. Saloons and gambling houses outnumbered other
enterprises for several blocks north, south, east, and west.
Across Main Street was the New York Store, to which Texas
men flocked for clothing, arms, and ammunition. Along
Douglas Avenue, at Horse-Thief Corner, stood the Texas
House, a rendezvous for cattlemen. Nearby were the
Douglas Avenue House and the Occidental. The Southern
and the Empire, two other famous frontier taverns, were
back on Main Street, and at the corner of Third and Main,
Judge Jewett had his courtroom close to the scenes which
provided customers.

Just across the toll bridge and outside the municipality,
Rowdy Joe Lowe and his wife, Rowdy Kate, ran a dance hall
and saloon which they bragged was "the swiftest joint in
Kansas." This claim was valiantly disputed by "Red" and
Mrs. "Red" Redfern, who operated a similar establishment
across the road along lines calculated to make idle their
neighbors' boasts of speed. Their rivalry continued until
Rowdy Joe, armed with a shotgun, and Red, with a six-
shooter, stepped into the road to settle the argument over
pace in incontrovertible fashion. Rowdy Joe downed Red,
but in the course of the killing a couple of stray buckshot
took the eyes out of an innocent bystander. Sheriff Meagher
deputized Wyatt to arrest the dance-hall proprietor, which

Wyatt did without difficulty, but Joe was promptly released when it was shown that the fight had been an even break. The bystander, it was held, could not prove legitimate business in the line of fire.

In a community of Wichita's size and propensities, little time was required for both permanent and transient residents to acquaint themselves with the newest recruit to the forces of law and order. More than half a century later, more than one old-timer who knew the cowcamp in its youth recalled the wave of interested speculation which followed Wyatt's first appearance in the village streets with his officer's badge and his Colt's persuaders.

In a sense Wyatt Earp was something new in the way of a Wichita peace officer. Theretofore the town had known either of two types. Early in its short history, professional killers had been hired to enforce some semblance of order, men deadly skillful with weapons, but who took the law as a license to shoot potential troublemakers without warning. Wild Bill Hickok had been the outstanding exponent of this school. He and his kind had rid the town of several undesirable visitors, but the manner of their so doing had left a bad taste in the mouths of fair-minded citizens. Apparently, it had affected the cowboy element only by inciting the Texas men to bloody vengeance for what they regarded as ruthless murders. From the Hickok regime the camp swung to the extreme of peace officers who were eternally compromising with the gun-toters, with the natural result that life at times was too unruly for local comfort.

Two Wichita pioneers who have contributed materially to this account of Wyatt Earp's career—Charles Hatton, Wichita's city attorney in 1874, later, United States Commissioner, afterward, a California jurist, and David D. Leahy, once a young reporter for *The Eagle,* Marsh Murdock's frontier newspaper, and later a distinguished journalist—have commented upon Wyatt's early appearances in the Wichita streets, the pronounced impression made by his splendid physique and the unobtrusively confident manner in which he went about his business.

"I met Wyatt the day he joined the marshal's force,"

Judge Hatton recalled. "I was told that he was the man who had arrested Ben Thompson in Ellsworth after the murder of Sheriff Whitney, and the rest of Wichita knew as much by nightfall. The Ellsworth exploit would have made him a marked man in any Western community, and when the town added to that the evidences of capability which showed in every inch of him, we began to hope that at last we had a peace officer who could fill our sizable bill. Later, I saw Wyatt, single-handed, go against some of the most desperate gunmen in the West—I stood not ten feet away from him on two such occasions—and in action he bore out my highest expectations."

"Also, Wyatt Earp was the handsomest, best-mannered young man in Wichita," interposed Mrs. Hatton, who had been listening to the reminiscences, and who, as a bride, had gone with her lawyer-husband to the booming cowtown.

While Wichita speculated upon possibilities latent in her new peace officer, he was making acquaintances. One was young Ed Doheny, a "pearl-diver," washing dishes for his board in the Texas House—that same Edward L. Doheny who eventually found enormous wealth in petroleum. Another, Jim Hemingway, who was hauling buffalo bones from the erstwhile hunting range, in later life was to be United States Senator from Indiana.

Dr. Andrew H. Fabrique was the cowcamp's pioneer physician and surgeon, for some years its only man of medicine, and demands of a practice which ranged from gunshot wounds to obstetrics and back again with every round of the clock, with patients scattered over several counties, drove him to extremities in search of occasional unbroken rest. There was no assistant trained in medicine at hand, so Dr. Fabrique did the best he might, and hired one trained in the law, a young man who had hung his shingle over the door of a shack on Douglas Avenue, but had yet to meet his first client.

Dr. Fabrique suggested that the embryo statesman sleep on a cot in the doctor's office and eat three meals a day at the doctor's expense. In return, the attorney would interview persons who sought the physician's services while the doctor was asleep. By examining a caller's wounds or considering symptoms, the lawyer could decide whether Dr. Fabrique should be aroused or rest undisturbed. The arrangement was in force at the time Wyatt Earp was deputy marshal. As Wyatt's prisoners were often in need of patching, and as most of them were arrested after nightfall, he and the lawyer soon became good friends. Between them they performed certain feats of surgery which must have made the good doctor turn over in his bed, at least, as he slept in the adjoining room.

Clark was the young attorney's name, Champ Clark, he said, and he was going to Missouri as soon as he raised the money to pay a few debts he had incurred in Wichita and to purchase transportation. Wyatt once offered to lend Champ enough money to get him out of Wichita with a clean slate, but the tender was not accepted. Then, one night, as the young men sat outside Dr. Fabrique's door where callers could be intercepted conveniently and Wyatt could keep an eye and an ear peeled toward the trouble zone around Keno Corner, Champ announced that, at last, he had a client.

One of Dr. Fabrique's patients had a son who for several years had been battling his way through college. The youth had finally reached senior grade only to find that between him and a degree loomed a graduation thesis. The boy had submitted three efforts which he termed essays, but the faculty had been unable to accept any one of them as such and had notified the father that, unless his son submitted a suitable paper before commencement, he would not receive the greatly coveted diploma. The distressed parent turned to his family physician for counsel and Dr. Fabrique struck a bargain in behalf of his lawyer-assistant.

Champ was to write a paper which the collegiate youth was to copy and submit to the faculty. If, on the strength of the essay, the son received his diploma, the father was to pay Champ's debts and buy his ticket to St. Louis. Otherwise, Champ's time would be wasted.

The essay was written in one day, Champ told Wyatt when he passed it over for criticism, the greatest difficulty having been to keep it from appearing far beyond the capabilities of the youth who was to copy the paper. The faculty's verdict, when reached, was favorable, and soon afterward, Champ left for Missouri and the career which was to all but make him President of the United States.

Texas trail herds awaiting shipment on the prairies south and west of Wichita had been swollen by daily arrivals to some 200,000 head. Outfits camped on the Cowskin and other Arkansas River tributaries could muster two thousand cowboys, among them riders for every cattle king in Texas and possibly one half under the leadership of professional fighting men, six-gun killers hired by the feudal lords of the unfenced range for their incessant wars with Indians, rustlers, and one another. As the throng of Texas men who hit town nightly was reinforced by later arrivals, the temper of the roisterers moved as steadily toward open battle against Wichita.

Among the hired gunmen in the Cowskin camps were Neil Kane and John Good, who promptly renewed their alliance with Ben Thompson and George Peshaur. Cad Pierce had been killed in a gunfight. That notorious quartet of gun-throwing brothers, Mannen, Gyp, Joe, and Jim Clements, were up with a gang of Texas men that included Tom, Bud, and Simp Dixon, Ham Anderson, Alec Barrickman, the Milligans, the Cunninghams, Billy Helfridge, Joe and Billy Collins, Brown Bowen, and, for a time, John Wesley Hardin—who had opened the shooting season by killing a buffalo hunter who appeared on Douglas Avenue wearing a silk hat—every last one noted for six-shooter proficiency and almost every one of whom had his boots on at his finish. With their clans in force, the cowboys told Jim Hope that if he didn't get rid of his new deputy at once, they'd do it for him.

"What do you want me to do about it, Wyatt?" the Mayor inquired.

"Nothing," his deputy marshal replied. "They've sent word to me several times that if I didn't leave town they'd get me. I'm staying in Wichita."

A day or so later, George Peshaur and several followers stopped Wyatt on Douglas Avenue and in the hearing of a half-dozen citizens threatened to kill him at his first attempt to interfere with whatever liberties the Texas men chose to take in the town.

"You're drunk, Peshaur," Wyatt answered; "go sleep it off," then walked down the street.

Within the hour Ben Thompson sought out Wyatt Earp.

"I never knew exactly why," Wyatt said, "but Ben hunted me up to tell me that, while he strung with his crowd against the town, this play was against me as an individual and he'd have no hand in it. He said he bore me no grudge for the Ellsworth business and wanted me to know that Peshaur and the others were going against his advice in their move to run me out of Wichita."

Wyatt proceeded characteristically with his preparations for encounter. He loaded several double-barreled shotguns with buckshot and placed them at strategic points behind counters and close to doorways of stores and saloons conducted by men in whom he had confidence. He inspected these weapons each afternoon and evening to make certain that their loads were in order. At whatever moment circumstance forced him to go against the Texans, he would be facing at close range, he knew, from twenty to one hundred six-guns. A shotgun would be the only weapon to give him anything like an even break against such overwhelming odds.

With his arsenal placed to suit, Wyatt went about his routine business.

10

A Cattle King Is Deposed

On a Saturday afternoon in early summer, a messenger dispatched by several Wichita merchants found Wyatt Earp on lower Douglas Avenue keeping tab on the cowboys streaming across the toll bridge for the Saturday carousal, which, in all well-regulated cowtowns, was several shades wilder and more widely inclusive than those of other days.

"They want you up on Main Street," the messenger told Wyatt. "Shanghai Pierce is drunk and raising Cain. Bill Potts [another deputy marshal] can't handle him. Shang says he'll kill the first man who lays hand on him."

Shanghai Pierce—christened Abel, but better known to his friends as Colonel, or Shang—was no gunfighting desperado; although a hundred of the six-shooter gentry on the Cowskin fed at his chuck wagons and five times that number would rally to his call. But he was, perhaps, the most colorful character of all those romantic figures whom the Old West dubbed its cattle kings and, unquestionably, a prime factor in whatever prosperity Wichita anticipated for 1874.

Sober, Abel Pierce was a jolly Connecticut Yankee transmogrified into a Texas beef baron, who, in personal appearance, mode of living, and domain governed, came closer to regal estate than any fellow sovereign who rode the Chisholm Trail. Six feet four he stood in his cowpuncher's boots, straight as an arrow with all his two hundred and twenty pounds, a fine full-bearded figure of a man. By his jovial personality and never-failing generosity he commanded a widespread loyalty and affection among cattlemen of the Southwest which no other of his time approached. Of him, George W. Saunders, president of the Old-Time Trail-Drivers' Association, has written, in "The Trail-Drivers of Texas":

Shanghai Pierce has a record in the cattle industry never surpassed, and I doubt if ever equaled by any man. My first recollection of Mr. Pierce was just after the Civil War when he bought fat cattle all over South Texas. I remember seeing him many times come to our camp where he had contracts to receive beeves. He was a large, portly man, always rode a fine horse and would be accompanied by a negro who led a pack-horse loaded with gold and silver. When the cattle were classed and counted out to him, he would empty the money on a blanket and pay it out to the different stockmen. We all looked upon him as a redeemer, as money was scarce in those days. Colonel Pierce was a great talker and would keep the boys awake until midnight laughing at his stories. He was a loud talker and no man who ever heard him or saw him ever forgot his voice or appearance. His steers became known from the Rio Grande to the Canadian line as "Shanghai Pierce's sea-lions." He was a money-maker, an empire-builder, and a wonder to his friends, and I believe to himself.

It was this same Shanghai Pierce who introduced the walking stick to Kansas, and who tickled the risibilities of the Young West with his offer, to a financially embarrassed

Nebraska, of a ten-thousand-dollar annual payment for the exclusive right to deal monte on railway trains within the state's borders. When the Nebraska legislators hesitated over granting such a lucrative franchise to an individual, he further convulsed an appreciative frontier by offering the same money for the exclusive privilege of dealing the game against only such passengers as professed to be clergymen or missionaries.

This second proffer meeting legislative rebuff, Shanghai played upon the mingled emotions of admirers and acquaintances by spending his ten thousand dollars for a bronze statue of himself clad in all the cowboy trappings which he loved, a statue forty feet high which he had erected at his Rancho Grande headquarters, at Tres Palacios.

"The statue was natural as life," wrote Charlie Siringo, who rode with Shanghai's outfit in the early seventies, "and when I looked at it, in imagination I could hear Shanghai's voice, which could be heard for half a mile, even when he whispered."

In a season when efforts to attract the cattle trade had started with open bribes to ranch foremen and trail bosses, Shanghai Pierce's drive to Wichita was the crowning glory of that cowcamp's labors. Practically every cattle owner of importance would follow Shanghai's lead in such matters. Wherefore, upon his arrival in Wichita with the first of his drives, for a stay which would terminate in September, Shanghai received whatever keys there were to the community. A redeemer for cash-shy cattle owners in South Texas, in Wichita he was nothing short of a business savior, and the town accordingly kowtowed. If Shanghai had been somewhat careless with a running iron in building his herds, so had others of his calling, and the Wichita of '74 was no camp to get squeamish over such gossip; so she laid herself out in welcome. Then Shanghai got drunk, and the entertainment committee put in a hurry-call for the new deputy marshal.

When Wyatt turned from Douglas Avenue into Main Street, he saw Shanghai Pierce sprawling on a chair in the middle of the walk outside of Billy Collins's saloon. At his right hip Shanghai wore the customary forty-five in an open holster, and as he roared defiance to anyone in Wichita who imagined that any such-and-such shorthorn village could tell the best so-and-so cattleman in Texas where to head in, he kept his hand on the gun butt. Particularly when Bill Potts presumed to request that he take himself indoors did Shanghai ascend to heights of noise and profanity that held Main Street's Saturday afternoon trade captivated to a standstill.

Pierce was too drunk to be deadly; danger lay in the chance that some bystander might be injured by wild shooting. And Wyatt saw that Shanghai's gun was wedged beneath his thigh, held tightly in the holster against the chair by pressure of the man's whole weight, against which Shanghai was tugging vainly.

With his fellow officer approaching, Potts grew bold enough to put a hand on the cowman's shoulder, a familiarity that Shanghai resented with a lurch that let his gun come free. Wyatt caught the cattle king's wrist.

"Drop that gun," he said.

Shanghai's outburst changed to a roar of pain as Wyatt clamped the forearm back and down against the chair.

The forty-five fell to the walk. Wyatt took the weapon inside to Collins's gunrack, and stepped back to the chair, where Shanghai was nursing an aching arm and cursing fluently.

"Get up and get inside," Wyatt ordered.

Shanghai bellowed colorful defiance.

"Hold the door open, Potts," Wyatt directed, seized the cattle king by the shirt collar with one hand, the belt with the other, yanked him from his seat, and hurled him halfway down the bar.

"If Pierce has any friends in here," Wyatt remarked to Collins's customers as a body, "they'll ride herd on him. If I see him drunk on the street again today, I'll heave him into the calaboose, and he'll stay there until morning."

When Wyatt returned to lower Douglas Avenue, he dismissed the Pierce affair as a closed incident. An hour later, an intuitive impulse took him back to Main Street. Scores of cowboys had crossed the toll bridge since Shanghai's man-handling and, as Wyatt idled along Douglas Avenue, it struck him that that thoroughfare was ominously quiet. Any lull in the uproar of a cowtown spree-day warranted investigation. Cairns was to come on duty in a few moments and he started uptown to meet him.

When Wyatt turned into Main Street, he did not know that word of his move had preceded him, or that he was under the eye of a lookout in Collins's doorway. When he was directly opposite the entrance through which he had hurled the cattle king, Collins's double-doors burst open and onto the walk surged a score of cowboys. In their midst towered Shanghai Pierce, still drunk and supported by two of his henchmen.

"There he is!" a cowpuncher shouted. "If he makes a move, let him have it."

Wyatt knew better than to go for his guns in the face of forty six-shooters ready for business. Ed Morrison, cowboy and professional fighting man, called the next turn.

"If you think you can arrest Shang Pierce, try it!" he taunted. "Come on! If you're so good with your guns, why don't you jerk 'em? We're taking Shang where he wants to go. Any move you make to touch him'll be your last one."

There followed a torrent of unprintable vituperation in which Morrison's followers joined, as with Pierce in their midst they backed toward Douglas Avenue. Until they reached the corner, the cowboys held Wyatt motionless under their weapons, but as the gang disappeared around the turn, the deputy marshal darted into an alley at the rear of the buildings fronting Douglas Avenue and with an entrance on Main Street. As he ran parallel to the course the Texas men were taking, he heard them whooping derision and shouting threats, above the steady roar of gunfire. Certain of their supremacy over the local peace officers, they were shooting up Douglas Avenue in wholesale Texas fashion.

From the northeast Wyatt heard, also, the resonant voice of the great iron triangle which hung before Judge Jewett's office and was sacred to the sole purpose of summoning

Wichita citizens to a finish-fight with the cowmen. In all the cowcamp's history no one had cried "Wolf!" with that triangle; the instrument had sounded the death knell of many a Texas gun-thrower, not, however, without the sacrifice of numerous townsmen. Wyatt had hopes of getting into action on his own before any posse of citizens could reach Pierce and the cowboys. Not only was there a chance that he thus could save some needless killing; in his first big play as a Wichita peace officer, the Texas men now had him studded.

Well in advance of the gang that was terrorizing Douglas Avenue, Wyatt ran by an alley entrance through a store to seize one of his cached shotguns. He jumped through the front doorway about fifty feet ahead of the Texans.

"Throw up your hands!" he shouted. "Throw 'em up or I'll blow hell out of you!"

"You, Morrison!"—the surprised cowboys, guns smoking but mostly empty, had halted in half-drunken confusion—"throw up your hands or I'll kill you."

Ed Morrison, thus singled out, with Wyatt's eye focused on him above the barrels of a weapon ready to spray eighteen buckshot across the roadway, chose discretion. His six-guns dropped in the dirt as his hands went skyward. Shanghai Pierce had been startled into something like sobriety and good sense.

"Throw 'em up, boys!" he bellowed, as he obeyed Wyatt's order. Retinue followed the royal example in a body.

Wyatt had the cowboys in line at the roadside when Marshal Smith and a citizen posse reached the scene. He held them that way while others took up their guns and gunbelts.

"Now," Wyatt said, "we'll go see Judge Jewett. Walk ahead of me to Main Street, turn and head for the courtroom. Keep in the middle of the road and don't try any funny business. Get going."

As the procession of crestfallen gun-toters scuffed its spur-jangling, high-heeled boots through the dust of Keno Corner under the muzzle of the double-barreled shotgun, a derisively raucous Rebel yell served notice that Ben Thompson was viewing the parade from the balcony of Whitey Rupp's establishment.

"Whoopee!" Ben jeered. "Paint that one on your chuck wagons! I told you he was poison!"

Judge Jewett fined each of the twenty-one Texas men whom Wyatt had arrested one hundred dollars, which Shanghai Pierce paid for all, with apologies to the municipality. As the culprits filed out, Wyatt turned to the judge.

"There's one favor you can do for me," he said. "As long as I'm an officer in Wichita, don't ring that triangle again."

It may be recorded here that, throughout Wyatt's subsequent service in Wichita, the triangle remained silent.

While his wholesale arrest of the Texas men gained for Wyatt additional confidence from Wichita citizens, and curbed for the time being the six-shooter celebrations of cowboy visitors, it also added to the animosity against him which motivated the guiding geniuses of the camps on Cowskin Creek. Wyatt's further employment of official tactics deliberately calculated to humiliate the cowboys increased their determination to get rid of him.

The deputy marshal speedily discovered that, while Wichita citizens generally believed with him that the surest method of holding gunplay in check was to enforce the ordinance against gun-toting, business, political, and less creditable interests withheld many townsmen from open support of this conviction. The cattle business meant five months of booming prosperity; the Texas men were the cattle trade; any edict which these roisterers might construe as an affront seemed impossible to obtain as long as Bill Smith was responsible to a certain group for what law enforcement was attempted. When repeated urging failed to elicit from Marshal Smith any wholehearted threat against gun-toters in the Wichita streets, Wyatt took it upon himself to enforce the ordinance, single-handed.

Unable to obtain court convictions for mere gun-carrying, Wyatt decided to complicate matters by charging all prisoners with drunkenness, the dereliction from which the Wichita judicial system derived supporting income. Arrests of this nature were commonly made in the late

113

afternoon and evening, and drunken prisoners were herded into the village bullpen to remain until court opened the next morning.

Wyatt's tests for intoxication were somewhat superficial; any unarmed man was sober; with a drink in him and a gun on him, he'd be thrown into the calaboose. Under this system, Wyatt corralled so many visiting cowboys that certain elements in the State of Texas nursed a grudge against him for the following half-century.

Shortly after the Shanghai Pierce incident, Wyatt encountered George Peshaur and a number of followers outside the Keno House. The Texan, who had been drinking heavily, greeted the deputy marshal with an outburst of invective and threats of violence which could not be entirely ignored. Wyatt waited for the end of the tirade.

"Peshaur," he said, "you couldn't talk to me like that if you were sober." With which observation, Wyatt stepped around the group and walked away. The epithet that Peshaur bawled after him was a particularly ribald allusion of the open range, to which Wyatt gave no heed.

On an afternoon of the following week, Wyatt again encountered Peshaur and his crowd, this time in front of Dick Cogswell's cigar store, where the deputy marshal stood talking with Charles Hatton.

"Peshaur," Judge Hatton recalled, "was a great, husky fellow, an inch or two taller than Wyatt and thirty or forty pounds heavier. With five or six cowboys to back him, he stepped up to Wyatt and ordered him in a loud voice and abusive language to stop arresting Texas men. The dare was too brash to ignore. Wyatt replied that he'd arrest any man who laid himself open to it, and that anyone who figured he could be bluffed out by a lot of cheap four-flushers was heading for trouble.

"At that, Peshaur got nastier. He taunted Wyatt about the Ellsworth affair and warned him that simply because Ben Thompson hadn't knocked him off was no reason for him to think he had everybody else buffaloed. Peshaur colored his taunts with insults that weren't pleasant to hear and I wondered why Wyatt didn't shoot him down in his tracks.

All Wyatt did was reply in that quiet, unperturbed way of his:

"'You were in Ellsworth, Peshaur, and had two guns on you at the time. What's more, I notice you haven't been wearing any in Wichita since I put out word it was safer not to.'

"That burned Peshaur up, and he cut loose with another string of abuse.

"'Be careful,' Wyatt warned him; 'you're sober today.'

"'You bet I am,' Peshaur replied, 'and if you didn't have two guns and a badge on and weren't looking for an excuse to murder me, I'd fix you so you wouldn't do any more arresting in a hurry.'

"Then Peshaur accused Wyatt of being yellow, in as vile a fashion as I ever heard a man talk. Wyatt paled under his tan—which was the only sign of emotion I ever knew him to display in any crisis—and turned to Dick Cogswell, who stood in his doorway.

"'Your back room empty?' he asked.

"Cogswell said that it was. Wyatt took off his guns and badge and handed them to Cogswell.

"'Come on, Peshaur,' Wyatt said; 'I'll give you a chance to make good.'

"The play just suited Peshaur. As I said, he was a bigger, rangier man than Wyatt, and I don't suppose he had any different idea of the outcome than the rest of us. Several men started to follow Wyatt and Peshaur to the rear room, but Cogswell stopped them. The pair went through the door, which Wyatt closed and locked behind them.

"There was an awful rumpus in that back room for about fifteen minutes; then the door opened again. I expected to see Peshaur walk out and to find Wyatt in there beaten half to death. Cogswell shared my fears, and said so; while the Texas men had been bragging of what their leader would do to that so-and-so deputy marshal. But it was Wyatt who came toward the front counter. His face was badly bruised, his shirt was torn, and his knuckles were bleeding. He picked up his gunbelts, buckled them in place, pinned his shirt together with his badge, and got himself straightened up a bit before he spoke to Cogswell.

"'Throw a bucket of water over Peshaur,' he said, 'and have his friends get him out of here.'

"Then Wyatt walked up Douglas Avenue. And, as intimately as I knew Wyatt Earp, I never heard him mention that fight to anyone after he left the cigar store.

"Cogswell and I went back to look at Peshaur. If he wasn't a spectacle, I never saw one. He was lying in a heap, moaning. Both his eyes were swollen shut, his nose was smashed and bleeding, and I don't think there was a square inch of his face that wasn't as raw as beefsteak. I've seen many a badly whipped man in my time, but never one who showed what had happened to him more plainly than Peshaur. Even after we soused him with water, he couldn't walk; his friends carried him to a room in the Texas House. Meanwhile, quite a crowd had gathered in front of Cogswell's, and their sight of Peshaur's condition didn't hurt Wyatt's reputation any."

More than fifty years after his fight with Peshaur, Wyatt gave his own story of the battle. It adds little to Judge Hatton's recollection, but so much of the true Wyatt Earp is revealed by the account that it merits quoting, *verbatim*.

"I had had some little trouble with Peshaur," Wyatt said, "and he had twitted me considerably about my work as an officer. One evening he got pretty drunk and prodded me rather sharply. I passed that by, but a few days later, when he was sober, he took to taunting me about the arrest of Ben Thompson in Ellsworth. Then he added that if I would remove my guns and badge, he would 'put a head' on me, and gave it as his opinion that I would be afraid of him if I was not armed. We were standing in front of Dick Cogswell's cigar store, which had a large back room, usually empty. I gave my guns and badge to Cogswell and went into the back room with Peshaur. During the fight which followed, I knocked Peshaur down several times; the last time, he couldn't get up, so the fight ended."

Peshaur's beating rankled with the Texas man and his

followers until they set out to organize the fighting men on Cowskin Creek for restoration of cowboy supremacy in the cowtown; if in the course of operations a few Wichita marshals could be put out of business, so much more successful would be the enterprise. The plan of action was carefully considered, rank and file were chosen on reputations as killers, and, for some reason never explained, the force was limited to fifty professional gunmen. This outfit planned as cold-bloodedly to tree Wichita as they might have organized a round-up.

The outstanding weakness in the cowboys' scheme was their propensity to boast, and their plans for attack became common property in Wichita barrooms. The gravity of the impending situation was indicated by the records of men of whom the Texans bragged as the nucleus of their avenging force, as well as those of other notorious individuals who, as soon as they reached the Cowskin with their trail outfits, were added to the hand-picked coterie.

The six-shooter expedition was recruited around a dozen desperadoes, owning allegiance, and most of them kin to the worst bad man in Texas history, John Wesley Hardin. No estimate of the outfit's qualities is required beyond knowledge that their mentor in affairs involving peace officers killed six men in six-gun battles before he was sixteen years old, fifteen before he turned his eighteenth year, and thirty-five before he was seven years older. Hardin left the Cowskin before the Wichita raid was completely organized, but his leader's boots were amply filled by his cousin, Mannen Clements, whose courage and proficiency with a six-gun had never been disputed successfully.

In sketching the career of Mannen Clements as a gunman, Owen P. White has written that he once asked Mannen how it felt to kill a man, to which the experienced authority replied: "Hell, kid, that don't amount to nothin'! For three hundred dollars I'd cut anybody in two with a sawed-off shotgun."

Somewhat prior to his Cowskin Creek leadership, Mannen Clements's reputation as a fighting man had been further enhanced by his single-handed victory in a gun battle with Joe and Dolph Shadden, also gunmen of the first order. The Shadden brothers had openly charged Mannen with cowardice, and Clements rode into their camp for a showdown. Both Shaddens went for their guns at sight of him, but Mannen drew, shot, and killed the pair before either got into effective action.

As lieutenants for the Wichita business, Mannen Clements had his brothers, Gyp, Jim, and Joe, almost as notorious in six-gun affrays as he; his cousins, Simp, Bud, and Tom Dixon, and several other clansmen. They joined forces with Peshaur, Kane, and Good, and their factions could have marshaled ten times the chosen number of kindred spirits.

By the time the Clements–Peshaur gang was organized, the Wichita authorities knew everything about it except the date on which the cowboys would attack the town, and this was a matter upon which the Texans had not settled. It was Wyatt Earp who precipitated action in a manner not without its humorous phases. Charles Hatton, city attorney, furnished the opportunity, and he has also furnished an account of the happening.

The high priestess of the Cyprian sisterhood in Wichita, known to the community as Ida May, had gathered a dozen of her kind in a honky-tonk on the outskirts of the village, where, she announced, Texans who enjoyed her hospitality would not be subjected to association with Northerners. Her house was a celebrated rendezvous for herd owners, trail bosses, winners at the gambling tables, the more highly paid of the professional gunmen—all Texans, in short, who had funds to meet the standards set for the establishment. Among her patrons Ida May numbered an ardent admirer in a wealthy young cowman who was notorious as a gunthrower. He and his crowd were to be found at her house every evening during the cattle-shipping season and constituted her best guarantee against intrusion.

In providing for entertainment, Ida May had purchased a square piano in Kansas City for one thousand dollars, paying two hundred and fifty dollars upon delivery, and agreeing to remit the balance as business warranted. Every effort made by the Kansas City dealer to collect any part of his seven hundred and fifty dollars met with an observation from Ida May that she'd like to see him get it. She had the piano, hadn't she? After one or two collectors had been severely manhandled by Ida May's gentlemen friends, the piano merchant came up from Kansas City to essay collection in person. What the Texas crowd, in high glee, did to him sent him to the courthouse, where he swore out a writ of replevin. Ida May ignored the writ and the piano dealer left for home after dropping a few caustic comments on Wichita's constituted authorities.

City Attorney Hatton was goaded by the piano dealer's remarks into stopping Ida May in the street one afternoon and telling her that if she didn't pay for the piano, he'd take it away from her. Fifty-odd years afterward, he told me, his ears burned like fire at recollection of Ida May's rejoinder, to which all Main Street listened. Hatton went to his office and summoned Wyatt Earp to consultation.

"Do you want the piano, or the money?" Wyatt asked.

"We'd prefer the money, but get one or the other," the city attorney answered.

"Do you care when, or how?"

"Suit yourself. You'll be allowed costs within reason, and we'll deputize anyone you want to help you."

"I'll need four men who can lift the piano and a wagon to put it in; I don't want any deputies," Wyatt asserted.

Later, the piano movers told Hatton what happened.

Wyatt rounded up four husky fellows whom he had known on the buffalo range and, late in the evening, when Ida May's place was crowded, took them and a wagon to the front door of the honky-tonk. Inside, the "professor" was making good use of the instrument to be replevined, and Wyatt and his helpers were in the midst of the merry-making before their presence was noted. Wyatt had two guns at his hips; by his order, the piano movers wore no guns in sight.

"Professor," Wyatt said, "shut up."

Whereupon Ida May stepped out to demand reason for the intrusion.

"I'll read it, if you insist," Wyatt told her. "It's an order to take your piano away because you haven't paid for it."

Ida May laughed.

"Put a finger on that piano," she jeered, "and my friends will throw you out the way they did others ahead of you."

"Your friends," Wyatt assured her, "if they're what I think they are, will not interfere with me. I'll give you one chance to keep your piano. Pay for it here and now, or out it goes."

Ida May burst into a run of that language for which she was celebrated. Wyatt's helpers, at his signal, stepped forward to upend the piano.

"Tom," Ida May screamed to her gun-toting admirer, "are you going to let this so-and-so such-and-such take my piano?"

Wyatt kept an eye on Tom while the piano legs were being unscrewed. The helpers reported that in Tom's company were a number of the prime movers in the conspiracy then developing on Cowskin Creek and that, in response to Ida May's urging, several sidled stealthily toward more advantageous positions. Wyatt remarked that the first move made for a gun would bring sudden trouble, and took to taunting the Texans for their stinginess when a friend needed assistance. With that cue Ida May changed the nature of her appeal and Wyatt aided her with a running fire of comment on the liberality of her callers which only four of his hearers appeared to relish. In rather discomfited fashion, Tom asked permission to confer with his fellows, and collected seven hundred and fifty dollars in greenbacks, in exchange for which Wyatt called off his helpers. The Texans were busy setting up the redeemed piano when Wyatt finished writing a receipt for the money, and the deputy marshal took a last jab at them before leaving.

"If you fellows'll take my advice," he said, "you'll never head into anything you can't buy out of."

With which not entirely cryptic remark he went downtown to turn seven hundred and fifty dollars over to a surprised city attorney, while his helpers embellished the yarn of his latest achievement at Texas expense in the Wichita saloons. About midnight Jim Earp warned Wyatt that Ida May's Tom and several friends had visited Keno Corner long enough to gather up such of the gunmen as were in town, including the Clements crowd and Peshaur, with whom they had started for Cowskin Creek.

Next morning, the cowboys moved to tree Wichita.

11

One Cowtown Gets Tamed and Curried

Mannen Clements was a first-class strategist as well as a fighting man. He started his half-hundred on the six-gun foray into Wichita about eight o'clock in the morning, an hour which all cowtowns devoted to catching up with sleep, and when ordinarily the Texans would have found few persons about to oppose them.

Clements and his crowd did not know that, as their threats shaped toward action, Wyatt Earp and Jimmy Cairns kept twenty-four-hour watch over the approach to Wichita from the Cowskin.

"It was not what you'd call an easy time," Cairns recalled. "Things were pretty hot, and we never knew at what minute hell might break loose. In front of each store on Douglas Avenue, under the awning, was a wooden bench for loungers, and in the early mornings Wyatt and I took turns trying to sleep on one of them, with one of us always awake in readiness for the expected emergency. This would be after spending the days and evenings at our regular work. For several days these bench naps were our only rest."

Thus it was that when a friendly cattleman sent word to Mayor Hope that the gunmen were starting their raid, Wyatt Earp was immediately available to head a reception committee. Jim Hope and Bill Smith wanted to sound Judge Jewett's triangle. Wyatt objected.

"In the first place," Wyatt argued, "if the Texas men find half the town lined up against them, they'll ride in shooting and there'll be a lot of promiscuous killing. You know Mannen Clements's gang well enough to gamble that, before you can put them out of business in such a fight, there'll be more dead citizens than there'll be dead cowboys. You may get 'em in the end, but the getting will be expensive.

"When you get down to cases, this is my fight. I'm the fellow they're after. Let me make my fight after my own fashion. If I win out, our troubles may be over for the summer; even if I lose, I'll guarantee there won't be as many bad ones left for you to handle. I don't want any crowd with me, to get excited and cut loose. I'll put a few fellows who won't go off half-cocked where I want 'em and make the play. If it goes against me, the men I'll pick can hold off the cowboys long enough for you to get organized."

Mayor Hope saw the sense of Wyatt's reasoning, gave him the authority he requested, and forbade sounding the triangle unless Wyatt asked for reinforcements. Wyatt picked a posse of ten, leaving out Bill Smith, but including Cairns, Deputy Marshal Jack Burns, and eight citizens, armed each with two six-shooters and a rifle, and set out for the toll bridge. Every man in town who was up and about followed the posse down Douglas Avenue, the procession constantly augmented by those who had been awakened with word of the impending battle.

By Wyatt's order, the Douglas Avenue roadway was cleared of spectators, most of these crowding the doors and windows of nearby establishments. Charles Hatton, for one, found a vantage point where he was eye and ear witness to all that followed.

Just below the cross-street nearest the river, Wyatt strung his men across Douglas Avenue so that they would not be bunched into a tempting target, and gave them a final order:

no matter what happened, the posse was not to fire until he had started shooting. Wyatt was armed with his Colt's peacemakers, and drawing them would not be the signal for cutting loose; when he actually fired a shot, then each could open up as it suited him. From the posse Wyatt walked on alone to a pole at the edge of the sidewalk, and took his station in what concealment this afforded.

On the flat across the river the cavalcade was heading for town at a steady lope. The Texas men clattered on to the far end of the bridge and slowed to a walk, the Clements brothers in the van as they reached the town limits.

At the sight of ten riflemen strung across Douglas Avenue, the leaders halted. Wyatt was fairly well hidden, and one of the cowboys admitted later that, when Mannen Clements and others fell to discussing ensuing tactics, they had not yet spotted their enemy; in fact, speculated somewhat over his whereabouts.

In the face of armed resistance the Texans decided to fight their battle afoot, in the interests of more accurate shooting as well as for such cover as buildings afforded. Ten cowboys were chosen to hold the ponies for forty who dismounted to advance on Keno Corner, drew their six-shooters, and awaited orders. Mannen Clements, a gun in either hand, turned from a last word with his following, walked to the middle of the road, and, with forty killers at his back, started uptown.

Wyatt Earp stepped from the walk, heading diagonally for the middle of the street and the cowboys. His guns were in their holsters, his hands swinging easily, but ready to drop to the butts faster than eye might follow.

It is possible that the cowboys were startled; in view of the known record of every man in their company, it is unfair to charge that they were frightened. They stopped short, Clements slightly ahead, and eyed this lone player defiantly.

"Mannen," Wyatt said evenly and so clearly that those behind him heard the command distinctly, "put up those guns."

Wyatt walked toward Clements steadily; the cowboy killer stood motionless.

"Mind me, Mannen," Wyatt repeated. "Put up those guns and take your crowd back to camp."

Again there followed one of those inexplicable denouements which won Wyatt Earp his place in Western legend. Clements hesitated, then without a word slipped his guns into their holsters, turned his back on Wichita, mounted and rode for the Cowskin. His troop of vaunted gunmen as silently followed his example. As Mannen turned, Wyatt halted; he stood alone in the middle of Douglas Avenue until the last cowboy had crossed the toll bridge. Then he turned and walked back to his posse.

The incident which definitely terminated the cowboys' attempts to hurrah Wichita during the summer of '74 followed closely upon Mannen Clements's abortive expedition. George Peshaur, by mixing flattery with cowtown whiskey, persuaded a youthful Texan who fancied his skill with a six-gun that getting Wyatt Earp would be a simple feat for one of his attainments. Peshaur coached his inebriated proxy carefully, then stood by to watch the killing.

The youngster—Wyatt said he could not have been more than eighteen—was posted with a dozen Texans in front of a Douglas Avenue saloon near the toll bridge, anticipating the deputy marshal's periodical patrol of the neighborhood. A few yards distant, a confederate held the boy's cayuse in readiness for a getaway, and immediately at hand was the bar at which the gunman's courage might be fortified if it appeared to ooze as he awaited the chance to blazon his name high up on the red list of Texas immortals.

Wyatt made his appearance at the expected hour, following a beat which would take him past the group of cowboys so disposed as to shield their champion from the official eye until the selected moment. As they were creating no disturbance, Wyatt gave them slight attention. He had walked several yards beyond them when he heard his name spoken. He turned to face a Colt's forty-five in the hand of the young cowboy, cocked and ready for action. The youngster's companions had stepped quickly from the probable line of fire.

"Earp," the boy declared, "I'm going to kill you, you—"

He trailed off into a string of epithets and an expletory recital of cowpuncher grievances against the peace officer.

Wyatt Earp did what he could for the moment, took the abuse without word or movement. The Texan had the drop. As his tirade reached its climax, he would shoot, might do so earlier if any gesture of Wyatt's seemed threatening. Unfortunately for Peshaur, the proxy's oratory went to his head along with the whiskey. He still had the drop, his steady gun vouched for nerves unshaken by liquor, but he was no longer single-purposed. With his determination to kill, he had mixed boyish fancy for melodrama.

"I'm going to kill you," he repeated, "but I wouldn't shoot even such a ———— as you are in the back. You've got a pair of guns on, you ————. Why don't you jerk 'em and —"

A forty-five flashed and roared. The youngster's six-gun clattered against the wall behind him as he clapped his left hand to his gun arm with a scream of mingled pain and terror.

"He's got me! He's got me!" the boy shrieked. "Peshaur, cut him down! You said you would if he went to shooting."

"Peshaur hasn't the guts," Wyatt cut in. "Shut up! You're not badly hurt."

With a Colt's in either hand—from the one in his right a wisp of smoke was curling—Wyatt faced the cowboys.

"Throw 'em up, all of you!"

Jim Earp arrived with those who had rushed into the street at the sound of shooting and to his brother Wyatt delegated the job of searching the cowboys for arms while he held them covered. None of them had weapons. The youngster who had threatened Wyatt had a flesh wound in his forearm. Wyatt literally had shot the gun from his hand; his bullet had struck the side plate and glanced upward.

"Take that kid to Doc Fabrique," Wyatt told Jim, and turned attention elsewhere.

"So this was your doing, Peshaur? A regular Peshaur trick. I notice you and the rest of your fighting men were careful not to have guns on when it came to a showdown. Got a boy drunk to try the dirty work you didn't have the nerve to tackle. You're short in this camp, Peshaur. Get out, and stay out."

Wyatt threatened no specific action, but within the hour George Peshaur rode across the toll bridge and was not seen in Wichita again that season.

At Dr. Fabrique's office, Wyatt found the wounded cowboy scared sober and ready to tell the whole story of the play against him.

"I suspected as much," Wyatt commented. "You're pretty young; you didn't look as tough as you talked, and you were pretty drunk. That's why I didn't kill you. Now, if you'll run an errand for me, I won't even arrest you.

"You go tell Mannen Clements what happened, and that I want to talk to him. I'll be outside the Texas House at eight o'clock."

Neither Wyatt nor Mannen Clements ever told in Wichita what they said to one another when Mannen answered the summons, but from that night on, the cowtown had no more serious difficulties with the Texas gunmen, and, almost without exception, every cowpuncher who rode into Wichita checked his guns at one of the numerous racks provided, before starting his carousal. Half a century later, Wyatt gave the gist of their conversation.

"To begin with," Wyatt said, "Mannen thanked me for not killing the youngster put up to gunning me. The boy happened to be one of Mannen's cousins, although I did not know that until Mannen told me. Then Mannen asked what I wanted.

"I answered that I wanted him to order his gang to quit toting guns in Wichita; that I knew such an order from him would be respected by most of the troublemakers; that I didn't want to make it too tough for the cowboys, but that if it came to a showdown, I'd stand at the lower end of Douglas Avenue and knock over every last cowpuncher who came across the bridge looking as though he might have a gun on him.

"'About the first fellows I'd have to kill,' I reminded Mannen, 'would be some of your brothers and cousins.' He had thirty or forty relatives in the different outfits.

127

"Mannen thought a minute, then said he'd do as I asked, but couldn't promise the boys would obey him. I told him I'd give him three days to spread the word; after that, I'd be at the bridgehead ready for business. He said he'd tell the boys he was going to obey my order and advise them to do so. I said that was all I wanted, and that's all there was to it.

"Mannen Clements's word was as good as gold, even if he was a killer, and I knew he'd do as he promised. I guess he made his advice pretty strong, because after that night we had no great difficulty with the general run of cowboys, none at all with his particular following."

Beyond the arrest of an occasional individual who struck town in too much of a hurry to inquire about changes in local law enforcement, Wyatt had no problems of pacification to solve for the balance of the cattle-shipping season. Late in November, however, the United States Government deputized him for a mission which had proved too much for three predecessors.

Frank McMurray was a tough citizen, outlaw killer and squawman, a leader of the renegade whites and halfbreed desperadoes who infested the Indian Nations. He made headquarters on the Washita River, near the Cheyenne and Chickasaw agencies, sold contraband whiskey to the Indians, held up, killed, and robbed white travelers, and otherwise conducted a business of which violence and lawlessness were the sole assets, and had as a partner Bill Anderson, who had served apprenticeship with Quantrell's Guerrillas.

The McMurray-Anderson gang had chased off a dozen cowpunchers driving sixteen hundred steers to Wichita over the Chisholm Trail for George Ulrich, a wealthy Texan, and had run the stolen herd into the Wewoka Valley. Ulrich appealed to Federal authorities and three posses under as many marshals, sent into The Nations to arrest McMurray and bring the herd to Wichita, returned with word that the outlaws were too strongly entrenched to be attacked successfully. In a final effort to recover his property Ulrich—a Texan, it is worth noting again—asked that Wyatt Earp be deputized.

Wyatt selected Jack Burns, of Wichita, as his deputy, and, from motives of economy, Ulrich's cowpunchers completed his posse. If Wyatt's enterprise was successful, he was to hold the steers in The Nations until spring, as climatic conditions would make it unwise to bring them into Wichita during the winter.

From his experience with the surveying party in 1870, Wyatt had intimate knowledge of the country which McMurray frequented and he led his men to the Wewoka by a route some distance from an established trail. McMurray and Anderson, therefore, had no advance word of his coming, were absent when the Earp posse rode into the rustlers' camp, and the fifteen or twenty men guarding the steers were drunk, the majority helplessly so, at the moment of the posse's arrival.

"There was no fight in McMurray's men," Wyatt said. "We simply took away their guns and booted 'em out of camp. Then we moved the Ulrich steers to another valley, where it would be easier to protect them and where there was good feed and water. I figured McMurray would try to recover the herd.

"The only way to get the cattle out was over the trail we had followed into the valley. We made camp so that we kept that trail covered constantly and, at the same time, could not be attacked from the rear. When the outlaws made their only serious effort to get the steers, they found a dozen rifles ready for them. They rode off when we started shooting, and I didn't see McMurray again that winter."

Before spring, Wyatt was called back to Wichita by Mike Meagher who was running for marshal against Bill Smith with the pledge to make Wyatt chief deputy with full authority over law enforcement in the event of his election. He wanted Wyatt's active support in his campaign. Meagher was elected and kept his pre-election promise, but before he took office, Jack Burns and Ulrich's cowpunchers rode in with the news that, as they were getting up the herd for the drive to Wichita, McMurray and Anderson at the head of a bunch of renegades had attacked their camp and again run off the cattle. Burns had followed the outlaws far enough to suspect that they were heading across Indian Territory to the Western country.

George Ulrich offered Wyatt twenty-five dollars a day and expenses if he would attempt another recovery of the cattle. With Meagher's consent, Wyatt accepted, and told Ulrich he would not need his cowboys.

"Burns and I'll bring in your steers," he promised, and with Burns, Wyatt set out in a buggy to cut the trails to the west until he struck that which the outlaws were using.

"I chose a buggy and a span of horses," Wyatt said, "because I figured that, while McMurray might be suspicious of any mounted men, he wouldn't figure a top-buggy on the prairie as carrying anybody but some tenderfoot land-grabber. For the plan I had in mind I carried a sawed-off shotgun."

Several days out of Wichita, Wyatt picked up McMurray's trail and timed his gait to reach the outfit as it halted for a noon rest at Skeleton Creek. Two men were riding herd and eight others, including McMurray and Anderson, were squatted near the chuck wagon, eating. Burns headed the team at a sharp trot toward the ford beside which the outlaws had camped; when nearly opposite the chuck wagon, he wheeled the horses suddenly. Wyatt jumped and had covered the rustlers with his shotgun before they recognized him. He held them thus while Burns hitched his horses and collected weapons. The two herd riders were called in and with the others listened to Wyatt's ultimatum.

"You can figure you're still working for McMurray," he said, "or go to work for me. String with McMurray, and you get going on foot; hire out to me, and you can drive these steers into Wichita, get paid for it, and be turned loose without argument. In either case, I'm keeping your guns."

To a man, the outlaws hired out to the marshal and, with McMurray and Anderson tied in the chuck wagon, the herd was pointed for Wichita, where Ulrich paid the riders what amounts Wyatt said was due them and their two leaders were placed in Federal custody.

Simultaneously with the arrival of the early Texas herds in

the spring of '75, a cowboy rode into Wichita with a message for Wyatt from Ben Thompson, asking if George Peshaur and he might come into town and open a faro game. Wyatt replied that they could come and go in his bailiwick as long as they behaved themselves. The pair spent the summer in Wichita and established a record for pacifism theretofore deemed impossible for either. Early in the season, Wyatt notified the arriving Texas outfits that gunplay in Wichita would not be tolerated and that the ordinance against gun-toting would be enforced to the letter. With few exceptions the Texas men heeded the warning and Wichita experienced her first trouble-free season as a cowtown. But one attempt at gunplay against Wyatt Earp is recorded in the town annals of '75.

The United States Army's most noteworthy contribution to the ranks of Western gunmen was one Sergeant King, at the age of twenty-eight a veteran of the Civil War, a frontier-hardened Indian fighter, and a non-commissioned officer of cavalry. He had participated in a score of troopers' gun battles against civilians in barroom brawls, had killed several men in six-gun engagements far removed from line of duty, and was a perennial thorn in the official side of every peace officer near whose territory his outfit was stationed. King was a finished artist with the six-shooter and a cold-blooded killer who found so many kindred spirits among the wilder Texas men that despite his alien service he was welcomed as their boon companion. It was his custom to take a furlough at the height of the cattle-shipping season, during which, in cowboy attire, he rode with his cowboy friends, and in a number of authenticated instances took part with them in hurrahing Kansas villages.

In July of '75, Sergeant King, in the parlance of the place, hit Wichita all spraddled out after trouble. He had heard, he announced to all and sundry at the Keno Corner, that there was a marshal in Wichita who reserved to himself the exclusive right to tote six-guns. If the bystanders would observe, he—Sergeant King—was wearing a pair of those weapons right out in plain sight where any blank-dashed-son-of-a-so-and-so marshal could see them, and what he would do to anyone who tried to tell him he couldn't wear them thus would be what six-guns were made for. With which introductory remarks he moved indoors for more of the riotous living he had come to town to purchase. After a few drinks, he returned to the sidewalk to advertise that he was about to blow Wichita wide open and would begin on Wyatt Earp the instant he laid eyes on him.

Ben Thompson, who had acquaintance with the soldier, approached King with a suggestion that he take his guns off, or himself inside, and, at any rate, stop his abuse of the marshal. Again, Charles Hatton, the city attorney, has furnished an eyewitness account of what followed.

"Wyatt Earp will kill you," Ben warned the sergeant. "You make any play for him and you won't live long enough to pull a trigger. Get inside before he gets word of the way you're acting."

King pulled a gun from the holster.

"I came to Wichita to get that son-of-a-bitch," he said. "All I want's a sight of him."

"You've got it," Ben said as he stepped to one side. "That's Wyatt rounding the corner."

"King," said Judge Hatton, "stood on the Douglas Avenue walk about fifty feet west of Main Street as Wyatt turned into the avenue. There was a crowd of about two hundred men on hand, and as they saw Wyatt they took to the roadway. King held his gun on Wyatt whose six-shooters were in their holsters. Wyatt never hesitated and never opened his mouth. He walked straight up to King, yanked King's gun away from him with his left hand, slapped King's face with his right, then jerked King's second gun from his belt. Wyatt threw both guns into the street, took King by the scruff of the neck, and marched him down to Ed Jewett, who fined the soldier one hundred dollars. That's all there was to the nerviest thing I ever saw in my life."

Again, in the interests of self-revelation, Wyatt Earp's account of an exploit in which he figured is of value in word-for-word entirety.

"I knew of Sergeant King before he came to Wichita," Wyatt said. "I had heard of him in Ellsworth, in Abilene, and other frontier settlements, and I knew, of course, that he was very friendly with the cowboy element. When I appeared on the scene that day in Wichita, King was surrounded by a large crowd. He was flourishing a gun and I heard him boasting of what he would do to Wyatt Earp as I turned the Keno Corner. I figured that he was a bluffer, so I stepped right up to him."

Here it may be added that, several months after his arrest in Wichita, this same Sergeant King shot it out with Bat Masterson at old Sweetwater—later, Mobeetie—near Fort Elliott, Texas. Bat, at the time, was a civilian scout with the army. King, entering the combination dance hall, gambling house, and saloon which the soldiers patronized, found Bat dancing with a girl whom the soldier regarded as his special property. King whipped out a six-gun, shot and killed the girl, and shot Bat in the leg. As he hit the floor, Bat jerked a Colt's and shot King through the heart. When King's fellow troopers would have taken up the sergeant's battle with Bat, as the latter lay on the floor, it was none other than Ben Thompson who leaped to the top of a faro layout with a gun in either hand and stood off the soldiers until Bat could be moved to safe quarters.

As the summer of '75 progressed, it became increasingly evident that Wichita had passed her peak as a wild and woolly cowtown. The rich valley lands along the Arkansas, the little Arkansas, and their tributary creeks were filling up with homesteaders. The "fool hoemen," as the cowboys called them, were fencing their quarter-sections, ending for all time enjoyment of the free and open range which had made it economically possible for the cattle kings to concentrate great herds within fair distance of the railroads. Cowboys and hoemen battled to the death on more than one occasion that summer over many a right of way across newly plowed prairie. The Chisholm Trail was narrowing its northern end to extinction between homesteaders' fences.

Too, the municipal temper of Wichita was changing with the influx of land-seekers. Once more in the course of history the man on horseback was giving way before the ruthless advance of the man who worked on foot, behind whom followed closely those who saw life eye-to-eye with the plodder. New business houses were established. Merchants who preferred the trade of peaceful farmers to the patronage of roistering, gun-wielding cowboys took a hand in community government. The gunman had to go, forced out by the growing sentiment against him, and by economic pressure which turned his employer elsewhere.

Long before the close of the shipping season, Wichita sensed that the ensuing year would see a tremendous falling-off in the cattle trade. Wyatt Earp would have left town had not Mike Meagher pressed him to stay through the winter.

"Maybe she'll open up again in the spring," Mike suggested.

"I'll stick until you find out what you're up against next season," Wyatt answered. "But from now on, about all Wichita'll need in the way of marshals will be a couple of fellows with blue uniforms."

Wyatt always remembered the winter of 1875–76 for the fact that at Christmastime he bought the first pair of shoes he ever owned. Theretofore he had worn the attire of the man who spends his waking hours in a saddle or ready to fork one.

"And that," he once recalled, "showed what was happening to Wichita."

By May of '76, it was apparent that no more big trail-herds would be driven to Wichita. In a general sense, the original Chisholm Trail was abandoned. At its Texas extremity the trace had been shifted from Red River Crossing westward to Doan's Store, and it now traversed The Nations to reach Kansas just below the point where Bluff Creek joins the Cimarron. Strictly speaking, the new route was the Jones and Plummer Trail; it led to the most famous cowtown in Western history then in the making as "the wildest, wickedest spot in the world, the bibulous Babylon of the frontier," Dodge City, or just plain Dodge, as the old-timers called her.

As early as May 1, Dodge was having trouble with the visiting cowmen, and a number of Wichita pioneers who had moved to the boom camp assured George Hoover, just elected as Dodge's first mayor, that if he wanted a man to ride herd on the Texans there was only one to send for. Hoover wrote to Wyatt and asked him to come to Dodge City; after a few more experiences with the Texas men, he took to telegraphing.

"You don't need me anymore," Wyatt told Mike Meagher, "and Dodge is booming."

"I don't blame you," Mike answered, somewhat enviously.

On May 16, Wyatt Earp started for Dodge City.

In later years, George Hoover told Bat Masterson that he asked Wyatt Earp to come to Dodge largely because of Wyatt's frontier-wide reputation as the fastest man with a six-gun then living and the assurance gained from his exploits in Ellsworth and Wichita that, no matter how bad and how tough might be the gunmen who would hit the camp, Wyatt would go against them.

The dominant trait of Wyatt's whole personality, it would seem from the achievements which brought this recognition, was absolute confidence—in himself, his strength, his proficiency, and his courage. His egotism did not necessarily amount to arrogance. Those who knew the man best have agreed that, rather, it was a calm, just estimate of his own capabilities, simply a well-grounded faith in his own talents.

12

The Cowboy Capital

Wyatt Earp reached Dodge City in the morning of May 17, 1876. By noon he had been appointed as the cowcamp's chief deputy marshal, succeeding the celebrated six-gun artist, Jack Allen, who had been run up an alley and out of town by a bunch of festive cowboys.

Officially speaking, Dodge was four years old. As early as '71, however, George Hoover and Jack McDonald had pitched a tent on the site of the future cowtown, from which they sold whiskey to Fort Dodge soldiers; Harry Lovett put up a second canvas saloon and Henry Sitler built a sod house. This trio of structures was known as "Buffalo City" until the spring of '72 brought railroad construction gangs, when a town was mapped on the north bank of the Arkansas River exactly five miles west of the fort. A general store and warehouse, three dance halls, and a half-dozen saloons were thrown up beside the ruts of the old Santa Fe wagon trail and the camp renamed Dodge City. To welcome the end of steel—the farthest advance of a railroad pushing southwest toward the Rio Grande—Dodge boomed with a roar that split a nation's ears and still echoes in her memory.

Given railroad facilities in her proximity to the buffalo range, Dodge City became the focal point of the hide business. Thousands of hunters flocked in to collect millions of dollars for skins and meat and to spend like amounts in uproarious carousals. In the peak year of the buffalo slaughter, more than two million dollars was collected by hunters trading in Dodge, and their greenback orgies were matched in scope and depravity by throngs of hard-bitten laborers drawing the railway payrolls. Out of Dodge a thousand ten-, twelve-, and sixteen-animal freight teams hauled supplies, south, north, and west; in the camp, while wains were loading, bullwhackers, mule skinners, and packers blew the wages of months in a night. For added measure, Fort Dodge harbored several hundred soldiers and Indian scouts who, once a month, could scatter money with any frontiersman.

Next came the cattle herds, up the Jones and Plummer Trail, with thousands of hard-riding, hard-spending guardians as wild and as fractious as their longhorns. Cattle owners, trail bosses, foremen, and cowboys collected millions of dollars in Dodge, and, as it was the only spot for spending which the majority would see for another twelve-month, blew the millions then and there.

Hundreds of blanket camps were pitched on the prairies at the edge of town. Dodge's two or three streets were so blocked by wagons and animals for days at a time that they were barely passable to a horseman. Buffalo hides, hind-quarters, and tongues were hauled in and transferred to railway trains by the carload; trainloads of supplies for camps and ranches were reloaded on wains that would distribute them over the great Southwest; cattle were shipped eastward by the tens of thousands.

Trouble was Dodge's synonym, that guaranteed by the diversity of elements which brought her roistering trade. Bullwhackers and mule skinners despised railwaymen and buffalo hunters, who not only returned the sentiment, but also abominated one another. Soldiers held themselves better men than any to be encountered out of uniform and were ready to support this contention with violence. A buffalo hunter might prefer knocking off a soldier to cracking down on a bullwhacker or mule skinner, because of animosity born in earlier trespass on some Indian hunting preserve, but as Dodge would tolerate the killing of any one of the three, he—like everyone else in the camp—shot first and established callings afterward.

The Texas men, as they transferred their patronage from Abilene, Ellsworth, and Wichita, carried their grudge against Northern men, and their contumacy was flaunted boldly as the cowboys swaggered from saloon to gambling hall to honky-tonk, with their jangling spurs on high-heeled boots, their broad-brimmed hats, their fancy neckerchiefs and their hair-trigger six-guns. From the moment the first cow outfit struck Dodge, these riders of the Southern plains jarred on the sensibilities of the established patrons of the camp and, knowing well the irritation which their strutting gave, comported themselves with an arrogance deliberately calculated to keep Dodge in smoking turmoil. Cowboys preempted the dance-hall belles, broke up variety shows, rode their ponies on the sidewalks and into the saloons, held up gambling games and openly spent the pilfered coin on further hilarity, shot the windows out of stores, the lights out of places of amusement and the same out of individuals who made protest. Texas men bragged that they intended to run the town and would welcome diversion in chances to prove it.

Life in such a camp was free and easy, to say the least, and as prosperity rode high an army of parasites flocked in for the pickings of a wild, wide-open community. Gamblers, gunmen, thieves, and thugs gathered from the corners of the earth and with them the hardier of the scarlet sisterhood. Gossip insists that the first gunfight in Dodge followed the quarrel of a buffalo hunter and a mule skinner over the temporary affections of the first Cyprian to reach camp. Whatever that case, history records that Dodge's first season as a cowtown saw exactly twenty-five gun-wielders planted on her Boot Hill and more than fifty others wounded in her six-gun battles. By the time Wyatt Earp reached the camp, some seventy or eighty argumentative visitors had been buried with their footgear in place—Dodge had lost accurate count. Although the cowboys suffered from the gunplay to the extent that the Boot Hill population was preponderantly Texan, incitement to most of the killings was charged against the cattlemen, and it was held, despite mute evidence that other plainsmen were better shots, that when Dodge curtailed the activities of the trail drivers she would lower her mortality to some respectability of cause and rate.

Dodge City's first earnest endeavor to slow up her killing pace had been the appointment of Billy Brooks, buffalo hunter, Indian scout, and all-around gunfighter, as guardian of the peace. Brooks killed or wounded fifteen men in the first thirty days of his incumbency. Single-handed, he shot it out with four brothers, cowboys who sought to avenge the death of a fifth brother whom Brooks had killed in an earlier fight. Brooks killed all four with as many shots from his six-gun while they cut loose at him ineffectively. Next, Brooks shot a rival for the affections of a dance-hall girl. Then he tangled with Kirk Jordan, a hide hunter, and got through, officially, in Dodge when he turned tail like a coyote before Jordan's buffalo gun. Billy Rivers, another notorious fighting man, stuck until a break went against him, when he, too, fled the camp. There followed a succession of professional killers in imposing array, called to the marshal's office, one by one, and in approximately that same order chased out.

Meanwhile, Dodge acquired a dozen dance halls, forty saloons and gambling houses, several stores, and incorporation papers. A temporary town council met to organize the camp on Christmas Eve 1875, and to pass ordinances "relating to council meetings, salaries of city officials, licensing of dramshops, defining misdemeanors and providing punishment for same," which were promulgated by handwritten posters tacked up on Christmas Day. P. L. Beatty, who, with James H. ("Dog") Kelley, owned the Alhambra Saloon, Gambling-Hall, and Restaurant, was to act as mayor until an election could be held.

There was no dispute over meetings, salaries, and licensing the establishments euphemistically grouped as "dramshops." For the last named it simply was ordered that liquor taxes should finance municipal administration, generally, while collections from gambling games, dance halls, and bagnios should establish and maintain schools. Revenues from like sources, it may be added, founded about every system of public instruction in the Western states.

Over "misdemeanors and punishment for same," the temporary council split in a difference of opinion which recurrently echoed in the roar of gunfire as long as Dodge stayed wild. Six misdemeanor ordinances were suggested. One, barred animals from the sidewalks; two, forbade riding an animal into any store, saloon, dance hall, gambling house, or honky-tonk; three, prohibited discharge of firearms within the corporate limits "other than by those empowered to employ same, except upon Fourth of July, Christmas and New Year's Days and the evenings immediately preceding these holidays"; four, proscribed firearms within the camp boundaries for individuals other than peace officers or persons actually proceeding into or out of the town; five, ordered that all visitors to Dodge should check their firearms immediately upon arrival at racks to be provided by proprietors of hotels, corrals, stores, and saloons, and forbade such proprietors to return weapons so checked to any claimant who was drunk; six, dealt with public intoxication and was calculated to blanket all possible offenses against outward order and decency not covered by the other five.

A minority of the council promptly opposed these six ordinances as inexpedient, to say the least. Their literal application, it was asserted, would spill more blood than the town had yet seen, if the objectors knew their trade—although, in the light of personal records, neither faction of the council had call to wax overscrupulous about a shooting or two. Secondly, it was argued, there was the certain effect upon the cash customers. When a cowboy couldn't wear his guns as he chose, couldn't spur his pony up and down the bar of some saloon, couldn't shoot out a few lights when the spirit moved, and couldn't whoop up and down Front Street to a salvo of forty-fives, he'd quit coming to town. The minute Dodge shut down on his celebrations, the cowboy would take his wages elsewhere to spend, as would the hunter, the bullwhacker, and the mule skinner.

The majority contended that as a hired hand the cowboy would end his trail drive and receive his wages at the point his boss preferred; the hunter, the bullwhacker, and the mule skinner, as one might say, likewise. Wholesale killings in the streets of Dodge had to stop; innocent bystanders were moving to town. The sure way to stop the killing was to remove the cause—promiscuous gun-toting.

On the strength of such reasoning, the six temporary ordinances were adopted by a vote of three to two and, a few weeks later, Dodge City went to the polls for her first election, to sanction or to overthrow the radical measures.

George Hoover was elected mayor on the law-and-order ticket, Beatty having declined nomination. Mayor Hoover announced forthwith that the original six ordinances would stay on the books and that Dodge was in the market for a marshal who could make them stick in practice against all the cowmen off the Jones and Plummer Trail.

The business-first element enlisted the aid of the all-powerful railroad, which felt privileged to suggest that it might be wiser to go easy with the Texas men as far as the letter of the new laws was concerned and, at any rate, advisable to engage a marshal who would compromise with cowboys rather than kill them. Mayor Hoover was in no compromising mood. It was time, he declared, that someone tapped this Texas bluff, and with her full hand of hog-tight, horse-high, and bull-strong ordinances, not to mention the kicker up her sleeve in the shape of Blanket Rule, No. 6, he figured Dodge was set for the call. If there was killing at the showdown, that would be unfortunate; but he figured on getting a peace officer who, kill or be killed, would shove Dodge's stack spang into the pot.

As a sop to the faction which objected to vesting the marshal's power in some stranger to the town, Hoover appointed Larry Deger as chief marshal and figurehead. For the real business of law enforcement the aforesaid Jack Allen, gun-thrower of the first order, was made chief deputy, with Henry Brown and Joe Mason under him.

Whereupon, one of the first trail outfits to hit camp broke all six of the new ordinances right under Allen's nose and hightailed the chief deputy to cover in the Santa Fe freight house. Jack sneaked aboard the first train west, left the mayor in the lurch and the cowboys hurrahing Dodge. Hoover telegraphed to Wyatt Earp.

"The message that took me to Dodge had offered me the marshal's job," Wyatt recalled, "but Hoover told me that for political reasons he wanted Deger to complete his year in office. He would pay me more money as chief deputy than Deger was drawing. I would have power to hire and fire deputies, could follow my own ideas about my job and be marshal in all but name. The marshal's pay was $100 a month, but Mayor Hoover said they would pay me $250 a month, plus $2.50 for every arrest I made. Brown and Mason were discharged from the force and I was to appoint three new deputies at wages of $75 a month, each, and make my own arrangements with them about the bonus.

"Bat Masterson's brother Jim was in Dodge, a good, game man who could handle himself in a fracas, and I picked him as one deputy, took Joe Mason back, and was looking for the third when Bat himself came in from Sweetwater, Texas, still limping from the leg wound he got when he killed Sergeant King. Bat's gun hand was in working order, so I made him a deputy. He patrolled Front Street with a walking stick for several weeks and used his cane to crack the heads of several wild men hunting trouble; even as a cripple he was a first-class peace officer.

"I told my deputies that all bounties would be pooled and shared, but would be paid only when prisoners were taken alive. Dead ones wouldn't count. Each officer carried two six-guns and I placed shotguns at convenient points, as I had in Wichita, but killing was to be our last resort.

"I figured that if the cowboys were manhandled and heaved into the calaboose every time they showed in town with guns on, or cut loose in forbidden territory, they'd come to time quicker than if we kept them primed for gunplay. Hoover had hired me to cut down the killings in Dodge, not to increase them. As far as that went, any one of the deputies could give the average cowboy the best of a break, then kill him in a gunfight, but even when gunplay was necessary, we disabled men, rather than killed them.

"With this policy, we organized for a fairly peaceful summer. There were some killings in personal quarrels, but none by peace officers. We winged a few tough customers who insisted on shooting, but none of the victims died. On the other hand, we split seven or eight hundred dollars in bounties each month. That meant some three hundred arrests every thirty days, and as practically every prisoner heaved into the calaboose was thoroughly buffaloed in the process, we made quite a dent in cowboy conceit.

"Buffaloing was a Western term generally applied to any manhandling, but, more specifically, to bending a six-gun over a man's head. If some obstreperous cowboy resisted arrest, a marshal could jerk his gun, bat him over the head, and end the argument.

"That brings to mind another misconception of Western practice, which often has a man 'club his gun,' that is, grasp the gun by the barrel and strike a blow with the butt. Turning a six-gun for such a blow would have been fatal in any frontier camp; the man who tried it would have been shot the instant he reversed the gun muzzle. With the proper method you had your man covered until you hit him and, moreover, the barrel of a three-pound Colt's forty-five applied full length to a man's head would stun without killing more certainly than a blow with the butt.

"We made no attempt to cut off the celebrations that the cowmen, teamsters, and hunters put on whenever they hit Dodge, but with a steady run of object lessons in the shape of buffaloed gun-toters, we certainly enforced a change in their ritual. And we held most of the hurrahing and fighting south of the Dead Line which we drew at the railroad.

"In 1876, Dodge was mostly Front Street, a wide road running east and west just north of the Santa Fe tracks, with the principal cross-street Bridge Street, or Second Avenue, which led to the toll bridge over the Arkansas River. For two blocks each way from Second Avenue, Front Street widened into the Plaza, with business establishments strung along the north side of the square. The depot, water tank, and freight house were at the east end of the Plaza, and immediately south of the tracks was the calaboose, a square, one-room building with floor, walls, and ceiling of solid two-by-six timbers spiked flatsides-to, on top of which the city judge and clerk perched a light board shack they used as an office.

"The Dodge House, Deacon Cox's famous hotel, was two blocks east of Second Avenue, at Railroad Avenue and Front Street—the northeast corner of the Plaza. Beebe's Iowa Hotel was at Third Avenue and Front Street. The post office and Wright and Beverly's store, then the most important commercial establishment on the plains, were at the Second Avenue four-corners. Between the store and First Avenue were the Delmonico Restaurant, the Long Branch Saloon, owned by Chalk Beeson and Bill Harris, with Luke Short running the gambling; Ab Webster's Alamo Saloon and City Drug-Store; Beatty and Kelley's Alhambra Saloon and Dodge Opera House, a gun store, and a couple of barber shops. That was the busiest block in town. The Wright House, another popular hotel, was on Second Avenue. South of the tracks were hotels, corrals, dance halls, and honky-tonks, the picayune gambling houses, and a bunch of saloons.

"Below the Dead Line, as far as the marshal's force was concerned, almost anything went, and a man could get away with gunplay if he wasn't too careless with lead. North of the railroad, gun-toting was justification for shooting on sight, if an officer was so inclined, and meant certain arrest. Any attempt to hurrah stores, gambling houses, or saloons along the Plaza was good for a night in the calaboose, and by proving that the Dead Line meant something every time anyone broke over its restrictions, we kept trouble south of the tracks.

"With the plank walks and wooden awnings which ran from storefronts to posts at the roadside, Front Street looked like any street in Ellsworth or Wichita. There were the same long lines of hitching rails, the benches, and the whiskey barrels filled with water for fire protection. Eddie Foy gave the best short description of the cowcamp that I ever read. Foy was the town's favorite comedian for several seasons and he wrote in his autobiography of the camp as he knew it in early years.

"'Dodge,' he recollected, 'was dust, heat, and prairie, but above all, dust.'

"If Foy had added, 'when it wasn't mud,' he'd have made the picture complete."

As the trail herds increased in size during the camp's first year of the cattle trade, the throng of cowboys in Dodge swelled to such proportions that Wyatt added another deputy to his force—Neal Brown, a breed of Cherokee Indian strain and a gunfighter of demonstrated proficiency. He had, also, as auxiliaries, Charlie Bassett, sheriff of Ford County—Dodge was the county seat—and Bassett's deputy, Bill Tilghman. Dodge boasted that this coterie of peace officers could maintain law and order in any community on earth. Wyatt Earp, Bassett, Tilghman, Bat Masterson, and Brown were names to conjure with where gunplay was concerned; in popular esteem Jim Masterson and Joe Mason never quite ranked with them.

Meanwhile, the fame of Wyatt Earp was spreading beyond the ken of those for whom he solved problems of law and order and word of his prowess brought Ned Buntline (E. Z. C. Judson) to Dodge. Buntline's prolific pen furnished lurid tales of life on the plains for consumption by an effete world that dwelled east of the Mississippi River and which, in the seventies, demanded that its portraits of Western characters be done in bloody red. Buntline's outstanding literary achievement had been to make William Cody, a buffalo hunter, into the renowned "Buffalo Bill," and from the exploits of Wyatt Earp and his associates he now obtained material for hundreds of frontier yarns, few authentic, but many the bases of fables still current as facts.

Buntline was so grateful to the Dodge City peace officers for the color they supplied that he set about arming them as befitted their accomplishments. He sent to the Colt's factory for five special forty-five-caliber six-guns of regulation single-action style, but with barrels four inches longer than standard—a foot in length—making them eighteen inches overall. Each gun had a demountable walnut rifle stock, with a thumbscrew arrangement to fit the weapon for a shoulder piece in long-range shooting. A buckskin thong slung the stock to belt or saddle horn when not in use. The walnut butt of each gun had the word "Ned" carved deeply in the wood and each was accompanied by a hand-tooled holster modeled for the weapon. The author gave a "Buntline Special"—as he called the guns—to Wyatt Earp, Charlie Bassett, Bat Masterson, Bill Tilghman, and Neal Brown.

"There was a lot of talk in Dodge about the specials slowing us on the draw," Wyatt recalled. "Bat and Bill Tilghman cut off the barrels to make them standard length, but Bassett, Brown, and I kept ours as they came. Mine was my favorite over any other gun. I could jerk it as fast as I could my old one and I carried it at my right hip throughout my career as marshal. With it I did most of the six-gun work I had to do. My second gun, which I carried at my left hip, was the standard Colt's frontier model forty-five-caliber, single-action six-shooter with the seven-and-one-half-inch barrel, the gun we called 'the Peacemaker.'"

At this point it may be advisable to correct one error to which the Buntline stories gave wide circulation. Buntline and a thousand successors to the contrary, Bat Masterson never was marshal of Dodge City. There is no detraction in a statement of fact which should obviate subsequent misunderstanding. The part that Bat actually played in taming Dodge City—a not inconsiderable one—is to be ascertained readily from the records. It can be told most fittingly here, as it is linked with the story of Wyatt Earp, by whom Bat's official career was advised and sponsored, for it is due largely to Bat's admiration for Wyatt that it is possible to recount certain incidents which bore weightily upon the latter's accomplishments as a peace officer.

As Bat spun his yarns of Wyatt Earp, no tales of gunplay offered such vivid pictures of prowess as the recollection of certain affrays in which Wyatt went against the handpicked bullies of the cow outfits with no further weapons than his two fists.

"Wyatt's speed and skill with a six-gun made almost any play against him with weapons 'no contest,'" Bat once explained. "Possibly there were more accomplished trick-shots than he, but in all my years in the West at its wildest, I never saw the man in action who could shade him in the prime essential of real gunfighting—the draw-and-shoot against something that could shoot back.

"In a day when almost every man possessed as a matter of course the ability to get a six-gun into action with a rapidity that a later generation simply will not credit, Wyatt's speed on the draw was considered phenomenal by those who literally were marvels at the same feat. His marksmanship at any range from four to four hundred yards was a perfect complement to his speed. On more than one occasion I have seen him kill coyotes at the latter distance with his Colt's, and any man who ever has handled a six-gun will tell you that, while luck figures largely in such shooting, only a past master of the weapon could do that.

"Most of the frontier gun-wielders practiced daily to keep their gun hands in. I have known them to stand before mirrors, going through the motions of draw-and-shoot with empty guns for an hour at a time. Outdoors they were forever firing at tin cans, bottles, telegraph poles, or any targets that offered, and shooting matches for prestige and money stakes were daily events.

"I never knew Wyatt to practice the draw beyond trying his guns in the holsters when he first put them on for the day, or slipping them once to make sure they were free when he was heading into a possible argument. He seldom did any target work when there was no competition.

"Wyatt had a keen sense of humor, and one of his favorite amusements was to horn into target matches at which professional gunmen were engaged. The way he'd outdo the best the braggart gun-throwers had to offer fairly burned those fellows up, and the casual manner in which he did it was not calculated to soothe injured pride. But there was more than humor involved; it was Wyatt's quiet way of reminding the bad boys that against him they stood small chance. He was certain of that, and after he had made monkeys out of a few who went against him, others were willing to forgo argument.

"Wyatt was the most perfect personification I ever saw of Western insistence that the true six-gun artist is born that way. A hundred men, more or less, with reputations as killers, whom I have known, have started gunplays against him only to look into the muzzle of Wyatt's Colt's before they could get their own guns half drawn. In such a call, if a gunman thought particularly well of himself, or had any record as a fighting man, Wyatt would bend the long barrel of his Buntline Special around the gunman's head and lug him to the calaboose.

"In the old days, to buffalo a gun-toter was to inflict more than physical injury; it heaped upon him a greater calumny than any other form of insult could convey. A man for whom a camp had any respect whatsoever was entitled to be shot at; so Wyatt took particular delight in buffaloing the gunmen who set great store by themselves.

"When circumstances made it necessary for Wyatt to shoot, he preferred disabling men rather than killing them. Offhand, I could list fifty gunfights in which Wyatt put a slug through the arm or the shoulder of some man who was shooting at him, when he might as certainly have shot him in the belly or through the heart. There were instances in which I thought Wyatt too lenient, when it would have been better for all concerned to have put some gunman completely out of business, then and there, and, what's more, I have told him so.

" 'Didn't have to kill him,' Wyatt would answer, and that would be all he'd say.

"Where human life was concerned, Wyatt was the softest-hearted gunfighter I knew. Yet, if circumstances demanded, he could kill more swiftly and more surely than any other man of record in his time."

To support Bat's estimate of Wyatt Earp as the speediest, deadliest gunfighter of the Old West, his recollections may

ьε interrupted, momentarily, with the summary of a sympo-
sium, to which Dr. O. H. Simpson, of Dodge City, devoted
fifty years, and which gains added weight from its inception
on the old Chisum Ranch in New Mexico—the seat of the
Lincoln County Cattle War—in the days of Pat Garrett,
John W. Poe, and Billy the Kid, and its further development
in the cowcamps of Kansas.

"When I was twenty-three," Dr. Simpson writes, "I came
to live and practice in this rendezvous of badmen. Dodge
was started by people from Abilene, Hays City, Ellis, and
Wichita, and I have heard the notorious gunmen who
frequented those places—Wild Bill Hickok, for one outstanding example—compared repeatedly with the gun-
toters who strutted the streets of Dodge.

"I had grown up in Western Missouri; the Younger–
Anderson–Quantrell mob was organized in my old home
town. Fifty per cent of the men I knew in the seventies knew
intimately the James Boys and their gang. I have heard all
the participants in their bloody affairs discussed by all
grades of men, from Governor Crittenden on down.

"My sister had married Walter Chisum, of the famous
Chisum Ranch down on the Pecos. It was the Chisums—
John and Walter—who imported Billy the Kid to fight for
them in the Lincoln County Cattle War. Pat Garrett and
John W. Poe were my brother-in-law's intimates. I visited
the Chisum Ranch frequently, and there, and at Roswell and
Santa Fe, heard their fighting men compared, time and
again.

"So, you see, I am steeped in such lore, without seeking it;
I just couldn't get away from it at the start—then it got into
my blood.

"Of all the famous 'pistoleers' I have heard discussed, Bill
Tilghman and Wyatt Earp are the only ones against whose
records some creditable witness, with names, dates, and
circumstances to back him, has not cited a 'hurdle' that was
refused in the face of too great odds.

"As far as six-gun proficiency is concerned: for fifty years
the men who were its most competent judges have been my
patients and my friends. They have agreed unanimously, for

example, that Hickok was a marvelous shot, much better than Buffalo Bill, and possibly the best at fancy shooting that the Old West knew. But the overwhelming consensus is that, trick-shooting aside—and you want to remember that in the minds of the old-timers grandstanding was of relatively small account—as a gunfighter of deadly speed and accuracy, Wild Bill and all others were clearly outclassed by Wyatt Earp."

To return to Bat Masterson's admiration for Wyatt Earp's muscular prowess, Wyatt explained it thus:

"In my first year at Dodge I found it necessary to engage in fistfights on several occasions. Two of these fights were with individuals who were considered mighty tough and against whom Bat and others were of the opinion that I stood no chance. Luck was with me, however, and thereafter Bat seemed to think that I was unconquerable."

"Did you ever lose a fight?" I asked Wyatt.

"Never," he admitted, and one had to know the man to comprehend the innate simplicity of his answer.

As Bat recalled the affairs, the two fistfights to which Wyatt referred were, in reality, three, deliberately planned to overthrow the marshal's rule of the cowtown. Despite their predilection for six-guns in settling questions of supremacy, the cowboys recognized the merits of the rough-and-tumble with a respect accorded to their most proficient bruisers barely less than that rendered to masters of the Colt's. Every outfit had its rough-and-tumble champion, as braggart over his accomplishments as any gun-throwing colleague.

The first gladiator chosen to polish off Wyatt Earp, Bat remembered, was a two-hundred-pound individual whose practice was to wear his spurs into action, to rake an adversary's shinbones or to gouge his face and body if he could bring an opponent to the ground. At the close of a hot summer day, this cowboy and some forty or fifty followers rode in from the shipping pens to the southeast of Dodge, put up their ponies, checked their guns, and strode north across the Dead Line to Front Street, where Wyatt, with Bat and one or two others, stood in front of the Long Branch.

With no preliminary small talk the Texan offered the suggestion that if Wyatt wasn't too yellow he'd take off his guns and take the beating of his life before he was run out of town.

In the sultry heat of Dodge's summer days and nights, Wyatt invariably went coatless, his guns belted at the waist of the dark trousers he always wore and his badge of office pinned to the bosom of a soft white shirt. At the cowboy's suggestion, he unbuckled his guns.

"Where do you want to do this fighting?" Wyatt asked.

"Right here," the Texan replied.

Wyatt handed his guns and badge to Bat and followed the tough customer into the road, where the camp bully continued his bluster.

"Don't talk so much," Bat said Wyatt suggested. "Let's get this over."

The fight was finished before the cowboy realized that it had begun. As the Texan lunged to grapple with Wyatt, the marshal sidestepped and hit him on the jaw, catching him off balance and dropping him in the dust. The cowboy got up and rushed again. Wyatt hit him twice, once in the stomach and, as he doubled with pain, again on the jaw. The cowboy did not get up this time until he was half-carried across the railroad tracks by his companions. Wyatt resumed his guns and badge without comment. His shirt, Bat swore, was scarcely mussed.

On the occasion of the second encounter, a cowboy leader of the fistianic school and a crowd of his fellows caught Wyatt alone at night in front of a South Side dance hall. Word that a trap had been set reached Bat at the calaboose and he reached the dance hall to find Wyatt with his back to the wall holding off the Texans with his guns. Upon Bat's arrival, Wyatt's attitude changed.

"This fellow has an idea he can put a head on me," Wyatt said. "Keep the rest of his crowd out while I let him try."

In the bruiser picked for this particular job, Bat recognized one of the toughest in the Texas camps, a hulking cowhand whom he had seen win a number of battles with his kind.

"Don't do it, Wyatt," Bat counseled; "he's bad."

"Maybe so," Wyatt replied, "but I run this camp, or I don't."

In the shadowy half-circle of light from a dance-hall flare, Wyatt and the Texas champion battled for cowcamp supremacy. The fight lasted well over half an hour, and long before it was finished the onlookers included a hundred residents of Dodge and several times their number of cowboys. The Texan employed every possible ruse to make his superiority of weight and height count for the utmost in a contest which took no heed of rules or human decency. Wyatt went down several times, but when the battle ended, he was on his feet; the cowboy champion had been so thoroughly punished that he had no fight left.

"Wyatt stood there naked above the waist," Bat recalled. "His shirt and undershirt had been torn off. He was badly bruised about the head and body and literally plastered with bloody mud. He was never a man to boast or gloat, but I don't suppose he could resist one fling.

"'Anybody else want any?' he asked.

"And someone else did.

"Another one of those cowboy champions stepped out. To appreciate the fool I made of myself, you must remember that Wyatt had just finished a solid thirty minutes of desperate rough-and-tumble fighting. My only excuse is that I was convinced that he was unbeatable. But when I tell you that this second battler was a bigger man than the first, what I did next sounds inexcusable.

"'Kill the ———, Wyatt,' I urged. Wyatt said afterward he never heard me. Whatever gave him the impetus, he hit that big cowpuncher square on the nose so hard it must have been heard in Tascosa. In all the professional prizefights I saw in after years, I never witnessed the like of what followed. For twenty solid minutes—there was no such thing as rounds with rest between—Wyatt carried the fight to that big bruiser every second. This Texas champion never got close enough to Wyatt to grapple with him. A smash on the nose is a fine way to greet an opponent in battle, and Wyatt followed this advantage to the full. He had the fellow whipped in the first five minutes, but he couldn't finish him immediately; in the process he punished him so that he must have been an object lesson to the cowcamps for some time after.

"Wyatt never did knock this second fellow out, but the fight ended with the cowboy on the ground, blubbering. He not only was punch-drunk; he had been punched into temporary imbecility.

"Wyatt was looking around for another battle, and I came to my senses. I took his arm, but he shook me off and stood there, glowering. He was no handsome spectacle; he was covered with blood and dirt, as a matter of fact, had taken two terrific beatings himself; but there was something magnificent about him. I've always believed that if I hadn't scattered that bunch of cowboys, Wyatt would have tried to clean 'em all out, single-handed. As it was, I got him to his room, where he washed, put on fresh clothes, and resumed his guns and badge. Then he went out and patrolled the town for the rest of the night.

"Those three fights, I suppose, are my strongest reasons for having said and written repeatedly that there was no man in the West who could whip Wyatt Earp in a rough-and-tumble fight when Wyatt was in his prime. Most of the men who saw that doubleheader have agreed with me."

As chief deputy marshal of Dodge, Wyatt's responsibility was the preservation of law and order within the cowtown limits only, and his efforts, except in emergencies, were bent to the temper of the community. Elimination of gunplay north of the tracks was held to be of first importance; next, was protection for residents and visitors in that end of town against holdups and homicide. Those in the honky-tonk district were supposed to look out for themselves, as were their thousands of roistering customers.

Early in his tenure of office, Wyatt established a reputation as small respecter of persons where his sense of duty was involved. Railway laborers and railroad officials, his old friends from the buffalo range and the Eastern agents who bought hides, cowboys, cattle buyers and cattle kings, gamblers, saloonkeepers, and merchants, all looked alike to

Wyatt Earp when guilty of infractions against any one of the six ordinances about which he bothered. So many of these were thrown into the calaboose for reflection on the new order of things that listing them and their battles would provide only repetitious detail. It should suffice to record that in no single instance in which Wyatt set out to arrest a man did he fail to take his prisoner, that on numerous occasions the services of Dr. T. L. McCarty, Dodge City's one and only surgeon, were required to patch up the offenders, and that, as soon as any one of them had recovered sufficiently to stand in court, he was fined from twenty-five to one hundred dollars—the amount usually depending upon the prisoner's financial circumstances—and discharged with an increased respect for the camp's newfangled ideas.

Late in July of '76, the excitement over gold discoveries at Deadwood, South Dakota, spread to Dodge. Cowboys up from Texas left their outfits to ride north as prospectors. Numerous Dodge residents started for the new diggings. Bat Masterson resigned as Wyatt's assistant and joined the rush. Wyatt was deterred by a promise to Mayor Hoover that he would serve out the cattle-shipping season as a marshal. Bat's place on the force was taken by Wyatt's younger brother, Morgan, who had come to Dodge on his way to Deadwood.

Morgan, then twenty-five, won speedy recognition as a second edition of Wyatt in the handling of gun-toting troublemakers. At the time of his arrival, however, the peak of the year's cattle business had passed, the number of cowboys in town was dwindling steadily, and by September 1, Dodge had toned down to a point where the Earps had little to do.

On September 9, Wyatt and Morgan left Dodge for Deadwood in a wagon drawn by the best four-horse hitch that money could buy. Behind him Wyatt left an enviable record as a fighting man, a peace officer whose specialty was taming wild towns and wilder humans, a business of which he swore he had washed his hands. Ahead was adventure and prospector's fortune.

At Sidney, Nebraska, Wyatt met Bat Masterson returning to Dodge. A long run of good luck at Cheyenne gambling tables had held him until he figured it was too late to go into the mining camp. Bat reported that Deadwood was jammed with prospectors far beyond its capacity to deliver profits and that every claim within miles of the original strike had been staked.

"I've started for Deadwood and I'm going in," Wyatt insisted. "I may strike something the rest have overlooked."

Before Bat left him, Wyatt had an inspiration.

"Why don't you run for sheriff of Ford County next year?" he asked Bat. "Charlie Bassett isn't going to run again. You tell Hoover and Jim Kelley that I suggested you as a candidate."

"I'm not quite twenty-two," Bat objected.

"You're as much of a man as you'll ever be," Wyatt replied.

With which counsel Bat Masterson struck out for Dodge to seek public office, while Wyatt and Morgan Earp struck northward to beat the snow to the passes which lead across the Black Hills.

13

The Boom Camp
of the Black Hills

Deadwood, in the late fall of '76, when Wyatt and Morgan Earp drove into the camp, was jammed with prospectors, miners, promoters, and fortune hunters so far beyond its apparent capacity to furnish pay dirt that Morgan returned to Dodge before the closing-in of the long Dakota winter. To Wyatt, who customarily was a winning gambler, the rich camp, running high, wide, and handsome, with a play as big and as continuous as any frontier town he had known, offered opportunity.

Wyatt's interests shifted when he learned that his horses would be about the only ones in Deadwood that winter. The complete absence of winter pasturage, coupled with a total lack of farmers to put up hay crops, made fodder prices almost prohibitive—corn sold at ten dollars a hundred-weight—so stock was driven over the mountains to remain until spring.

Despite the warning of costliness, Wyatt arranged to keep his team in the mining camp, and, with the onset of real winter, Deadwood awoke to an acute realization that in the business of booming she had neglected a matter of prime importance, namely, her fuel supply. There was firewood in the hills, but unless it was toted, man-back or on handsleds, the camp might subsist on uncooked rations until it froze beyond need of them. Even with corn at ten dollars a hundred, Wyatt's team could earn its keep.

"The man from whom I rented a stable," Wyatt said, "had filed on a timbered hillside a few miles from town where he had been cutting and piling wood during the fall, expecting to sell it when winter set in. But, like the rest of the camp, he had forgotten all about transportation. I had a hunch that a fuel shortage was coming, so I tied up that wood supply with a contract to pay the owner two dollars a cord, at his property. As it was mostly deadfall, he made a fine profit. I rigged a wagon-box for use on wheels or runners that would carry two cords to the load, and hired a man to help me load and throw off at two dollars a trip. Buyers did their own piling. I could haul four loads a day, sometimes five, which meant eight or ten cords daily. I sold it in Deadwood at twelve dollars a cord, cash in hand before unloading. Every haul was contracted for in advance, and many a time I have driven down the main street of the camp with men running alongside bidding twenty, thirty, and even fifty dollars a cord for what I was obligated to sell at my regular price to someone to whom I had promised delivery. For special night hauls I charged stiff premiums. Once a man routed me out of my blankets for wood to keep a big poker game going until morning. He paid one hundred dollars a cord and ten dollars for my helper—the thermometer was at forty below zero that night and there was a forty-mile northwest wind howling.

"I didn't gamble much that winter. I delivered wood seven days a week and when night came I wanted to sleep. But I was young and tough, so were my horses, and we came through to spring in fine shape physically, with a profit of about five thousand dollars.

"As compared to the Kansas cowtowns, Deadwood was a law-abiding community. There were plenty of tough citizens in the camp, with the usual run of saloons, gambling houses and honky-tonks wide open twenty-four hours a day, and more crooked gamblers, thieves, and outlaws than the cattle centers knew. On the other hand, the braggart bad men from Texas did not reach Deadwood in any numbers, and the few who did come soon learned that tactics employed in hurrahing the cowcamps meant disaster in the mining town, free and easy as that was. For one thing, there were no business influences which inclined Deadwood to leniency with the cowboys, such as they enjoyed in the Kansas trail terminals.

"One bunch of cowboy-prospectors in camp, known as the Texas gang, took to holding up stagecoaches, but as far as I knew never made any organized effort to run the place. If they had, they would have been knocked off promptly. There was a crowd of gun-wielders in Deadwood that, collectively speaking, was never surpassed in proficiency by the residents of any Western community, except possibly Tombstone.

"Seth Bullock was sheriff; John Mann and Jerry Lewis were marshals. Offhand, I recall others, as Johnny Bull, Billy Allen, Scott Davis, Tom Hardwick, Tom Mulqueen, Charlie Clifton, Boone May, Laughing Sam, Tom Dosier, Charlie Rich, Doc Pierce, Lew Shoenfield, Bill Hillman, Johnny Oyster, Jim Levy, Charlie Storms, and Colorado Charlie Utter. Of the group, Jim Levy, Charlie Storms, and Tom Mulqueen were possibly the outstanding six-gun artists.

"There were a few killings in the camp that winter, but all were in the settlement of purely personal differences and everyone concerned got an even break; I don't recall that any of the survivors were arrested. I happened to witness one shooting scrape that gives Deadwood's attitude toward such affairs far better than any generalities. Also, it had a direct bearing upon later events in my life.

"One day in the Montana Saloon, Turkey Creek Jack Johnson had an argument with two partners which all three agreed should be settled by gunplay. If the partners had teamed up on the spot against Turkey Creek, they might have been hanged for murder. Such an affair ought to have been fought out with Turkey Creek going first against one partner, then, if he survived, taking on the second. But that wasn't Turkey Creek's caliber, and, as he had the greatest risk to run, he was allowed to dictate terms of battle. I drove up with a load of wood as the three started out to settle things and my helper and I joined twenty or thirty others who followed along to see the shooting.

"Turkey Creek was no slouch with a six-gun, but the rules he laid down for this fight were certainly foolhardy. A cemetery had been fenced off at the edge of camp and Turkey Creek stood in the road opposite one fence corner, while the partners faced him at the other fence line. At signal, all three could start walking and shooting. The cemetery plot bordered the road for about fifty yards and it was to be two against one over as much of that distance as marksmanship determined.

"We tried to get Turkey Creek to take the partners on singly, but he wouldn't listen. I remember his saying that he had picked the road in front of the cemetery as the place for the fight because at least one man, and probably two, would be buried, and he aimed to make things as convenient as possible for those who would have to do the undertaking.

"Here let me call to mind what I have said before about taking time in a gunfight. At the signal both partners cut loose as they started toward Turkey Creek. Each had two guns in his hands and each had exhausted the loads of one gun and shifted weapons before he had walked ten yards. Turkey Creek, meanwhile, was walking steadily down the road, one Colt's in his gun hand, the other in its holster; he had not fired a shot up to the time the pair against him shifted weapons. With the range reduced to about thirty yards, Turkey Creek let 'em have it. His first shot got one partner through the middle of the body and dropped him in his tracks, where he died in a few moments. The second partner kept walking and shooting. Turkey Creek stopped and I thought he was hit. But he fired again, deliberately, and this slug he put clean through the surviving partner's heart. This fellow was killed instantly, and when we turned him over, we found his six-gun still in his hand, the hammer cocked and his finger on the trigger. Out of ten shells he had to start with, a single cartridge was unexploded. He had fired nine shots and the other dead man had fired seven. Turkey Creek had two or three minor flesh wounds where some of this lead had grazed him. He had taken his time and fired twice with results that were indisputable.

"Turkey Creek hired a couple of fellows to dig graves for his victims—I remember the ground was frozen so hard they had to blast it—and spectators went back to the Montana, where I went to unloading wood. Disillusioning as the truth may be, I can't recall that Turkey Creek bought drinks for the camp; if he issued such an invitation, I didn't hear it; anyway, I didn't drink; the time I had taken to watch the battle had cost me a trip to the woodlot and I was too busy to be interested. I know that Turkey Creek was not arrested.

"When warm weather finally made prospecting possible, I roamed over the Deadwood hills long enough to be certain that everything looking like the suspicion of pay dirt had been staked by some earlier arrival. I was pretty much disappointed, my wood business had petered out, and by the middle of June I was ready to leave the country."

In a crudely hand-lettered notice which was displayed on the bulletin board outside the Wells-Fargo Express Company's Deadwood office in the early summer of 1877, there was evidence of the status which the whole frontier now accorded to Wyatt Earp. The distinction unquestionably was based on Wyatt's achievements in the Kansas cowtowns and provides a measure of the man that is indispensable to his proper appraisal.

In June, Wells, Fargo and Company faced the responsibility of transporting the spring cleanup of the Deadwood mines—a bulk shipment of more than $200,000 in bullion —to Cheyenne by stagecoach. Ordinarily, this task might have involved risk, to lives of Wells-Fargo employees as well as to the shipment itself, by virture of the highwaymanly propensities of numerous Deadwood citizens. On this occasion, it was rendered extraordinarily hazardous by the presence of the Dunc Blackburn gang of stage robbers in the hills just outside the village limits.

Blackburn and seven companions, all notorious outlaws with prices on their heads in a number of Western communities, had shown full appreciation of opportunities for their kind in the richness of the Deadwood diggings, and in the spring of '77 had setup camp in the nearby hills, whence they could maintain surveillance over all stage lines. They had spies in the camp, and when it was evident that any day might see the shipment of the cleanup, they took to holding up every stage that left Deadwood. The gang obtained some small booty and, for good measure, robbed several incoming stages of currency shipments and such of the passengers' property as appealed to them. Under threat of their activities, however, the bullion was withheld from shipment. Several posses were organized to go after the highwaymen, but these were eluded and holdups continued. After all, getting the bullion through was the express company's business, and most of Deadwood felt that chances involved in going against a crowd like Dunc Blackburn's might reasonably be left to those whom Wells, Fargo and Company paid for such services.

In the course of their depredations, Blackburn and his followers killed or wounded a number of stage drivers and shotgun messengers, as the armed guardians of express company treasure were called, from the weapons they generally favored for repelling boarders. In a majority of instances, when Dunc stepped into the road—neither he nor his followers attempted to conceal their identities—with the command, "Whoa-up, and throw off the box," the stage team was pulled to a halt and the treasure chest heaved to the roadside. Occasionally some more daring driver had run for it while the messenger cracked down on the highwaymen, efforts that had led to fatal consequences. The climax to the Blackburn series of highway murders came when the outlaw shot Johnny Slaughter, possibly the most famous and most fearless of all Black Hills drivers.

Gray, the Wells-Fargo agent at Deadwood, might have organized an escort of gunfighters to take out the bullion, or have sent to the nearest army post for troops, but two factors deterred him. Wells, Fargo and Company was in business for profit, charges for handling bullion were fixed, and the cost of a special escort would have been excessive. Second, was the loss of prestige which the famous express company would have suffered in abandoning standard practice for a gang of bandits. Of the two, in the frontier West, the latter was by far the more important consideration. The whole structure of Wells, Fargo and Company's business had been founded on the company's reputation—the proud boast was far from idle—for the safe conduct of all commerce with which it might be entrusted, through all the hell or high water that could be raised by human or natural forces.

When Wyatt Earp went to the stage office to reserve a seat in the Cheyenne stage—he had sold his team to a Dead-wood resident—his plan to leave camp furnished the Wells-Fargo agent with the possible solution for a pressing problem. After persuading Wyatt to postpone his departure, Gray posted a bulletin on the door of the Wells-Fargo office:

NOTICE TO BULLION SHIPPERS

The Spring Clean-up will leave for Cheyenne on the Regular Stage at 7:00 A.M., next Monday. Wyatt Earp, of Dodge, will ride shotgun.

On Monday morning, with more than $200,000 in the box and Wyatt in the boot, the Cheyenne stage rolled out of Deadwood as per advertisement.

"I was a traveling arsenal that morning," Wyatt recalled. "On that particular occasion my six-guns were auxiliary weapons. Across my knees, for the first fifty miles, I carried a regulation Wells-Fargo sawed-off shotgun loaded with buckshot, nine to the barrel, and a Winchester rifle. If Blackburn jumped us from the roadside, I would use the shotgun; for anything but short-range surprise, I figured to hold off the outlaws with the rifle while the team ran for it. In case an animal was shot down in a long-distance attack, I believed that, by using the stage as cover, I could pick off the six or eight men in the Blackburn gang before they could get close enough to do much damage."

162

Gray's advertising had the desired effect. Dunc Blackburn's spies carried word of the warning poster and the spring cleanup went through to Cheyenne under Wyatt Earp's escort with no stop other than for team changes. About ten miles out of Deadwood, however, two parties of four horsemen each kept pace with the stage for a time along the base of the hills at either side of the road. Certain that these were Blackburn men, Wyatt fired several rifle shots at each party. One group stopped abruptly and, as the stage drew ahead, the second bunch rode to join the first.

"I never heard what happened," Wyatt said, "but I always thought I hit a horse. That would account for the sudden stop. When I saw the two parties holding abreast of us, one on either side, I figured they were preparing for a long-range attack, and would close in on us if they could down one or more of the animals. In dealing with such men, I have always found that advantage is gained by taking the initiative, and I figured that if shooting was to be done, I might as well start it. We saw no more of Blackburn's gang. Later, Scott Davis ran Dunc into his hole and wound up his career as a road agent. We reached Cheyenne about four o'clock Wednesday afternoon with every ounce of dust intact. We had changed drivers during the three-hundred-mile trip, but I was on duty every minute. Wells, Fargo and Company had provided my stagecoach passage, and at the end of the run paid me fifty dollars."

In Cheyenne, Wyatt witnessed one of the most talked-of six-gun battles in the annals of the Old West, the street duel between Jim Levy and Charlie Harrison.

Bat Masterson characterized Harrison as a man of impetuous temperament, quick of action, of unquestioned courage, and an expert with a pistol.

"He could shoot straight faster when shooting at a target than almost any other man I knew," Bat said. "When you add that few men possessed more courage, the natural conclusion would be that he would be deadly in a gunfight."

Neither Levy nor Harrison was armed when they quarreled in Bowlby's gambling house, and both left to get their pistols. They were to shoot it out on sight. Each returned to the street wearing a Colt's forty-five and they met in front of the Dyer House.

"I have often cited that Levy–Harrison duel," Wyatt said, "as additional support for my contention that, given anything like an even break, the man who takes his time wins gunfights.

"In an interval between quarrel and return to the street, Levy and Harrison inspired considerable betting on the outcome of their battle. Harrison ruled favorite because of his courage and his fame as a marksman. Cheyenne didn't know much about Levy––he had just come down from Deadwood –but I had seen him in action and knew him as a top-notch gun-wielder, a nervy fellow of the deliberating type that I have always regarded as the most dangerous. I made no bets, but I did warn one or two fellows that Levy was not to be regarded lightly.

"Jim Levy came out of the Dyer House as Harrison rounded a nearby corner. Charlie Harrison shot first and so fast that he fairly set his Colt's on fire. He turned loose all five chambers before Levy let go with one, the one that ended the argument. Levy's slug tore through Harrison's belly and Charlie dropped. He died soon afterward. All Levy got was a couple of scratches.

"Without question Harrison was as game as Levy, as good a shot, and in the fight itself, he demonstrated that he was much faster. But Harrison lacked deliberation, was too anxious, wanted to shoot too fast, and that lost for him. Jim Levy took his time, only a split second, but enough to hold his shooting to its single purpose, accuracy."

While idling in Cheyenne, Wyatt received a telegram from Jim Kelley, newly elected mayor of Dodge City, urging him to return to the cowboy capital to resume his job as marshal at an increase of one hundred dollars a month in wages over his pay of the preceding summer.

In that year of 1877, Dodge was to reach high mark as the longhorn cattle center of the universe and by June the camp was overrun by Texas cowboys. In the absence of any peace officer of sufficiently forceful attainments to ensure respect for the local ordinances—fat Larry Deger and Joe Mason were supposed to preserve order—gun-toters were swaggering along Front Street, gunplay was an hourly occurrence, hurrahing the camp in the roar of six-gun fusillades was once again the favorite relaxation. When Mayor Kelley wired to Wyatt Earp at Cheyenne, Dodge, if she was not exactly treed, certainly had been upended. Deger had resigned, and the peace officer's job had been entrusted to Joe Mason as the only available substitute. Wherefore, the town authorities faced Fourth-of-July festivities with grave forebodings.

In Cheyenne, Wyatt telegraphed acceptance of Kelley's offer, but while he sped to the relief of the cowcamp, hell popped on the holiday. There were no fatalities among the peace officers, and none were inflicted by them, but several killings were recorded among cowcamp visitors. For more than twenty-four hours every saloon and honky-tonk in Dodge saw almost continuous free-for-all battle, in which pistols, knives, and fists were employed impartially.

Charlie Siringo, who in 1877 rode up the trail from Texas for George Littlefield, has set down his experiences in Dodge on that Fourth of July in a manner that furnishes the essential details.

"We arrived in Dodge on the third day of July," Siringo wrote. "I drew my pay and quit the job to celebrate the glorious Fourth of July in the toughest cattle town on earth. That celebration came near costing me my life in a free-for-all fight in the Lone Star Dancehall, in charge of the now noted Bat Masterson. The hall was jammed full of free-and-easy girls, long-haired buffalo hunters, and wild and woolly cowboys.

"In the mix-up my cowboy chum, Wess Adams, was severely stabbed by a buffalo hunter. Adams had started the fight to show the long-haired buffalo hunters they were not in the cowboy class. We had previously taken our ponies out of the livery stable and tied them near the hall. I had promised Adams to stay with him until Hades froze up solid. After mounting our ponies, Joe Mason, a town marshal, tried to arrest us, but we ran him to cover in an alley, then went out of town yelling and shooting off our pistols.

"This incident," Siringo comments, "shows what fools some cowboys were after long drives up the trail and after filling their hides full of the poison liquor manufactured to put red-shirted railroad-builders to sleep. Instead of putting a cowboy to sleep, it stirred up the devil in his make-up and made him a wide-awake hyena."

Wyatt Earp reached Dodge City early in the morning of July 5. He was appointed marshal immediately, and cowboy celebrants, awakening from their Fourth-of-July drunks, learned in short order that further hurrahing of Dodge was hazardous.

14

The Toughest Town
on the Trail

Wyatt Earp's return to Dodge as marshal in July of '77 was bitterly resented by the faction which had opposed Mayor Kelley's election. Ostensibly, this animosity was born of party politics; actually, it derived from business jealousies, personal grudges, and undercover alliances with a powerful Texas element.

"Dog" Kelley, as the mayor of Dodge was known across the frontier, was no rabid reformer; he was, himself, half-owner of the Alhambra Saloon and Gambling-House, the Dodge City Opera House, a dance hall, and other establishments dependent for prosperity on the cowboy trade. He saw, nevertheless, that unbridled lawlessness could kill prosperity for his bailiwick quicker than any other influence; and no one ever denied that Jim Kelley owned the courage to support convictions with entire disregard of personal consequences.

Kelley was a retired sergeant of United States Cavalry, who for years had been orderly to Brigadier-General George A. Custer. He had the soldier's holy regard for authority, had been elected, as he saw it, to the duty of law enforcement, and intended to obey orders; others could do likewise or take punishment made and provided.

As far as "Dog" Kelley was concerned, Wyatt Earp's appointment as marshal of Dodge was settled when the mayor's three fellow Republicans on the council sanctioned his choice and the two Democrats voted against him.

"You know what we want," Kelley told Wyatt. "I'll back you in any play you make to get it."

Opposition was not to be routed thus readily.

Before Wyatt had been in the official saddle twenty-four hours, Mayor Kelley learned that immunity had been assured to any gunman who could kill his new marshal and get beyond the town limits. Reply to the threats was largely in terms of action. Kelley reiterated that the gun-toting ordinances would be enforced, and Wyatt set about making the cowboys believe him.

Morgan Earp and Bat Masterson were now deputy sheriffs under Charlie Bassett. Bat had acquired a half-interest in a dance hall and variety theater and was campaigning to succeed Bassett as sheriff. Larry Deger, erstwhile marshal, had jumped the political fence and was the Democratic, anti-Kelley candidate against Masterson. Wyatt named Neal Brown and Jim Masterson as his deputies and later appointed Frank McLean, Ed Masterson, Bill Tilghman, and, for a few weeks, his brother, Virgil Earp, to assist him. As long as he was marshal of Dodge, he drew when possible upon this group for his subordinates.

In July of '77, 200,000 head of Texas cattle grazed on the Dodge prairies; with them were two thousand cowboys. The calaboose was filled nightly to overflowing with those who refused to heed the marshal's edicts, a majority well manhandled in the arresting process and a few who forced the gun-toting issue to a shooting point disabled by official gunfire. In a month's intensive effort, Wyatt took the fight out of the cowboy crowd to such an extent that Eddie Foy, who reached the camp as a tenderfoot actor early in August, could write in his autobiography: "I can testify that the majority of days passed rather peacefully in Dodge, with no killings and few fights."

Fuller appreciation of the tribute conveyed may be had from a partial roster of gunmen who made headquarters in Dodge during the summer of '77. Among them were Bob Robertson, Cal Polk, Bill Moore, Lon Chambers, Lee Hall, Tom Emory, Bob Williams, Louis Bozeman, Jimmy Oglesby, Fred Leigh, Tom Monroe, Charlie Coffee, King Fisher, and John Culp, professional fighting men for the great cattle outfits. To these add Dave Rudabaugh, Billy Wilson, Mike Roarke, Ed West, and Charlie Bowdre, later partners of Billy the Kid; Tom Pickett, Ed Norwood, Jimmy Carlysle, Johnnie Maley, Fred Chilton, Frank Valley, Lem Woodruff, Ed King, Charlie Emory, Smoky Hill Thompson, Pat Garrett, Doc Skurlock, and the Catfish Kid. There, to the old-timer of the cattle camps and trails, is the cream of the Old West's six-shooter talent. Yet these, and hundreds of others none the less accomplished in lethal exploit, and no whit less resentful of interference with their pleasures, fell victim to Dodge City's demands for a measure of tranquillity.

"The $2.50 bounty on a prisoner was still in force," Wyatt recalled. "Incidentally, a cowboy got the same for breaking a bronco. We got it for taming a cowboy, and for the first month after my return from Deadwood our bounty pool was nearly $1,000. Then, I guess, the Texas men saw the light, for never afterward did we corral them in such numbers."

In their wholesale arrests of gun-toting troublemakers—cowboys, buffalo hunters, and local residents—Wyatt and his deputies gathered in several highly influential citizens. Numerous large cattle outfits were family enterprises and riders sent up the trail often were brothers and cousins under leadership of older relatives. The youngsters were fully aware of their economic importance to Dodge and, moreover, in that heyday of the cattle king were too liberally supplied with money and credit, a combination which made them one of the cowtown's most difficult problems. To the average cowboy's attitude toward towns and town men, they added greater conceit and ability to finance unlimited deviltry.

About these Texas clans gathered hundreds of retainers, that great range-run of cowboys who, for forty dollars a month, horses to ride, ammunition, and chuck, returned to employers a loyalty in matters of work or play, life or death, that few man-to-man relationships have seen equaled. And, as every cowboy who rode the trail was of necessity as familiar with a pistol as with rope and running iron, results which calls upon that loyalty entailed have been written in red in the annals of the cattle country.

Two families which annually sent large herds and large outfits of uproarious retainers up the trail were the Rachals and the Driskills. The four Rachal brothers drove as many as 30,000 head of cattle in a season; one of their sales could put $600,000 into circulation. The six Driskills, under Tobe, the eldest, drove herds of like proportions, with an array of cousins to match the Clements–Hardin aggregation. No Texas clan exceeded either for downright arrogance.

Under Larry Deger's rule influential cattlemen had enjoyed such special privilege that, even after Wyatt Earp's punitive measures had demonstrated for ordinary cowhands the error of hurrahing Front Street, wealthy herd-owners continued to insist they'd wear guns as they chose and celebrate cattle sales on the north side of the Dead Line likewise. That they were encouraged in this attitude by a Dodge City faction was no secret. Several minor beef barons had suffered indignities of arrest at the hands of the Earp forces and were demanding a showdown in the camp when no less an individual than Tobe Driskill, a sure-enough cattle king, decided that the time was ripe for him to cut loose on Dodge in wholehearted Texas fashion.

In celebrating a sale of cattle, Tobe acquired, with his liquor, delusions of a call to shoot Front Street wide open. A Dodge citizen of anti-Kelley leanings returned Driskill's guns to him from the check rack of his establishment after Tobe stated his purpose, and with others of like affiliation stood in the doorway of the saloon from which Driskill sallied, to watch the fireworks.

Momentarily Dodge reverted. With a six-gun smoking in either hand, the Texan bellowed his intent to stand the camp on her ear and invited attempts to stop him, emphasizing his remarks with gunfire too promiscuous for the safety of bystanders.

As Driskill halted before the Alhambra Saloon and bawled an obscene invitation to Mayor Kelley and his customers to step out and see what was being done to the community, Wyatt Earp ran across the Plaza. Someone called a warning, and Driskill turned, but, before Tobe could collect the poise for a course of action, he was knocked sprawling. Next he knew, his guns had been taken from him, a muscular hand had seized the scruff of his neck, and he was walking turkey toward the calaboose, into which he was heaved headlong.

"I would have been justified in shooting Driskill," Wyatt said in after years, "but there was no need for gunplay. His identity did not influence me. I handled him as I would have any cowboy, but to a man of Driskill's standing and conceit, the mauling I gave him would rankle deeper and longer than any other punishment. He never would live down the fact that I had held him in too small esteem to draw a gun on him. And I wanted every move I made against the Texas men to belittle them as much as possible."

Word that Wyatt Earp had thrown Tobe Driskill into jail spread quickly. Numerous persons hastened to Mayor Kelley to demand that the wealthy herd owner be released.

"As long as I was marshal of Dodge," Wyatt recalled with no small satisfaction, "Jim Kelley backed me to the limit. The Tobe Driskill case was no exception. His only reply to demands for Tobe's release was that I had full authority. When pressure was brought to bear on me, I insisted that Driskill was entitled to less consideration than if he had been some poor, ignorant cowpuncher, and that he'd stay in the calaboose until morning."

Tobe Driskill's friends were not to be turned thus easily from retaliation. Frank Warren, at the time a bartender in the Long Branch Saloon, has furnished an eyewitness account of immediately subsequent happenings.

News of Tobe's predicament was sent to the Driskil outfit, with a suggestion for rescue. Presently Tobe's foreman, a professional fighting man of note, led twenty-five cowboys of like proclivities over the toll bridge into town, yelling like mad, leading a riderless pony which Tobe was to use in his getaway. Several dismounted before the jail and one ran to Tom Nixon's blacksmith shop for a sledgehammer. Others sat their ponies about the door with guns drawn and, in the custom of their kind, bawled their boasts that they were taking Tobe Driskill out of jail and dared Dodge's fighting men to stop them.

Wyatt Earp reached the calaboose as a cowboy started pounding at the door with the sledgehammer. Frank Warren took cover in a shed beside the jail. Wyatt, he said, walked straight into the group of cowboys, alone and without drawing a weapon.

"Quit pounding on that lock," Wyatt ordered. "You fellows better not start something you can't stop."

There followed another of those remarkable tributes to the force of Wyatt Earp's personality.

"In an instant," Frank Warren testified, "it was as quiet as a churchyard around that calaboose. The pounding stopped and the cowboys quit yelling."

"Put up your guns," Wyatt continued, "and get out of town. Before you go, put that sledgehammer back where you got it."

Wyatt had his eye on the gunfighting foreman, and that individual undoubtedly figured that he was marked for Boot Hill with the first move toward further hostilities. The marshal afterward confirmed the accuracy of the foreman's reasoning. The leader of the rescue party wheeled his pony and started out of Dodge, followed by his troop of killers. Wyatt watched the last one cross the toll bridge, then went back to Front Street. Next morning, Tobe Driskill was fined one hundred dollars.

Hard on the heels of the Driskill affair, Bob Rachal also got drunk enough to defy Dodge City regulations.

At the evening hour, when Dodge took supper, Wyatt was

called from the Delmonico Restaurant by the noise of gunfire. He stepped into Front Street to see an undersized fellow, whom he recognized as a violinist with a traveling theatrical troupe, running toward him.

"I'm shot! I'm shot!" the musician screamed, and as blood streamed from a wound across his scalp, it was not difficult to believe him. Behind him at some distance, a drunken man made such speed as he might, waving a Colt's in either hand and calling upon the fugitive to stop and be killed, which demand he emphasized with profanity and punctuated with pistol shots.

"Get in out of sight," Wyatt directed, pushing the little man into the Long Branch doorway. The marshal recognized the pursuer as Bob Rachal, and prepared to deal with him. As Rachal saw his quarry disappear, he, too, started for the doorway. Wyatt stepped out to meet him.

"Drop those guns, Rachal," the marshal ordered.

"Get to hell out of the way, you blankety-blanked short-horn!" Rachal answered. "I'll kill that little fiddling son of a so-and-so."

Whereupon the twelve-inch barrel of the Buntline Special was laid alongside and just underneath the Rachal hatbrim most effectively. The buffaloed cattleman dropped to the walk, unconscious.

The sound of gunfire had brought Neal Brown on the run, and when Rachal's gunbelts had been removed, Wyatt and his deputy started for the calaboose, lugging their senseless prisoner between them. By the time they were halfway to the lockup, the cowman's Dodge City friends were intervening. When their suasion failed to turn the marshal from his purpose, they sent for Bob Wright, a founder of Dodge, half-owner of the cowcamp's most important business establishment, Ford County representative in the Kansas Legislature, astute politician, warm friend to numerous Texas men, and by all odds the wealthiest of the local citizenry. Wright reached the calaboose as Wyatt unlocked the door.

"Here, Earp; you can't lock up Bob Rachal," Wright said.

"What makes you think so?" Wyatt asked.

"Why, his business is worth half a million dollars a year to Dodge."

"I know that," Wyatt admitted, while Neal Brown sloshed water over the cattle king to hasten his return to consciousness. Wright's anger mounted as the marshal answered further protestations by heaving Rachal into jail. Emboldened possibly by the crowd which had gathered, Wright made open threats.

"You'll let him out if you know what's good for you," he warned the marshal.

Wyatt locked the calaboose door. Wright seized his arm.

"You let Rachal out or Dodge'll have a new marshal in twenty-four hours," he stormed.

"Take your hand off my arm," Wyatt said.

Bob Wright erred. He snatched at the key in Wyatt's hand and grappled with him, mixing with muscular efforts a highly colored prophecy of the marshal's immediate future. Thereupon Wyatt swung open the door of the calaboose and pitched the irate legislator into jail with Rachal, turned the key, and went across the railroad tracks to ascertain the extent of the violinist's injuries.

Rachal, it appeared, had invited the musician to battle over the way certain tunes had been played by the traveling orchestra. When the violinist demurred, the cowman struck him over the head with a gun barrel, splitting his skin with the wound which bled so profusely. Rachal started to shoot and the panic-stricken fiddler started to run, and thanks to inebriation the scalp wound was the only one inflicted.

Jim Kelley, at the Alhambra, was besieged with demands for the release of Rachal and Wright. Kelley heard his marshal's report and refused to interfere. Wyatt, when arguments were turned upon him, declined to discuss the matter. Someone persuaded Bat Masterson to intervene, and Bat never forgot the thinly veiled reproof which met his proposals.

"After I was all through," Bat said, "Wyatt reminded me, of what I knew all along, that he'd never hold the Texas men in line if he played favorites with anyone; and that when Bob

Wright tried to run a bluff on him before half of Dodge and a whole crowd of Texans, he left but one course, as Wyatt saw it—to call Wright's hand. Then it was Wright's move, to make good or crawfish.

"'If I had done anything else,' Wyatt said, 'I'd have to leave town, because I'd have lost whatever edge I've got on these troublemakers. Now, I've put the play squarely up to Bob Wright and everybody knows it.'"

On the second day after Rachal's arrest, Wyatt Earp was informed that a standing offer of one thousand dollars had been posted for any gunman who would kill him, in a fair fight or otherwise, and with this went a guarantee against prosecution if the killer could escape Dodge City jurisdiction. The first attempt to collect this bounty was made early one morning, as Wyatt crossed the railroad tracks at First Avenue. Three shots were fired from behind a freight car, two missing the target entirely, the third cutting a hole through the marshal's sombrero. A few nights later, when Wyatt reached his room on the ground floor of the Dodge House, and stepped quickly to the window for a look outside before he lighted the lamp, the roar of a double-barreled shotgun brought the sash around his head in splinters.

"The fellow was too anxious," Wyatt said, "and shot high. I saw him run for the South Side and went through the window after him. I wanted to get him in talking condition, so I shot him in the leg, and he tumbled.

"Tom Finnerty and I lugged the fellow to the calaboose and sent for Dr. McCarty. I told my prisoner that if he'd tell me why he tried to kill me and who put him up to it, I wouldn't make any charge against him. He was just an ordinary cowboy, who didn't know anything about the men back of the business. He had lost his year's pay, pony, saddle, and guns, gambling, he said, and a herd-boss had promised him a thousand dollars if he'd kill me, provided a shotgun for the job, and posted him on my habit of looking out of my window, which showed how well the gang had me spotted."

When Wyatt Earp next appeared on Front Street, all

Dodge knew of the conspiracy against him. "Dog" Kelley suggested a bodyguard and a number of Dodge's foremost gunfighters volunteered for regular turns of duty in Wyatt's company. The marshal declined their offers.

"I told my friends," Wyatt recalled, "that I would not give my enemies the satisfaction of seeing me take precautions against them. That was foolish, but where Texas men and their kind were concerned, I've never denied that what I wanted most of all was the personal satisfaction of winning with a lone hand against the whole outfit."

Dodge and her cowboy hangouts now went agog with excitement.

"They've sent for Clay Allison to cut down Wyatt Earp," the news ran; "Clay Allison of the Washita!"

Confirmation came with Texas boasts that Clay Allison, a six-gun killer with twenty-one men to his "credit"—of whom six were frontier marshals or sheriffs—was coming over from Las Animas to shake up Dodge in smoke, to go against Wyatt Earp in his own bailiwick.

"They've sent for Clay Allison, sure enough," "Dog" Kelley told Wyatt. "Clay's made talk in Las Animas that he's been invited to come over here and run you out, or knock you off, and that he's heading for Dodge to fill the order. What do you want me to do?"

"Nothing," Wyatt answered. "I'll decide what to do with Clay when the time comes."

Jim Kelley always maintained that Wyatt made no preparation for the reception of the man who was coming to kill him. The rest of Dodge awaited feverishly what it was freely predicted would be the six-gun classic of the century.

Clay Allison was a Tennessee-born Texan, whose six-gun skill, at the age of twenty-six, had filled graves from Dodge to Santa Fe. He was strikingly handsome, six feet two inches in his socks, weighing about one hundred and eighty pounds, broad-shouldered, slim-hipped, muscularly powerful, lithe, quick as the proverbial cat, with remarkably slender hands and feet of which he was inordinately vain. A profusion of wavy black hair set off his high forehead, dark blue eyes, and aquiline nose; the boldness of his countenance was further enhanced by the black mustache and beard which he wore more neatly and closely trimmed than was current fashion. Allison was a fastidious dresser, affecting all the cowboy trappings for horse and man, but holding to a single black-and-white color scheme. He complemented this distinctive attire through ownership of two cow ponies, each with a thoroughbred cross; one, coal black; the other, cream white, and referred to as his "warhorse."

Upon the mountain man's inherent aptitude for firearms Clay grafted the six-shooter tradition of the range-riders. So assiduously did he cultivate the development, that by 1873 the frontier settlements in Texas, Colorado, New Mexico, and Kansas knew and feared him as a killer who would shoot a man to see him kick.

"Sober," one of his earlier associates has written, "Clay Allison could be a mighty good fellow. Throw a couple of drinks into him and he was a hell-bound turned-loose, r'arin' to shoot—in self-defense."

Next to out-and-out gunplay, Allison found his chief delight in standing the Western camps on end, and for a number of years he paid scheduled visits to a regular list of communities and hurrahed them to a finish. Christmas and Fourth of July, for example, he regularly devoted to running Las Animas up a tree, although he was not averse to standing that particular town on her ear at such other odd times as the spirit moved him.

The temper of Clay's celebrant moods is exemplified in his visit to a Las Animas dentist for relief from a toothache. The dentist pulled the wrong tooth, an error which later came painfully to Clay's attention; whereupon Allison returned to the dentist's office, buffaloed the practitioner, and pulled a half dozen teeth from the dentist's jaws with that gentleman's own forceps.

On another occasion, Clay treated Canadian, Texas, to a cowboy version of Lady Godiva's Ride. He took his black pony to the edge of camp, stripped to his skin, barring gunbelts and boots, tied his clothing to his saddle and headed down Main Street on a whooping, shooting gallop, standing full length in his stirrups, stark naked above the shins except for his cartridge carriers. When this exhibition palled, he pulled up in front of a saloon, dismounted, and, without dressing, went inside for a drink. Not all of his celebrations were as harmless.

Allison once rode into Cimarron, New Mexico, and while in Lambert's saloon, accumulating inspiration for scheduled festivities, met Marshal Pancho, a well-known frontier peace officer. Lambert said that Pancho, while trying to talk Allison out of his contemplated spree in the interests of the community, removed his sombrero and let the hand which held the hat drop to his waist. Clay jerked a gun and shot Pancho dead.

Allison asserted that the marshal had used his sombrero as a shield behind which he had tried to draw his gun, and that, as the marshal had no warrant for his arrest, he had shot in self-defense.

Again in Las Animas, Clay shot and killed Marshal Charlie Faber, who had ordered Clay and his brother, John Allison, to check their guns while in a local dance hall. The brothers refused, and Faber left the hall to return with a double-barreled shotgun. He ordered John Allison to throw up his hands. John went for his Colt's and Faber shot him through the gun arm. Clay Allison, from a far corner of the room, shot the marshal through the chest and killed him. Again, Clay pleaded self-defense, on the ground that Faber had a load in the second barrel of his gun and was after either Allison he could get. After a Las Animas jury cleared him on the strength of that argument, Clay added the courts to his list of playgrounds.

Allison had himself appointed foreman of a grand jury and kept that august body in a twenty-eight-day-and-night session during which the jurors transacted no business, but did keep hilariously drunk on liquor which Clay purchased with county warrants. Again, when he reached Las Animas to find court in session, Clay rode into the courtroom on his warhorse and ordered the tribunal of justice adjourned to stay that way until he had left town. The judge accommodated him.

In Clifton, New Mexico, Clay met another killer, one Chunk, who with eleven notches in his gun had announced that he would cut Number 12 for Clay Allison whenever he met him. So highly regarded was Chunk's proficiency on the draw-and-shoot that in the frontier camps the betting was at even money on the outcome of the anticipated battle.

Clay rode up to the Clifton House to find Chunk there ahead of him, with neither man previously aware that the other was on that trail. To work up to fighting pitch, the men bought drinks for one another, then matched ponies in a race which Chunk won. Next, Chunk invited Clay to dine with him at a restaurant. The men sat at opposite sides of the table and ordered food, but gave their best attention to whiskey. Clay got impatient, reached across the table and slapped Chunk's face. Chunk went for his gun, but Clay beat him to the draw and shot him through the head. As Chunk had advertised his intention of killing Allison, Clay was not held.

The only killing credited to Clay Allison's account in Dodge had taken place in the early days of that camp, when Wyatt Earp was in Wichita. Clay was eating in a restaurant when a drunken man with whom he had quarreled entered with a gun in his hand and the announcement that he was hunting Allison.

"Here I am," Clay called, and while his inebriated enemy was trying to focus his wavering eye and sights, Allison drew a gun and shot him. Legend adds that Clay went on with his meal while someone else dragged his victim to Boot Hill. He strutted in Dodge for several weeks that season, but eventually returned to his Las Animas stamping ground.

Wyatt Earp, while marshal of Dodge, was on active duty in the streets until four o'clock each morning and, unless court business called him, slept until noon. Thus it happened that when Clay Allison hit Dodge City one morning, Wyatt was in bed. The marshal's first knowledge of Allison's arrival came with a message from the mayor that the gunman was in town, had been in several saloons buying drinks, and was boasting of the purpose of his visit. Clay was rapidly approaching the stage of intoxication at which he was most dangerous. Wherefore Mayor Kelley and his supporters were anxiously awaiting Wyatt's appearance.

"I'll be right along," Wyatt said in response to the summons, then went about the routine of shaving and breakfast.

"With Clay in town the time for fussing was past," Wyatt commented. "Now, it was up to me to leave Dodge by the back alley or go down Front Street and meet Allison.

"I did not intend to give Clay the satisfaction of thinking he had hurried me. He knew that I'd been sent for before I did, and I knew enough about the average braggart killer to be certain that a lot of Clay's fight would go into all the talk he'd be making while he waited. And the more I could irritate him by tardiness, the less sure of himself he'd be at the showdown.

"I wore my guns at breakfast on the chance that Clay might bring the fight into the dining room. While I was eating, several men came to ask if they could help any, but beyond asking Bat Masterson and Charlie Bassett to make sure I was not ambushed by Allison's friends, I declined their offers. About ten o'clock I walked down Front Street toward Second Avenue."

Accounts of men who witnessed Wyatt Earp's meeting with Clay Allison do not differ in essential details, but few who have told their stories occupied positions as commanding as those of Chalk Beeson and Bill Harris, proprietors of the Long Branch in front of which the marshal met the gunman, and Luke Short who ran the Long Branch gambling concession.

Between gunfighter and gunman, one marked similarity was noted, in the colors of their clothing. Clay Allison had followed his predilection for black and white from the toes of his fancy boots to the tip of his huge sombrero, through the full array of white buckskin and silver-trimmed accoutrements. Wyatt Earp was dressed as for any other midsummer morning. He wore no coat and his dark trousers were pulled down over the tops of his boots; a gun was belted to either hip; on his soft white shirt was his marshal's badge; for shade, he wore a sombrero as large and as black as Allison's.

As Wyatt started toward Second Avenue, the north side of Front Street cleared instantly, a few spectators taking vantage points in stores and saloons, a majority utilizing the ditch beside the railroad. As Wyatt neared the Long Branch, three doors from Second Avenue, Clay Allison came out of Wright and Beverly's door on the corner.

Wyatt stopped and leaned against the wall of the Long Branch, just west of the doorway. Allison came along the walk, turned, as if to enter the saloon, and halted abruptly.

"Are you Wyatt Earp?" the killer demanded.

"I am Wyatt Earp," the marshal replied.

"I've been looking for you."

"You've found me."

"You're the fellow who killed that soldier the other night, aren't you?" Allison continued.

"What business is it of yours if I am?" Wyatt countered, although the charge implied was without foundation.

"He was a friend of mine," Allison retorted.

As Allison talked, he had stepped close, and was actually leaning against Wyatt, thus shielding his right side and his right hand from the marshal's view.

"Clay was working for his gun all the time," Wyatt said, "trying to get into such a position that I couldn't see him start after it."

"I'm making it my business right now," Allison snarled.

Wyatt felt the muscles of the body which pressed against him tauten.

The watchers in the Long Branch said that Clay Allison had his thumb hooked around the hammer of his Colt's and the weapon half out of the holster when stark amazement replaced the fighting scowl which had distorted his face, he dropped his gun as though the butt had turned red-hot, and jerked both hands, empty, above his waist. Then onlookers saw the reason for the transformation, although none had caught the action which brought it. The muzzle of Wyatt Earp's forty-five was jammed into Allison's left side, just underneath the ribs.

With his gun against Allison's body, Wyatt waited for the other to move or speak.

A few seconds of threatening suspense brought the strain to a pitch Clay could not endure. Hesitantly, Allison backed across the walk. With several feet between him and the muzzle of Wyatt's forty-five he found voice.

"I'm going around the corner," Clay suggested.

"Go ahead," Wyatt told him. "Don't come back."

Allison backed out of sight beyond Wright and Beverly's. A moment later, when the marshal peered around the same corner, Second Avenue was empty. From across the road, Bat Masterson called. Armed with a shotgun, the deputy sheriff had taken his stand in a doorway to command three approaches to the Front Street intersection, thus precluding any attempt to gang up on Wyatt from those quarters. Bat called that Allison had gone into Wright and Beverly's by the side entrance and that there were some twenty other men in the place who would bear watching. Then he pointed across the Plaza to Sheriff Charlie Bassett, guarding against a shot in the back from that direction. Wyatt returned to his post beside the Long Branch door. Allison's war-horse was hitched to the rail before Wright and Beverly's front doorway. Harris, Beeson, and Short could forestall any bushwhacking operations through the saloon. To reach his pony, Allison would have to come into Wyatt's line of vision, and from where he stood the marshal could keep cases until the killer made his next move.

Allison probably was taking on liquid courage in Wright and Beverly's, and while Wyatt waited, the door of the Long Branch opened behind him and a double-barreled shotgun was thrust within reach of his hand.

"Take this and give him both barrels," Chalk Beeson counseled.

The proffered gun, incidentally, was the same fine English-made piece with which Bill Thompson killed Sheriff Whitney in Ellsworth. The gun belonged to Bill's brother Ben, and was his favorite weapon. Early in '77, Ben Thompson went broke in Dodge and posted the shotgun with Chalk Beeson for a loan of seventy-five dollars. Chalk kept the gun back of the bar while waiting for Ben Thompson to redeem it.

Wyatt Earp, without taking his eye from the Wright and Beverly door, shook his head at Chalk's suggestion. Bill Harris joined his partner.

"Don't be a fool, Wyatt," Harris counseled. "Take the shotgun and use it."

"All Clay's got is a pair of six-guns," Wyatt answered.

Allison strode out of Wright and Beverly's door; Beeson and Harris ducked back through their own. The gunman, pistols in their holsters, walked straight to his war-horse, swung into the saddle, and sat staring savagely. He turned to the marshal.

"Come over here, Earp," he suggested. "I want to talk to you."

"Make your talk," Wyatt answered. "I can hear you."

"You, Bob Wright!" Allison bellowed. "Bob Wright!"

Wright stepped to the walk in front of his store.

"Now, Clay—" he began, but Allison cut him short.

"You're a hell of a fellow," the gunman shouted so that half of Dodge City heard. "You made some promises about this morning, and agreed to have some fighting men here, but I haven't seen any signs of them."

"What do you mean, Clay?" Bob Wright inquired suavely.

"You know what I mean," Allison answered with a string of oaths, "and so do the fellows you sent to Las Animas after me."

With which telling observation, Clay Allison wheeled his war-horse and started for the toll bridge on a run. As he reached the bridgehead, Clay pulled up and turned to face the Plaza. With a wild whoop, he jerked a gun, put spurs and quirt to his mount, and headed back toward Wright and Beverly's.

"Watch the store, boys," Wyatt called to Masterson and Bassett, "I'm going to get him."

The marshal walked to the middle of Second Avenue. Clay came at a gallop, gun in his right hand, quirt flailing in his left, yelling madly. When he was about fifty yards distant, Bat Masterson saw the Buntline Special move slowly from Wyatt's side to a level slightly above his waist. As Bat and the others waited for the roar of gunfire that would relieve the West of a killer or rob it of a peace officer, Clay yanked his war-horse to his haunches, in the sliding stop that only a highly trained cow pony can achieve, wheeled, and rode breakneck again for the toll bridge. This time he kept on, out of Dodge, toward Las Animas. The showdown had come, and gone. Clay Allison had quit the fight.

Wyatt turned from the roadway to face Bob Wright and several of the legislator's friends who had watched Allison's departing gesture.

"I thought so," Wyatt remarked. No one answered.

Some two weeks later, Clay Allison found it necessary to visit Dodge if he was to close a cattle deal. He rode to the south bank of the Arkansas with his cowboys and sent one to ask the marshal if he might come into town.

"Tell him to come in and do his business," Wyatt answered.

With this assurance Allison rode into Dodge, checked his guns, sold his cattle, and rode away without known reference to his recent fiasco.

"I saw Clay and spoke to him several times while his cattle deal was pending," Wyatt said; "the last time just as he was leaving town. He waved a hand to me as he rode toward the bridge. I never laid eyes on him afterward."

The extent to which Wyatt's prestige held even the most powerful and most influential cattlemen from browbeating Kansas to utter docility is indicated by Judge John Madden, of Tulsa, Oklahoma, who practiced law on the plains for half a century and who for years was counsel to the Missouri, Kansas and Texas Railroad. In handling "hoemen" who preempted open range, the cattle barons found their most effective weapon in fear-inspired control of the Kansas county courts. Judge Madden, then a young attorney, was retained to defend certain homesteaders whom the cowmen were "railroading" to prison on a trumped-up charge of cattle stealing, as the easiest means of ousting them from desirable grazing areas.

When the Texans attempted to follow their custom of furnishing a jury for a Kansas court from the ranks of Texas cowboys, Wyatt Earp and Bat Masterson, each wearing his badge and guns, took places at Madden's side. The prospective jurors, every last one an armed Texan, were called and each was challenged by young Madden as Wyatt prompted him. The volunteer jurors resented the challenges with open threats, but when it became increasingly evident that Wyatt and Bat were backing a play which they had instigated, a deputy was sent out to bring in enough *bona fide* Kansas citizens to fill the jury box.

"The judge was Jerry Strong, a one-armed man who was strong for the cattlemen," Judge Madden wrote me in recalling the case. "It was a ticklish job for a young tenderfoot lawyer to refuse men for the jury who wanted to serve and who carried guns belted on them in open court. But Wyatt and Bat sat by my side and told me whom to challenge in a manner that did not leave their purposes in doubt. Thanks to them, I got away with it. My clients were found 'not guilty.'

"I may be giving you information that Wyatt would never have disclosed, as he was very modest. But he and a few others like him were the vanguard of law and order in the early days of Kansas.

"I find myself shrinking from writing about the badmen of the Old West. I knew so many of them that they palled on me. However, I never classified Wyatt Earp with the badmen. He was a gunfighter, but he stood for law and order.

"God bless old Wyatt Earp, and his kind! They shot their way to Heaven."

At about this time, Morgan Earp resigned as a deputy under Sheriff Bassett to try his luck in Montana, where his career was shaped by the touch of Wyatt's celebrity. Butte was in need of a marshal who could maintain some semblance of order in the booming camp, against the frontier riffraff which had responded to the lure of mining excitements. An erstwhile resident of Wichita mistook Morgan Earp for Wyatt, with the result that the local council sought him to handle the peace officer's problems. When Morgan established his identity, Butte decided that if it couldn't have one Earp, it would take another.

Morgan never was Wyatt's equal in any respect which made for Western preeminence. He was not as steady of habit, was more easily swayed from that calm sagacity which was Wyatt's outstanding attribute, and at times could be goaded into hunting trouble. On the other hand, neither his courage nor his proficiency as a gunfighter ever was successfully questioned; the exploit for which he is best remembered in Montana established his reputation.

Billy Brooks, that remarkably expert gunman who had preceded Wyatt as marshal of Dodge, was in the mining camp. Billy resented Morg's appointment, and advertised that he would gun the new officer at first opportunity. Brooks had killed a number of men after leaving Dodge and in Butte was held to be cock-of-the-walk in affairs of gunplay.

When told of Brooks's threats against him, Morgan Earp sent word to Brooks that he would shoot him on sight. A few hours later, the men met in the main street of the camp. Two shots roared as one. Morg was hit in the shoulder, but he put Billy Brooks out of business with a slug that struck the killer full in the stomach.

In Dodge, Wyatt was facing the high point of the greatest cattle-shipping season the West had known. But, with a force of deputies which included Virgil Earp, Frank McLean, Neal Brown, Jim and Ed Masterson, Wyatt held the Texas men so completely in awe that standing the camp on her ear generally had come to be listed with the cowboys' lost accomplishments.

15

Wyatt Earp Meets Doc Holliday

Despite the ebullient idiosyncrasies which distinguished those early citizens and visitors whose memories have outlived a half-century of prosaic tranquillity, Dodge City's social order did not exist solely on debauch and gunplay. The village had its quota of legitimate mercantile establishments, and as residents, their proprietors, employees, and families.

The racket of saturnalia, the roar of gunfights and news of casualties sounded across the railroad tracks, but in 1877 probably three hundred men, women, and children in Dodge had no more intimate knowledge of such goings-on than was to be gained from gossip and the columns of cowtown newspapers. Law-abiding residents lived to the north of Front Street, almost entirely. Between them and trouble Wyatt Earp and his deputies drew the Dead Line. Occasionally some drunken cowpuncher might whoop his way into the precincts of decent existence, but was summarily dragged out to repent of his social error in the calaboose.

The Dead Line not only limited gunplay in Dodge; it served also to demarcate the community's castes of society. Men and women from south of the Plaza simply did not belong with the group on the north, and made no attempt to break the unwritten law which barred them. There were as many saloons and gambling houses to the north of Front Street as there were to the south, but those corresponding to Messrs. Kelley and Beatty's Alhambra, Mr. Webster's Alamo, and the Long Branch of Messrs. Beeson and Harris were held to be perfectly respectable and persons connected with them were accorded full privileges of polite intercourse. When a little church was built in the north end of town, it quickly developed a circle not unlike that of any contemporary village.

"Entirely aside from the offerings of the South Side joints, which, to read most accounts, you'd think were all the camp had in the way of recreation, there was plenty of amusement in Dodge when we could spare time for it," Wyatt Earp recalled. "Almost everyone in town did a long, hard day's work, every day in the week. We had our keep to earn and couldn't devote our lives entirely to round after round of the saloons and gambling houses, stopping now and then to shoot out a difference of opinion, and winding up each evening with a wild racket in some dance hall. Not everyone in town got drunk every day, either.

"It may surprise some to learn that the church supper was Dodge City's most popular institution. The camp ran strongly to bachelors, and what few wives and daughters of local businessmen there were followed the customs of other villages with their sewing circles, church entertainments and parties, for raising church funds. We single fellows certainly turned out for a chance at good home cooking, and usually there'd be big delegations of Texas men on hand at the suppers for the same reason. The cowboys behaved at such times and the women made them welcome.

"The only available gathering places for the run of Dodge businessmen were the saloons along Front Street. There were gambling tables and restaurants connected with each of them, they were open day and night, Sundays included, and catered to all comers. Evenings, you'd find the average Dodge City man in some Front Street saloon, yarning with friends, taking an occasional drink, or, maybe, gambling.

"But, without any attempt at whitewashing Dodge's widely advertised iniquity, I'd like to go on record with the statement that she offered a lot of fun outside her saloons and hurdy-gurdies.

"Where firearms were of such common usage, there naturally was a good deal of competitive shooting. Target matches were standard entertainment, often for high stakes and large side bets. The camp had a six-man rifle team, headed by Billy Dixon and Wes Wilcox, which kept a ten-thousand-dollar purse hung up for all comers to match and shoot at. Numerous Western camps sent their crack shots to Dodge for many a try at that purse, but the Dixon-Wilcox team never was beaten during my time in Kansas. Billy Dixon and Wes Wilcox were possibly the best rifle-shots then living.

"There was a good deal of hunting for sport, as well as business, but two attractions which lured us all, townspeople and visitors alike, were horse racing and dog coursing.

"Almost every man in Dodge had a horse or two of which he thought highly, some from the run of cow ponies, others with marked thoroughbred crosses. The same held true of about every cow outfit that came up from Texas. I had four or five animals that could show a turn of speed, Dog Kelley had several, Ham Bell had some, and so had army officers at Fort Dodge. Even the Indians would bring in their best ponies and hang around looking for match races on which the bucks would bet everything they owned. It was generally understood that any man with a horse could find a race in Dodge for any sum he cared to stake. One result was that in good weather there were races every afternoon in the week and often all day on Sundays. On more than one occasion I have seen a pair of ordinary cayuses race a quarter of a mile with thousands of dollars bet on the outcome.

"In greyhound coursing Dodge stacked up with any town in the United States for size of stakes and breeding of dogs. Mayor Kelley got his nickname 'Dog' from his devotion to this sport. His string of hounds began with a pair given to him by General Custer, but he sent to Europe for others. There were a great many fine dogs owned in and around Dodge, a number of Texas cattlemen had big kennels, army officers at the fort had some, and greyhound meetings were held regularly. The matches were run across the open range after jackrabbits, and in one match I umpired, one of Kelley's dogs coursed against an army officer's hound for a stake and side bets of more than twenty thousand dollars. We rode our ponies out to the prairie and followed the hounds across country."

In support of Wyatt's recollections of the lighter side of life in Dodge there are the reports of the cowtown journals.

Horse-racing just east of town every day now [the editor of *The Globe* records], with plenty of fun for the boys.

The Louie Lord Troupe at the Opera House last night done Guy Mannering to a delighted audience, the playing being very fine.

Messrs. Chapin and Taylor are engaged for the season by the Opera Troupe.

Foy and Thompson at the Comique are simply immense and well worth going to see.

These are followed by news of South Side recreational pursuits, a single item sufficing to provide the tenor:

The boys and girls across the Dead Line had a high old time last Friday. They sang and danced and fought and bit and cut and had a good time generally. Five knockdowns, three broken heads, two cuts, and several incidental bruises. Unfortunately none of the injuries will prove fatal.

"The closing weeks of the cattle-shipping season of '77 were fairly quiet," Wyatt commented. "We had the run of South Side fracases and heaved the daily grist into the calaboose. We made a few arrests north of the Dead Line and knocked over an occasional gun-toter, but there were no major affrays that I remember. One shooting scrape was amusing, but I probably would have forgotten all about that if it had not been for the later eminence of the principals, one, Eddie Foy the actor, and the other, also an actor at the time, Charles E. Chapin who became a newspaper editor in Chicago and New York.

"Chapin and Foy were lads who had come to Dodge with traveling theatrical companies, Foy as a comedian and Chapin in a troupe that played melodramas. Neither one could have been classed as a gunman by any stretch of the imagination, but when young Chapin got the idea that Foy was trying to steal his girl, he bought a gun and went after Eddie. He took a few potshots at his rival one night at a distance of about twenty feet and ran without checking up on the damage. As it happened, he missed Eddie completely. While we soon learned who had done the shooting, we didn't arrest Chapin, although Foy had not been armed when Chapin shot at him. I would have remembered the incident only for Foy's participation if I hadn't run into the celebrated newspaper editor, Charlie Chapin, years later and recognized him as Dodge City's worst gun-thrower of record.

"As the cattle business fell off, my brother Virgil lost interest in his job under me and started for Prescott, Arizona, then booming as a mining center. I stuck in Dodge for the fall elections, at which Bat Masterson was elected sheriff over Larry Deger by a two-to-one majority. Late in November, the Santa Fe Railroad asked me to round up the Dave Rudabaugh—Mike Roarke gang of outlaws which was robbing construction camps and pay trains.

"Rudabaugh was about the most notorious outlaw in the range country, rustler and robber by trade with the added specialty of killing jailers in the breaks for liberty at which he was invariably successful whenever he was arrested. He was the same Rudabaugh who later ran with Billy the Kid, down in the Pecos country. After a series of holdups, word came that Rudabaugh and Roarke were in Texas and as I was a deputy United States Marshal I was offered ten dollars a day and expenses if I'd go get them. I left after promising Kelley that I'd come back to Dodge City.

"Dave Rudabaugh's trail had been cold for several weeks when I took it up, but he had been reported last at Fort Griffin, Texas, some four hundred miles from Dodge. So I struck for Doan's Crossing and the Brazos.

"About the first man I met at Fort Griffin was John Shanssey, whom I had last seen when he fought Mike Donovan in the Cheyenne prize ring on the Fourth of July, '68. Shanssey was running a saloon and gambling house, and from him I learned that Dave Rudabaugh's gang had left Fort Griffin; but he didn't know whether the outlaws had headed across the Staked Plains for New Mexico or south toward the Rio Grande."

John Shanssey's Fort Griffin establishment housed bar, gambling tables, dance hall, and eating-house in one great room, thronged day and night by cowmen, prospectors, bullwhackers, mule skinners, horse thieves, cattle rustlers, scouts, soldiers, gamblers, dance-hall women, and roving adventurers, some one of whom, sooner or later, was certain to have word of Rudabaugh.

"Your best bet in this camp," the saloonkeeper told the marshal, "is Doc Holliday. Know him?"

"By reputation," Wyatt answered, "and I wouldn't figure him to be friendly toward a peace officer. He's the killer, isn't he?"

"He's killed some," Shanssey admitted, "but none around here. Doc's in my debt for some favors and will help you if I say so."

With this prelude began that extraordinary association of Doc Holliday with Wyatt Earp, which has long been cited as an enigmatic wonder of the Old West and about which so much claptrap of mysterious motive, secret design, and fantastic surmise has developed.

Doc Holliday was a hotheaded, ill-tempered, trouble-hunting, and, withal, cold-blooded desperado, rightly placed by history in the gunman-killer category of Ben Thompson, John Wesley Hardin, and Clay Allison. He was no sooner out of one scrape than he was into another, and was greatly feared and genuinely disliked by all except a very few of the men who knew him.

"Doc had few real friends," Bat Masterson said. "He was selfish and of a perverse nature, characteristics not calculated to make a man popular on the frontier. I never liked Holliday; I tolerated him and helped him at times solely on Wyatt Earp's account, as did many others. As far as I can recall, Doc had but three redeeming traits. One was his courage; he was afraid of nothing on earth. The second was the one commendable principle in his code of life, sterling loyalty to friends. The third was his affection for Wyatt Earp. The depth of this sentiment was shown not only by Doc's demonstrated willingness to stake his life for Wyatt without second thought; it was even more clearly established by the fact that, despite his almost uncontrollable temper and his maniacal love of a fight, Doc Holliday could avoid trouble when there was a possibility that some encounter might prove embarrassing to Wyatt. On more than one occasion Doc actually backed down before men whom he easily could have killed, simply because gunplay at the time would have reacted unfavorably against Wyatt. To appreciate that fully, you had to know Holliday."

In latter-day accounts Doc Holliday has been branded as the coldest-blooded killer of the West, the merit of which description no one disputes. Carried beyond the bounds of fact, however, quite possibly by the crimson hue of Holliday's colorful career, certain ones have hailed him as "the fighting ace of the Earp faction," when the most perfunctory examination of Western history establishes that where fighting was in order, the Earps could do their own.

The actual development of Doc Holliday's friendship for Wyatt Earp and its results are of considerable significance in any study of the peace officer's career. Moreover, their proper comprehension, essential to an understanding of events, is so dependent upon an accurate appraisal of Holliday, that Wyatt Earp's own estimate of his six-gun satellite may well be quoted exactly.

"Of all the nonsensical guff which has been written around my life," Wyatt commented, "there has been none more inaccurate or farfetched than that which has dealt with Doc Holliday. After Holliday died, I gave a San Francisco newspaper reporter a short sketch of his life. Apparently the reporter was not satisfied. The sketch appeared in print with a lot of things added that never existed outside the reporter's imagination, and the account repeatedly has been picked up and further manhandled.

"One shining example of the purely fictitious figure which Doc grew to be in print went like this: 'When deputized to assist the Earps in any little emergency that happened to arise, the doctor appeared with a sawed-off shotgun, deadliest of weapons, swung to his shoulder under his coat.'

"I have chosen this to illustrate my point, because Doc Holliday never carried a sawed-off shotgun into a fight but once in his life and upon this one occasion he threw the gun away in disgust after firing one shot and jerked the nickel-plated Colt's which for years was his favorite weapon.

"I am not picking on one so-called historian to the exclusion of a dozen others who have made Doc Holliday out as much that he never was; the sentence I quoted happens to be fresh in memory, although it is by no means as unfair as much of the stuff I resent. Mind me, Doc Holliday was no saint, and no one knows that better than I. But even the Devil is entitled to his due, and for reasons which will appear I'd like to see Doc Holliday get his.

"When Shanssey and I were discussing the chances of locating Dave Rudabaugh, we were sitting in a small room where Shanssey kept his strongbox and from which he commanded a view of the bar, gambling tables, and dance hall. There were times when Shanssey found it advisable to address his customers with a sawed-off shotgun in hand and the door to this room was set to provide advantage when doing so. To get hold of Doc Holliday, he merely called to a man sitting at a nearby table.

"The young fellow who came into the office was so slim as to give a mistaken impression of his height, and was unusually pallid for the plains country. He was about five feet ten inches tall, but couldn't have weighed more than one hundred and thirty pounds. If his face had not been emaciated, he might have been handsome; he looked to be a man of intelligence and good breeding. From the moment I laid eyes on him, Doc Holliday's appearance haunted me—it does to this day—with his large blue eyes set deep in a haggard face, his heavy head of wavy, ash-blond hair, and his neatly trimmed mustache, his really fine nose and his very expressive mouth.

"When Shanssey introduced us, Doc had to postpone shaking my hand until a fit of coughing passed. I then guessed what I later found to be true; he was tubercular. As a matter of fact, he had come West to die and had surprised himself by continuing to live. When he did take my hand, I had a surprise myself. In a rough-and-tumble fight Holliday could not have whipped the average fourteen-year-old boy; but the grip of his long, slender fingers was as strong and steady as steel, the secret, perhaps, of his great skill at manipulating cards and with a gun.

"When Shanssey told Holliday what I wanted, Doc said he'd learn Rudabaugh's whereabouts if I'd give him time. Within the next week or so I saw a great deal of Holliday and I learned, then and later, more than anyone else in the West knew of his earlier life and his family. Whatever attachment may have existed between us at that time was entirely one-sided. I certainly had no suspicion of anything permanent in relationship with a man who regarded every peace officer as a natural enemy. If I encouraged intimacy, it was only because I wanted information about Rudabaugh.

"Doc was born John H. Holliday, in Valdosta, Georgia, son of a major in the Confederate army. After the Civil War, the family was in financial straits, but managed to send John to Baltimore, where he studied dentistry. Just after he finished college, Holliday was warned that he had consumption and should seek the dry atmosphere of the Western plateau if he wished to live. His physician told him he couldn't last more than two or three years, at best. Doc went from Valdosta to Dallas, Texas, and opened a dental office. Doc really liked his profession. He once told me that the only times he wasn't nervous were when he was in a fight or working on someone's teeth.

"By the time I met him at Fort Griffin, Doc Holliday had run up quite a record as a killer, even for Texas. In Dallas, his incessant coughing kept away whatever professional custom he might have enjoyed and, as he had to eat, he took to gambling. He was lucky, skillful, and fearless; there were no tricks to his new trade that he did not learn and in more than one boom-camp game I have seen him bet ten thousand dollars on the turn of a card.

"Doc quickly saw that six-gun skill was essential to his new business, and set out to master the fine points of draw-and-shoot as cold-bloodedly as he did everything. He practiced with a Colt's for hours at a time, until he knew that he could get one into action as effectively as any man he might meet. His right to this opinion was justified by Doc's achievements. The only man of his type whom I ever regarded as anywhere near his equal on the draw was Buckskin Frank Leslie, of Tombstone. But Leslie lacked Doc's fatalistic courage, a courage induced, I suppose, by the nature of Holliday's disease and the realization that he hadn't long to live, anyway. That fatalism, coupled with his marvelous speed and accuracy, gave Holliday the edge over any out-and-out killer I ever knew.

"Doc's first fight in the West ended a row over a Dallas card game. He shot and killed a top-notch gunman, and as Doc was comparatively a stranger where his victim had many friends, Doc had to emigrate. He went to Jacksborough, at the edge of the Fort Richardson military reservation, where he tangled with three or four more gunmen successfully, but eventually killed a soldier and again had to take it on the run. Next, he tried the Colorado camps, where he knocked off several pretty bad men in gunfights. In Denver, Doc encountered an ordinance against gun-toting, so carried a knife, slung on a cord around his neck. Bud Ryan, a gambler, tried to run one over on Doc in a card game and when Doc objected, Ryan went for a gun he carried in a concealed holster. Doc beat him into action, with his knife, and cut him horribly.

"Doc gambled in the Colorado and Wyoming camps until the fall of '77, and fought his way out of so many arguments that, by the time he hit Fort Griffin, he had built up a thoroughly deserved reputation as a man who would shoot to kill on the slightest provocation. The reputation may have had some bearing on the fact that when I first met him, he had not yet found anyone in Fort Griffin to provide him with a battle.

"It was in Shanssey's saloon, I think, that Doc Holliday first met Kate Fisher, a dance-hall girl better known as 'Big-Nosed Kate.' Doc lived with Kate, off and on, over a period of years. She saved his life on one occasion, and when memory of this was uppermost Doc would refer to Kate as Mrs. Holliday. Their relationship had its temperamental ups and downs, however, and when Kate was writhing under Doc's scorn she'd get drunk as well as furious and make Doc more trouble than any shooting scrape.

"Perhaps Doc's outstanding peculiarity was the enormous amount of whiskey he could punish. Two and three quarts of liquor a day was not unusual for him, yet I never saw him stagger with intoxication. At times when his tuberculosis was worse than ordinary, or he was under a long-continued physical strain, it would take a pint of whiskey to get him going in the morning, and more than once at the end of a long ride I've seen him swallow a tumbler of neat liquor without batting an eye and fifteen minutes later take a second tumbler of straight whiskey which had no more outward effect on him than the first one. Liquor never seemed to fog him in the slightest, and he was more inclined to fight when getting along on a slim ration than when he was drinking plenty, and was more comfortable, physically.

"With all of Doc's shortcomings and his undeniably poor disposition, I found him a loyal friend and good company. At the time of his death, I tried to set down the qualities about him which had impressed me. The newspapers dressed up my ideas considerably and had me calling Doc Holliday 'a mad, merry scamp with heart of gold and nerves of steel.' Those were not my words, nor did they convey my meaning. Doc was mad, well enough, but he was seldom merry. His humor ran in a sardonic vein, and as far as the

197

world in general was concerned, there was nothing in his soul but iron. Under ordinary circumstances he might be irritable to the point of shakiness; only in a game or when a fight impended was there anything steely about his nerves.

"To sum up Doc Holliday's character as I did at the time of his death: he was a dentist whom necessity had made a gambler; a gentleman whom disease had made a frontier vagabond; a philosopher whom life had made a caustic wit; a long, lean, ash-blond fellow nearly dead with consumption and at the same time the most skillful gambler and the nerviest, speediest, deadliest man with a six-gun I ever knew."

Within a week after their meeting, Doc Holliday brought word to Wyatt Earp that Dave Rudabaugh had gone to Fort Davis, west of the Pecos and more than five hundred miles away. At Fort Davis the marshal found that, while Holliday's information had been correct, Rudabaugh had left that camp for Fort Clark. From Fort Clark the outlaw's trail led to Fort Concho, to Fort McKavett, then back to Fort Griffin, which Wyatt reached for the second time on January 20, 1878, learning upon arrival that in his absence Doc Holliday had killed Ed Bailey in a fight over a poker game.

Bailey's friends in Fort Griffin were numerous. Doc had none in the camp except Big-Nosed Kate and John Shanssey. The dance-hall girl met the emergency. The Fort Griffin marshal was holding Doc a prisoner in a hotel room while Bailey's friends absorbed the stimulus for a lynching-bee at the adjoining bar. Kate Fisher threw a few of her own and her lover's belongings into a bag, took two saddle-ponies to a convenient spot, and then set fire to the rear end of the hotel.

As the redoubtable woman had foreseen, every free man in Fort Griffin but one ran out to fight the flames, the dreaded scourge of flimsy frontier settlements, and Doc was left with a single guard. Six-gun in hand, Kate stepped into the room and ordered the surprised deputy to throw up his hands, took his guns and ammunition, rearmed Doc with his favorite Colt's, and hustled her lover out to the waiting ponies. By the time the fire had been extinguished and pursuit organized, Doc and Big-Nosed Kate were miles away on an unknown trail. Weeks later, Doc sent a teamster to John Shanssey for his trunk and by him a message for Wyatt Earp, which was that he'd see the marshal in Dodge City.

At Fort Griffin, Wyatt now had word from Dodge that Rudabaugh's gang had doubled on their trail of the preceding fall and again ridden north into Kansas to hold up a Santa Fe pay train at Kinsley, Kansas, and steal ten thousand dollars. Bat Masterson had led a posse which surprised the robbers in camp on the southern trail, Rudabaugh had been arrested, but Mike Roarke had escaped. Wyatt's new orders were to find Roarke, and about April 1, after trailing him over half of Texas, Wyatt rode into San Antonio less than forty-eight hours behind the fugitive, to learn that Roarke was making for his old home near Joplin, Missouri. Wyatt reached the Missouri city ahead of his quarry, and was awaiting the outlaw's arrival when he received a message from Dog Kelley urging him to return at once to Dodge. Kelley had been reelected mayor by a vote of 200-to-13, but was ending his first term and beginning his second in the midst of difficulties with which Ed Masterson, as marshal, seemed unable to cope. His problems were set forth repeatedly in items by the Dodge City journalists.

"Some of the 'boys' in direct violation of the city ordinances carry firearms on our streets without being called to account for the same," the editor of *The Globe* complained on March 5, 1878. "They do so in such an open manner that it doesn't seem possible that our city officers are in ignorance of the fact."

From week to week *The Globe* renewed caustic criticism, observing that, despite a police strength increased to a marshal and three assistants, the wild bunch which heralded the arrival of another cattle-shipping season was standing Dodge on her ear and breaking every ordinance in the municipal books.

On April 9, Ed Masterson was killed in a gunfight with Jack Wagner and Alf Walker.

A few weeks earlier, Wyatt Earp's substitute had diverged from the main business before him to argue with a gun-toter about the right and the wrong of the ordinance he was attempting to enforce. While Masterson was talking, the gunman shot him through the shoulder. Ed drew and shot as he fell, and downed the cowboy with a slug through his hips. The officer had barely recovered from this experience when Wagner and Walker flaunted their opinion of his official ability in the face of the entire camp by shooting up Front Street in good, old-fashioned style. Instead of putting these disturbers out of business and remonstrating later, Ed again chose to do his talking first.

Bat Masterson, who helped Ed in handling local law-breakers as his sheriff's duties allowed, rounded the corner of Second Avenue on the way to his brother's assistance just in time to see Walker and Wagner down the marshal. Ham Bell, who witnessed the shooting from a window of the Lone Star, has told me of what followed.

Bat Masterson, fully sixty feet away as his brother fell, fired four shots. The first slug hit Wagner squarely in the pit of the stomach and killed him. Bat came on, shooting at Walker, who was shooting back. Walker was hit three times, once in the lung, and twice in the right arm. None of his shots at Bat took effect. With his gun arm out of commission, the cowboy turned and ran for cover in the Lone Star.

"Catch me!" Walker gasped to Ham Bell as he reeled through the door. "Catch me! I'm dying."

"That corner's as good a place as any," Ham replied, and, as no one in the place offered additional succor, Walker went on out the rear door. He escaped Bat's further vengeance because the sheriff believed that Walker was mortally wounded and because word that his brother had but a few minutes to live was shouted to him from Hoover's saloon, into which place Ed had been carried. Walker got down the trail into Texas, where he died of pneumonia induced by the lung wound.

For days following Ed Masterson's death, the cowboys played havoc with the ordinances, hoorahed the Front Street establishments as thoroughly as they did the South Side district, and so cowed the citizens that Bat Masterson was unable to recruit a force adequate to restore order. Only lack of numbers due to the earliness of the season prevented the gunmen from taking over Dodge completely.

On April 30, *The Globe* announced that the season's first large herds of northbound Texas cattle had forded the Red River at Doan's Store, with 265,000 head in the vanguard in charge of 1300 cowboys and 250 owners, and that the leaders would reach Dodge about May 15. In the same issue the editor chronicled several gunfights and the burial on Boot Hill of several losers in such arguments. This item was followed by the announcement that the Dodge City Council was about to prohibit further burials on Boot Hill and was looking for a suitable piece of ground which might be set aside for purposes which Boot Hill theretofore had served.

In *The Globe* for the week of May 7, the editor commented that street fights were too numerous to recount.

On the morning of May 12, Wyatt Earp reached Dodge in response to Mayor Kelley's message. At noon, with his marshal's badge and his guns in place, he walked down Front Street to meet two Texas men who came across the Dead Line with pistols slung openly from their hips.

The cowboys were turning into the Long Branch when Wyatt stopped them.

"You can't wear guns in this end of town," the marshal announced.

"Who said so?" the Texans rejoined, or words to that effect.

For answer each was buffaloed so quickly and so effectively that neither knew an eighteen-inch Colt's had been bent over his head until he recovered consciousness in the calaboose. The balance of that day, and several to follow, Wyatt Earp devoted to dealing in similar fashion with Texans and others who refused to believe that he had returned to Dodge with a purpose.

"I always disliked beating up the general run of cowboys," Wyatt said, "and I could handle many of them without employing extreme measures. But at that particular time their long period of license had made the whole crowd so unruly that the only way to get the situation in hand was to knock over every man who looked twice at me."

In *The Globe* for May 14, all local news is subordinated to this brief item:

> Wyatt Earp, the most efficient officer Dodge ever had, has just returned from Texas. He was immediately reappointed Marshal by our City Dads, much to their credit.
>
> Hurry up with that new cemetery [the editor suggests pointedly]. We know not the day, or the hour.

That week the first of the large herds reached the banks of the Arkansas, three outfits arriving at Dodge on the 19th and seven more on the 20th, whereupon the South Side boiled.

> Bill Thompson, well known on the cattle trail in Texas and Kansas, arrived last week [*The Globe* records in its summary of news of the drives].
>
> Numerous cowboys "under the influence" in town yesterday.
>
> We understand that a "brace" game was dealt from the outside last week; this ain't the usual way it comes.

Immediately subsequent issues of *The Globe* furnished numerous accounts of fracases and fights in which cowboys figured, each notable only for the fact that participants ran afoul of Wyatt Earp and wound up in the calaboose. On June 18, *The Globe* sums up a week of Wyatt's accomplishments thus:

> Three dancehalls in full blast on the South Side, stables jammed full, hundreds of cowboys perambulate daily, but two cases in police court. Who says we aren't a moral city!
>
> Wyatt Earp is doing his duty as a marshal, adding new laurels to his splendid record every day.

Upon his return to Dodge, Wyatt had found Dr. and Mrs. John H. Holliday—otherwise, Doc and Big-Nosed Kate—living in the most luxurious fashion that Deacon Cox's Dodge House offered. Doc was at the height of a long run of good luck at the gambling tables and, as far as trouble was concerned, the pair were exemplary citizens.

In a camp the size of Dodge, Wyatt naturally met Doc frequently in casual fashion. But, to the best of Wyatt's recollection, he held Holliday in no particular esteem until the gunfighting dentist took a hand in a game of life and death which had been stacked against the marshal.

16

Doc Holliday Calls the Turn

While dissatisfaction over Wyatt Earp's reappointment as marshal of Dodge again was profanely and forcefully expressed by a minority element of business boomers—to which the visiting cowmen wholeheartedly subscribed—it is a matter of record that he speedily restored his forty-five-caliber rule over the cowtown. The season was to set a new peak for the cattle trade. Money was in hand in far greater sums than the Texas men, the gamblers, and the frequenters of South Side establishments had ever seen, yet, week in and week out, *The Globe* found no police news worth printing.

By late July, however, the cumulative effect of Wyatt's steady manhandling of Texas celebrants had once more aroused resentment to the point where a conspiracy to get rid of him was discussed openly. When an attempt of cowmen to carry a wild celebration across the Dead Line ended with sore heads in the calaboose, it was followed by a renewal of the one thousand dollars bounty on Wyatt's head which had been advertised in the preceding summer.

"Getting Wyatt Earp was another matter," Bob Vandenberg told me.

Vandenberg reached Dodge City in 1872 and remained until the close of the trail-driving era. He was deputy sheriff of Ford County, and marshal of Dodge from '81 to '85.

"Ordinarily, when the cowboys wanted to put some man out of the way," Bob Vandenberg said, "one of their top-notch gun-artists would goad the other fellow into a fight, after which the cowboy could plead self-defense, or a crowd would start a gunplay so mixed up that no one could tell who did the killing. They usually paved the way for this by getting their victim pretty well liquored before the shooting started, in which shape he'd be easy for a sober gunman. Another method was to get some dance-hall girl to do the dirty work, and first thing the marshal knew he'd be paying more attention to the girl than he did to his job. If the victim wasn't decoyed into a fix where some gun-thrower could knock him off, he'd get so tied up with the dance-hall crowd that the authorities would have to fire him.

"Wyatt Earp was too good a general to let any bunch of cowpunchers head him into a jam. There wasn't a man on the plains who'd go against him in a gunplay that was anything like an even break, and the way he'd come out on top in any number of scrapes where the odds were all against him had cured the Texans of any idea they could gang him. He didn't drink, and I never heard so much as a suspicion that Wyatt had what you might call an entangling alliance in any South Side dance hall; his worst enemy never hinted that he could be bribed. Wyatt had his shortcomings, but, except for overconfidence in his friends, they weren't the kind to head him into trouble.

"I knew Wyatt intimately for years, and it has struck me that two of his outstanding qualities have been overlooked in the efforts to play up his courage. Mind you, I'm not belittling that; no braver man than Wyatt ever lived. But two things in his makeup that I would like to see credited were his generalship and his sense of duty.

"I spent four years in the United States Cavalry, on

Western campaigns with and under some of the most famous scouts and Indian fighters this country knew, and I was a cowtown peace officer, marshal and sheriff, for ten years more. In all that time I knew no keener, shrewder strategist than Wyatt Earp, nor any man in whom the sense of duty was more deeply rooted. Once Wyatt made up his mind that he was under moral obligation to accomplish a certain end, all hell couldn't hold him from the course he decided upon. And moral obligation to the law was one thing that few men on the frontier could comprehend."

The first attempt in the season of '78 to collect the bounty on Wyatt's head was made July 26. Eddie Foy and his partner, Jim Thompson, were playing at the Comique Theater, and as Wyatt's duties precluded his presence inside the theater, he stood in the street just outside the thin board stage wall where he could hear the songs and jokes, while keeping an eye and an ear out for trouble.

Foy had just started his celebrated "Kalamazoo in Michigan" when Wyatt noticed a horseman pass in the road, turn, and jog by again. A block away he turned once more and came down the road at a gallop. As the pony sped by the point where Wyatt stood, the roar of a forty-five and a flash of flame sent a heavy slug through the plank at the marshal's side, across the stage, and into the opposite wall. A second, then a third bullet followed.

Inside the theater, Eddie Foy has written, the act terminated suddenly in the scream of lead. The comedian threw himself flat on the stage and half of his audience dropped from their seats to the floor.

Outside, Wyatt went into action toward the horseman, jerking his Colt's as he jumped.

The rider had a mount of more spirit than steadiness. At the roar of gunfire the cayuse shied, plunged, and reared. Wyatt grabbed for the pony's tail with his left hand, to throw himself onto the animal's hindquarters and hold himself so closely against the pony's legs that he could not be hurt by flying hoofs while his weight would be more effective than hobbles against a speedy getaway. As he lunged, so did the pony, and Wyatt missed the hold. The rider shot at Wyatt again, and missed. The bucking spoiled his aim.

Wyatt shot in reply, but also missed, as the pony jumped sideways, and was off toward the toll bridge on a dead run. The horseman turned in his saddle and fired once more, flipping the brim of the marshal's sombrero with the slug. Wyatt squatted on his haunches to bring his target into greater relief against the dark sky and shot a second time. The pony's hoofs clattered on the bridge at a decreasing pace, then halted. The rider had fallen from the saddle, and at the south end of the bridge Wyatt found him, unconscious, with a bullet through the small of his back. At the calaboose Dr. McCarty pronounced him mortally wounded.

Next morning the wounded man was identified as George Hoyt, a Texas cowboy, but, as he recovered consciousness only to go into a delirium, Wyatt was unable to question him. Hoyt was still delirious when Wyatt took leave of absence from his marshal's job.

Kansas took her politics seriously, and in her formative years the interparty differences often were acrimonious to the point of bloodiness. Internal dissensions and factional disputes regularly split the major groups to the extent that neither Republicans nor Democrats could rely upon their delegates to caucuses and conventions to carry out the instructions of the electorate. Both parties were sold out from the inside repeatedly. In the unusually bitter campaign of '78, the Republicans were attempting to reunite their wrangling ranks by the selection of leaders who could be depended upon to carry out instructions. Wyatt Earp went as Dodge City's delegate to the Republican State Convention held at Topeka, the second week in August, and as the delegate of Ford County Republicans to the Congressional Convention which followed.

The Globe for August 27 reports:

George Hoyt, the Texas cowboy, died on Wednesday, August 21st, and was buried on Boot Hill in grand style.

Wyatt returned from the Congressional Convention to learn that as Hoyt was dying he had given full information concerning the plot against the marshal, other than identities of the men who had hired him for the killing. *The Globe* verified and later published Hoyt's story.

The cowboy, it appeared, had come to Dodge a fugitive from Texas justice. Hoyt said that certain influential cattlemen had promised him that if he killed Wyatt Earp, the Texas warrant against him would be quashed and that he would be paid one thousand dollars. With this assertion on his lips, he died.

On August 6, *The Globe* had published the following item of significance:

> Dutch Henry is again on his old stamping ground south of Dodge.

About a week after Hoyt's death, two shots were fired at Wyatt as he walked along First Avenue. The gunman sat his pony in the shadows of a cross-street and as he fired wheeled, turned, and galloped for the toll bridge. Neither shot hit the marshal and Wyatt commandeered the first cow pony to hand in a string nearby.

Beyond the south bridgehead, Wyatt could see the rider streaking down the trail which branched toward the camp of the Dutch Henry–Tom Owens gang of rustlers. Chancing a shortcut, he reached the outlaws' fire in time to see Tom Owens rip the saddle from a pony and drop down with four or five of his fellows. Dismounting, Wyatt walked straight to Owens.

"Get up!" he commanded.

Dutch Henry edged away from the light. He stopped as Wyatt's gun flashed from his holster.

"On your feet, all of you, hands in the air!" Wyatt ordered. The rustlers obeyed and Wyatt disarmed them.

"Head for town, Owens," the marshal continued. "You're walking, I'm riding behind you."

Wyatt slung the collection of confiscated belts and weapons over his saddle horn.

"Get going, Owens," he said. "The rest of you'll find your guns wherever you find Owens in the morning. In the meantime, keep out of Dodge."

On the way into town, Wyatt wrung from Owens the admission that the horse thief had hoped to collect the thousand-dollar bounty on the marshal's head, although Owens swore he had no definite knowledge of who was to pay the money for the killing. Wyatt locked the outlaw in the calaboose for the night, saw him fined one hundred dollars in court the next morning, and started him for his camp on foot, carrying the weapons which had been confiscated from his associates.

"Don't come into Dodge again, any of you, as long as I'm in town," Wyatt warned the rustler.

Owens was another individual who owed his life to a magnanimity which Bat Masterson criticized sharply, but there may be some justification for Wyatt's attitude in the fact that thereafter, while the Owens–Henry gang operated extensively in Kansas, none of the leaders ever ventured into Wyatt Earp's bailiwick.

The summer of '78 had been marked by weather conditions which kept the beef market booming until late in the fall.

On September 16, word was brought to Dodge that a large band of Northern Cheyenne Indians under Chief Dull Knife had broken out of Indian Territory, and were making for their old home in the Dakotas, pillaging ranches, homesteads, and white settlements. Troops were sent in pursuit, but when the red warriors crossed the Cimarron at the Kansas Line, raided Meade City, a trading post on Crooked Creek, and pillaged the Chapman and Tuttle Ranch on the Mulberry eighteen miles from the cowtown, Wyatt Earp went out at the head of a force of civilian volunteers to reinforce the cavalry. His part in the chase ended when he returned to town about September 24, with a few Indian prisoners placed in his custody by the military authorities.

Wyatt barely had locked his prisoners in the Ford County jail when some twenty-five Texas cowmen, under the leadership of his ancient enemies, Tobe Driskill and that Ed

Morrison whom he had run out of Wichita, rode into Dodge under the impression that Wyatt was still absent, and with the single purpose of hurrahing the camp as they long had felt she must be hurrahed for the satisfaction of Texas.

There is small doubt that the instigators of the cowboy expedition were Tobe Driskill, nursing his memory of a manhandling by Wyatt Earp, and Ed Morrison, whose grudge against Dodge was in reality one against that same marshal, but dating back to the Shanghai Pierce affair in Wichita. Furthermore, in view of subsequent records made as peace officers, it is of interest to note that two of the Driskill–Morrison troublemakers on this occasion were none other than Pat Garrett and Smoky Hill Thompson.

The Driskill–Morrison outfit left their chuck wagon at Cimarron Crossing, west of Dodge, late in the afternoon. The wagon was to continue southward while the riders were taking Dodge by surprise, shooting up the South Side honky-tonks, shaking up sacrosanct Front Street, hightailing the citizenry, and otherwise disporting themselves in such forty-five-caliber pleasantries as opportunity and a few quick drinks might combine to inspire.

Driskill and Morrison led their gun-toters into Dodge by way of Front Street to Second Avenue, crossed the railroad, and dismounted in front of a saloon, where they fed and tethered their ponies and from which point they figured to make their getaway once such fighting men as might be left in Dodge gave signs of getting organized. The cowboys ate an early meal at a South Side restaurant, and then, with the streets of Dodge deserted for the supper hour, went into uproarious action.

To the best recollection of Dodge citizens who saw something of the Driskill–Morrison raid, the cowboys devoted less than five minutes to the South Side joints, and headed across the Dead Line, whooping, shooting, and inviting Dodge out to oppose them. Their first stop on the North Side was a saloon at the corner of Front Street and Fourth Avenue, where they ran the bartender and a few hangers-on to cover, helped themselves to liquor, wrecked the interior, and piled out again. Thence they hurrahed

Front Street systematically, every light and every pane of glass they saw a target for fifty six-shooters.

As the Texans proceeded eastward toward the camp's main four-corners, their evident intentions so disorganized Dodge's customary aplomb that, as the cowboys moved, the lights in various establishments ahead of them were doused by frantic merchants and saloon-keepers as they and their patrons took to Tin Can Alley. Front Street was soon in darkness, except for the incessant flares from the roaring six-guns and the glow through the windows of the single place of business which had not completely abandoned camp to the mercy of the gunmen—the Long Branch Saloon, in which Cockeyed Frank Loving sat dealing faro for a lean, pale-faced, ash-blond gambler who could not be chased from a run of luck by all the gun-throwers in Texas.

When the cowboys fired their first fusillade, Wyatt Earp was at the northeast edge of town feeding his Indian prisoners. By the time he had his charges locked up for the night, the cowboys had been across the Dead Line for some minutes.

As Wyatt turned into Front Street, the Texas gang was at Second Avenue, showering lead along that cross-thoroughfare. As the marshal reached First Avenue, the cowboys were in front of Wright and Beverly's. Wyatt noted the light in the Long Branch, and hurried to reach that doorway and one of his shotguns, ahead of the Texans. He was late by the fraction of a second. Driskill and Morrison were at the door discussing in loud voices what they'd do to the Long Branch when Wyatt stepped from the shadow. For a moment, possibly, the cowboys were startled, but liquid courage made them quick to act on their advantage.

Wyatt's Colt's were in their holsters. Each cowboy had a pair of guns in his hands. Furthermore, every Texan was sufficiently flushed with alcohol and success to be at his deadliest.

"By God," Driskill roared, "it's Earp!"

"You son-of-a-bitch," Morrison added, "I've waited five years for this!"

211

"I owe him some myself," Driskill observed, with a string of epithets.

"We've got him," Morrison said, "and, by God, he's going to get it! You're such a fighter, Earp; here's your chance to do some."

Morrison called to the crowd behind him.

"If he makes a move, boys, let him have it."

He addressed himself once more to Wyatt.

"You white-livered Northern this-and-that," he raged, "if you've got any praying to do, get at it."

That night in Dodge was one of two occasions in Wyatt's career when he figured he was about to go out with his boots on.

"Those Texans were in an ugly mood," he recalled. "They had held the upper hand long enough to make them believe they could maintain it; they had taken on enough liquor to be vicious, but not enough to be unsteady; they were led by men who hated me; they had me at complete disadvantage as far as gunplay went, and a getaway so well arranged as to be almost a certainty. Those last two items always influenced the cowboy attitude.

"While Driskill and Morrison were threatening me, I was trying to get where I could make one jump through the Long Branch door, and the only praying I did was that the door hadn't been locked. There was a chance I could make such a jump, or that I might get so close to Driskill or Morrison that with all the talking they were doing, I could catch one of them off guard long enough to shove a gun into his belly, while he shielded me from the rest. I hadn't much hope that either move would succeed, but I didn't dare jerk a gun until I was ready for one or the other. I had edged almost to the doorway, with my eye on Morrison while he cursed me. Then I saw a look in his eye that made me abandon all ideas but that of taking a few Texans with me to where I knew I was going.

"It all took place in so much less time than is required to tell about it that the speed of the action is hard to make clear. Not more than two minutes elapsed from the time the cowboys first saw me until Morrison told me a second time to hurry with my prayers. Like all Texans of his stripe, he had to do a certain amount of bragging before he got down to shooting. I recall his final threat as vividly as though he made it yesterday.

" 'Pray, you son-of-a-bitch,' he said, 'or jerk your gun and—' "

"Throw 'em up!" challenged a voice at Wyatt's shoulder as the door of the Long Branch burst open and a long, lean, ash-blond individual with a six-gun in either hand leaped into silhouette against the light.

"Throw 'em up, you blank-dashed so-and-so murdering cow thieves!"

"There were times," Wyatt commented, "when Doc Holliday swore beautifully, and what I next heard over my shoulder—I didn't dare look around—made Morrison's ranting sound like a Sunday School lesson.

"The interruption was all I needed. Before Driskill, Morrison, or any of their crowd caught up with their surprise, I had jerked both my guns, and there we stood, Doc and I, with four guns against fifty, but with the break closer to even."

To understand what had happened, it is necessary to revert to the time at which the cowboys made their move on Front Street and business places were deserted in the path of their roaring progress. Messrs. Beeson, Harris, and Short were absent from the Long Branch at supper; a bartender was in charge, with Cockeyed Frank Loving dealing faro for the benefit of Doc Holliday. When everyone else in the place decamped ahead of the oncoming cowboys, the bartender reported, Loving and Holliday continued their game without comment that he heard before he fled to the alley.

Frank Loving was a cool, courageous fellow who would have gone quickly to Wyatt's assistance. He said later that, before he could move, Doc Holliday had run to the six-shooter rack at the end of the bar, grabbed his own nickel-plated weapon which hung there and another beside it, and jumped through the door.

Under the guns of Doc Holliday and Wyatt Earp, the temper of the Texas crowd altered instantaneously. Doc was quick to turn their hesitancy to advantage.

"What'll we do with 'em, Wyatt?" he asked as though the question of ascendancy had been fully determined.

In reply, Wyatt Earp took a single step toward Ed Morrison and, before that individual or any of his followers sensed what was happening, laid the barrel of his Buntline Special over the cowboy's head. Morrison dropped as though he had been shot instead of buffaloed.

"Throw 'em up!" Wyatt commanded. "All the way and empty! You, Driskill! You're next!"

Six-shooters clattered to the walk as the cowboys' hands went skyward, but in the rear of the crowd, one Texan took a chance.

"Look out, Wyatt!"

Quicker than speech, however, Doc cut loose at the cowboy who tried a potshot at the marshal. Two reports roared almost as one, but a howl of pain established the accuracy of Holliday's gunfire—the cowboy was a split-second late and missed.

"Years afterward it was told that Doc Holliday killed that Texan," Wyatt said. "He didn't. He hit him in the shoulder. The result disappointed Doc, but it was all I needed.

"With the gang grabbing air, Doc and I herded them across the tracks and into the calaboose. Then we went back and picked up about fifty guns in front of the Long Branch. Next morning Driskill and Morrison were fined one hundred dollars apiece, and each of the others, twenty-five dollars. I put their guns in a couple of gunnysacks and told them not to distribute them until they were well out of town. What's more, they minded me, and the last I saw of that crowd they were riding off to catch their chuck wagon. I never heard that they painted 'Dodge' on the cover, either.

"One thing I've always believed: if it hadn't been for Doc Holliday, I'd have cashed in that night. There was no real call for Doc to make the play he did; everybody else in camp had hightailed it, including some of my deputies, and why Doc wasn't knocked off is more than I can tell you. He wasn't, and if anyone ever questions the motive of my loyalty to Doc Holliday, there's my answer. In the old days, neither Doc nor I bothered to make explanations; I never was given to such things and in our case they would have been contrary to Doc's sense of decency. The only way anyone could have appreciated the feeling I always had for Doc after the Driskill–Morrison business would have been to have stood in my boots at the time Doc came through the Long Branch doorway."

The termination of the Driskill–Morrison raid marked the end of organized opposition to Wyatt Earp's rule over the cowtown. Further resistance to his enforcement of the local ordinances was an enterprise in which the few individuals who attempted it could find no wholesale backing. Whatever criticism a later generation may make of Wyatt's tactics, this record of their accomplishment is the point invariably emphasized by those who had firsthand acquaintance with the frontier marshal's problems.

17

Dodge City Goes Humdrum

"The Comique Theater is closed for the season. The hurrah-look which pervaded our streets is gone, and we now linger in peace," the editor of *The Globe* observed as the month of September 1878 drew to a close in Dodge City. "It looks," he added, "like a slow winter."

Seven days later, the weekly blazoned news of the first killing in a long and lurid list of deaths by violence which Dodge, as a community, was inclined to view as unjustifiable homicide.

Murder was a term but rarely employed in the language of cowcamp courts. There were killings aplenty, but if killer and killed were armed, the unwritten law of "the even break" ordinarily established justification. A fine might be imposed for carrying the weapon with which the killing was done; where the death occurred below the Dead Line, there often was no official cognizance whatsoever. When prisoners were arraigned for killings, courts were notoriously lax and susceptible to improper influence none too surreptitiously brought to bear—procedure which was responsible for the frontier Vigilante societies as well as the preference of marshals for keeping the law in their own competent hands.

In the course of business as joint proprietor of the Alhambra Saloon and Gambling-House, Mayor Dog Kelley had ejected one Jim Kennedy from his establishment with more force than thoughtfulness. Jim was the son of Captain Mifflin Kennedy, whose partner, Richard King, gave the term cattle king to Western idiom, whose firm of King and Kennedy owned the largest cattle ranch in Texas and drove the largest trail-herds to Kansas.

In planning revenge, Jim Kennedy elected to kill Kelley in his sleep, by shooting through the flimsy wall of the bedroom at the front of the mayor's two-room shack which Kelley customarily occupied. Unknown to Kennedy, Kelley had rented his shack to Dora Hand and Fannie Garrettson, belles of the Dodge City dance halls. Dora Hand was in the bed which Dog Kelley previously had used and Kennedy's bullet killed her instantly.

As the roar of the gunfire echoed in the street, Kennedy was seen riding due west out of Dodge at breakneck speed, but it was almost certain that he would try to reach The Indian Nations, where he would be reasonably safe from Kansas authorities. At this time, it must be borne in mind, Kennedy did not know that he had killed a woman. If his luck had been good, as he saw it, he had simply knocked off the mayor of Dodge, an achievement for which he most certainly would not be delivered to an avenging posse by any man below the Cimarron.

It has been generally conceded by the men and women pioneers of Dodge City that, saint or sinner, Dora Hand was the most graciously beautiful woman to reach the camp in the heyday of its iniquity, and in no other community on earth is it probable that she could have occupied the anomalous position in which the cowtown placed her. By night, she was Queen of the Fairy Belles, as old Dodge termed its dance-hall women, entertaining drunken cowhands after all the fashions that her calling demanded. By day, she was the Lady Bountiful of the prairie settlement, a demurely clad, intensely practical, generous, forceful woman, to whom no appeal for the succor of another's trouble would go unheeded. Once, Dora Hand had been a singer in grand opera. In Dodge, she sang of nights in the bars and honky-tonks. On Sundays, clad in simple black, she crossed the Dead Line to the little church on the North Side hill to lead the hymns and anthems in a voice at which those who heard her forever after marveled. A quick change of attire after the Sunday evening service, and she was back at her trade in the dance hall. Every man and woman in Dodge, good, bad or indifferent, knew all sides of Dora Hand's life among them, and, as one of them put it, fifty years after: "The only thing anyone could hold against her was her after-dark profession, and, by Godfrey, I'm allowing she elevated that considerably."

Because Wyatt Earp, who held the commission of Deputy United States Marshal jointly with his municipal office, could be relied upon to take Jim Kennedy from under the guns of all his father's henchmen, the mayor ordered Wyatt to lead a posse after the fugitive. Wyatt selected Bat Masterson, Charlie Bassett, and Bill Tilghman, and the quartet took the trail a few hours behind their quarry.

"Bring him in alive, Wyatt," Kelley told his marshal. "Dodge'll want to deal with him as a community."

Kennedy's ruse of riding west convinced Wyatt that the fugitive would avoid the Jones and Plummer Trail, and circle to ford the Cimarron near Wagon Bed Springs, about seventy miles from Dodge, whence he could cut the Texas Trail well down in The Nations. To those not skilled as plainsmen, any attempt to cut across country for this ford would have been disastrous; Wyatt's posse struck out over the prairie.

Late in the afternoon, the posse was hit by a hailstorm of such ferocity that the men were forced to seek shelter for their frantic animals under a stream bank. When the hail ceased, they rode the rest of the night through a terrific downpour of rain which drenched and blinded them and did not stop until dawn the next morning. Yet sunup found the posse within a mile of the ford which was their destination. Examination showed that no horseman had crossed the Cimarron since the rain, and Wyatt did not believe that Kennedy could have reached the ford in time to have had the storm obliterate his tracks entirely.

Near the crossing was a homesteader's sod house, forerunner of the thousands which were to force the cattle herds from all the Kansas trails, and to this the posse turned for information and breakfast. They learned that no rider was known to have passed since before the storm set in, fed their tired ponies, and arranged to take turns watching the trail while breakfast was under way. The men had barely finished eating when Bill Tilghman reported a horseman heading in from the north. Through his field glass Wyatt identified Kennedy. To forestall possible injury to the homesteader's family, the marshal took his posse away from the house to a bank of earth which had been thrown up in sinking a well.

"We'll stop him out here," Wyatt said. "I don't think he'll make a fight; most likely he'll run for it."

"If he does," cut in Bat Masterson, "I'll drop him."

"Shoot his horse," Wyatt ordered. "Kelley wants Kennedy alive. Stop his horse and we'll get the man."

"I'll kill him if he makes a run," Bat insisted.

Developments vindicated Wyatt's method of man-hunting as against that advocated by Masterson. At a range of approximately fifty yards, Kennedy sighted the posse and wheeled his horse as Wyatt shouted a command to halt. Bat shot first with his rifle. Kennedy lurched in his saddle, but recovered and kept on. Then Wyatt cut loose.

"I hated to do it," he admitted in recounting the incident. "Kennedy's horse was a beauty. My first slug hit the horse in the barrel just back of the foreleg. He dropped in the middle of his stride, pinning Kennedy."

When the posse pulled Kennedy from under the dying animal, they found that Bat's rifle bullet had shattered the Texan's right arm, but that otherwise he was uninjured. Kennedy's first question was for Dog Kelley.

"Did I kill him?" he asked.

Wyatt told his prisoner that the bullet intended for the mayor had killed Dora Hand. Noting the rifle in Masterson's hand, Kennedy turned on Bat in sudden rage.

"You blank-dash so-and-so of a this-and-that," he snarled, "you ought to have made a better shot than you did."

"Well," the astounded Bat managed to reply, "you blank-blanked murdering son-of-a-likewise, I did the best I could."

When Wyatt reached Dodge with his prisoner, the county authorities asserted jurisdiction. Kennedy's wealthy father was summoned from Texas, and, after proceedings at which Dodge City officials protested vainly, Dora Hand's murderer was freed on the ground that convicting evidence could not be marshaled against him. His father took him back to Texas.

With the last of the cowmen off on the Southern trail, Dodge City settled down to that slow winter which the editor of *The Globe* had prophesied. Between cattle seasons but two events were chronicled as of sufficient interest to stir the camp from cold-weather lethargy. One was a religious revival about which the editor of *The Globe* could arouse no enthusiasm; the second was the cowcamp's first baby contest, which stirred Dodge well-nigh to frenzy, and in which the irrepressible Messrs. Earp and Masterson stole the show from married acquaintances with a more vital interest in the competition.

After several abortive attempts at founding a church, on the part of overly zealous ministers whose dogmatic tendencies the cowboy capital resented, the Reverend O. W. Wright had come to town with a tolerant, broad-gauge brand of religion, appealing strongly to Dodge through the common quality of its creed and the humanism of its preacher. When the Reverend Mr. Wright observed that he needed a church, the Front Street gambling houses, in two days of play, "kittied" out enough money to build one for him, and that with rough lumber at fifty dollars a thousand. Further evidence of the Reverend Mr. Wright's standing in Dodge is to be found in the record that Marshal Wyatt Earp and

Sheriff Bat Masterson were chosen as his deacons, thereby solving in advance any problems of congregational deportment.

The wives and daughters of Dodge City's few businessmen, who formed the first Ladies' Aid Society, promptly started to raise a missionary fund, for the bulk of which they were dependent upon the liberal souls who frequented the Plaza hangouts. Throughout the cattle-shipping season these women rang the changes of church suppers and box socials; with the cowboys gone, they cast about for another method of money-raising.

Someone in the Ladies' Aid discovered that there were a half-dozen yearling citizens in the camp, and arranged a babies' popularity contest, the only conditions being that candidates for honors must be under one year of age and Dodge City born. Decision was to be reached through votes cast for each entrant; the ballots sold at six-for-a-quarter. The women needed a prize, and again Front Street ran true to form; Luke Short gave them one hundred dollars in gold for the youngsters to shoot at. After the women had recovered from that flabbergasting generosity, the fond mamas and their supporters two-bitted the camp nearly to death; every time a man turned around, someone was waiting to solicit votes for this or that baby. It is stating a fact rather mildly to say that in the last week of the contest feeling in Dodge ran high. The Ladies' Aid itself was badly split into cliques, each coterie tearing in to bring one infant home a winner. No one who knew old Dodge could expect the he-end of the camp to pass up such an opportunity.

To mark the close of the contest and to corral a few extra dollars, the Ladies' Aid Society was putting on a church supper the night the ballots were to be counted. Voting was to stop as supper started, and the result was to be announced after tables had been cleared and all were seated in front of the platform.

On the last day of the contest, the Front Street crowd took to voting steadily without solicitation, at ten- and twenty-dollar clips, and several open games, it was known, were running kitties to finance this voting. Conditions of the contest held the ballots secret and, as has been aptly stated, the Ladies' Aid was milling like a bunch of Matagorda mosshorns. As the supper bell sounded, a crowd from the Long Branch filed past the ballot box to deposit votes totaling more than two hundred dollars, running the profit for the church to something over two thousand dollars.

When the minister mounted the platform to award the prize, the mothers of entrants were seated in a semicircle just below him, each holding the infant she'd have bet her last chip was to draw down the hundred dollars. The preacher read the official standing, starting with the lowest and working up to the leaders. When he had given the totals for all but one of the babies present, so an old account has it, that particular youngster's mother jumped up to make for the purse of gold, while the baby's father let out a whoop of exultation.

"Just a minute," the minister interposed. "The winner of this contest is"—and he read a name long since forgotten, but which it is vividly recalled no one present appeared to recognize.

"I am not acquainted with this child," the preacher continued, "but if the parents will produce him and establish his right to the prize under the conditions imposed, I shall be glad to hand over Mr. Short's purse of gold."

In the rear seats the boys with no family ties to worry them were doubled over in glee, but a majority of the crowd was as much mystified as the minister. Then Wyatt Earp arose to say that he knew the baby who had been declared winner and that he could have the child brought to the church within a few minutes. The minister asked him to do so, and Wyatt and Bat went out together.

While the two deacons were absent, the waiting audience buzzed with excitement. There had been a dark horse in the race, but who he could be and where he had been dug up, no one had any idea.

The door at the rear of the hall opened and Wyatt and Bat came down the aisle, escorting a very tall, very fat, and very black sister from a South Side dance hall which catered exclusively to Negro patronage. In her arms the Negress carried a pickaninny, not more than two weeks old and just as black as she was.

The preacher's jaw sagged a little, but he was game and asked the girl if her baby had the name that he read as winner. She said that he had, and who was to give her the hundred dollars that the white gentlemen had told her she would be paid for waiting outside the church that evening with her baby, and would they count the ten dollars that had been paid her to make certain she'd be there?

At that point a chagrined mother yelled, "Who's the father?"

"That," said the minister, "is this lady's business"—and handed over the money.

Following the close of the baby contest, life in Dodge, insofar as it affected Wyatt Earp, moved with uneventful routine toward the opening of another cattle-shipping season.

For weeks not even the editor of *The Globe* could dig out any news items of lasting interest, until on April 1, 1879, he reported that 250,000 cattle had been started over the Texas Trail to Dodge City.

Doc Holliday and his inamorata reached another periodical parting of their ways. Big-Nosed Kate announced that she intended to spend the forthcoming cowboy season in Dodge, so there was nothing for Doc to do but move elsewhere. He started for Colorado, telling Wyatt he'd return to Dodge as soon as Kate left it.

Wyatt's preparation for the summer was to impress upon all early arrivals his determination to prevent gun-toting north of the Dead Line. So well did he succeed that when Levi Richardson, one of the frontier's most noted six-shooter exponents, quarreled with Cockeyed Frank Loving on the night of April 5, Levi had to go to his room in a South Side hotel to arm himself for a fight. The Richardson–Loving affair was one which Wyatt often cited in support of his contention that hurry-up six-gun work of the show-off variety could not stack up in a gunfight against plain straight-shooting.

"Levi Richardson," Wyatt said, "had been a buffalo hunter, and was one of the best shots with rifle or pistol on the range. He had a touchy disposition that often got him into trouble, but he had the courage to back it, so was regarded as a dangerous fellow. With his plain, unvarnished style of shooting, Levi had killed several badmen in gun-fights, but then he took up gun-fanning. I have seen him on the outskirts of Dodge practicing his new tricks by the hour and on a number of occasions before his fight with Loving I saw him show off his new methods in target matches. There were few men around Dodge who could beat Levi at the targets.

"Frank Loving was not more than twenty years old. He owned a forty-five and was a fair shot, but until the Richardson affair he had never fired at a man in his life. The extent of his courage can be judged by what happened when Levi returned to the Long Branch.

"Loving was well back in the room, and partly concealed by the stove from a clear path to the door. Levi was no assassin and he yelled a warning to Frank that he was going to kill him. Loving took his gun from the drawer of the layout and stood up, waiting.

" 'Go to shooting! Go to shooting!' Richardson yelled.

" 'It's your turn,' Frank told him.

"With that Levi cut loose, fanning his gun and firing so fast you couldn't count the shots. Not one of his slugs hit a fair mark, his last one scratched Loving's hand. While Levi was pumping lead at him, young Loving raised his gun as cool as you please and fired three shots. Every one hit Richardson in a vital spot, and Levi was as good as dead when he hit the floor. Crack shot and courageous man that he was, Levi Richardson had tried to hurry. Frank Loving had taken his time when the split-second of deliberation took a nerve that was far beyond mere physical courage.

"I've speculated a good deal about that Richardson–Loving scrape, wondering how a man of Levi's skill with a pistol could have missed a man's body with five shots at a distance of twenty feet. Hurry is the only satisfactory answer.

"Cockeyed Frank was not locked up for killing Richardson; everyone knew he had shot in self-defense. Several years later, Frank was killed in a gunfight at Trinidad, Colorado, by that same Jack Allen whose place I had taken as marshal when Allen was chased out of Dodge. I never knew the details of this fight, but Allen went loose on the grounds of self-defense, which meant that probably there'd been an even break. Allen afterward turned street-preacher and traveling evangelist."

By June 1, the trail season of '79 was booming Dodge in unprecedented fashion, yet the cowcamp newspaper could find no gunplays to report until June 10, when *The Globe* records:

> Last night the marshal disarmed a squad of cowboys who had neglected to lay their six-shooters aside while visiting the city. War was declared, several shots were fired, one cowboy was shot in the leg, and the rest were disarmed.

Wyatt Earp recalled the incident as one in which a dozen inebriated Texans met his order to stay south of the Dead Line with gunfire which stopped when he dropped their leader with a slug through his thigh, and which ended with the customary fines in court the following morning.

July 3, however, was marked by the arrival in Dodge of an individual who ever since has remained the cowcamp's outstanding mystery. He rode into town alone, astride an excellent and oft-branded cross-bred cow pony properly caparisoned for warfare, straight to Wright and Beverly's corner, where he dismounted, hitched a pair of six-guns into hand-position at his hips, and stepped to the walk. During his very short stay in Dodge, the stranger revealed neither his identity, his antecedents, his home address, nor his destination upon leaving. Beyond hinting that he was from

Texas, he went into no conversational details except those pertaining to the purpose of his visit, which he stated promptly and fully.

"Is Wyatt Earp still marshal of Dodge?" the stranger inquired of a lounger.

Informed that such was the case, the visitor stepped into the nearest bar, where he bought two or three drinks and asked where Wyatt Earp might be found. He was told to try the Long Branch.

"Wyatt may drop in here any minute," the Long Branch bartender, Adam Jackson, informed the stranger, "but you'd better shed your guns before you meet him. He won't stand for gun-toting."

"So I've heard," the visitor replied, "and that's the point I intend to argue with him."

"Have one on the house," Jackson suggested. "What was that you said?"

Possibly Dodge City liquor was too potent.

"I said I've come to Dodge to make Wyatt Earp eat his guns."

Bystanders caught the drift of the conversation and the stranger was surrounded by those who sensed possibilities. With each drink the mysterious visitor became more emphatic and more extensive in his description of what was about to happen to Wyatt Earp.

"He's run it over our Texas boys too long," he explained, with the proper touch of profanity, "so I've come up to cut him down."

"You rate yourself pretty high, don't you?" someone inquired.

"See that!" The stranger flipped a gun from the holster. "Twenty credits, and every one a marshal."

Chalk Beeson interposed a request that the killing take place in the open air and the visitor led his auditors to the Plaza, where the crowd of listeners was augmented as the visiting gunman discoursed upon the scores his friends had chalked against Wyatt Earp and the method by which he proposed to pay them. He stood with a gun in either hand and was well into a tirade in which Wyatt was mentioned repeatedly in uncomplimentary fashion when the crowd about him melted. A tall, slender, blue-eyed fellow, wearing a black sombrero, with a badge pinned to the breast of his soft white shirt and a pair of guns swung low in his hip-holsters, stood before him.

"I've been listening to your talk for several minutes," this person observed. "I gather you're looking for me. I'm marshal of Dodge. My name's Wyatt Earp."

With which introduction Wyatt slapped the stranger's face with his open hand, vigorously, first on one side, then on the other. With a downward sweep of both hands the marshal seized the guns for which twenty credits had been boasted. Then, to the equal surprise of the gunman and the onlookers, Wyatt shoved both of those guns back into the holsters from which they had been drawn for advertising purposes.

"You can go back and tell your Texas friends," said the marshal of Dodge, "that I didn't bother to take your guns or lock you in the calaboose. Or, if you insist on a gunplay, I'll get you a rifle and a shotgun to go with your pistols and you can go down on the riverbank where nobody'll get hurt when you do your shooting. When you send word you're ready, I'll come down and start you for Texas with a boot in the seat of the pants that'll lift you clean into The Nations."

As he concluded this offer of an alternative, Wyatt took the stranger's earlobe between his thumb and forefinger and led him to the side of his pony, where he hoisted him to the saddle. With a slap of his hand the marshal started the pony toward the toll bridge. Halfway to the bridgehead, the mysterious horseman stopped, turned, and shook his fist at the marshal. Then he rode on toward Texas.

"And that," Wyatt commented, "was the last gunplay made against me while I was marshal of Dodge City."

The summer of '79 passed so peacefully in Dodge that the marshal's job degenerated into a humdrum vocation. The greatest herds in the history of the Texas trail drives grazed on the prairies outside the camp, the town was filled with cowboys in larger numbers than had ridden north before, business in Dodge was at the financial high-water mark.

But—and this is the sole criterion on which to base any estimate of Wyatt Earp's accomplishments in three years of warfare against the gun-toters and the so-called badmen—rebellion against the law was at a standstill.

As Wyatt recalled, he spent more time in gambling than he did rounding up obstreperous visitors, and for the first time in his career was more often to be found gambling on the "inside" than on the "outside," which is to say that he now was playing for the house. He was an adept at faro and monte, and, with time heavy on his hands, dealt regularly for Luke Short at the Long Branch, his interest in the game a percentage of house winnings.

As Dodge had grown, Wyatt had sold certain land-holdings at a profit. Jim Earp had come to town and the brothers were contemplating establishment of a cattle ranch in the Texas Panhandle when a series of letters from Virgil, now half-owner of a mine near Prescott, Arizona, turned their attention to the new camp of Tombstone, some rumors of which had reached Dodge and which within a few short months was to be hailed as the mining sensation of the century. Virgil had made a hurried trip to Ed Schieffelin's facetiously dubbed discovery in the desolate hills of south-eastern Arizona, and had written Wyatt of his conviction that early arrivals in the district would be richly rewarded. The cowtown seemed to have lost that earlier appeal which held the men of restless blood. To phrase this determining factor of Wyatt Earp's decision in his own words: "Dodge's edge was getting dull." So Jim and he decided to move westward.

Wyatt was not unfamiliar with conditions which would prevail in any camp under a typical mining excitement. From tales of the outlaw depredations for which Arizona Territory already was notorious, he believed that if Tombstone developed into a producer of great wealth—another Bannock, Deadwood, or Virginia City—there would be a place in the community for a man of certain reputation and attainments. He had no thought of a peace officer's job. It was his intention to establish a stage line which would connect Tombstone with the railroad, over which he would transport passengers, mail, express, and bullion shipments with his personal guarantee of protection against the gangs of highwaymen who would swoop down on transportation lines with the first news that they were carrying booty.

As Wyatt planned his Arizona enterprise, Virgil was to do the prospecting for the family, the brothers sharing alike in all fortunes which attended their ventures. Jim was to have charge of a stage depot and corral to be set up in Tombstone. Morgan was to be summoned from Montana to share with Wyatt the dangers of riding shotgun on the stages which Wyatt planned to operate between Tombstone and Tucson. Friends connected with frontier transportation assured Wyatt that he could have the Wells-Fargo contract for carrying bullion, and it was reasonable to assume that with it would come the mail contracts.

On September 9 the editor of *The Globe* reported:

> Wyatt Earp, the most efficient marshal Dodge City ever had, has resigned and is leaving for Arizona.

Wyatt had turned in his badge on September 8.

"I'm finished with this marshal business," he told Dog Kelley. "I'm tired of being a target for every drunken gun-toter who goes hunting a reputation."

On September 9, Wyatt set out for Tombstone.

For the long drive overland, Wyatt had purchased twelve horses somewhat heavier than the run of cow-pony stock. Six of these were to draw each of two wagons which he had equipped and stocked with supplies; and later to work the stages; the thirteenth animal was his favorite saddle horse, a traveler and a stayer with which he had done most of his out-country work while a peace officer in Kansas. Jim Earp, his wife and daughter rode in one wagon; Wyatt drove the second.

The cattle-shipping season was at an end, and Wyatt always remembered Dodge City as he drove out of it in the early morning, the littered streets empty to the point of desertion, the ramshackle camp, dirty, dusty, and forlorn in the brilliant September sunshine, a few scattered head of cattle along the Arkansas bottoms. Except for a brief visit four years later, Wyatt Earp had no further part in the dramatic epic of the cowtown; it is of interest to note, however, that soon after he left, a new administration of city officials went into office and at the height of the first cattle-shipping season to follow, the Texas gun-toters once more were hurrahing the Plaza.

Some two weeks after leaving Dodge, as Wyatt was breaking camp near Trail City, in The Indian Nations, he looked up at the sound of an approaching horseman.

"Where you going, Wyatt?" Doc Holliday inquired as casually as if the two had parted the night before.

"Tombstone," Wyatt answered.

"That's what they told me in Dodge," Doc said. "Guess I'll go with you."

Holliday threw his duffle into Wyatt's wagon, hitched his pony with the led animals, and took a place beside Wyatt.

Upon leaving Dodge after his quarrel with Kate, Doc had gambled and fought his way through numerous Western camps, adding three names to the list of his six-gun victims, then struck Las Vegas, New Mexico, a construction center on the Santa Fe Railroad. Here he prospered until Big-Nosed Kate reached town. As she showed no disposition to patch up their quarrel, and Dodge was five hundred miles from Kate, Doc had chosen the cowtown as sanctuary. Upon learning that Wyatt was on the Tombstone trail, he had ridden to overtake him.

Wyatt Earp's two-wagon train reached Prescott about November 1. Virgil sold his mining interests and with his wife joined the Tombstone party.

Doc Holliday struck a run of luck at faro which he refused to break by leaving Prescott.

"I'll see you in Tombstone," he promised, and remained to hit the Prescott game for more than forty thousand dollars.

As the party left Prescott, it consisted of James and Virgil Earp, with their families, and Wyatt; Morg was on his way down from Montana. From Prescott, Wyatt drove to Tucson, from which point he intended to strike across the desolate reaches of the Santa Rita and the Whetstone Mountains, down the Barbacomari, and over the desert bottoms of the San Pedro to the boom camp of Tombstone, already glamorous in an awestruck public mind with its wild community boast of "a man for breakfast every morning."

18

Tough and Turbulent Tombstone

At Tucson, Arizona, Wyatt Earp met Charles Shibell, sheriff of Pima County, a wild and brutal bailiwick covering twenty-eight thousand square miles of sagebrush, rock, and cactus which included the Tombstone district and for which Tucson was the seat of government.

"If you're going to Tombstone," Shibell told Wyatt, "I'll make you deputy sheriff."

"Much obliged," Wyatt answered, "but I'm aiming to run a line of stages."

"There are two lines running out of Tombstone already," Shibell countered, "with mail and express contracted."

Even when convinced that no third stage line could succeed, Wyatt was loath to return to his Kansas calling.

"You're a Democrat and I'm a Republican," he objected further. "Your organization wouldn't stand for me."

"Politics don't count," the sheriff replied. "The sheriff is tax and fee collector as well as a peace officer. He gets a percentage of collections, plus mileage. We should get ten or twelve thousand dollars a month from Tombstone, but a lot of fellows in there figure they're too tough to pay taxes, and what little is collected never reaches us. I'm after a deputy who's man enough to collect what's due, and honest enough to make certain the county gets it. I'll guarantee you five hundred dollars a month, if you'll take the job."

"I understand," Wyatt observed, as he considered this last inducement, "that Tombstone sets up to be a pretty tough camp."

"There won't be much criminal work," Shibell asserted. "Tombstone's going to organize and will appoint a marshal to handle law and order. Get the county's money and you can suit yourself about the gunmen."

Wyatt weighed personal disinclination against responsibility. Virgil's prospecting must be financed, while the other Earps lived decently.

"I'll take your job," he told the sheriff.

On December 1, 1879, Wyatt Earp rode into the boom silver camp as a deputy sheriff of Pima County, but not a Deputy United States Marshal, as has been generally recorded. His Federal commission came later.

At the age of thirty-one, Wyatt had altered but slightly in outward appearance since his early days in the Kansas cowtowns. The small mustache he had cultivated in Dodge was now the sweeping growth of current fashion. But he was the same deceptively slender, tawny-haired, blue-eyed six-footer; weighing possibly one hundred and fifty-five pounds, square-jawed, flat-muscled, as lithe and uncannily effortless in his physical exertions as ever.

On the eastern slope of the San Pedro Valley, where the Mule and Dragoon Mountains met in a range of jagged foothills vaguely known as an Apache stronghold, Ed Schieffelin had prospected in defiance of army officers' warnings that all he'd find would be his tombstone. In August of 1877, he located ore bodies assaying twenty thousand dollars a ton. At Tucson, in recording discovery, he was required to identify his claim.

"What do you call it?" the Federal agent asked.

Schieffelin recalled the army officers' forebodings.

"Tombstone," he answered.

His second strike, Schieffelin named the Graveyard, and when he returned to the district the following spring with his brother Al and Dick Gird, whom he had taken into partnership, the trio located the Lucky Cuss, with values running to fifteen thousand dollars. News of the strikes spread over the West like wildfire, and hordes of adventurers stampeded to the Tombstone hills.

Stamp-mills were set up in the San Pedro Valley, where there was water. Charleston was built around them. Galeyville, Harshaw, Paradise, Contention, Fairbanks, Bisbee, and a score of smaller camps mushroomed out of the desert. The first stamp dropped on Tombstone ore in June of '79—forerunner of a hundred and fifty which would grind out $30,000,000 in bullion—and Tombstone evolved, with a roar, from mesquite mesa to mining metropolis.

Isolated on a mile-high ledge of bedrock in the heart of a great desert, Tombstone was a mining camp that boomed in a cattle country, on a par with Pioche, Deadwood, and Alder Gulch for sudden riches, ranking with Abilene, Wichita, and Dodge for rough-and-ready lawlessness. When Wyatt Earp took charge of the sheriff's office, he was the only peace officer within seventy-five miles. The camp had a population of five hundred, and possibly six one-story, one-room adobe cabins. The rest of the community was in tents, wagons, mesquite wickiups, Apache-fashion, or under blankets.

Six months later there were five thousand people in Tombstone; a year later, ten thousand and within eighteen months, a population of nearly fifteen thousand. From the cactus roots down, the camp's foundation, in spots, was solid silver. In the middle of Toughnut Street, for example, there gaped a forty-foot hole from which a fortune in pure metal was taken with picks and shovels. "The Million Dollar Stope," it was dubbed, in accord with mint records of production.

The tale of Tombstone's boom is the story of Wyatt Earp's ascendancy to eminence as a frontier marshal and, for its accurate recounting, a few truths about old Arizona are necessary.

John C. Frémont, possibly the most incompetent administrator of public affairs on record in the United States, was Governor of Arizona Territory from 1878 to 1881. Frémont was a Republican, appointed by President Hayes. Internally, Arizona was a Democratic stronghold, her elective offices filled with men of that persuasion. Governor Frémont appears to have deemed an alliance with a local element essential to his personal ambitions. Wherefore there came into existence in Arizona a working combination of practical politicians and outlaw killers which, for wholesale infamy, has seldom been equaled.

Fundamentally, it was the age-old system. Government offices were filled with unscrupulous tricksters. Under their protection desperadoes robbed, smuggled, rustled cattle, held up stages, and murdered all who opposed them. The boldest and the most remunerative of the depredatory gangs operated in Pima County and, with the boom of the silver camp, Tombstone became their rendezvous.

The field forces of Arizona's organized outlawry are typified in Old Man Clanton and his following. Clanton was a tough old Texas renegade who had gone to California in '49, been chased out by Vigilantes, drifted to Arizona, where he took up a ranch near Fort Thomas, and existed for some years through his ability to out-Apache the Apaches. With the Tombstone strike, Clanton—his initials were N. H., but even in court records he was designated as Old Man— moved to Lewis Springs, just up the San Pedro from Charleston, where ore was turned into bullion and booty.

With Old Man Clanton rode his sons, Joseph Isaac, the notorious Ike; Phineas, called Phin; and William, Billy; all three born and raised in outlawry. Curly Bill Brocius, John Ringo, Frank and Tom McLowery, Joe Hill, Jim Hughes, Pony Deal, Frank Stilwell, and Pete Spence were other lieutenants. Under them, three hundred outcasts of frontier society dominated human rights and life in southern and eastern Arizona.

Clanton followers, in the guise of ranchers, squatted on every desert water hole from Old Mexico to the Mogollon, and from the Huachucas to Las Animas. One of the few surviving cattle kings of Old Arizona has told me that in 1880–82 there were not a dozen cowmen in the Territory who dared brave the wrath of the Clanton–Curly Bill-McLowery gang by subscribing openly to the campaign against them undertaken by the Arizona Cattlemen's Protective Association. The majority of stockmen either paid grudging tribute in fear of vicious reprisals, or built up their herds with stolen cattle.

Curly Bill and John Ringo ranked next to Old Man Clanton in outlaw councils. Brocius—he sometimes gave his name as Graham—and Ringo—family name, Ringgold—were fearless gunmen of the first order, professional killers, trained in the wars of the Texas cattle barons. Each had encountered Wyatt Earp as marshal in Wichita and Dodge City. Their followers were renegade cowboys, fugitives from border justice, a majority with killings to their credit and likewise acquainted with Wyatt's record. For this crowd, and their political patrons, Old Man Clanton's son Ike—a craven soul if ever an outlaw was one—acted as go-between.

Curly Bill Brocius was a swart and muscular six-footer, with a heavy shock of kinky black hair, and coarse, ugly features. In leisure hours he could be a good-natured, open-handed fellow. On business bent, he was a brutal thug to whom murder was routine.

John Ringo was tall, slender, auburn-haired, and handsome. Though he robbed, killed, and caroused with his fellows, he was of a sullen temperament and periodically so vicious that even his friends avoided him.

Curly Bill demonstrated repeatedly that he would shoot a man in the back rather than give him an even break. Ringo, a week after Wyatt Earp reached Tombstone, invited a chance acquaintance in a saloon, one Louis Hancock, to have a drink, and shot his guest through the throat when Hancock ordered beer as Ringo took whiskey.

With Tombstone skyrocketing to fame, Arizona's astute politicians sensed that the new camp would hold the balance of territorial power at the polls, with a rapidly growing leaven of Eastern capitalists, businessmen, clerical employ-

و., and laborers, who it was suspected might vote the Republican ticket. So, the practical politicians financed a newspaper, *The Tombstone Nugget*.

In early issues *The Nugget* referred to the Clanton gang so fulsomely as "cowboys" that the outlaws and their protectors became known as "the cowboy party." A newspaper dispatch from the boom camp observed:

> *The Nugget* has so far identified itself with the rustlers that it is generally known as the cowboy organ.

In the spring of 1880, John P. Clum, with an Arizona-wide reputation for courageous honesty gained as head of the San Carlos Apache Indian Reservation, arrived in Tombstone to start another newspaper. Clum was thoroughly cognizant of territorial politics and as he intended to fight the outlaw machine was welcomed by the law-and-order faction. Asked what he intended to call his newspaper, Clum replied that every Tombstone should have its Epitaph, and thus was named the journal that for years was the daily delight of every editorial paragrapher in the country.

The Nugget railed bitterly against continuance of the black Republican, Wyatt Earp, as deputy sheriff, and attacked him savagely. *The Epitaph* supported Wyatt's activities as an officer.

Fires which swept early Tombstone destroyed files of *The Epitaph*. By chance, *The Nugget* files were preserved for later consultation. Of greater misfortune to historians has been the absence of documents pertaining to Wyatt Earp from archives in the Tombstone Courthouse. This building was first occupied in 1883; for prior times few official records were available.

In territorial times, publication of Arizona court proceedings often was prohibited throughout a hearing. Afterward, a newspaper might print the evidence. There has been, for some years, a growing suspicion that *The Nugget* news reports were shaped to fit political policies, but, in the absence of documentary contradiction, they have found popular acceptance as Tombstone history.

Considerable responsibility is attached to flat denial of much that a hundred historians have transcribed as fact. However, if this narrative is to merit consideration, it must be definitely established that here for the first time in print is a full account of Wyatt Earp's contribution to the taming of the last frontier. To the good fortune upon which denials and consequent contentions are largely based, Mr. J. E. James, currently clerk of the Superior Court, Cochise County, Arizona, can testify. Mr. James and his father-in-law, Mr. James Marrs, between them, have had supervision over Cochise County records for nearly half a century.

Search for material to complement Wyatt Earp's own story of his life led to Tombstone. After examining the few known documents, Mr. Marrs was led to reminiscence.

"Come to think," he said, "the old 'dobe courthouse wasn't burned in '82. A bunch of prisoners brought a load of papers and stuff over here, and dumped 'em into a storeroom out back that's been shut off for years. What's in there, no one knows. If you don't mind dust, you could find out."

Assertion that dust was no barrier at all was made in ignorance of what desert sand can pile upon and permeate a few thousand papers in the course of forty-seven years. But at the end of a week, hundreds of hand-written documents salvaged from a mass of ancient correspondence, torn ledgers, minute books, and whatnot had been identified as worthless, or otherwise.

Near the bottom of the pile we found the court reporter's complete, hand-written, official transcript of the most celebrated of all frontier court proceedings, the case of Organized Outlawry *vs.* Wyatt Earp. In that hearing, which lasted for thirty days in the fall of '81, the full history and workings of the cowboy party were revealed to an extent that astounded even lawless Tombstone. It was all there, each transcript of testimony signed and certified.

Both Mr. Marrs and Mr. James agreed that within the last forty years no one had had access to the rediscovered documents. They added that to have any writer make inquiries of them was an entirely unique experience.

Further corroboration is due to the support which Wyatt

Earp had from Wells, Fargo and Company in his war on the Arizona outlaws. Arizona history repeatedly mentions a Charleston saloon operated by J. B. Ayers, in which the outlaws made rendezvous and where Ayers was regarded as their ally. Also, there are numerous references to Fred Dodge, characterized as a gambler. J. B. Ayers, of Charleston notoriety, was in reality a cleverly spotted undercover man for Wells-Fargo and the Southern Pacific Railroad who reported the doings of the Clanton gang to Fred Dodge. Fred Dodge, in his true character, was confidential special agent for John J. Valentine, president of Wells, Fargo and Company.

John Thacker and James B. Hume were openly Wells-Fargo officers, and with them Fred Dodge worked secretly, when ostensibly he was owner of a faro bank running in Hafford's saloon at Tombstone. Reports which Messrs. Thacker, Hume, and Dodge sent to Wells-Fargo headquarters at San Francisco were destroyed by fire in 1906. Thacker and Hume died, but Wells, Fargo and Company officials agreed that after passage of half a century there could be no harm in publishing the firsthand information about the old Arizona politico-bandit gang which Fred Dodge alone possessed.

Not even Marshall Williams, Wells-Fargo agent at Tombstone in the boom days, knew of Fred Dodge's connection with his company. Three Vigilante leaders and the Earp brothers were the only men in the camp to be trusted with that knowledge. So Fred Dodge ran his faro bank and mixed with the "cowboys" at Hafford's bar, or rode over to Charleston to play hail-fellow-well-met with Curly Bill, Ike Clanton, Milt Hicks, Joe Hill, Johnny Barnes, and the rest in Ayers's saloon, and to gather information. Fred Dodge's account of Arizona happenings has been drawn on freely for these pages, as has a scrapbook kept by John P. Clum, *Epitaph* editor, Tombstone's first mayor and postmaster.

Tombstone fulfilled Shibell's prophecy. Wyatt Earp's first thirty days as deputy sheriff netted him seven hundred dollars in fees and mileage; not once while he held the office did his monthly income fall below that figure.

On January 6, 1880, a citizens' committee appointed Fred White, erstwhile army officer, first marshal of Tombstone.

Morgan Earp reached Tombstone early in January, followed closely by Doc Holliday. To Wyatt's surprise, Big-Nosed Kate came with Doc. The gunfighting dentist's faro bank winning in Prescott had led to reconciliation.

Wyatt invested heavily in Tombstone real estate, including land at the southwest corner of First and Fremont Streets, where he erected two houses; Virgil Earp moved into one, James into the other. At times, Wyatt and Morgan boarded with their brothers, although for the most part they bached, at first in an adobe cabin with Fred Dodge near the calaboose on Allen Street, later at the Cosmopolitan Hotel owned by Albert C. ("Chris") Billicke.

As bullion shipments increased, Old Man Clanton's rustlers gave more attention to the Tombstone stages. Outgoing coaches carried bullion; incoming, the currency to meet payrolls and other needs of a booming community; passengers customarily were supplied with funds. Mine owners cast their treasure in alloy-bricks weighing three hundred pounds each, hoping thus to discourage the outlaws. Old Man Clanton's boys retaliated by driving wagons to their holdups. Whereupon Jim Hume, chief of Wells-Fargo officers, visited Tombstone.

Hume engaged Wyatt Earp to guard treasure shipments between Tombstone and Tucson, later shifting the run to Benson. Wyatt deputized Morgan as assistant in the sheriff's office and went to riding shotgun. For six months thereafter, when a bullion shipment left Tombstone or currency came in under Wells-Fargo auspices, Wyatt Earp rode with it. When the sheriff's business demanded Wyatt's time, he sent Morg out as messenger.

It is notable that coincidentally with Wyatt Earp's first trip in the boot, highway robbery of Tombstone stages stopped abruptly. Throughout all that follows it should be kept in mind that not once, when an Earp was riding shotgun, was any stage so much as threatened by any outlaw.

Crawley P. Dake, United States Marshal for Arizona, now appointed Wyatt United States Marshal for the Tombstone district, and Wyatt told the bandits bluntly just what they could expect from him. Wyatt's cowtown experiences had acquainted him with a majority of the badmen now terrorizing Arizona and identities of Old Man Clanton's followers were such common knowledge that he stopped individual outlaws in the Tombstone streets to deliver his ukase. Stage robberies ceased, but close on the heels of these warnings, Wyatt's favorite horse was stolen. For months, Wyatt got no trace of the animal.

Resentment against the high-handed manner in which Wyatt Earp handled the stagecoach problem rankled, but the outlaws voiced no open threats against the marshal until he took up a matter of stock rustling.

Curly Bill, Frank and Tom McLowery, Frank Patterson, and Billy Clanton ran off a bunch of Government mules from Camp Rucker. Captain Hurst, with four troopers, rode to Tombstone to ask the marshal's aid in recovering the animals. Wyatt, Virgil, and Morgan took the trail with Hurst and tracked the mules to the McLowery ranch, near Soldier Holes in the Sulphur Springs Valley, where they found six of the stolen animals.

Captain Hurst held parley with Frank Patterson, and reported that the outlaws would give up all Government animals they had if the Earps went back to Tombstone, but that he must be satisfied with six if he kept the Earps in his posse.

"You say the word," Wyatt told Hurst, "and I'll bring out every mule on the place. This is a trick to get us out of the way. If we leave, you won't get a mule."

The army officer insisted that eight men would be no match for the fifteen or twenty rustlers at the ranch, and that his first duty was to recover stolen property, not to fight outlaws.

"Virg, Morg, and I will attend to the fighting," Wyatt assured him, but Hurst preferred the compromise.

A few days later, Captain Hurst rode into Tombstone without any mules, but with a message for Wyatt.

"The McLowerys sent word that if you or your brothers interfered with them again, they'd shoot you on sight."

"Tell 'em they'll have their chance," Wyatt answered.

Three weeks later, Wyatt met Frank and Tom McLowery in the street at Charleston.

"That army officer give you our message?" Tom Mc-Lowery asked.

"He did," Wyatt replied, "but in case you didn't get my answer, I'll repeat it."

The McLowerys wanted no gunplay that morning.

"If you ever follow us again," Frank McLowery promised, as he and his brother walked away, "your friends'll find what the coyotes leave of you in the sagebrush."

19

Arizona Sees a Showdown

In the spring of 1880, Tombstone was the howling wonder of the Western world. Red-blooded fortune hunters streamed in by thousands. Stores, hotels, restaurants, saloons, gambling houses, dance halls, and honky-tonks jammed an area half a mile long and quarter of a mile wide in frame and adobe buildings, a few of two stories, with wooden awnings shading dirt walks to the hitching rails along sixty-foot roadways. Allen Street, from Mexican dance halls at one end to cribs at the other, was a seething night-and-day thoroughfare of mercantile enterprise, hilarious entertainment, and uproarious iniquity.

Tombstone transported to the desert for the delectation of wild and woolly frontiersmen the metropolitan fancies and luxuries, offering in crude structures of weatherboard and adobe all the gilded amusement and glittering sin that New York and San Francisco housed in marble and brownstone. Her shops, shows, restaurants, and recreational establishments were epitomized in a dispatch of August 3, 1880, by

243

Clara S. Brown, most prolific of the boom camp's newspaper correspondents:

> Saloon openings are all the rage. The Oriental is simply gorgeous. The mahogany bar is a marvel of beauty, the gaming-room carpeted with Brussels, brilliantly lighted and furnished with reading matter and writing materials for its patrons. Every evening there is the music of a violin and piano which attracts a crowd, and the scene is a gay one.

There, in a paragraph, is the Oriental Saloon and Gambling-Hall, the Crystal Palace, the Alhambra, and a dozen others along Allen Street. Also, there is Tombstone, when barren hills and torrid desert spouted riches faster than three eight-hour shifts of bartenders, game dealers, and dance-hall ladies could glaum them.

Buckskin Frank Leslie killed Mike Killeen in a gunfight on the steps of the Commercial Hotel; Roger King killed Johnnie Wilson—they were professional fighting men—in a six-gun battle in the middle of Allen Street and both Leslie and King were turned loose. Pima County's roster of six-gun victims was getting longer than her Apache casualty list, and the adherents of law enforcement in the outlying precincts threw in with their Tombstone friends for a housecleaning.

The first move was to elect a sheriff in place of Charlie Shibell, and as candidate the Law and Order Party selected Bob Paul, of Tucson, a Deputy United States Marshal and shotgun messenger for Wells-Fargo. Wyatt Earp resigned as Shibell's deputy.

"I'm supporting Bob Paul," Wyatt told the sheriff.

Shibell moved to offset opposition by appointing Johnny Behan to succeed Wyatt Earp as deputy sheriff and to repair political fences. One result was the prompt renewal of rustler activities. A second was the return of the Clanton–Curly Bill crowd to hurrah Tombstone.

In the evening of Wednesday, October 27, 1880, Wyatt Earp reached home from Tucson to find the camp in an uproar. "The cowboys" had possession of Allen Street.

Wyatt saw Curly Bill, Frank Patterson, Frank and Tom McLowery, Ike and Billy Clanton, and Pony Deal going into a saloon and noted that all wore guns. A few minutes later, Marshal White sent for him.

White told Wyatt that the outlaws had been carousing in town for two days, had made several gunplays, and that when he appealed to Deputy Sheriff Behan, Behan had refused to help arrest them.

As the marshal talked, the roar of six-guns again filled Allen Street.

"Will you help me arrest those fellows?" White asked.

"Come on," Wyatt answered.

Diagonally across Allen Street was a vacant lot, later site of the Bird Cage Theater, at the rear of which was the cabin shared by Wyatt, Morgan Earp, and Fred Dodge. From the shadows someone was howling for Tombstone to come out and fight.

"You go in from this side," Wyatt instructed White. "I'll come in from the other."

As the officers closed in, they saw that their quarry was Curly Bill, half-drunk and waving a pistol. White seized the outlaw's weapon by the barrel. The forty-five roared, and Marshal White dropped, shot in the abdomen. Curly Bill hit the ground beside him under a blow from Wyatt's gun barrel; he was still unconscious when Morgan Earp and Fred Dodge reached the spot.

"Wyatt's coolness and nerve never showed to better advantage than they did that night," Fred Dodge wrote me recently. "When Morg and I reached him, Wyatt was squatted on his heels beside Curly Bill and Fred White. Curly Bill's friends were pot-shooting at him in the dark. The shooting was lively and slugs were hitting the chimney and cabin. All of us squatted. In all that racket, Wyatt's voice was as even and quiet as usual.

"'Put out the fire in Fred's clothes,' he said. White had been shot at such close range that his coat was burning."

Wyatt had White carried to his cabin, and ordered Morgan and Fred Dodge to put Curly Bill in the calaboose.

"I'll get the others," he said.

Before he finished, Wyatt had thrown Frank Patterson, the two McLowerys, Billy Clanton, and Pony Deal in with Curly Bill, walking up to each as he found him and buffaloing him in his tracks. Word of his execution had Allen Street cleared of rustlers by the time he had polished off five.

Marshal White lived for some days, and in the county court Curly Bill was admitted to bail. His companions were discharged with reprimands.

"They remembered their sore heads longer than they did the judge's warning," Wyatt remarked in later years. "They never forgave that manhandling. If I do say so myself, I was thorough."

Before he died, Fred White exonerated Curly Bill of murderous intent, explaining that the hair-trigger Colt's had been discharged by his attempt to jerk it from the outlaw's hand.

On the Tuesday following White's death, Pima County went to the polls. When the votes were counted, Shibell apparently had been reelected sheriff by a majority of 47. Wyatt noted that the San Simon precinct, an outlaw stronghold voting at Galeyville, showed 104 votes cast, 103 for Shibell and 1 for Bob Paul.

"There aren't fifty votes in that precinct," Wyatt declared. "You demand a recount," he told Bob Paul, "and if I can make Curly Bill talk, you'll be sheriff."

Wyatt rode to Charleston and told Curly Bill flatly that he could reveal what had happened in the San Simon on election day or be hanged for the murder of Marshal White.

"Come through about the Galeyville votes," Wyatt told the outlaw, "and I won't dispute White's dying statement. Otherwise, I'll swear you shot White as he reached for your gun. If the law doesn't hang you on that, Fred White's friends will."

Wyatt's bluff stood up. Curly Bill agreed to get affidavits from the men who had stuffed the San Simon ballot box.

Immediately after White's death, Virgil Earp was appointed temporary marshal of Tombstone. The camp had scheduled her first municipal election for January 4, 1881.

Virgil refused to be a candidate for the regular term of office, but for his brief tenure he took a leaf from Wyatt's book and the rustlers transferred recreational headquarters to Charleston.

In December, on the strength of affidavits which Wyatt obtained through Curly Bill, the Board of Elections threw out the San Simon ballots and declared Bob Paul's election. Shibell appealed to the courts and held office pending decision. Curly Bill was arraigned for the death of Fred White and discharged on the strength of White's *ante-mortem* statement.

At the January election, John P. Clum, candidate of the Citizens' Safety Committee, was elected first mayor of Tombstone by a vote of 532 against 165 for Mark P. Shaffer, running with the support of *The Nugget*. Ben Sippy, erstwhile soldier, was elected marshal by a similar majority over Howard Lee, exponent of cowboy liberality.

On January 12, Virgil Earp gave way to Ben Sippy. Three days later, in the Tombstone streets, a mob of five hundred of the toughest citizens that Tombstone and Charleston could muster made wild and woolly Arizona's first real play against this Wyatt Earp, who, the more desperate characters had been insisting, was overly feared and greatly overrated.

Johnny-Behind-the-Deuce (John O'Rourke) was a tinhorn gambler. Aside from his predilection for playing the two-spot open when in funds to buck a faro bank and through which he gained his frontier sobriquet, there was nothing notable about him. He was an insignificant runt who hung around Charleston gambling houses, figured himself as one of the outlaw gang, but never stacked high enough to enjoy serious consideration until he got his "man for breakfast" one morning.

After an all-night poker session at Charleston, in which Henry Schneider, burly chief engineer of the Tombstone Mining and Milling Corporation, was a heavy loser, the tinhorn passed some comment on the engineer as a gambler. Words led to violence, and as Schneider drew a knife, Johnny-Behind-the-Deuce jerked a six-gun and killed him.

George McKelvey, Charleston constable, heard that a

bunch of Curly Bill rustlers had suggested to a crowd of Schneider's employees that there'd be a morning's entertainment in trying and hanging the tinhorn and that the lynching party was organizing in Quinn's saloon. McKelvey hitched a pair of mules to a buckboard and started his prisoner for Tombstone.

Halfway up the San Pedro slope, McKelvey looked back to see a mob of horsemen hot after him, and poured leather. Three miles out of Tombstone, the riders opened fire at long range on the buckboard. Half a mile ahead was Jack McCann's adobe, "The Last Chance Saloon." McKelvey took the final ounce from his team to reach this dubious haven three hundred yards ahead of his pursuers.

At this point legendary accounts of the episode differ from contemporary records. Yarn spinners have sent Jack McCann to the constable's aid on his race mare, Molly McCarthy. The horseman who met McKelvey by chance was Virgil Earp, riding Dick Naylor, a thoroughbred animal belonging to Wyatt.

"That gang's aiming to lynch this fellow," McKelvey shouted to Virgil. "These mules are done."

Virgil, who did not know Johnny-Behind-the-Deuce from Adam, worked Dick Naylor close to the buckboard.

"Jump on behind," he yelled. The tinhorn obeyed, and Dick Naylor started for Tombstone.

The powerful thoroughbred, carrying double, easily distanced the cow ponies which had come ten miles upgrade on a dead run. At Tombstone, Virgil found Wyatt and Morgan at the Wells-Fargo office. Johnny-Behind-the-Deuce got out enough of his story to let Wyatt know that John Ringo and other cowboys were leading his pursuers before Jim Earp ran over with word that the Charleston mob had ridden up Toughnut Street and dismounted to mix with the "graveyard shift" of miners from Dick Gird's property on the hill. They had recruited about three hundred Tombstone men employed by this company for which Schneider had worked, were getting rifles and shotguns from the mine arsenal, and planned to storm the calaboose to which they assumed Johnny would be taken.

Wyatt picked up a double-barreled, sawed-off shotgun. Across Allen Street was Jim Vogan's bowling alley, a long, narrow, solid, adobe building, walls sealed on either side by adjoining structures, a small door and high windows at the rear, double doors fronting Allen Street.

"Take him into Vogan's," Wyatt told Virgil and Morgan. "If they try for the back, you can pick 'em off faster than they can crowd in. If they get by me in front, give this fellow a gun and let him help you."

Five hundred blood-lusting frontiersmen poured into Allen Street as Virgil and Morgan got Johnny-Behind-the-Deuce into the bowling alley. Wyatt stood alone at the curbline, his shotgun in the crook of his right arm. The mob was to the east. To the west, Allen Street had cleared of traffic with ominous celerity.

"Where is he?" the mob clamored.

"Over in Vogan's," someone shouted. The five hundred executed a surging flank movement that filled Allen Street from curb to curb, faced the United States Marshal, and halted abruptly.

"Go in and drag him out!" the jamming rear ranks called.

Again folklore departs from history. Wyatt's version of what followed is borne out by Jack Archer, old-time stage driver, who stood that morning in the Wells-Fargo doorway.

"Wyatt didn't swear, or call names," Archer insists. "He didn't have to raise his voice. The mob wasn't thirty feet from him."

"Most accounts have me cursing that crowd plenty," Wyatt commented, "but that was no time for hot language. "'Boys,' I said, 'don't you make any fool play here; that little tinhorn isn't worth it.'"

The lynchers were not to be turned thus readily from their bloodletting.

"Go in after him!" those in the rear kept yelling. "Earp can't stop you!"

Under pressure the front rank edged forward. The surging movement shifted to the rhythmic stamp of an Indian war dance. This was no mob of the cities. Half of the men in the crowd had fought Apaches. The rest were highwaymen, rustlers, cowboys, and boom-camp miners on a rampage. Shouts and catcalls merged in the whooping staccato of the red man's war cry.

Wyatt threw his shotgun before him, left hand on the fore-end, right on grip and triggers.

In the crowd every man had a shotgun, rifle, or six-gun, ready to pour lead into the lone peace officer. At the rear, those who could not see the marshal's eye waved and fired their guns in the air, their rage increasing as those in front bore back from the threat of Wyatt's weapon.

"Yi-yi-yi-yi-yi! Ya-a-a-hoo!"

Tapping his mouth with his hand, an old-timer screeched an Apache death yell. The mob took up the familiar signal.

"Rush him!" someone called. "He'll quit! If he doesn't, let him have it! Get that tinhorn strung up and get this over!"

Wyatt swung the twin muzzles slowly back and forth across the crowded street.

"Don't fool yourselves," he cautioned the front ranks. "That tinhorn's my prisoner, and I'm not bluffing."

His eye traveled swiftly over the maddened faces.

"The most dangerous mob in the world," he observed fifty years afterward, "is a leaderless one, for the reason that there's no one on whom you can pin anything. The crowd that wanted to lynch Johnny-Behind-the-Deuce had shown no leader, so I picked one for them, and gave him a few assistants. There in the front row, with a rifle in his hand, was Dick Gird, multi-millionaire, employer of half of the men at his back, as popular a fellow as there was in the camp and one of the best friends I had in Tombstone. He told me afterwards he never knew how he went crazy enough to get there."

Again the rear ranks tried to force action.

"Cut him down! Turn loose on him! You'll get him!"

The front rank surged to within twenty feet of the marshal.

"Stop where you are," Wyatt ordered. "Sure you can get me. But I'll take eight or ten of you along. There's eighteen

250

buckshot in this gun and the wads are slit. One step more, and you get it."

Jack Archer and two others who saw the play have said that Wyatt paled beneath his tan until he looked as though he had jaundice.

"Nice mob you've got, Mr. Gird," Wyatt remarked in a casual tone, fixing leadership as he had determined. "I didn't know you trailed with such company."

He swung his gun muzzle on the mine owner's belly.

"If I have to get anyone, Mr. Gird," the marshal continued, "you're first. Three or four will go down with you." He named the men at Gird's right and left in the same matter-of-fact fashion. "Your friends may get me, but there'll be my brothers. It'll cost good men to lynch that tinhorn, and Number One'll be Dick Gird."

The rear ranks pressed forward. Those in front bore back from the step into eternity. One man against five hundred. This was a showdown.

Wyatt sensed the high point.

"Don't be a fool, Dick," he suggested.

Gird grinned sheepishly, turned and shouldered through the crowd. One by one, others followed. The front rank grew ragged, broke up. The Tombstone residents edged to the far sidewalk and the rear, leaving forty or fifty Charlestonians, mostly of the Clanton crowd, to face the marshal. Wyatt dropped his shotgun into the crook of his elbow, and eyed his professional enemies scornfully.

"Jim," he called to his brother, who, unarmed, had stood in a doorway at one side, "have Charlie Smith drive his wagon up here. I'm taking the prisoner to Tucson."

Johnny-Behind-the-Deuce broke jail in Tucson while awaiting trial. Customarily he is dismissed from frontier history with the statement that he escaped to Old Mexico and was not heard of again in Arizona. In reality, the tinhorn gambler returned to the Tombstone country months later, to exact vengeance against the outlaws who had led the mob after him. The nature of his revenge has been buried for half a century in confidential reports of Fred Dodge to

Wells, Fargo and Company, wherefore its result often is cited as an unsolved mystery of old Arizona.

While Wyatt Earp held the lynch mob at bay, Deputy Sheriff Johnny Behan, two of his deputies, and Ben Sippy, the Tombstone marshal, stood across Allen Street from the bowling alley and made no move to assist Wyatt.

Closely following Wyatt's play against the lynch mob, news reached Tombstone that the Territorial Legislature had set off seven thousand square miles in the southeast corner of Pima County as a new district, to be named Cochise County, with Tombstone as county seat. The political ring was anxious to set up the new bailiwick. Cochise County, properly exploited, could provide millions of dollars annually for the politicians, and none of its officers could be chosen by voters until November 1882. Johnny Behan announced his candidacy for appointment as first sheriff of Cochise County. Tombstone's law-and-order faction asked Wyatt to oppose him.

"I don't want the job," Wyatt answered. "I can make more money with my Federal job and the Wells-Fargo business. If Frémont appoints me, I'll accept, but I won't ask for it."

A law-and-order delegation went from Tombstone to present its views to the Governor. Several days later, Johnny Behan stopped Wyatt Earp on Allen Street.

"Let's get off the street," he said. "I want to talk to you."

The two walked through Dave Cohen's cigar store into a card room at the rear. Behan locked the door behind him.

"I hear you're fighting me for the sheriff's job," Behan began.

"You're wrong," Wyatt answered. "I don't want the job but I've agreed to take it if it's offered to me."

"It won't be," Behan assured him. "The only thing that'll keep me from getting the appointment is the fight your friends may make against me. They can't get the job for you, but they may keep me out. If they do, my friends can force Frémont to appoint a compromise candidate. What do you think the sheriff's job'll be worth in this new county?"

"Several thousand a year, I suppose," Wyatt answered.

Behan laughed.

"Thirty to forty thousand," he corrected. "That's what I want to talk about.

"You telegraph your friends at Prescott to withdraw your name and I'll get the job, sure. I'll appoint you under-sheriff. I'll run the civil business; you can run the criminal end and appoint your own deputies. We'll hire a clerk to handle all collections and split even. Somebody's going to earn this money and it might better be us than a stranger. Is it a deal?"

Wyatt realized that Johnny Behan was not overstating the influence his crowd had on the Governor, and at this time neither he nor anyone else in Tombstone had any conception of Behan's alliance with the outlaws. Moreover, as under-sheriff with Morg and Virg as deputies, Wyatt could keep his United States Marshal's job and the Wells-Fargo position.

"All right, Johnny," he said. "It's a bargain."

The two went to the telegraph office, where Wyatt filed the message agreed upon. Behan started for Prescott, and returned with his commission as first sheriff of Cochise County.

"Johnny Behan never mentioned our agreement to me afterward," Wyatt recalled, with a chuckle over his own gullibility. "But the outcome is the best line on him I can furnish.

"Behan picked Harry Woods, editor of *The Nugget,* as under-sheriff, and appointed Dave Campbell, Dave Neagle, Frank Stilwell, Lance Perkins, Frank Hereford, and William Breakenridge as deputies. Neagle was not very shrewd, but he was honest and courageous; he did all of Behan's work that needed a fighting man. Stilwell was openly one of the Clanton gang. Hereford and Breakenridge were process-servers.

"By the time Johnny Behan returned from Prescott, I wouldn't have taken his partnership if he had offered it, and I expected to tell him so. I'd been offered a chance at double the money the sheriff's office could have paid, and could keep my Federal and Wells-Fargo jobs along with it."

Jim Vizina owned the Oriental Building and rented the restaurant and bar to Mike Joyce. Lou Rickabaugh, a noted gambler from California; Dick Clark, of San Francisco; one Dunlap; and William H. Harris, erstwhile partner with Chalk Beeson in the Long Branch at Dodge City, jointly leased and operated the luxuriously furnished gambling rooms, which enjoyed by far the largest play of any Tombstone establishment.

Other gamblers, envious of the Oriental's popularity, hired a corps of professional fighting men under Johnny Tyler to hurrah the Rickabaugh place so consistently as to scare away patronage. Tyler had a record of six-gun victims scattered from Kansas to California. Dunlap had been taken ill and had left Tombstone. Neither Clark nor Harris was a fighting man. Lou Rickabaugh was game, but age and excess weight had slowed him down. Bill Harris got Luke Short and Bat Masterson in from Dodge to deal at the Oriental, but even their presence did not cow the hired killers. Lou Rickabaugh got a price on Dunlap's-interest and went to Wyatt Earp.

"I saw your play against that lynch mob," he told Wyatt, "and from what Harris, Masterson, and Short have told me, I figure you're the man I need. The quarter-interest will net you a thousand dollars a week, that much a day sometimes. Do you want it?"

Wyatt accepted Rickabaugh's offer.

Opposition gunmen had been usurping the Oriental bar and gambling tables during hours which should have been the most profitable, and driving customers out by gunplay and other violence. The first evening of Wyatt's partnership, Johnny Tyler led a dozen followers in to continue the intimidation. Wyatt sat in a chair against the rear wall of the gambling room.

While his companions lingered at the bar, Tyler walked to a faro layout where Rickabaugh was dealing and changed in one hundred dollars. After a steady run of bickering and abuse of Rickabaugh, Tyler jerked a six-gun to shove his stack of chips across the layout to the Queen.

"Deal 'em, you big so-and-so," he challenged, "and if the Queen loses, I'll blow that stack into your bank!"

Rickabaugh filled the dealer's slot to overflowing and a shot that scattered the stack of chips would send the forty-five-caliber slug tearing through his body. Lou looked the gunman in the eye, and made a turn. The Queen did not show.

Johnny Tyler screamed with pain. A muscular thumb and forefinger was hoisting him from his seat by an earlobe. If he had an idea of gunplay, he abandoned it when he saw who had him.

"I didn't know you had an interest in this place," Tyler exclaimed.

"I have," Wyatt Earp assured him, "and you can tell your friends it's the fighting interest."

Using the ear as a lever, Wyatt propelled Tyler to the door. With a shove and a boot he sent the gunman sprawling into Allen Street. As he turned back into the Oriental, Wyatt saw Tyler's followers lined up at the bar, hands in the air, and looking into Doc Holliday's nickel-plated six-gun.

"Much obliged, Doc," Wyatt said. "Herd 'em outside with their friend."

Whatever gamblers' war might have been under way in Tombstone was called off, and the Oriental business quickly brought Wyatt's profits to the figure Rickabaugh had estimated. The gambling partnership was now forced to purchase the Oriental bar, when Mike Joyce was appointed to Cochise County's newly formed Board of Supervisors, and threw in politically with their enemies.

Johnny Behan had barely taken office when his deputy, Frank Stilwell, Pony Deal, and several others of the Clanton –Curly Bill crowd held up a stage without a guard, on which no mail or express was carried, and took one hundred and thirty-five dollars from the passengers. Sheriff Behan did not send out a posse, and as neither Federal nor Wells-Fargo shipments had been involved, Wyatt Earp was without jurisdiction.

While Bob Paul awaited decision in his contest against

Shibell, he continued to ride shotgun for Wells-Fargo. About ten o'clock at night on March 15, Wyatt, while dealing faro at the Oriental, received a telegram from Paul at Benson, stating that an attempt had been made to hold up the stage on which he had left Tombstone at six o'clock with a bullion shipment of eighty thousand dollars. Paul reported the attack as near Drew's Ranch, six miles out of Contention toward Benson. He had saved the bullion, but Bud Philpot, the stage driver, and Peter Roerig, a passenger, had been killed by highwaymen.

Wyatt deputized Virgil and Morgan Earp, Bat Masterson, and Marshall Williams as his posse and started for Drew's Ranch.

20

Johnny Behan Tips His Hand

Wyatt Earp suspected that Bill Leonard, Jim Crane, Harry Head, and Luther King, of the Clanton outfit, who had been camping for a week in an abandoned adobe on the Contention Road, were the Benson stage bandits, a suspicion speedily confirmed after his posse reached Drew's and was joined by Sheriff Behan and his deputy, Breakenridge. Bob Paul and passengers who had ridden through the attack gave details of the attempted holdup.

The Sandy Bob stage had changed teams at Contention and gone on past Drew's Ranch. As the horses slowed on a grade, three men stepped out of the chaparral, two at the left of the road, one at the right, each with a rifle at his shoulder. It was a clear, moonlit, desert evening. The highwaymen were masked, but Paul and two passengers recognized Crane and Leonard.

"Whoa-up!" one of the pair on the left shouted. This was Bob Paul's side of the road.

"We don't hold up for anybody!" Paul yelled defiantly.

"Go on, Bud," he urged Philpot, as he threw his shotgun to his shoulder.

Philpot was a courageous old-timer who had been through more than one brush with frontier road agents. He yelled at his horses and cracked his whip in the signal which sent the six animals into their collars.

One bandit on Paul's side let go with his rifle, the bullet crashing into the seat at Paul's elbow. The messenger replied with his shotgun. A highwayman screamed. The bandit on the right cut loose. His bullet hit Bud Philpot squarely in the heart, and the driver pitched onto his wheelers. Bob Paul jerked his six-guns, but as Philpot's body struck them, the wheel horses jumped, and the whole hitch bolted. As the terrified animals leaped into a run which carried the bullion shipment beyond the bandits' reach, the road agents opened rifle-fire on the receding stage. Peter Roerig, riding in the dicky seat, tumbled dead into the road.

When Philpot died, the reins dropped to the ground where they dragged as the stage careened and jolted. Bob Paul clambered along the swaying tongue, retrieved the lines, regained the box, slid into Philpot's seat by the brake, and guided the stage into Benson. This gave color to later rumor that Paul had been driving at the time of the attack, having tricked Bud Philpot into a change of seats in anticipation of a holdup. Acceptance of this fabrication as truth was necessary to success of a scheme by which the outlaws sought to shift responsibility for the murder, but it was discredited entirely by passengers who had been riding outside just back of Paul and Philpot.

At daylight, Wyatt found seventeen empty rifle shells in the road where the highwaymen had stood while pumping lead after the vanishing bullion. In the mesquite, he located the spot where one man had held four horses, from which three other men had gone on foot to and from the road, and in the nearby brush four cloth masks covered with frayed rope to simulate long hair and whiskers. Certainty that four men had taken part in the holdup strengthened Wyatt's certainty of identification, and he knew to his own satisfaction how they had operated.

In support of later innuendos, *The Tombstone Nugget* inquired pointedly how robbers could know which stages were carrying treasure unless they were tipped off by someone in the confidence of the express company. *The Epitaph* answered with a truth familiar to everyone in Tombstone.

"The solution is easy to all who know anything about affairs here," Mr. Clum stated in his columns. "Whenever treasure is shipped, a messenger is sent on that stage; when there is no treasure, there is no guard. Under these circumstances any intelligent person can deduce whether the coach is *en bonanza* or *en borusca*."

Wyatt Earp and Bob Paul agreed that when King, on watch outside the adobe cabin, saw the stage pass with a shotgun messenger at Philpot's side, he had been certain that the regular Tuesday shipment of bullion was going out and that he and his companions had mounted and followed. While the teams were being changed at Contention, the outlaws had detoured across country to intercept the stage at a point where they knew the horses would be held to a walk.

Sheriff Behan sought to discourage pursuit of the bandits by picturing the hopelessness of a desert trail that was twelve hours old. Marshal Earp, however, had confidence in his ability to pick up sign. Then Behan protested that Wyatt would have no authority to take prisoners if he caught up with them, and stated that, as sheriff, he would make no arrests on suspicion. Wyatt replied that the stage had carried mail, and took up the trail. Behan and Breakenridge followed.

East to the Dragoon foothills, northwest to Tres Alamos, and on up the valley the rustlers' trail was covered by every trick they knew and every resource of the desolate country. They doubled on their tracks, rode for miles in the riverbed, followed long reefs of barren rock, and rounded up a bunch of cayuses which they drove along to cover the sign of their own ponies. Smart as the outlaws were, they were followed by men as skilled at reading ruses of escape as any Indian.

Early in the morning of March 19, the posse rode up to Wheaton's abandoned ranch on the San Pedro, after one hundred and fifty miles of tortuous trailing. In Wheaton's old barn they found a badly done cow pony, which Wyatt recognized as an animal Luther King had ridden into Tombstone a week earlier.

From Wheaton's the trail led to a ranch owned by Hank Redfield, known to be on good terms with the Clantons. Redfield swore that no horsemen had passed his place for several days. Nearby, Morgan Earp picked up fresh sign, which was followed to a ranch four miles farther on, owned by Len Redfield, Hank's brother.

As the posse rode up to Len Redfield's, Luther King climbed the far side of the corral and made for the brush. Morgan Earp ran him down. King had a rifle slung across his shoulders, two six-guns and belts of cartridges at his waist, and twenty boxes of rifle and pistol ammunition in the slack of his shirt above his trousers.

King disclaimed all knowledge of any holdup, denied that the spent pony found at Wheaton's was his and that he had been near Tombstone in two weeks. Len Redfield stood by, watching, as his brother Hank rode in. Wyatt and his deputies started a search for King's companions, leaving King in Sheriff Behan's custody.

"Don't let King talk with the Redfields," Wyatt warned the sheriff.

The marshal returned unexpectedly and caught King talking with both Redfields, while Behan and Breakenridge stood by unconcernedly. Hank Redfield rode off quickly, and when Wyatt reproached the sheriff for his laxity, Behan answered sharply that no one had made any charges against either King or the Redfields, and that he, as sheriff, did not propose to take orders from Wyatt, anyway.

Wyatt and Bob Paul took King to one side and for the astounded rustler's benefit sketched rapidly, as they had reconstructed the action, every move the highwaymen made from the time the stage passed the adobe cabin until they started their getaway from the scene of the double murder.

"Bill Leonard, Harry Head, Jim Crane, and you pulled that job," Wyatt concluded. "Three of you stood by the road, stuck up the stage and killed Philpot and Roerig; the fourth held the horses in the brush. I don't know which one he was, but, whoever he was, he's lucky. The other three will swing for this job."

"I held the horses! I held 'em!" King cried. "Honest, I did! I didn't do any shooting."

In the presence of Bob Paul, Virgil and Morgan Earp, Marshall Williams, Sheriff Behan, and Deputy Sheriff Breakenridge, Wyatt had Luther King repeat the full story of the attempted robbery, and admit that the horse found at Wheaton's was his. King added that he had ridden one of Hank Redfield's horses down to Len's for ammunition and money and that when the Earp posse rode in, he was just saddling a fresh mount to rejoin Leonard, Head, and Crane, who were camped near Hank Redfield's. They had obtained fresh horses from Hank Redfield earlier that morning.

"Just where are they camped?" Wyatt asked.

The rustler was about to answer when his attitude changed swiftly to defiance. Some undetected influence had rebolstered his courage.

"You'll never get 'em!" King boasted. "They know you've got me, and you'll never catch 'em. I'm not talking anymore, either."

"You'll talk plenty when the time comes to stretch rope," Wyatt assured him. "Your kind always does."

Behan interposed.

"King's my prisoner," he declared. "I'm arresting him for murder. That's a county offense, not Federal. I'm taking him to Tombstone."

Wyatt nodded to Marshall Williams.

"I'll go with you," the Wells-Fargo agent told Behan.

"You don't have to," the sheriff retorted.

As Wyatt and his posse started after Leonard, Head, and Crane, Marshall Williams rode with Behan, Breakenridge, and King on the back trail for Tombstone.

Near Hank Redfield's, Wyatt's posse found a spot where

three men had rested for some hours and had broken camp hastily. Hank Redfield had been well ahead of them with his warning.

For more than three hundred miles over the most desolate section of Arizona, Wyatt tracked his quarry after leaving Redfield's, north and west along the Tanque Verde, Rincon, and Santa Catalina Mountains, through the Oracles and Cañada del Oro, east through the Santa Cruz, across the San Pedro, and back to the Dragoons. At Helm's Ranch, in the Dragoons, Behan and Breakenridge rejoined the posse, bringing with them Buckskin Frank Leslie, ostensibly because of Leslie's great skill as a trailer. Forty years afterward, when Leslie was a broken old vagabond, he told Wyatt Earp that Johnny Behan had hired him to throw the marshal's posse off the trail of the Benson stage robbers.

"What did you do with King?" Wyatt asked Behan when the sheriff rejoined him.

"Locked him up," the sheriff answered.

The outlaw trail now led toward Galeyville, down the San Simon to Joe Hill's ranch in the Cienaga, then toward the Cloverdale section of New Mexico, where Leonard and Head, Curly Bill, the Clantons, and other outlaws had ranches. In ten days and nights of trailing, the posse covered more than four hundred miles, for the greater part over endless wastes of rock and cactus, where for a hundred miles at a stretch there was no sign of human habitation, and, as their horses slowed down with fatigue, it might be forty-eight hours between water holes.

The outlaws, as they fled, were gaining. They had been able to get fresh ponies at rustler hangouts in the desert, while Wyatt's men were riding the animals on which they had left Tombstone. Bat Masterson's horse gave out, and Bat returned to Tombstone with a passing teamster. At a spring in the Guadalupe foothills, where signs indicated the outlaws were two days ahead, Jim Hume overtook the posse.

"King's loose," the Wells-Fargo officer told Wyatt as he dismounted.

The marshal turned on the sheriff.

"That right?" he demanded.

"Guess it is," Behan admitted.

"Why didn't you tell me this before?"

"I didn't figure it was your business," the sheriff answered.

"How'd he get away?" Wyatt asked.

Behan began the story of King's escape to which he and his followers clung thereafter in their attempts to square themselves with Tombstone.

John Dunbar, county treasurer, and Behan were partners in the Dexter Corral and Livery Stable at Tombstone, and on the way in with King, the sheriff said, he had bought the horse which King had abandoned at Wheaton's. After reaching Tombstone, King was taken to the sheriff's office, where Dunbar was to pay over the money. Behan said that Breakenridge and he were called away, leaving Under-Sheriff Woods and Dunbar with the prisoner. While a bill of sale was being drawn, King slipped out the door and escaped on a horse which a friend had saddled and waiting.

Hume contradicted this flatly. The Wells-Fargo officer said that when Behan, Breakenridge, and Marshall Williams rode into Tombstone with King, Behan announced that he would not put King in the calaboose, but would take him to the lodging house at the edge of town run by the wife of Under-Sheriff Woods. Marshall Williams objected, but Behan persisted and assigned a single deputy, Lance Perkins, to watch King. During the night, King walked out of the room which he shared with Perkins, mounted a horse waiting at the rear of the house, and rode off, taking with him a pair of guns and ammunition belts which were property of the sheriff's office. Later, the truth of Hume's story was incontestably established.

Wyatt and Jim Hume decided to return to Tombstone and attempt to pick up King's cold trail. Virgil and Morgan Earp and Bob Paul were to keep after Leonard, Head, and Crane.

Sheriff Behan stayed with the posse bound for New Mexico, but thereafter the two factions rode and camped separately. The Earps and Bob Paul did all the sign hunting and trailing. Behan, Breakenridge, and Leslie merely followed along, never letting the first three out of their sight.

Under Virgil's leadership the trail of the three murderers was followed to the Leonard and Head Ranch, thence over the desert into Old Mexico. Food for Paul and the Earps ran out, although the sheriff's party had some which they did not offer to share. For miles on end there was no water. With Leonard, Head, and Crane well down on alien soil, there seemed no other course than to turn back for Tombstone. The die was cast when Virgil Earp's horse dropped dead under him.

With Morg and Bob Paul taking turns at carrying Virgil behind them, the posse turned north. As the sheriff's animals were comparatively fresh, Behan, Breakenridge, and Leslie went along easily. Under the double burden, Morg's horse gave out, then Bob Paul's; the Earps and Paul had to lead two horses and follow on foot the trail left by Behan's men as they drew rapidly ahead of them. The three on foot and the two horses had been without water or food for forty-eight hours when they reached a desert water hole at the edge of San Simon Valley. Behan, Breakenridge, and Leslie were there, animals rested, fed, and watered.

Certain that the marshal's men had abandoned pursuit of the outlaws, the sheriff's party left them. Riding at night, the Behan party reached Joe Hill's ranch, forty miles distant, about daylight. Hill was a Clanton follower, and a friend of Behan's. No help for the marshal's men was sent from his place. Late the next night, Behan and his two deputies reached the San Simon Ranch, where they reported the plight of the Earp posse. The rancher immediately sent cowboys to the rescue with provisions and fresh ponies. When succor reached them, Virgil, Morgan, and Bob Paul had been without food for five days. However, they immediately started across country and made Tombstone but a few hours after Behan.

Wyatt had reached home to find that Luther King had ridden into Old Mexico the morning after he walked out of Sheriff Behan's custody. So far as Wyatt knew, King never returned to the Arizona country. Of greater import was discovery of a scheme to shift public suspicion of guilt in the Benson murders to Wyatt, Virgil and Morgan Earp, Doc

Holliday, Bob Paul, and Marshall Williams. *The Nugget* during Wyatt's absence had published the charge that Doc Holliday had taken part in the holdup as representative of the Earps and had fired the shot which killed Bud Philpot. In so doing, *The Nugget* dealt with Luther King's getaway thusly:

> It was a well-planned job by outsiders to get him away. He was an important witness against Holliday.

In this connection, and throughout all that follows, it must be kept in mind that the editor of *The Nugget* was that same Under-Sheriff Woods, from whose house and custody King walked, unhindered.

Next, *The Nugget* stated that proof of Holliday's participation in the holdup rested on the following reasons, quoted as published:

> On the afternoon of the attempted robbery he engaged a horse at a Tombstone livery, stating that he might be gone for seven or eight days, or might return that night. He left town about four o'clock armed with a Henry rifle and a six-shooter. He started for Charleston, and about a mile below Tombstone cut across to Contention. When next seen it was between ten and one o'clock at night, riding back into the livery at Tombstone, his horse fagged out. He at once called for another horse which he hitched in the street for some hours, but he did not again leave town. Statements attributed to him, if true, look very bad, and, if proved, are most conclusive as to his guilt, either as a principal or an accessory after the fact.

The story was followed by others of similar purport. The Earps and the Wells-Fargo officers kept their own counsel. Doc Holliday's only public reaction to *The Nugget* yarns was resentment at the slur on his ability.

"If I had pulled that job, I'd have got the eighty thousand," he said. "Whoever shot Philpot was a rank amateur.

If he had downed a horse, he'd have got the bullion. As for riding out of town with my six-gun and rifle, I did go over to Charleston that afternoon, and, as it's the hangout of certain persons who dislike me intensely, I went prepared for any attentions they might offer."

It was difficult, however, to offset rumors concerning trips which Doc had made to the adobe cabin where the four highwaymen had camped. Holliday denied that he had been there the afternoon of the crime, but admitted other visits.

Bill Leonard, as all Tombstone knew, had come to the camp to open a jewelry store, from Las Vegas, where he had been a respected businessman. In that New Mexico town, Doc Holliday had once practiced dentistry with his office in Leonard's store building. The two had become good friends, a relationship resumed in Tombstone. Leonard's calling got him in with the Clanton–Curly Bill outfit; it was his job at first to recover gold and silver from stolen amalgam or alloy. Eventually, he sold his store and rode with the outlaws openly. To Doc, this made no difference. Holliday liked Leonard and associated with him whenever he felt like it.

Gossip connecting Doc Holliday with the Philpot murder was dying out when Doc quarreled with Big-Nosed Kate. Kate went on a spree, during which several of Wyatt's enemies persuaded her to sign an affidavit charging Doc with participation in the attempted holdup. On the strength of this, Sheriff Behan arrested Holliday for the murder of Bud Philpot and Peter Roerig.

Wyatt promptly posted five thousand dollars cash bail for Doc's release, and Virgil Earp locked Big-Nosed Kate in a hotel room to get her sober. At the hearing, Kate disappointed Johnny Behan woefully. She had signed some paper, she said, while drinking with Behan, Mike Joyce, and some of their friends, but what it was or had in it she could not remember. Then Wyatt called his witnesses.

Doc Holliday admitted riding to Charleston; he had heard of a big poker game under way in that camp, but had found the game closed upon arrival. He had returned to Tombstone immediately, reaching town about six o'clock, had supper, and played faro the rest of the night. About ten o'clock, Wyatt Earp had shown him a telegram from Bob Paul telling of the holdup and had asked him to be ready to join a posse if necessary. Doc had sent to a livery for a saddle horse and kept it tied outside the gambling house all night, in case Wyatt sent for him in a hurry.

Old Man Fuller, who hauled water for the town of Tombstone from The Wells, ten miles out on the Charleston Road, testified that just after he left The Wells about four o'clock on the afternoon before the holdup, Doc Holliday had come along, hitched his horse at the rear of the water wagon, and ridden into Tombstone on the seat beside him. They had reached Tombstone a little after six o'clock, Old Man Fuller said, and in front of the livery, Doc had unhitched his horse and left him.

Wyatt Earp testified that he had seen Doc Holliday in a restaurant about six-thirty, and that within five minutes after he received Bob Paul's telegram, he had found Doc playing faro at the Alhambra. A faro dealer and several men who had been in the game testified that Doc had been bucking the bank for several hours when Wyatt came and talked to him, that Doc had sent a messenger for a horse, and had stayed at the faro table until daylight.

Doc Holliday was discharged from custody.

"You say the word and I'll leave Tombstone," Doc told Wyatt as they left the courtroom.

"You send that fool woman away and I'll be satisfied," Wyatt answered.

What Doc said about the woman was scarcely fit for repetition. That afternoon, Doc asked Wyatt for one thousand dollars in currency from a roll Doc kept in Rickabaugh's safe. That evening Big-Nosed Kate left Tombstone, and as far as Wyatt Earp ever knew, she and Doc Holliday parted company forever.

Bob Paul replaced Charlie Shibell as sheriff of Pima County. As far as Cochise County officers were concerned, the Benson stage holdup apparently was a closed incident. Wyatt Earp, however, sensed keenly that the prestige accruing to the outlaw organization, with continued immunity from punishment for the murder of Philpot and Roerig, would make his own position intolerable.

Open pursuit was no longer feasible, wherefore Wyatt resorted to craft. Destiny upset strategy, and organized outlawry embarked on a vendetta without parallel in frontier history.

21

Ike Clanton Makes a Deal

Sheriff Behan entrusted law enforcement in Charleston and Bisbee to Frank Stilwell, who had held up so many stages, it was said, that stage teams obeyed his voice as they would their drivers'. With Stilwell, Behan teamed a deputy, Gates, also a Clanton follower. Wyatt heard that Deputy Sheriff Gates was riding the horse which had been stolen from the marshal months earlier, and Sherman McMasters reported one morning that within the hour he had seen Gates ride the horse into Frank Stilwell's corral at Charleston. Wyatt reached the corral as Billy Clanton was riding out on the stolen animal.

"Get off my horse!" Wyatt commanded.

"Get out of the way or I'll ride you down!" Billy Clanton answered.

Wyatt dropped his hand to a gun butt.

"Get off," he repeated, "and get that saddle off, *pronto.*"

Clanton swung to the ground and removed saddle and bridle. Wyatt dropped a rope over the horse's head, turned suddenly, and jerked the rustler's guns from their holsters.

"I'll take these along for a spell," he said. "You'll find 'em in the road on the other side of the bridge."

"Next time it won't be your horse we'll get," Billy Clanton called after Wyatt in highly colored allusion; "it'll be you."

"Come anytime, and bring your friends," the marshal replied as he started for Tombstone.

The Clantons still maintained headquarters at Lewis Springs, and had preempted a string of water holes reaching to Las Animas Valley in New Mexico. On the Babocomari, west of Charleston, the McLowerys, Pattersons, Hicks brothers, Johnny Barnes, the Lyles, and others had cabins. East, the McLowerys, Joe Hill, the Pattersons, and numerous rustlers had additional camps at Soldier Holes in the Sulphur Springs Valley and beyond. Curly Bill held forth at Galeyville and Paradise.

Ranchers, mining operators, and traders in isolated sections complained that their taxes were assessed and collected by Clanton riders, in more than one instance by a deputy from Behan's Tombstone office accompanied by Curly Bill himself. Behan and his deputies treated this as a huge joke. There is no record of levity with the men who rode into Tombstone with tales of amounts assessed against them and methods employed for collection.

About every prisoner finding his way into the sheriff's custody who could establish connection with the Clanton crowd promptly walked out of the calaboose. *The Nugget* usually printed Johnny Behan's explanations of the escapes, and the roster of getaways equaled that of arrests, included half the "cowboy" gang, and involved every crime from horse stealing and highway robbery to arson and murder. Also, as compared with money collected in the name of the law, funds for legitimate county purposes were inexplicably lacking.

What understanding existed at this time between Sheriff Behan and the outlaws, no competent authority has stated. Boom-camp journalists, however, provided a day-to-day record of the outlawry upon which Old Man Clanton and his following embarked, and their freebooting attained such notoriety that newspapers the country over featured reports of Cochise County crimes and killings. The Congress of the United States took the scandal under discussion, and President Garfield was asked to remove Frémont as Governor of Arizona Territory.

Tombstone organized a fighting branch of the Citizens' Safety Committee, one hundred business and professional men, commanded by Captains W. B. Murray and J. L. Fronck, retired soldiers. These vigilantes were to report on call for duty under Wyatt Earp within the Tombstone limits. As John P. Clum has stated the case:

"The situation in Tombstone was aggravated by the general feeling among the citizens that the peace officers of the county under Sheriff John Behan were in sympathy with the lawless element which roamed southeastern Arizona and it was deemed wise to guard against possible depredations of these outlaws. Our plans for law enforcement and protection of our lives and property were fully and freely discussed with Wyatt Earp and his brother Virgil. This fact establishes beyond any question the high esteem and confidence which the leading citizens of Tombstone entertained toward both Wyatt and Virgil.

"I was a great admirer of Wyatt Earp," Mr. Clum continues, "although it would have embarrassed him to know it. He was tall, erect, manly, serene, with hair a bit long, but trimly kept, a royal mustache, and in neat attire topped with a broad-brimmed Stetson, he looked the part of the capable and courageous peace officer that he was. I still have a clear vision of that dignified figure walking calmly along Allen Street."

To this William J. Hunsaker, in 1931 dean of the Los Angeles, California, bar, but as a young man a pioneer Tombstone attorney, has added: "I knew Wyatt Earp well. He was a quiet, but absolutely fearless man; as a peace officer, above reproach. He usually went about in his shirt-sleeves, and with no weapons. He was cool and never excited, but very determined and courageous. He never stirred up trouble, but he never ran away from it or shirked responsibility. He was an ideal peace officer and a fine citizen."

With Johnny Behan in the county saddle, the outlaws resumed their swaggering in the Tombstone streets, boasting openly to bartenders and dance-hall girls of the sources of swag they squandered. Innumerable warrants for the arrest of the rustlers were sworn to by their victims, but neither Behan's force nor Ben Sippy, the Tombstone marshal, could be prevailed upon to serve them. There was a growing suspicion that Sippy had thrown in with the Behan faction. As the boldness of the outlaws increased, certain of them bragged that Leonard, Head, and Crane, the Bud Philpot murderers, had returned to Arizona soil and were riding again with Old Man Clanton.

At Wyatt's suggestion, Wells, Fargo and Company flooded the territory with posters offering two thousand dollars reward, each, for the captures of the road agents. As Wyatt had anticipated, this brought scores of persons to him with information. He listened, but took no action.

Wyatt believed he knew Ike Clanton's makeup better than Ike knew it himself. His plan of action hinged on the accuracy with which he gauged this outlaw's character.

On May 30, Ike Clanton rode into Tombstone, and stayed several days. On two or three occasions the outlaw sought to discuss the reward posters with the marshal, but Wyatt shut off the overtures.

"I let Ike itch a bit," Wyatt said.

In the afternoon of June 2, Wyatt met Ike Clanton alone in front of the Eagle Brewery Saloon.

"Ike," the marshal asked without prelude, "how'd you like to make six thousand dollars?"

"What d'ya mean?" Clanton countered.

"Meet me out back of the saloon in ten minutes and I'll tell you," Wyatt answered.

At the appointed time, Wyatt found Ike Clanton waiting, and knew he had judged his man correctly.

"Ike," Wyatt said, "you help me catch Leonard, Head,

and Crane, and you can have every cent of the Wells-Fargo reward."

Ike displayed no resentment at the inference, and for half an hour marshal and outlaw discussed means whereby Leonard, Head, and Crane might be captured, after which Ike left for Sulphur Springs Valley to get the help of Joe Hill and the McLowerys. On June 6, he returned to Tombstone with Hill and Frank McLowery.

"Any strings on your offer?" Joe Hill asked the marshal.

"None," Wyatt answered.

"We can use the money," Frank McLowery said, "but if the rest of the crowd ever learns who turned up these fellows, we won't live twenty-four hours."

"I won't give you away," Wyatt assured the trio. "You get Leonard, Head, and Crane where I can grab them, then I'll collect the reward and turn it over to you in cash. You won't appear in the business."

"You'll never take them alive," McLowery said, which led Ike Clanton to another question.

"How about that?" he asked. "The reward is offered for their arrest. Does that go, dead or alive?"

From this point the rustlers refused to proceed without official assurance that blood money would be paid regardless of condition in which the highwaymen were taken. Wyatt asked Marshall Williams to telegraph the necessary query to San Francisco. The reply came next morning, but as the conspirators would not take Wyatt's word for its content, he was forced to ask Marshall Williams for the message. Williams saw Wyatt show the telegram to Hill, Clanton, and McLowery.

The whole fabric of the later Clanton–Behan conspiracy against Wyatt Earp was woven around Ike Clanton's denial that there had been any such telegram as Wyatt received. So much has been made of the doubt that the message existed, even in official histories of Arizona, that it appears advisable to quote the much-discussed telegram, exactly as copied from the original found in the long mislaid court records of Cochise County. The message read.

SAN FRANCISCO, CALIF.
June 7, 1881

Marshall Williams,
Tombstone, Arizona.
Yes, we will pay rewards for them dead or alive.
L. F. ROWELL

Rowell was assistant in San Francisco to John J. Valentine, president of Wells, Fargo and Company.

The three rustlers now agreed to go through with the betrayal. They were to report to Wyatt as soon as they could set a proper trap for their victims.

Before Wyatt saw the conspirators again, Tombstone had her first disastrous fire, on June 25, which destroyed a large section of the business district. Looting which followed the fire brought the Safety Committee's decision to get rid of Ben Sippy as marshal, and suggestion that he resign was made in such manner that he complied immediately. Virgil Earp was appointed to serve Sippy's unexpired term.

On Fourth of July, Ike Clanton, Joe Hill, and Frank McLowery rode into Tombstone to report that Leonard, Head, and Crane were camping near Eureka, New Mexico, and that they planned to lure them to Rabbit Springs on the Bisbee Road, at which later spot Wyatt could surprise them. The bait was to be a pretended holdup of the stage carrying the Copper Queen payroll.

Setting the trap was again delayed while the conspirators rode with Old Man Clanton, John Ringo, Jim Hughes, Rattlesnake Bill Johnson, Jake Gauze, and Charlie Snow to the massacre of Skeleton Canyon. A mule train carrying seventy-five thousand dollars in silver bullion was ambushed and nineteen muleteers slaughtered. Old Man Clanton pocketed most of the loot, but enough was distributed to send the whole crowd on a two weeks' orgy in Galeyville and Charleston. Details of the massacre were bragged about as the killers caroused, but Johnny Behan, the only peace officer with jurisdiction, made no arrests. It was two weeks before Joe Hill, Ike Clanton, and Frank McLowery recovered from their debauch.

Then, Curly Bill, Joe Hill, Milt Hicks, and several others

rode into Sonora and rustled a herd of Mexican steers back to the Clanton Ranch at Cloverdale. Old Man Clanton was to drive them to market. While Hill and Brocius waited for the Clantons to round up another stolen herd, Mexican vaqueros, who had followed them across the line, caught the outlaws napping and recovered the stolen stock. Curly Bill, Joe Hill, John Ringo, and several others started after the Mexicans. They caught them in San Luis Pass, shot fourteen vaqueros out of their saddles, and started the steers back to Las Animas. On the back trail, Curly Bill and his men tortured, mutilated, and killed after the Apache fashion eight wounded Mexicans who had not succumbed to the first gunfire.

Old Man Clanton with five cowboys started his drive to market, and the immunity which he enjoyed may be gathered from his announced intention of selling the stolen steers in Tombstone. On the way through Guadalupe Canyon, the cattle thieves were ambushed by relatives of the bullion-train victims. Old Man Clanton and four of his men were killed, Harry Earnshaw alone escaping.

Two days later, Joe Hill rode into Tombstone with word that Jim Crane had died with Old Man Clanton in Guadalupe Canyon. Wyatt urged Hill to keep after Leonard and Head, and after another talk with Ike Clanton and Frank McLowery, Hill started for the New Mexico hideout.

Joe Hill found Bill Leonard and Harry Head, but in their coffins; he reached Huachita, New Mexico, a few hours after the two bandits were killed by Ike and Bill Haslett, brothers who ran a small store which the outlaws attempted to rob. Wyatt sent Morgan to Huachita to verify Hill's story.

Morgan learned that Leonard lived for some hours after the Hasletts shot him, and that his groin showed a festering flesh wound which Leonard admitted had been inflicted by Bob Paul's shotgun in the attack on the Benson stage. Leonard's dying statement identified Luther King, Jim Crane, and Harry Head as his only associates in the holdup. Crane, he declared, had fired the shot which killed Bud Philpot. Who had killed Roerig, he could not say, as Crane, Head, and he had stood in the road and shot at the back of the stage. Morgan had barely returned to Tombstone when Curly Bill and John Ringo rode up to the Haslett store, shot and killed the Hasletts without warning, in revenge for the deaths of Head and Leonard.

Curly Bill succeeded Old Man Clanton as titular head of the Cochise County outlaws; John Ringo shared leadership, and the pair boasted openly of their working alliance with the sheriff's forces. Outlaws stole cattlemen's monthly payrolls as well as their animals. Behan's deputies were regular visitors at the Clanton, McLowery, and Patterson ranches, and with Curly Bill in Galeyville. The recognized method of recovering stolen stock was to dicker with the rustlers through the sheriff's office.

Wyatt and Morgan Earp went to board with their brothers in the houses at First and Fremont Streets, and Pete Spence moved into a house directly across First Street. Spence was a tall, lanky Texan, whose true name was Lark Ferguson. He had killed a dozen men in Texas and New Mexico and had taken part in several Curly Bill forays before moving into Tombstone as spy for the outlaws.

On September 8, at eleven o'clock at night, the Tombstone–Bisbee stage was held up near Hereford and robbed of twenty-five hundred dollars in the Wells-Fargo box and a mail sack. Jewelry and seven hundred and fifty dollars in currency were taken from four passengers. There was no shotgun messenger on the stage, and Levi McDaniels, the driver, offered no resistance when two masked men, one with a shotgun, the other with a Colt's, stepped into the road with the order to halt and throw off the box. McDaniels recognized the bandit who relieved the passengers of their cash and jewelry as Pete Spence, and the second as Sheriff Behan's deputy, Frank Stilwell. Off in the chaparral McDaniels saw two other men whom he could not identify.

Wyatt Earp joined McDaniels at Hereford, to take the trail at daylight. Morgan Earp, Marshall Williams, and Fred Dodge were with him. Sheriff Behan sent out his deputies, Breakenridge and Neagle. There had been rain, and in the damp sand beside the road Wyatt noted a number of prints from the narrow, high heels of a cowpuncher's boots, each track showing the imprint of four nailheads in pattern. Again, in the chaparral where the mail sack had been slit and rifled, similar tracks were found. From this spot the trail of four horsemen led into the hills.

In Hereford, Wyatt had learned that Frank Stilwell, Curly Bill, and Pony Deal had been together all afternoon and evening, until just before the robbery they were joined by Pete Spence, when the four rode out the Bisbee Road. Wyatt believed this quartet had left the sign he noted until the fugitives separated and he chose to follow the trail of a single horseman into Bisbee.

As the posse rode through town, Frank Stilwell stepped into a saloon just ahead of them. Wyatt's eye caught the broad, flat heels on Stilwell's boots, such an anomaly in that country that Wyatt wheeled to the hitching rail, dismounted, and went into a bootshop.

"Frank Stilwell been in here?" Wyatt asked Dever, the shoemaker.

"He just went out," Dever answered.

"Have the heels changed on his boots?"

"Yes, I made him some new boots the other day, and he came in and had me put on low heels in place of high ones."

"Got the heels you took off?"

Dever handed over a pair of narrow heels with four nailheads in each one forming a pattern that every man in the posse recognized.

Wyatt announced that he intended to arrest Stilwell for the stage robbery.

"I'm going to get something to eat," Breakenridge remarked.

"Don't let us catch you eating with Stilwell," Morgan Earp called after him.

Wyatt went into the saloon, where Stilwell submitted to arrest with the boast that he'd be turned loose ten minutes after he saw Johnny Behan.

Fred Dodge and Marshall Williams started Stilwell for Tombstone while Wyatt and Morgan headed for Charleston on the chance of finding Pete Spence. They overtook Spence on the trail and had him in Tombstone soon after Stilwell's arrival.

Sheriff Behan tried to hold jurisdiction over Stilwell and Spence, but Wyatt swore out Federal warrants and took the men to Tucson, where they were bound over for robbing the mails, with bail at five thousand dollars.

While Wyatt was at Tucson, Ike and Billy Clanton, Frank and Tom McLowery, John Ringo, Milt Hicks, and Joe Hill rode into Tombstone. They met Morgan Earp on foot in Allen Street, and circled around him.

"I'm telling you Earps something," Frank McLowery began, in the hearing of Ed Byrnes and Charlie Smith, who were loafing nearby. "You may have arrested Pete Spence and Frank Stilwell, but don't get it into your heads you can arrest me. If you ever lay hands on a McLowery, I'll kill you."

Morgan was alone, and unarmed.

"If the Earps ever have occasion to come after you, they'll get you," Morgan replied, and walked away.

Wyatt reached home on October 17. Ed Byrnes, Charlie Smith, Ed Winters, Farmer Daly, and Old Man Fuller—whose son Wes was a hanger-on with the outlaw gang—were among those who warned him that the Clantons, McLowerys, Ringo, Hicks, and Hill all had openly boasted around the saloons that they'd kill the Earps and Doc Holliday.

Tombstone recognized Ike Clanton and Frank McLowery as mouthpieces for the outlaws.

"If the Earps were not men of great courage," read a *Star* news dispatch sent out of the camp, "they would hardly dare to remain in Tombstone."

Efforts to force Frémont's resignation as Governor of Arizona had been held in abeyance from the assassination of President Garfield in July until his death on September 19, but upon succession of Chester A. Arthur to the presidency they were renewed. President Arthur announced Frémont's resignation as of October 15, with selection of

John J. Gosper as acting governor pending appointment of a full-fledged successor.

To cap the political worries incident to the change in governors, Johnny Behan now suffered a blow at a more vulnerable point, his conceit of himself as Tombstone's most accomplished charmer. Behan was a spender, and lavished no small portion of the forty or fifty thousand dollars which came his way each year upon the assumption that he was Tombstone's most popular beau. The dapper little sheriff set himself up as arbiter of the camp's social affairs and sartorial style, once journeying clear to San Francisco for dancing lessons to clinch his position. The young lady whom he might honor with attentions was expected to be duly appreciative.

As Wyatt Earp followed the run of Tombstone's social activities with no particular pretenses, Tombstone was considerably amused to learn that the object of Johnny Behan's most ardent affections had given Johnny the mitten and was publicly exhibiting a decided preference for the marshal's company.

Johnny Behan always talked too much, and over his love affair he waxed bitter, voicing the first of his open threats to run Wyatt Earp out of Tombstone. This bitterness unquestionably led the sheriff to further abetment of the outlaws in their conspiracy against the Earps and was a determining factor in the course which that vendetta followed.

Wyatt Earp returned from a lengthy conference with Governor Gosper and Marshal Dake in Tucson, to find Ike Clanton awaiting him in great trepidation. Ike accused the marshal of having told of the plot to betray Leonard, Head, and Crane, and swore that he'd be killed as soon as the news reached his fellow outlaws. Wyatt truthfully denied that he had mentioned the conspiracy to anyone.

"Marshall Williams knows all about it," Clanton insisted. "He just told me so."

"He's shooting at the moon," Wyatt said. "Is he drinking?"

"Some," Ike answered.

As Wyatt suspected, the Wells-Fargo agent, with that shrewdness of intoxication, had drawn conclusions from the telegrams he handled and the meetings he saw while the plot for betrayal of the three stage robbers was under discussion. Ike Clanton had given himself completely away by his rise to Williams's speculations.

Three days later, fear-stricken Ike again sought Wyatt and accused him of having told Doc Holliday of the proposed betrayal. When Ike insisted that this was true, Wyatt said:

"Doc's been out of town for ten days. I don't see how he could have spread much around. He's coming in on the six-o'clock stage. We'll see what he has to say."

Wyatt and Ike were at the Wells-Fargo office when Doc climbed out of the stage.

"Doc," Wyatt asked bluntly, "did I ever tell you that Ike Clanton and I were in any deal together?"

"No," Doc replied.

"Ike says I did."

"Ike's a liar."

Clanton insisted that his secret had been divulged. Doc inquired ingeniously what the secret might be, and Ike, in hearing of numerous bystanders, burst into a full account of the deal he said he was accused of having made, thus giving first public knowledge of the outlaws' agreement to betray their fellows.

Now, the cardinal tenet of Doc Holliday's perverted creed was loyalty. Moreover, Doc had liked Bill Leonard. The gunfighting dentist owned a vocabulary rich in scurrilous idiom and the wit to apply it, which he turned in full force and flavor upon Ike Clanton to tell him what he thought of a murdering cow thief who'd sell out his kind. For fifteen minutes and for all Allen Street to hear, Doc Holliday berated Ike Clanton vigorously and profanely. He finished, turned, and walked away, while Ike shouted after him threats to kill the next man who coupled his name with that of Wyatt Earp.

That night Ike Clanton rode out of Tombstone to the McLowery Ranch in Sulphur Springs Valley.

On October 22, Ike and Billy Clanton, Frank and Tom

McLowery rode into Charleston and obtained the release of Billy Claiborne, who was being held for the murder of James Hickey. Claiborne was a tough young Curly Bill satellite who, after the death of Billy the Kid (Bonney), in New Mexico, aspired to succeed that outlaw in public notoriety. He insisted upon being called Billy the Kid, and before shooting Hickey, had killed two men who refused to accord him that title.

On October 23, four of Sheriff Behan's prisoners walked out of the Tombstone calaboose: Milt Hicks, Jim Sharp, Yank Thompson, and Jesse Harris, all Curly Bill followers, Hicks under arrest for cattle stealing, the others on murder charges. Tombstone received Behan's explanation of their escape somewhat dubiously, and, as the town filled with cowboys, doubt increased.

Curly Bill, John Ringo, Ed and Johnny Lyle, Frank Patterson, Frank Stilwell, Pete Spence, and fifty kindred spirits swaggered up and down Allen Street. In the saloons and dance halls the outlaws bragged that the Earps were to be run out of Tombstone. They had set a time limit now, the cowboys said. The showdown would come within forty-eight hours.

The Citizens' Safety Committee offered to back Virgil Earp in herding the whole bunch of rustlers out of town. Wyatt advised against such a move, certain to bring on a free-for-all street battle. The Safety Committee then deputized Wyatt and Morgan Earp and Doc Holliday as marshals of Tombstone under Virgil Earp and left the situation to them.

"We'll wait," Wyatt counseled with Virgil. "The Clantons and McLowerys are back of this show. You haven't seen them in town for three or four days. They'll get nervous when nothing happens and come in. The longer we keep them waiting, the tougher we make it for them."

In the late afternoon of October 25, Ike Clanton and Tom McLowery rode into Tombstone. They made considerable show over checking their six-guns and rifles at the Grand Hotel and separated. Tom sat into a poker game at the Occidental Saloon, a cowboy hangout, where Sheriff Behan also was playing. Ike made the rounds of Allen Street saloons alone.

Word was sent from Charleston by J. B. Ayers that Frank McLowery, Billy Clanton, and Billy Claiborne were in his saloon, armed and apparently awaiting a call of definite nature. It was suggested that the trio expected to join Ike and Tom in Tombstone.

"I expect so," Wyatt agreed.

"What are you going to do about it?" the vigilance committee asked.

"Nothing," Wyatt replied. "Have you noticed there aren't a dozen cowboys in town? They cleared out when Ike and Tom came in. I don't think there'll be any fight. Ike Clanton seems to be running this, and Ike would rather talk than fight. I say, let him."

22

At the O. K. Corral

Whiskey has made more fight-talk than fights, and more brag has been slept off with its liquor than ever has made good in battle. Frontier benders pretty generally followed the alcoholic rule, but the red-eye that set Ike Clanton's tongue wagging in the Allen Street saloons during the evening of October 25, 1881, was to precipitate the most celebrated encounter between outlaw and peace officer in the history of untamed Arizona. It was also to furnish Ike with dubious immortality through a gunfight over which the West has wrangled for half a century, and can still argue as heatedly as while the roar of six-shooters echoed in the streets of Tombstone.

Potency under Ike's belt found vent in loose-mouthed boasts that he would kill Wyatt Earp and Doc Holliday before the setting of the next day's sun. When Farmer Daly and Ed Byrnes suggested that the rustler had laid out quite a job, Ike sneered:

"The Earps are not so much. You'll see, tomorrow. We're in town for a showdown."

About midnight Ike went to the Occidental Saloon where his friends were playing poker. Doc Holliday entered and walked directly to Clanton.

"Ike," Doc said, "I hear you're going to kill me. Get out your gun and commence."

"I haven't any gun," Clanton replied.

"I don't believe you," Doc retorted. "I'll take your word for it this time, but if you intend to open your lying mouth about me again, go heeled."

Morgan Earp, who passed the saloon as Holliday was berating Clanton in picturesque profanity, pulled Doc to the sidewalk. Clanton followed with Tom McLowery, insisting that he was not armed, but promising he soon would be and would shoot Doc on sight. Wyatt and Virgil Earp came along and took Doc to his room, where Wyatt ordered the dentist to keep away from Clanton.

"A gunfight now, with you in it," Wyatt warned Holliday, "would ruin my chance to round up this bunch."

"All right," Doc promised regretfully, "I'll keep away from him."

Half an hour later, Ike found Wyatt at the Eagle lunch counter.

"You tell Doc Holliday no man can talk about me the way he did and live," Ike began. "I'm wearing a gun now and you can tell Holliday I aim to get him."

"Doc's gone to bed," Wyatt replied. "You're half drunk. You'll feel better when you've had some sleep."

"I'm stone-cold sober," Ike retorted. "I'm telling you to tell Holliday I'll gun him the first time I see him."

"Don't you tangle with Doc Holliday," Wyatt advised. "He'll kill you before you've started."

"You've been making a lot of talk about me, too," Ike said.

"You've done the talking," Wyatt corrected.

"Well, it's got to stop," Ike declared. "You had the best of me tonight, but I'll have my friends tomorrow. You be ready for a showdown."

"Go sleep it off, Ike," Wyatt suggested. "You talk too much for a fighting man."

Virgil Earp came in the door, as Ike started out. Ike paused and shouted over his shoulder:

"I said tomorrow. You're to blame for this, Wyatt Earp. What I said for Doc Holliday goes for you and your so-and-so brothers."

Wyatt and Morgan Earp went home about four o'clock. Virgil went to the Occidental to keep an eye on Behan, Clanton, McLowery, and the other cowboys until their game broke up; he reached home after daylight.

The Earps were awakened in the morning of October 26 by word that Ike Clanton was at Fifth and Allen Streets, armed with six-guns and a Winchester, bragging that his friends were on the way to Tombstone to help him clean out the Earps. A second message warned that Billy Clanton, Frank McLowery, and Billy Claiborne had just ridden in to join Ike and Tom McLowery and that the five outlaws were at Fourth and Allen Streets. Ike and Frank had been in several saloons asking if the Earps or Holliday had been around that morning. In Vogan's they had boasted they would shoot the first Earp who showed his face in the street.

"Where's Holliday?" Wyatt asked.

"He hasn't been around."

"Let him sleep," Wyatt ordered.

Ike Clanton had not given the Earps much concern, but Billy Clanton, Claiborne, and the two McLowerys, whatever else they might be, were game men, crack shots and killers. The McLowerys were possibly the two fastest men with six-guns in all the outlaw gang. Frank McLowery was admittedly better on the draw-and-shoot than Curly Bill or John Ringo, and held by some to surpass Buckskin Frank Leslie.

Warren Earp was in California with his parents. Jim Earp was physically unable to take a hand. But, outnumbered as they were, none of the three brothers, as he buckled on his guns, had any idea other than that they would go directly to Fourth and Allen Streets.

"You and Morg go up Fremont Street," Wyatt instructed Virgil. "I'll take Allen Street."

He was giving his brothers the better chance of avoiding the outlaws. They knew it, but obeyed, as was their habit.

"If you see Ike Clanton, arrest him," Wyatt said. "But don't shoot unless Ike does. Take his guns away in front of the whole town, if you can, and show him up."

At Fourth Street, Virgil and Morgan turned south and reached the midblock alley as Ike Clanton eased out of the narrow passage, rifle in hand, eye on the Allen Street corner.

"Looking for me?" Virgil asked in Ike's ear.

Clanton swung around, lifting the rifle. Virgil seized the Winchester with his left hand, jerked a Colt's with his right, and bent the six-gun over Ike's head. Virgil and Morgan lugged their prisoner through the street to Judge Wallace's courtroom, where Morgan guarded him while Virgil went to find the judge. Several persons who had seen Ike arrested went into the courtroom, among them R. J. Coleman, a mining man who figured in later happenings, and Deputy Sheriff Dave Campbell. Ike was raving with fury.

"I'll get you for this, Wyatt Earp!" he yelled as Wyatt came through the door.

"Clanton," Wyatt answered, "I've had about enough from you and your gang. You've been trying for weeks to get up your nerve to assassinate my brothers and me. The whole town's heard you threaten to kill us. Your fight's against me, not my brothers. You leave them out of this. I'd be justified in shooting you on sight, and if you keep on asking for a fight, I'll give it to you."

"Fight's my racket," Ike blustered. "If I had my guns, I'd fight all you Earps, here and now."

Morgan Earp offered one of Ike's sequestered six-guns, butt foremost, to the owner.

"If you want to fight right bad, Ike," Morgan suggested, "take this. I'll use my fists."

"Quit that, Morg," Wyatt snapped. Deputy Sheriff Campbell pushed Ike into a chair.

"All I want with you," Ike shouted, again identifying Wyatt with a few choice epithets, "is four feet of ground and a gun. You wait until I get out of here."

Wyatt walked from the courtroom. At the door he literally bumped into Tom McLowery, hurrying to Ike's assistance.

"You looking for trouble?" McLowery snarled as he recovered his balance.

"I didn't see you coming," Wyatt answered.

"You're a liar!" McLowery retorted.

Bystanders said Wyatt paled an ominous yellow under his tan.

McLowery's gun was at his hip. Faster than the outlaw could think, Wyatt slapped him full in the face. Tom made no move for his pistol.

"You've got a gun on," Wyatt challenged. "Go after it."

McLowery's right hand dropped downward. Wyatt Earp's Buntline Special flashed and the marshal buffaloed Tom McLowery his full length in the gutter. Wyatt turned his back and walked toward Allen Street.

Judge Wallace fined Ike Clanton twenty-five dollars for breach of the peace. As Ike realized he was to get off thus lightly, more of his bravado returned. The courtroom was filled and before this audience the outlaw took a fling at Virgil Earp.

"If I'd been a split second faster with my rifle," he boasted, "the coroner'd be working on you now."

"I'm taking your rifle and six-guns to the Grand Hotel," Virgil replied. "Don't pick them up until you start for home."

"You won't be here to see me leave town," Ike retorted.

Wyatt Earp had posted himself outside of Hafford's. Frank and Tom McLowery, Billy Clanton and Billy Claiborne passed him, all wearing six-guns, and went into Spangenberg's gun shop. Virgil Earp came along, carrying Ike Clanton's weapons to the Grand Hotel, and joined Wyatt at a point across Fourth Street from the gunsmith's. They and several vigilantes who stood with them could see plainly all that went on in the gun store.

Ike Clanton now hurried into Spangenberg's. He purchased a six-shooter and the five rustlers loaded their cartridge belts to capacity. Virgil Earp went on to the hotel.

Frank McLowery's horse moved onto the walk in front of the gun store. Wyatt strode across the road and seized the animal's bit. The two McLowerys and Billy Clanton came running from the store.

"Let go of my horse!" Frank shouted.

"Get him off the walk," Wyatt rejoined.

"Take your hands off my horse!" McLowery insisted.

"When he's where he belongs," Wyatt replied, backed the horse into the road and snubbed him close to the hitching rail.

The three rustlers had their hands on their gun butts, spectators later testified.

"That's the last horse of mine you'll ever lay hands on!" Frank McLowery assured Wyatt with a string of oaths.

Wyatt turned on his heel and recrossed the street.

The cowboys left Spangenberg's in a group, going to the Dexter Corral on the south side of Allen Street, between Third and Fourth Streets, owned by Johnny Behan and John Dunbar. Wyatt joined Virgil and Morgan at Hafford's corner, where the brothers stood for possibly half an hour while the rustlers made several trips on foot between the corral and nearby saloons, during which most of Tombstone was apprised of their intention to wipe out the Earps.

Captain Murray and Captain Fronck, with half a dozen Vigilantes, were conferring with Wyatt when R. J. Coleman, heretofore mentioned, reported that he had followed the rustlers to the Dexter Corral and on the way back had met Johnny Behan. Coleman said he had told Behan he should disarm the outlaws, as they were threatening to kill the marshal and his brothers, and that Behan had gone on into the corral. As the Earps and the Vigilantes went into Hafford's to get away from the crowd that gathered, Coleman again went down Allen Street to watch the cowboys.

While Virgil Earp was talking with the Vigilantes, Sheriff Behan entered Hafford's and cut into the conversation.

"Ike Clanton and his crowd are down in my corral making a gun-talk against you fellows," Behan said. "They're laying to kill you. What are you going to do about it?"

"I've been hoping that bunch would leave town without doing anything more than talk," Virgil answered. "I guess they've got to have their lesson. I'm going to throw 'em into the calaboose to cool off. I'll put somebody on to see that they don't walk out, too."

"You try that and they'll kill you," Behan warned Virgil.

"I'll take that chance," Virgil replied. "You're sheriff of Cochise County, Behan, and I'm calling on you to go with me while I arrest them."

Behan laughed. "That's your job, not mine," he said, and left the saloon.

Virgil Earp went into the Wells-Fargo office and returned with a sawed-off shotgun, as Coleman came back to Hafford's with word that the rustlers had transferred headquarters from the Dexter to the O. K. Corral and recruited a sixth to their war party in the person of Wes Fuller, hanger-on and spy for the Curly Bill crowd. Ike Clanton, Tom McLowery, Billy Claiborne, and Fuller had crossed Allen Street to the O. K. Corral without horses, Billy Clanton had ridden his horse and Frank McLowery had led his. All were wearing six-guns, Coleman said, while Billy Clanton and Frank McLowery had rifles slung from their saddles. They had gone past the stalls near the Allen Street entrance to the corral and into the rear lot which opened on Fremont Street. They had posted Wes Fuller on lookout in the alley and Tom McLowery had gone out into Fremont Street, returning within a few minutes.

The reason for Tom's brief absence was established later by Chris Billicke and Dr. B. W. Gardiner who had been standing on the courthouse steps. Tom walked from the corral to Everhardy's butcher shop, better known as Bauer's. This business had been placed in Everhardy's name after Bauer was indicted as purchaser of cattle which the Curly Bill crowd rustled, but Bauer continued to work at his block. Chris Billicke and Dr. Gardiner saw Tom McLowery talk with Bauer and stuff a roll of bills into his trousers pocket as he left the shop, revealing as he did so the butt of a six-gun at his belt, an item to be noted.

After Tom's return, Coleman started to walk through the

corral yard and was stopped by the cowboys, who asked if he knew the Earps. When he replied that he did, Frank McLowery and Ike Clanton gave him two messages, one for the Earps as a whole, the other for Wyatt, in particular.

"Let's have 'em," Wyatt said.

"They told me to tell the Earps that they were waiting in the O. K. Corral, and that if you didn't come down to fight it out, they'd pick you off in the street when you tried to go home."

The strategy which had moved the outlaws from the Dexter to the O. K. Corral now was apparent.

Allen and Fremont Streets ran parallel with the numbered streets crossing them at right angles, and with an alley running east and west through each block. The O. K. Corral had its covered stalls on the north side of Allen Street, and an open yard across the alley on the south side of Fremont. On Fremont Street an adobe assay office stood at the west line of the corral yard, while to the east was C. S. Fly's photograph gallery.

On the north side of Fremont Street, facing the yard, was the original Cochise County Courthouse, a rambling two-story adobe with courtroom on the ground floor, and on the upper the offices of county officials. These offices opened onto an outside gallery, the west end of which was about opposite the west line of Fly's studio. Then came the *Epitaph* office, and an adobe store occupied by Mrs. Addie Bourland, a milliner.

To return to the O. K. Corral, the alley which ran between the stalls and yard gave onto Fourth Street, and in this passageway Wes Fuller was stationed to keep an eye on the Allen Street corner.

The Earps, in going to and from their homes at First and Fremont Streets, customarily followed Fremont Street past the O. K. Corral yard. The only other direct route available took them by the Allen Street entrance. The Clantons and McLowerys could command with their guns, on a moment's notice, either path; thus outlaw strategy forced the Earps to call the turn or quit the play.

"What's the special message for me?" Wyatt Earp asked Coleman.

"They said to tell you that if you'd leave town they wouldn't harm your brothers," Coleman answered, "but that if you stayed, you'd have to come down and make your fight or they'd bring it to you."

Wyatt looked at Virgil and Morgan. Without a word the three Earps started for the door. Captain Murray stopped them.

"Let us take this off your hands, boys," he offered. "Fronck and I have thirty-five Vigilantes waiting, ready for business. We'll surround the corral, make that bunch surrender, and have them outlawed from Tombstone."

"Much obliged," Wyatt answered for his clan, "but this is our job.

"Come on," he said to Virgil and Morgan.

As the Earps swung out of Hafford's door and started, three abreast, along Fourth Street, Doc Holliday came up on the run.

"Where are you going, Wyatt?" Doc demanded.

"Down the street to make a fight."

"About time," Holliday observed. "I'll go along."

"This is our fight," Wyatt said. "There's no call for you to mix in."

"That's a hell of a thing for you to say to me," Doc retorted. "I heard about this while I was eating breakfast, but I didn't figure you'd go without me."

"I know, Doc," Wyatt said, "but this'll be a tough one."

"Tough ones are the kind I like," the gunfighting dentist answered.

"All right," Wyatt agreed, and Doc Holliday fell into step with the only person on earth for whom he had either respect or regard.

Holliday was wearing a long overcoat and carrying a cane, as he often did when his physical afflictions bore heavily.

"Here, Doc," Virgil Earp suggested, "let me take your cane and stick this shotgun under your coat where it won't attract so much attention."

Holliday handed over the stick and drew his right arm from the overcoat sleeve, so that the garment hung cape-like over that shoulder. Beneath it he held the short Wells-Fargo weapon. As the four men passed the Fourth Street alley, Wes Fuller ran back into the corral where the Clantons and McLowerys were waiting.

"You ought to have cut him down," Doc Holliday observed.

Beyond this laconic suggestion, not one of the quartet of peace officers spoke as they walked rapidly toward Fremont Street.

Johnny Behan and Frank McLowery had been standing together at the corner of Fourth and Fremont Streets as the Earps left Hafford's. The sheriff and the rustler hurried to the corral yard; Behan talked for a moment with the five cowboys, then hastened back toward the corner, some fifty yards away. He had covered less than half the distance when the marshal's posse came into view.

Tombstone's Fremont Street of 1881 was a sixty-foot thoroughfare with the wide roadbed of the hard-packed, rusty desert sand bordered by footpaths at no marked elevation from the road level. The walks, where buildings adjoined, ran beneath the wooden awnings with their lines of hitching rails. At the O. K. Corral yard, there was necessarily a gap in the awning roofs and rails, which gave unhindered access for the width of the lot. Johnny Behan apparently expected the marshal's force to follow the sidewalk to the corral and hurried along it to meet them.

Along Fourth Street the Earp party had been two abreast, Wyatt and Virgil in the lead, with Virgil on the outside, Morgan behind him, and Doc Holliday back of Wyatt. Each sensed instinctively what could happen if they rounded the corner of Fly's Photograph Gallery abruptly in close order, and at the street intersection they deployed catercorner to walk four abreast, in the middle of the road.

Half a dozen persons who saw the four men on their journey down Fremont Street have described them. The recollections agree strikingly in detail. No more grimly portentous spectacle had been witnessed in Tombstone.

The three stalwart, six-foot Earps—each with the square jaw of his clan set hard beneath his flowing, tawny mustache and his keen blue eyes alert under the wide brim of a high-peaked, black Stetson—bore out their striking resemblance, even in their attire; dark trousers drawn outside the legs of black, high-heeled boots, long-skirted, square-cut, black coats then in frontier fashion, and white, soft-collared shirts with black string ties to accentuate the purpose in their lean, bronzed faces. Doc Holliday was some two inches shorter than his three companions, but his stature was heightened by cadaverousness, the flapping black overcoat and the black sombrero above his hollow cheeks. Holliday's blond mustache was as long and as sweeping as any, but below it those who saw him have sworn Doc had his lips pursed, whistling softly. As the distance to the O. K. Corral lessened, the four men spread their ranks as they walked. In front of Bauer's butcher shop, Johnny Behan ran out with upraised hand. The line halted.

"It's all right, boys. It's all right," the sheriff sputtered. "I've disarmed them."

"Did you arrest them?" Virgil Earp asked.

"No," Behan said, "but I will."

"All right," Virgil said. "Come on."

The politician's nerve deserted him.

"Don't go any farther," he cried. "I order you not to. I'm sheriff of this county. I'll arrest them."

"You told me that was my job," Virgil retorted.

The three Earps and Holliday moved on in the road. The sheriff ran along on the walk.

"Don't go down there! Don't go down there!" he cried. "You'll all be killed!"

The four men in the road cleared the line of Fly's studio. Virgil, Wyatt, and Morgan turned sharply left into the corral, Virgil a few feet in the lead, Wyatt and Morgan following in the order named. The wise Doctor Holliday halted with an uninterrupted sweep of Fremont Street. The door of Fly's gallery banged. Johnny Behan had ducked into the building, where a window gave him view of the corral yard and farther along a side door opened. Across the lot the five rustlers stood, backs to the assay office wall.

The outlaws were vigorous, sinewy fellows—Ike Clanton, burlier than the rest, wearing, as did each McLowery, a thin mustache in Mexican-dandy style—all with a similarity of attire as marked as, but contrasting sharply with, that of the Earps. Huge sand-hued sombreros, gaudy silk neckerchiefs, fancy woolen shirts, tight-fitting doeskin trousers tucked into forty-dollar half-boots—a getup so generally affected by Curly Bill followers that it was recognized as their uniform—set off the lean, sunbaked hardness of these desert renegades. Ike Clanton and Tom McLowery wore short, rough coats, the other three, fancy sleeveless vests in the best cow-country fashion.

Billy Claiborne was farthest of his group from the walk, perhaps thirty feet from the street line. Next, on his left, was Ike Clanton, then Billy Clanton, Frank, and Tom McLowery. They had avoided bunching and Tom McLowery was about ten feet from the street. Posted to blank possible fire from the assay office corner were two cow ponies, one Frank McLowery's, the other Billy Clanton's, each carrying a Winchester rifle in a saddle boot.

One glance at the cowboys revealed that, despite Johnny Behan's declaration, all were armed. Tom McLowery had a six-gun stuck in the waistband of his trousers. Frank McLowery, Billy and Ike Clanton, each had similar weapons slung from their belts. Claiborne had a Colt's at either hip.

The Earps moved in. From the road, Doc Holliday referred to Johnny Behan in one unprintable phrase. Virgil Earp was well into the corral, Wyatt about opposite Billy Clanton and Frank McLowery, Morg facing Tom. Not a gun had been drawn. Wyatt Earp was determined there'd be no gunplay that the outlaws did not begin.

"You men are under arrest. Throw up your hands," Virgil Earp commanded.

Frank McLowery dropped his hand to his six-gun and snarled defiance in short, ugly words. Tom McLowery, Billy Clanton, and Billy Claiborne followed concerted suit.

"Hold on!" Virgil Earp shouted, instinctively throwing up

his right hand, which carried Doc Holliday's cane, in a gesture of restraint. "We don't want that."

For any accurate conception of what followed, one thing must be kept in mind: action which requires minutes to describe was begun, carried through, and concluded faster than human thought may pick up the threads. Two witnesses swore that its whole course was run in fifteen seconds, others fixed the time at twenty seconds, Wyatt Earp testified that it was finished thirty seconds after Frank McLowery went for his gun. Also, careful note of that action furnishes, more than any other episode of his life, the key to the eminence of Wyatt Earp.

Frank McLowery and Billy Clanton jerked and fired their six-guns simultaneously. Both turned loose on Wyatt Earp, the shots with which they opened the famous battle of the O. K. Corral echoing from the adobe walls as one.

Fast as the two rustlers were at getting into action from a start with guns half-drawn, Wyatt Earp was deadlier. Frank McLowery's bullet tore through the skirt of Wyatt's coat on the right, Billy Clanton's ripped the marshal's sleeve, but before either could fire again, Wyatt's Buntline Special roared; the slug struck Frank McLowery squarely in the abdomen, just above his belt buckle. McLowery screamed, clapped his left hand to the wound, bent over and staggered forward. Wyatt knew Frank as the most dangerous of the five outlaws and had set out deliberately to dispose of him.

In this fraction of a second, Tom McLowery jumped behind Frank's horse, drawing his gun and shooting under the animal's neck at Morgan Earp. The bullet cut Morgan's coat. Billy Clanton shot a second and a third time at Wyatt, missing with both as Morgan turned loose on him, aiming for Billy's stomach, but hitting the cowboy's gun hand.

Sensing that Tom McLowery was now the most dangerous adversary, Wyatt ignored Billy Clanton's fire as Tom again shot underneath the pony's neck and hit Morg.

Tom McLowery must be forced into the open. Wyatt shot at the pony behind which the cowboy crouched, aiming for the withers. The pony jumped and stampeded for the street, the excitement taking Billy Clanton's horse with him. As his brother's horse started, Tom McLowery grabbed for the rifle in the saddle boot, but missed it.

At the upper end of the lot, Virgil Earp had been delayed in going for his gun by the position of his hand and his grasp of Doc Holliday's cane. Before Virgil could jerk his Colt's free, Billy Claiborne fired at him twice and missed. Claiborne started across the corral toward the side door of Fly's gallery which opened for him, firing point-blank at Virgil as he passed him and missing again. When Ike Clanton saw Johnny Behan open the door for Claiborne, his braggart heart funked. Ike had not drawn his gun; it swung at his hip as in his panic he headed straight for Wyatt Earp.

Tom McLowery's second slug had hit Morgan Earp in the left shoulder, glanced on a bone, ripped across the base of his neck, and torn a gaping hole in the flesh of his right shoulder.

"I've got it!" Morg gasped, as he reeled under the shock.

"Get behind me and keep quiet," Wyatt said.

As Morgan was hit, Virgil Earp fired his first shot in the fight, breaking Billy Clanton's gun arm as it covered the cowboy's abdomen. Billy worked the "border shift," throwing his gun from right to left hand.

Far from obeying Wyatt's command, Morgan, who saw Billy Clanton's maneuver, shot Billy in the chest as Virgil put a slug into Clanton's body, just underneath the twelfth rib.

Before Wyatt could throw down on Tom McLowery, as the pony plunged away, Ike Clanton had covered the few feet across the corral and seized Wyatt's left arm.

"Don't kill me, Wyatt! Don't kill me!" the pot-valiant Clanton pleaded. "I'm not shooting!"

"This fight's commenced. Get to fighting or get out," Wyatt answered, throwing Ike off. The gallery door was held open and Ike fled after Claiborne.

Tom McLowery was firing his third shot, this at Wyatt as Ike Clanton hung to the marshal's arm, when Doc Holliday turned loose both barrels of his shotgun simultaneously from the road. Tom's shot went wild and McLowery started on a run around the corner of the assay office toward Third

Street. Disgusted with a weapon that could miss at such a range, Holliday hurled the sawed-off shotgun after Tom with an oath and jerked his nickel-plated Colt's. Ten feet around the corner, Tom McLowery fell dead with the double charge of buckshot in his belly and a slug from Wyatt Earp's six-gun under his ribs which had hit him as he ran.

Frank McLowery was nearing the road, left hand clutching his abdomen, the right working his gun as he staggered on. Billy Clanton was still on his feet and following. Frank shot at Wyatt. The slug struck short. So did another he sent at Morg.

Wyatt heard the crash of glass from the side window of Fly's gallery, where Claiborne and Sheriff Behan stood. Two shots from the window followed.

"Look out, boys!" Wyatt called. "You're getting it in the back!"

Morgan Earp wheeled to face this new danger, stumbled and fell, but Doc Holliday sent two bullets through the window. Shooting from the gallery stopped. At this juncture Ike Clanton darted from a rear door across the alley and into the stalls of the O. K. Corral, flinging his fully loaded six-gun into a corner of the yard as he ran. Doc sent two shots after Ike, but was a split second late. Doc wheeled to face Frank McLowery, who had reached the street, drawn himself upright and, less than ten feet away, was steeling himself for steady aim at Holliday.

"I've got you, you so-and-so such-and-such," McLowery snarled.

"Think so?" Doc found wit to inquire.

When Morgan fell, he rolled to bring his gun arm free and brought up at full length on his side facing McLowery and Holliday.

"Look out, Doc!" Morg called, shooting as he lay.

McLowery's, Holliday's, and Morgan Earp's pistols roared together. Doc winced and swore. Frank McLowery threw both hands high in the air, spun on his bootheels, and dropped on his face. Morg got to his feet. Morgan's bullet had drilled clear through Frank McLowery's head, just behind the ears; Doc's had hit the outlaw in the heart. Either would have killed him instantly, while Wyatt's first shot, which had torn through his abdomen, would have brought death in another few seconds. Frank's last bullet had hit Doc Holliday's hip holster, glanced, and shaved a strip of skin from his back.

Meanwhile, as Wyatt sent a bullet into Tom McLowery when he ran, Virgil Earp and Billy Clanton were shooting it out. Billy was making for the street, firing as he went, when he hit Virgil in the leg. Virgil kept his feet and returned the fire as Wyatt shifted his attention to Billy Clanton. Wyatt's shot hit Billy in the hips, and as the cowboy fell, Virgil's bullet tore through his hat and creased his scalp. With his last ounce of gameness, the rustler raised to a sitting posture and tried to steady his wavering gun on his knee. While Wyatt and Virgil hesitated over shooting at a man who plainly was done, Billy Clanton slumped in the dust. The firing ceased. Billy Claiborne ran from the rear of Fly's on through toward Allen Street. Holliday's trigger clicked futilely.

"What in hell did you let Ike Clanton get away like that for, Wyatt?" Doc complained.

"He wouldn't jerk his gun," Wyatt answered.

The fight was over.

Frank McLowery was dead in the middle of Fremont Street. Tom McLowery's body was around the Third Street corner. Billy Clanton was still breathing but died within a few minutes.

Virgil's leg wound and Morgan's, in the shoulder, were ugly, but not serious. Doc Holliday's scratch was superficial.

Four of the cowboys had fired seventeen shots; Ike Clanton, whose brag and bluster brought on the battle, none. They had scored just three hits, not one of which put an adversary out of action.

The three Earps and Holliday had fired seventeen shots, four of which Doc Holliday had thrown at random into the gallery window and after Ike Clanton. The remaining thirteen had been hits. Any one of Frank McLowery's wounds would have been fatal. Billy Clanton had been hit six times, three fatally. Either of Tom McLowery's wounds would have killed him, and Wyatt's shot which stampeded the cow ponies was a bull's-eye; it served Wyatt's exact purpose, stinging the animal to violent action, but not crippling him beyond ability to get out of the way.

As the smoke of battle lifted, Wyatt turned to look up Fremont Street. A yelling mob was headed toward him. The Citizens' Safety Committee had started for the corral in a column of twos, but excitement overcame discipline.

"I distinctly remember," writes John P. Clum, "that the first set of twos was made up of Colonel William Herring, an attorney, and Milton Clapp, cashier of a local bank. Colonel Herring was tall and portly, with an imposing dignity, while Milton Clapp was short and lean and wore large spectacles. The striking contrast in stature and bearing between these two leaders of the 'column' registered an indelible picture which still intrudes as a flash of comedy in an exceedingly grave moment."

Virgil and Morgan Earp were taken to their homes by the Vigilantes and a guard of twenty posted around the Earp property to prevent retaliation by friends of the dead outlaws. Other Vigilante squads patrolled the Tombstone streets.

Ike Clanton was found hiding in a Mexican dance hall, south of Allen Street, and Billy Claiborne nearby. They were taken to the calaboose and guarded to prevent either escape or lynching. Ike, at least, had small desire for freedom; he begged to be locked up and protected.

After his brothers had been cared for, Wyatt Earp walked up Fremont Street with Fred Dodge. Across from the sheriff's office, above the O. K. Corral, Johnny Behan stopped them.

"Wyatt," the sheriff said, "I'm arresting you."

"For what?" Wyatt asked in astonishment.

"Murder," Behan answered.

Wyatt's eye turned cold and his voice hard.

"Behan," he said, "you threw us. You told us you had disarmed those rustlers. You lied to throw us off and get us murdered. *You* arrest *me?* Not today, nor tomorrow either. I'll be where any respectable person can arrest me any time he wants to, but don't you or any of your cheap errand boys try it."

The sheriff walked away.

That afternoon a coroner's jury refused to hold the Earps and Holliday for death of the cowboys. Johnny Behan, principal witness at the inquiry, was deeply chagrined. At this time Behan thought himself the sole eyewitness to the fight in the corral, other than the participants. He so boasted to C. S. Fly. Fly had seen something of the battle and had noted other witnesses of whom Behan was unaware. Fly was a Vigilante, and closemouthed. He reported Behan's belief to the Safety Committee, which sagely decided to give the talkative little sheriff all the rope he'd take.

One item which the coroner did uncover was that the three dead outlaws had, among them, more than six thousand dollars in currency, and that Ike Clanton and Billy Claiborne also had carried large sums of cash into the battle. This substantiated subsequent testimony that the rustlers had planned to kill the Earps and Holliday and ride for Old Mexico to stay until public resentment subsided.

The Cochise County grand jury was sitting at Tombstone at the time of the battle in the O. K. Corral and the Vigilantes asked that body to investigate the killings immediately. Behan, still believing there were no nonparticipating witnesses to contradict him, testified before the grand jury, as did Ike Clanton. Numerous Tombstone citizens were called, but the Earps did not appear. The grand jury announced that it could find no reason to indict four duly appointed peace officers for performance of necessary duty.

Ike Clanton left the calaboose and went with Johnny Behan to the office of *The Nugget*. Wes Fuller and Billy Claiborne were called into conference. With the next issue, *The Nugget* began the prosecution for Outlawry *vs.* Wyatt Earp.

23

A Frame-up Fails

On the day after the fight at the O. K. Corral, the bodies of Frank and Tom McLowery and Billy Clanton were dressed in the finest "store clothes" that money could buy, placed in ornate caskets, surrounded with what Tombstone could provide in the way of floral decorations and put on public view in the parlors of a Tombstone undertaker. Above the bodies the exhibitors placed a large sign:

MURDERED IN THE STREETS
OF TOMBSTONE

The Nugget, in publishing an invitation for all citizens to come and see what could happen to three peaceable, law-abiding cowboys, quoted Sheriff Behan, Ike Clanton, Billy Claiborne, and Wes Fuller as authority for the charge that the McLowerys and Billy Clanton had been shot down ruthlessly while their hands were in the air in compliance with Virgil Earp's command, and that of the cowboys in the fight only Frank McLowery and Billy Clanton had been armed. Claiborne, it was naively suggested, did not count, as he had merely chanced to be in the corral. Whereupon Claiborne, Behan, and Fuller were offered as disinterested witnesses to corroborate Ike Clanton's story. Furthermore, so *The Nugget* stated, the cowboys had been on their way home when surprised by the Earps.

The fight at the O. K. Corral had taken place on Wednesday. On Thursday and Friday, with the bodies on display, the Clanton–Curly Bill following was noticeably absent from Tombstone streets and saloons, but Saturday brought the renegades of the ranges into town in such numbers that their hangouts were crowded. Late that afternoon, Ike Clanton and Johnny Behan went before Judge Wells Spicer and jointly swore to warrants charging Wyatt Earp, Virgil Earp, Morgan Earp, and John H. Holliday with the murder of William Clanton, Frank and Thomas McLowery.

Behan had deputized a dozen rustlers to help serve the warrants, and set the time for arrests after the close of the banks and county offices, which would leave the Earps and Holliday defenseless in the calaboose over Sunday, the day set for a cowboy demonstration in Tombstone in connection with the funeral of the McLowerys and Billy Clanton. What might have happened to the Earps and Doc Holliday as Behan's prisoners on such an occasion must remain a matter for surmise.

Wyatt Earp learned of Johnny Behan's plans and appeared in Judge Spicer's court, with Doc Holliday, while Behan was out looking for them. When Behan and Ike Clanton hurried in with the five firms of lawyers they had retained to prosecute, Wyatt's attorney, Tom Fitch, had arranged that Virgil and Morgan Earp, bedridden by wounds, were to remain at liberty pending decision in the hearing against Wyatt and Doc.

The Behan–Clanton attorneys demanded that bail for Wyatt Earp and Holliday be set at fifty thousand dollars each. Tom Fitch asked for a few minutes' delay. Anson T. K. Safford, formerly Governor of Arizona, and H. Solomon, Tombstone's leading bankers, would open their safes to produce cash for the bonds. Judge Spicer replied that the sum asked was preposterous, released Wyatt and Doc in ten thousand dollars bail, each, and set the hearings for Monday morning.

On Sunday, the Clanton–McLowery funeral procession paraded Tombstone, attended by two hundred rustlers. Cowboy sympathizers had planned to crowd the courtroom for the Earp–Holliday hearing, but, on Monday, to quote from *The Epitaph* of October 31, 1881: "No one excepting officers of the court, and the witness whose testimony was being taken, was allowed inside."

A news dispatch sent out of Tombstone that night reported:

> Everything is quiet in town, and the investigation is proceeding with closed doors. Under statutory rules none of the testimony is allowed to be published. There is a more assured feeling of security now than since the shooting. The friends of the cowboys will have to fight it out in court without resorting to any more bloodshed.

Thus, Sheriff Behan, Ike Clanton, Billy Claiborne, and Wes Fuller each was forced to tell his story to Judge Spicer without exact knowledge of what the others had sworn to. As matters transpired, they had over-rehearsed their act.

Ike Clanton based his testimony on the attempt to rob the Benson stage, with the consequent murder of Bud Philpot and Peter Roerig. He swore that Doc Holliday had confessed to him that it was he who killed Philpot, and, further, that Morgan Earp, Virgil Earp, and Wyatt Earp each had sought him out to confide that they had arranged the robbery and to beg him, Ike, to keep Leonard, Head, and Crane from revealing the officers' part in the crime. The fight in the O. K. Corral, Ike said, was the Earps' desperate effort to get him out of the way, because he knew too much of their undercover criminal activities. Ike, in telling the story of the actual fight, charged that Holliday had fired the first shot from a nickel-plated six-gun, and explained that he had grappled with Wyatt Earp to keep Wyatt from shooting at his brother. He testified that only Frank McLowery and Billy Clanton were armed, and that all had thrown up their hands at Virgil Earp's command.

Johnny Behan supported Ike's general description of the fight. However deeply the sheriff may or may not have been involved in the conspiracy of the O. K. Corral, it is worth noting that on the witness stand Behan could recall nothing of his association with the cowboys the night before the battle, his meeting with Virgil Earp and the Vigilantes in Hafford's saloon or the "gun talk" which the rustlers had made in his corral. The sheriff testified that his first intimation of impending trouble came while he was in a barber's chair a few minutes before the shooting, that he had hurried to the corral, where he made certain that none of the cowboys was armed except Billy Clanton and Frank McLowery, who agreed to surrender their weapons if he would disarm the Earps. He told of the first shot, fired from Holliday's nickel-plated gun, made no mention of any shotgun, said that he held Fly's door open as sanctuary for Claiborne and Ike Clanton, but recalled no shots fired from or into the window.

Claiborne testified that Doc Holliday fired the first shot from a nickel-plated six-gun, and then went Ike and Johnny Behan several better. He swore that Morgan Earp fired the second shot of the fight, placing his gun against Billy Clanton's belly and pulling the trigger as Clanton stood with hands in the air, crying, "Don't shoot me! I don't want to fight!" Claiborne could not recall that he fired his own pistol.

Wes Fuller supported much the others had said, but wove in extra details which later were to confound his associates.

With the preliminary statements on record, Judge Spicer opened the case for public hearing. The prosecuting witnesses repeated their charges on the stand, and quickly involved one another in a mass of perjury.

Wyatt Earp and Doc Holliday brought no countercharges against Behan and the cowboys, but confined their efforts to refuting the accusations of murder. Their first witnesses were Dr. H. M. Matthews, coroner, and Dr. George Goodfellow, who had conducted post mortem examinations of Billy Clanton and the McLowerys. The surgeons established incontestably that neither Clanton nor McLowery could have been shot at powder-mark range or with hands in the air. Next, it was proved that both Ike Clanton and Tom McLowery had gone into the fight armed, by reputable witnesses of whose presence neither Behan nor Ike Clanton had been aware. A dozen Tombstone citizens told of threats to kill the Earps on sight which the Clantons and McLowerys had voiced, and established the intimate association of Behan with the outlaws just before the fight. Several swore that Doc Holliday had gone into action with a shotgun only after everyone else in the corral was shooting, and it was proved that Billy Clanton had fired at least two shots, possibly three, before he himself was hit. Among others, two eyewitnesses of the battle had been Judge Lucas, of the probate court, who had watched the fight from the gallery of the courthouse, and Addie Bourland, who had seen it through the window of her milliner's shop.

Then Wyatt Earp took the stand to tell the inside story of his long campaign against organized outlawry in Arizona, beginning with the incident of the stolen Government mules and ending with the fight in the O. K. Corral. In so doing he employed the full results of his own investigations with all the corroboration which Wells, Fargo and Company employees and other Federal officers had unearthed. The Behan–Clanton forces objected vigorously, but, as Ike Clanton had testified at length on the same subjects to support his charges, the marshal was allowed to continue. Wyatt supported his statements with documentary evidence, and when he had finished, Cochise County had for the first time an accurate conception of the extent to which she had been exploited by the politico-cowboy gang. *The Nugget* did not publish this portion of the proceedings.

Progress of the Tombstone hearing was a national newspaper sensation of 1881. One result was the receipt by Judge Spicer, on November 16, of two documents which he filed without making public and which have remained unpublished to the present day. Wyatt Earp was not aware of their existence. The originals were found with other records of the case buried in the dust of half a century. One, dated at Dodge City, Kansas, November 4, 1881, reads:

TO ALL WHOM THESE PRESENTS MAY COME, GREETING:

We the undersigned residents of Dodge City, Ford County, Kansas, and vicinity, do by these presents certify that we are personally acquainted with WYATT EARP, late of this city; that he came here in the year 1876; that during the years 1877, 1878 and 1879, he was Marshal of our city; that he left our place in the Fall of the year 1879; that during his whole stay here he occupied a high social position and was regarded and looked upon as a high-minded, honorable citizen; that as Marshal of our city he was ever vigilant in the discharge of his duties, and while kind and courteous to all he was brave and unflinching and on all occasions proved himself the right man in the right place; and, hearing that he is now under arrest charged with killing three men termed, "Cow Boys," from our knowledge of him we do not believe that he would wantonly take the life of his fellow man, and that if he was implicated he only took life in the discharge of his sacred trust to the people, and we earnestly appeal to the citizens of Tombstone, Arizona, to use all means to secure him a fair and impartial trial, fully confident that when so tried he will be fully vindicated and exonerated of any crime.

With this was a similar paper, from Wichita, Kansas:

We the undersigned citizens of Wichita are well acquainted with WYATT S. EARP and were intimately acquainted with him while he was on the Police Force of this city in the years, 1874, 1875, and a part of the year, 1876. We further certify that said WYATT S. EARP was a good and efficient officer, and was well known for his honesty and integrity, that his character while here was of the best, and that no fault was ever found with him as an officer or as a man.

Appended to the documents were the signatures of scores of the leading citizens of Kansas, including—it should be noted—those who had been Wyatt's political opponents as well as his supporters and friends, and not a few upon whom his official hand, in times past, had fallen heavily. Of even greater significance is the fact that Dodge City and Wichita knew the Curly Bill gang of so-called "Cow Boys" all too well; a majority of the Arizona rustlers had ridden the Texas Cattle Trails.

The Clanton–Behan prosecution eventually wound up in such a tangle of self-contradiction that Judge Spicer called a halt. In his decision, on December 1, Judge Spicer dealt at length with the threats sent to the Earps by the cowboys while they were strutting the streets of Tombstone heavily armed, reviewed the details of the fight, and commented with considerable insight upon the shift of base from the Dexter to the O. K. Corral. He then took up the discrepancies and perjuries of the Behan–Clanton side.

"Witnesses for the prosecution," Judge Spicer observed, "state unequivocally that William Clanton fell, or was shot at the first fire and, Claiborne says, was shot when the pistol was only about a foot from his belly. Yet it was clear that there were no powder burns or marks on his clothes, and Judge Lucas says he saw him fire, or in the act of firing, several times before he was shot and, he thinks, two shots afterward.

"Addie Bourland, who saw distinctly the approach of the Earps and the beginning of the affray, says she cannot tell who fired first; that no hands were held up; that she would have seen them if there had been."

The court stressed the surgeons' testimony that Billy Clanton's first two wounds, one on his gun hand, the other breaking that arm, were received while that hand was lower than the muzzles of the pistols from which the wounding shots were fired, and their findings on the body of Tom McLowery. Doc Holliday's double charge of buckshot had made a wound in Tom's lower abdomen, the whole of which could have been covered by the palm of a man's hand, but in so doing had torn away the flesh of his lower arm as it must have been held against his stomach in the normal position for most effective wielding of a pistol.

"These circumstances, being indubitable facts," Judge Spicer held, "throw great doubt upon the correctness of witnesses to the contrary."

In concluding his detailed discussion, Judge Spicer discounted Ike Clanton's testimony completely with the observation that Ike's yarn of vengeance upon himself fell short of being a sound theory because of the fact most prominent in the whole matter: Ike could have been killed first and easiest, but was suffered to flee unharmed. Behan's confessed dickerings with the outlaws, Judge Spicer termed "a proposition both monstrous and startling," and stated that, in view of all the facts and circumstances, the characters and the positions of the parties, he could not "resist the conclusion that the defendants were fully justified in committing these homicides, that it was a necessary act in the discharge of an official duty." He thereupon ordered Wyatt Earp and Doc Holliday discharged and their bonds exonerated, and quashed the warrants for Virgil and Morgan Earp.

Judge Spicer's decision was attacked by *The Nugget* with the charge that Spicer was an Earp partisan. So he was, and so were hundreds more in Tombstone if active support of peace officers, whose integrity was never questioned by reputable citizens, against a gang of highwaymen and murderers constituted partisanship. In commenting upon the Spicer findings as a long step toward ridding Cochise County of outlaws a news service dispatch sent out of Tombstone on December 2 read:

The other side [the cowboy faction] accepts the verdict with bad grace and a smouldering fire exists which is liable to break forth at any moment. It is well known that several prominent residents of Tombstone have been marked for death by the rustlers.

Wyatt Earp's name led the roster of those marked for assassination. Virgil, Morgan, and Doc Holliday followed, then Mayor Clum, Judge Wells Spicer, Marshall Williams, E. B. Gage, James Vizina, Tom Fitch, and five others active with the Vigilantes.

On December 14, Frank Stilwell, Ike Clanton, and John Ringo were recognized in a gang of twenty which attempted to assassinate Mayor Clum as he rode from Tombstone to Benson in the stage. Sheriff Behan refused to send a posse after the attackers.

Shortly after this, Doc Holliday and John Ringo had their famous encounter in Allen Street. The yarn generally told is that Ringo suggested that he, as representative of the cowboys, and Doc, representing the Earps, shoot it out in the middle of Allen Street to decide which faction should leave Tombstone. Charles Liftchild, partner in Tombstone's first men's clothing store, and George W. Parsons, mine-owner and one of the Council of Ten of the Citizens' Safety Committee, do not recall it that way. Both saw and heard what took place, were but a few feet from Holliday and Ringo.

The Earps, at the request of the Vigilantes, had moved to the Cosmopolitan Hotel, where it would be simpler to protect Virgil and Morgan, disabled by their wounds. Wyatt took a room adjoining those occupied by his brothers; Doc Holliday moved in on the other side. The Cosmopolitan Hotel was directly across the street from the Grand Hotel, where Curly Bill, John Ringo, Ike Clanton, and their followers made headquarters.

On the afternoon in question, Doc Holliday walked up Allen Street to find John Ringo awaiting him in front of the Cosmopolitan. Ringo wore a heavy ulster with slit-pockets in which he kept his hands.

"I understand you've been talking about me, Holliday," Ringo snarled.

"I have," Doc replied pleasantly. "I have said, and I repeat, I'm sorry to see a first-class cow thief like yourself fall in with a bunch of cheap bushwhackers."

Doc's nickel-plated six-gun was slung underneath the skirt of his square-cut coat. In each of his slit-pockets John Ringo had a thumb on the hammer of a Colt's forty-five, as Doc well knew.

Ringo began to berate Holliday in a style of which the gunfighting dentist need not have been ashamed, demanding that Doc retract publicly all that he had said about the rustler. He was trying to goad Holliday into a move for his gun. But Doc could be exasperatingly even-tempered when he chose. He stepped close to the outlaw leader; George Parsons heard what he said.

"Let's move into the road where no one else'll get hurt," Holliday suggested. "What I said about you goes. And, if you get what I'm driving at, all I want of you is ten feet out here in the road."

Doc turned his back on Ringo and started off the walk. Before Ringo could follow, he was seized from behind by a husky young fellow named Flynn, who had been appointed to the police force by Virgil Earp.

"Turn him loose, Flynn," Doc Holliday called, "and you, Ringo, when you start, start shooting."

Flynn held Ringo in a bear-like grip and Holliday was urging the officer to let go when Wyatt Earp stepped into the street. Wyatt's eye caught one factor in a possible battle which Holliday had overlooked.

"Quit this foolishness, Doc," Wyatt said, nodding at a shuttered window in the Grand Hotel, from which the muzzle of a rifle was withdrawn as Wyatt spoke. "That fellow would have dropped you at your first move for a gun."

In each of Ringo's ulster pockets Flynn found a loaded Colt's. He took the rustler and his weapons to the calaboose, where, according to the statement of one of Behan's deputies, who relates the incident with great gusto to show what a good fellow he was, Sheriff Behan got Ringo into his office, placed the outlaw's guns in plain view on his desk, then walked out. A few minutes later, and Ringo was back at the Grand Hotel with his six-guns in his pockets again.

That evening, Jack Altman, a clerk at the Grand Hotel.

informed Wyatt that Curly Bill, Ike Clanton, Pony Deal, Frank Stilwell, Pete Spence, John Ringo, Hank Swilling, and one or two others of their crowd had been renting a front room in the hotel for the last week, going and coming from it at intervals. Wooden strips had been removed from a window shutter, he said, so that gun muzzles could be sighted into Allen Street, and also into the rooms which the Earps occupied in the Cosmopolitan.

Wyatt immediately posted Doc Holliday, Texas Jack Vermillion, and Sherman McMasters, armed with rifles, at the window of his own room, and for an hour walked up and down, or sat on the second-floor gallery, hoping to draw gunfire from across the street, which would have been the signal for his own men to pour a hail of lead through the altered shutter in the Grand Hotel. No shooting materialized and Wyatt went over to investigate. Altman told him that Ringo, Frank Stilwell, and Pony Deal had just left in a hurry by the back door. In their vacated room, Wyatt found the shutter as Altman had described it and a loaded rifle in a closet.

Attention of the Vigilance Committee was next directed to information that the Curly Bill gang was plotting to kidnap United States Senator George Hearst, then on an inspection tour of Cochise County mining properties, and to hold the capitalist for ransom. Senator Hearst, however, insisted upon making his trip, so the Safety Committee asked Wyatt to accompany him. With Wyatt, Hearst spent a week riding and camping in the mountains and desert, without molestation. Hearst's decision not to invest in Tombstone mining properties was a bitter pill for the community; it strengthened a conviction which for some months had been growing stronger; Tombstone had passed the peak; as a boom camp she was on the downgrade.

While Wyatt was absent with Hearst, Lou Rickabaugh, Dick Clark, and Bill Harris had decided to sell the Oriental back to Mike Joyce, the first owner. To the sense of this, Wyatt agreed. During the fall of '81, it had become increasingly evident that easy money no longer circulated. Tombstone had become a city of hardworking day laborers, miners getting four dollars a day, and clerks earning like wages. These fellows gambled, but were of necessity pikers. Moreover, the silver market was falling. The days when every man in the camp was flush, when thousands of dollars changed hands hourly, and hundreds of thousands almost daily on the strength of new strikes, twenty-foot prospect holes, or even a new set of corner monuments, were days of glamorous history. Mining claims, including those owned by the Earps, had been bought up and consolidated by corporations; bullion now went East to stockholders who never saw the frontier. The Oriental had as many players about the tables as ever, but the money changing hands and the profits were no longer attractive to a man of Rickabaugh's talents.

The arrangement was that Joyce was to take over the place on January 5, 1882. Joyce said that he had a partner to run the gambling, but would not identify him.

Just before midnight of Wednesday, December 28, Virgil Earp, once more on duty as marshal, stepped from the Oriental, and crossed Fifth Street. As he was silhouetted against the lighted windows of the Eagle Brewery Saloon, five shotguns roared from a building under construction across Allen Street. Three double loads of buckshot splintered the windows and riddled the corner post of the saloon, a fourth load tore a gaping hole in Virgil's left side, a fifth shattered his left arm above the elbow.

Virgil kept his feet, and saw five men run out of the ambush, three going in one direction, two in another. He managed to reach and open the door of the Oriental, where he met Wyatt who had started up at the gunfire.

"They got me, Wyatt," Virg said as he collapsed.

Again George Parsons has furnished eyewitness corroboration of Wyatt's account of what followed. Mr. Parsons was in Dr. Goodfellow's office when the surgeon was called to attend Virgil and went with him.

While the surgeon was working over Virgil, Wyatt went to the building where the assassins had hidden. There he picked up a sombrero with Ike Clanton's name in it. A few minutes later, a watchman at an icehouse on Toughnut

Street told him that Ike Clanton, Frank Stilwell, and Hank Swilling, all carrying shotguns, had run by. The trio was seen a few minutes later by a miner, mounting horses they had tethered in Tombstone Gulch and starting toward Charleston on the gallop. John Ringo had been recognized as one of the two gunmen who had run down Allen Street. Who the fifth man was no one appeared to know.

Meanwhile, Dr. Goodfellow was removing four inches of shattered bone from Virgil's left upper arm, and twenty-odd buckshot from his body. The surgeon told Wyatt that his brother's recovery was doubtful.

In the files of newspapers the country over for December 30, 1881, may be read the news dispatch from Tombstone, Arizona, which tells of the attempt on Virgil's life with this concluding sentence:

The county authorities are doing nothing to capture the assassins.

That was the exact truth. With the identities of four of the potential murderers known, and one of them a deputy in his own office, Sheriff Behan refused to send a posse after them. This attitude consolidated the forces of decent citizenship against Behan and his henchmen. A contemporary editorial in *The Epitaph,* published during John P. Clum's absence, exemplifies the temper of ten thousand Tombstone residents. It reads, in part:

The time has come when the Bible's injunction, "Choose ye this day whom ye will serve," applies with particular force. There can be no halfway business in this matter. He who is not for law and order is against it. . . . The people are not fools. They will mark these things down on the tablets of their memories where they cannot be erased by the sophistical tongues of aspiring politicians. The San Simon vote will not elect next November. The next vote polled in what is now Cochise County will be on the principles of safety n life and protection to property.

First opportunity for Tombstone to choose at the polls between Behan henchmen and Vigilante partisans came six days after Virgil Earp was shot. Municipal election was set for Tuesday, January 3, 1882. Behan and *The Nugget* had a ticket in the field to wrest all city offices from the law-and-order party.

24

The Cost of Shooting Square

Virgil Earp's wounds precluded his further service as marshal of Tombstone, and Dave Neagle, who had broken with the sheriff over Behan's outlaw alliance, was named in his stead on the ticket with John Carr, law-and-order candidate for mayor.

Sheriff Behan deputized one hundred Curly Bill–Clanton followers "to keep order at the polls," and on election day rustlers with six-guns and rifles paraded the Tombstone streets. Their campaign of intimidation was cut short when two armed Vigilantes took posts beside each of the cowboy deputies. Carr and Neagle were elected by large majorities.

On the following day, Johnny Behan billed Cochise County for two thousand dollars, as pay for his election day posse.

The Safety Committee now swore out warrants charging Ike Clanton, Frank Stilwell, and Hank Swilling with the attempt to murder Virgil Earp. The trio surrendered to Sheriff Behan; a dozen cowboys testified that the three rustlers had been miles away from Tombstone on the night

315

of December 28; Ike Clanton produced witnesses to swear that the hat found in the ambush was one he had lost months earlier, and the alibi held up. The cowboys left court with renewed confidence in their immunity from the law.

Mike Joyce took over the Oriental, as scheduled, his gambling partner none other than Johnny Behan. Despite the huge sums which he drew from the Cochise County coffers, Behan was always in financial straits and the Oriental venture was an attempt to recoup his shaky fortunes. Behan placed his games in charge of a dealer known as Fries, and Wyatt Earp was tipped off that Behan's bankroll was a bare five thousand dollars. That night Wyatt and Dick Clark walked into the Oriental to buck a faro bank with Fries dealing and Johnny Behan in the lookout's chair. Wyatt changed in one thousand dollars, other players promptly withdrew, and Clark went to keeping cases. Luck seesawed for an hour, before Wyatt won ten straight turns.

"I'm cashing in," he announced.

"What's the matter?" Johnny Behan inquired.

"There's more than six thousand dollars in my stack," Wyatt replied. "We put a thousand into your game and five thousand's the size of your bankroll."

"That's all right. That's all right," Behan declared. "I'm good for anything you win."

Wyatt distributed his odd chips above six thousand dollars among the hangers-on.

"Have a drink, boys," he suggested. "Mike'll take these over the bar."

"I'll take mine in cash," he said to the sheriff. "Your credit with me doesn't cover a white chip."

Fries paid over what he had in the money drawer. Johnny Behan drained the other tables and his roll in the safe. Before the sheriff's eyes, Wyatt divided the money with Clark.

"Come on, Dick," Wyatt said. "We've got what we came for."

Behan closed his games for the night. For that matter, Johnny Behan never did make any money from his Oriental tables. In his first heavy loss, however, was additional bitterness for his growing hatred of Wyatt Earp.

Johnny Behan had bested Wyatt Earp just once, in politics. Thereafter at every turn Wyatt won. One must sense Behan's inordinate vanity to measure the gall this brought to the sheriff's soul. It illuminates much that otherwise was inexplicable, as does the deliberation with which Wyatt at every opportunity impressed upon Behan that in the company of men the practical politician was out of his class.

Late in the afternoon of Friday, January 6, the Tombstone–Bisbee stage was held up in the Mule Mountains by five bandits and robbed of an eighty-five-hundred-dollar payroll for the Copper Queen Mine. The handkerchief mask dropped from the face of one bandit, revealing the familiar countenance of Sheriff Behan's deputy, Frank Stilwell. Two of his companions laughed and pulled off their masks— Pony Deal and Curly Bill. Billy Waite, the driver, and Charles Bartholomew, shotgun messenger, identified the others as Pete Spence and Ike Clanton. Pony Deal cut out a stage horse to lead away; Curly Bill took Bartholomew's shotgun with the remark that he'd take his next Wells-Fargo box at the muzzle of the express company's own weapon.

At daylight next morning, as Wyatt Earp took up the trail of the payroll bandits, he got word that the Tombstone–Benson stage had been held up near Contention and robbed of mail and express worth twenty-five hundred dollars. At the scene of the second holdup, Wyatt found J. B. Hume, the Wells-Fargo officer, who had been asleep inside the coach when it was stopped. There had been no shotgun messenger on this stage.

Pony Deal and Curly Bill had pulled off this second robbery without assistance; neither had worn a mask and both had talked with the driver and Hume freely. Curly Bill took from Jim Hume a pair of ivory-handled, gold-mounted six-guns, and joked about his growing collection of Wells-Fargo weapons. Hume had recognized the shotgun which Curly Bill threw down on him as express company property and the driver had spotted Pony Deal's mount as one of Waite's horses.

Wyatt Earp, with Sherman McMasters and Jack Johnson —who was Turkey Creek Jack of Deadwood fame— followed the trail of Curly Bill and Pony Deal to Hank Redfield's ranch, found fagged horses which the bandits had traded for fresh animals, and picked up sign which indicated that the robbers were heading back toward Charleston.

While Wyatt was chasing the highwaymen, John Ringo was arrested under a grand jury indictment for a robbery at Galeyville and taken to Tombstone. Soon afterward, a Vigilante messenger brought warning that twenty rustlers were in ambush at the Charleston bridge awaiting Wyatt Earp's attempt to arrest Curly Bill and Pony Deal. Ten Vigilantes under John H. Jackson were sent to ride with Wyatt into the outlaw stronghold.

Johnny Behan promptly turned John Ringo loose, sending him to Charleston to warn and help his friends. Ringo, armed with a rifle, was one of three rustlers on watch in the Charleston street when Wyatt started into the town. Impatience betrayed the presence of the posse, and the outlaws vanished. Curly Bill and Pony Deal had fled when Wyatt reached their hangout.

Judge William N. Stillwell, of the district court, warned Behan that he would be held responsible for Ringo's escape. Behan and Breakenridge began a frantic search for the outlaw, finally reaching him with word that brought his surrender in time to save their official skins.

The decent Democrats of Arizona now read the Cochise County gang out of the party. Their official newspaper, *The Prescott Democrat,* after an extensive résumé of the situation, observed:

> One thing is certain, if the people of that county take the law in their own hands and commence hanging, there is no knowing when it will stop.

Which paragraph illuminates the visit to Tombstone

made by Acting Governor Gosper and Crawley P. Dake, United States Marshal for Arizona Territory. After conferences with Tombstone businessmen, Vigilantes, Judge Stillwell, and others, Sheriff Behan was, to all intents and purposes, superseded as a peace officer. Governor Gosper invested Marshal Wyatt Earp with complete powers of law enforcement and appointed under him seven deputies named by the Vigilantes: Morgan and Warren Earp, Doc Holliday, Sherman McMasters, Texas Jack Vermillion, and Turkey Creek Jack Johnson. He authorized Wyatt to appoint other deputies, and placed five thousand dollars to Wyatt's credit in the local banks. Wells, Fargo and Company and the Southern Pacific Railroad matched this sum, and the citizens of Cochise County subscribed another five thousand dollars. With this cash, Wyatt was to arm and equip his posses, meet payrolls and traveling expenses. The preliminaries arranged, Governor Gosper issued final orders.

"Judge Stillwell will give you the warrants you need," the Governor told Wyatt. "Now, go out and clean up this county."

As Judge Stillwell handed over a sheaf of warrants, he offered some advice, which Wyatt also carried in his memory.

"If I were serving these warrants, Wyatt," Judge Stillwell suggested, "I'd leave my prisoners in the mesquite where alibis don't count."

At the time of Governor Gosper's visit, Joe Hill had come into Tombstone under pressure brought by a brother who could see the handwriting on the wall, and had substantiated in detail Wyatt's account of the conspiracy in which Hill, Ike Clanton, and Frank McLowery had agreed to betray Leonard, Head, and Crane and had exonerated Doc Holliday from all connection with the attempt to rob the Benson stage. He disclosed also numerous additional operations of the cowboy-politico gang.

On January 23, Marshal Wyatt Earp started on his cleanup of organized outlawry. Curly Bill and his followers fled into the Chiricahuas. On January 24, there was distributed throughout Tombstone a handbill, which read:

PROCLAMATION

To the Citizens of the City of Tombstone:

I am informed by his Honor, William H. Stillwell, Judge of the District Court of the First Judicial District, that Wyatt Earp, who left this city yesterday with a posse, was intrusted with warrants for the arrest of divers persons charged with criminal offenses. I request the public to abstain from any interference with the execution of said warrants.

JOHN CARR, *Mayor*

Dated, January 24, 1882.

This would seem to establish, beyond all carping, the official status which Wyatt Earp enjoyed in Arizona. Behan's reception of the proclamation was characteristic.

For two weeks Wyatt Earp and his posse rounded up Curly Bill followers and sent them into Tombstone or ran them into Old Mexico. Purposely they were throwing the fear of death and disaster into the souls of the rank and file, which would simplify the final campaign against the leaders. This strategy had disrupted the outer circle of the rustler organization when Johnny Behan again took a hand.

On February 10, Sheriff Behan and Ike Clanton went before a cowboy justice of the peace at Contention and swore to warrants charging Wyatt, Virgil, and Morgan Earp and Doc Holliday with the murder of William Clanton, Frank and Tom McLowery in the O. K. Corral. Behan deputized Ike Clanton and other rustlers to help serve the warrants. Word of Behan's play reached Wyatt in the San Simon country, and he came into Tombstone on February 11, the day that President Arthur announced appointment of Fred A. Tritle as Governor of Arizona Territory. Wyatt telegraphed an offer to resign as marshal, which Governor Tritle answered with an order for Wyatt to continue his work.

Marshal Earp, on the advice of Judge Stillwell, sent word to Behan that Morgan, Doc Holliday, and he would answer the murder charges at Contention on February 14, but that any attempt to serve a warrant before that date, or on the bedridden Virgil at any time, would mean trouble. The sheriff took the hint.

On the morning set, Wyatt, Morgan, and Doc Holliday rode up to Behan's office, each armed, and wearing his Federal badge. Sheriff Behan, Under-Sheriff Woods, Deputy Breakenridge, and Special Deputy Ike Clanton were awaiting them, mounted, but with a buckboard for their prisoners.

"You men are under arrest," Behan said. "Give me your guns and get into the buckboard. One of you'll drive. We'll ride behind you."

"And herd us down the road where your friends can shoot us in the back?" Wyatt observed. "Not much. Get going, and ride ahead."

As Behan argued, a posse of heavily armed Vigilantes, led by Colonel William Herring, the attorney, rode out of a side-street to join the Contention party. Behan abandoned his buckboard idea and rustlers stationed along the road to assassinate the Earps and Holliday took to the brush when the cavalcade hove into view.

In the Contention courtroom the three prisoners lined up wearing their weapons, Colonel Herring beside them with a rifle in the hollow of his arm and Vigilantes against the wall.

"This is the murder case against the Earps and Holliday," Behan began, but Colonel Herring interposed.

"We're here for justice or a fight and ready for either," the attorney said to the court. "You haven't any more jurisdiction over this matter than a jackrabbit. If there's any hearing, it'll be in Tombstone."

The cowboy justice of the peace took a look at the attorney, and his fellow Vigilantes.

"Case transferred to Tombstone," he decided.

In a competent court, Wyatt, Morgan, and Doc Holliday were promptly discharged. Wyatt resumed his campaign against the outlaws with the added support of proclamations from President Arthur and Governor Tritle.

The Arizona Cattlemen's Association now offered a reward of one thousand dollars for Curly Bill, dead or alive. A few days later, Ike Clanton rode up to Sierra Bonita Ranch, home of General Henry C. Hooker, president of the association, and rolled from a sack the head of a swarthy individual whose death was of recent date. Ike said it was Curly Bill's head and demanded one thousand dollars. General Hooker and Billy Whelan, his foreman, who knew Curly Bill all too well in life, laughed at Ike's pretensions, and Clanton left, swearing vengeance. The head, it was later established, was that of an itinerant Mexican with a curly thatch whom Ike had killed in his scheme to collect the cattlemen's cash.

Wyatt's roundup of the small fry was producing results. Ranchers in outlying districts found courage to lynch several rustlers who fell into their hands while separated from their gangs, and sent information which enabled Wyatt to catch Frank Stilwell and Pete Spence. This pair gave bonds to appear before the Federal grand jury in Tucson on the morning of Tuesday, March 21.

On Friday, March 17, Pete Spence and Frank Stilwell rode into Tombstone with a halfbreed, Florentino Cruz, better known as Indian Charlie, a hanger-on with Ike Clanton and Curly Bill. Later, they were joined by Hank Swilling, also a halfbreed. Stilwell went to the law office of Briggs Goodrich to retain him as attorney for the holdup case. Saturday morning, Goodrich met Wyatt Earp in Allen Street.

"Wyatt," the lawyer said, "I'm not supposed to betray professional confidence, but there are four men in town who plan on getting you tonight. They expect others to join them. I can't tell you who they are, but you'd better watch out."

"I'll tell you who they are," Wyatt answered—"Frank Stilwell, Hank Swilling, Pete Spence, and Indian Charlie are in town now, and they're waiting for John Ringo."

"Except for Ringo," Goodrich replied, "you're a good guesser. Ringo knows there's trouble coming, and has asked me to tell you that he'll have nothing to do with it, that from now on he's going to take care of himself and let others do the same."

"That's good with me," Wyatt said. "Thanks for the tip."

That afternoon, Wyatt and Morgan combed Tombstone in vain search for Stilwell, Spence, Swilling, and Indian Charlie. They learned that the four had taken their horses from the West End Corral at noon, with announced intention of riding for Tucson. Night fell with no further trace of them.

Had Wyatt been a better guesser, he might have found four horses in a gulch near the Tombstone cemetery under guard of Hank Swilling. Pete Spence, Indian Charlie, and Frank Stilwell were hiding in Spence's house at First and Fremont Streets.

The Lingard Opera Company, a traveling theatrical troupe, was playing "Stolen Kisses" that night in Schieffelin Hall. Just after eight o'clock, Wyatt and Morgan Earp joined the audience.

About ten o'clock, according to testimony given later by Pete Spence's wife, someone whistled outside the Spence home. Pete, Indian Charlie, and Stilwell left, Pete armed with a pair of six-guns, each of the others with two six-guns and a rifle.

Wyatt and Morgan Earp came out of Schieffelin Hall in a group of friends with whom they walked to Allen Street. Wyatt announced that he was turning in and started for the Cosmopolitan Hotel. Morgan said that he was booked for a game of billiards with Bob Hatch, owner of the billiard hall on Allen Street which had been headquarters for the marshal's forces since the sale of the Oriental.

"Better come to bed, Morg," Wyatt suggested.

Morgan looked at his brother quizzically.

"You trying to baby me?" he asked with a grin, then clapped a hand on Wyatt's shoulder.

"I'll be up in an hour," he promised.

In his hotel room, Wyatt sat for some minutes of indecision, one boot off, the other half drawn. In response to that intuition which he never disregarded, he pulled on his boots again, belted his six-guns at his hips, put on his coat and sombrero, and went to Bob Hatch's billiard hall.

The billiard tables were beyond the bar as Wyatt entered Bob Hatch's place from Allen Street. Morgan and Bob were at a table next to the rear wall. Wyatt walked through to a chair nearby, from which he could command full view of the place. Morgan looked up.

"It's too early to go to bed," Wyatt explained, in answer to the unspoken query. As the marshal took a seat with his back to the wall, he did not know that a man who left the front bar simultaneously hurried around into Fourth Street.

The only opening in the rear wall of Bob Hatch's building was a narrow door at the north corner which gave onto the alley, between Fourth and Fifth Streets. The lower door panels were solid wood; the upper half was quartered with glass, the lower panes painted white, the upper two clear.

Bob Hatch was making a shot. Morgan stood at one side, chalking his cue, back to and almost against the alley door.

The panes of glass in the door frame crashed and shattered in a thousand fragments; flame, lead, and smoke spurted through the jagged openings as the roar of six-guns filled the room.

Morgan Earp wheeled to face the door, dropped a hand to his holster, and fell on his face in the splinters of glass.

Two bullets thudded into the plaster just above Wyatt Earp's head. A shot struck George Berry, the proverbially innocent bystander, in the thigh, and Berry died in his tracks from shock.

Wyatt Earp's Buntline Special flashed into action as he sent three shots into the alley darkness, and leaped to Morgan's side. The door was bolted and seconds elapsed before Bob Hatch, Dan Tipton, Sherman McMasters, and Pat Holland could rip it open to gain the alleyway. They heard men running, muffled shouts, and the confused hoof-drumming of cow ponies jumped from a stand into full gallop.

Morgan Earp was conscious as his brother carried him to a couch in Bob Hatch's office.

"Put my legs straight," he said to Wyatt.

"They are straight, Morg."

Morgan smiled.

"My back's broken," he said. Then to Hatch, "I guess I've run out my string, Bob."

Dr. Goodfellow quickly verified Morgan's belief. A forty-five slug had entered the small of his back at the left, and passed out at the right, smashing his spine.

"It won't be long, will it, Doc?" the wounded man asked.

"No, Morg, not long," the surgeon replied.

"We know who did it, don't we, Wyatt?" Morgan said.

Wyatt nodded and Morgan closed his eyes. He opened them a few minutes later when Virgil Earp appeared on the shoulders of Jim and Warren Earp, the first time that Virgil had left his bed since wounded by assassins eleven weeks before. Morgan spoke to his brothers, then appeared to fall asleep. He had been shot at eleven-thirty. It was after midnight when he opened his eyes again.

"Bend down close to me, Wyatt," Morgan requested. He whispered briefly in Wyatt's ear.

For half a century Morgan's last words to Wyatt have been the subject of lurid speculation in the West, of legends largely devoted to red oaths of vengeance and other melodramatic foolishness.

When I asked Wyatt Earp just what Morgan had whispered as he was dying, Wyatt hesitated over his reply.

"I've never told anyone what Morgan said to me then, not even Virgil," he began. "I can't say why, unless it was that Morgan and I were particularly close, and I hung on to this one thing as a memory of him the others might not understand. Sometimes it strikes me I've been silly about it. Hundreds have asked me what the secret was, but in telling you it will be the first time I've uttered the words aloud since I heard them from Morgan's lips. I have repeated them to myself, many, many times. To make their meaning clear, I'll have to go back a little. What I'm going to tell you may sound foolish, but it should put an end to all the claptrap about Morgan's last few minutes of life.

"Morgan had a boyish curiosity which I never knew to be satisfied. He had been much interested in reported experiences of persons who were said to have had visions of heaven when at the point of death, and who had rallied long enough to leave behind them word of what they saw. Morg got me to read one of his books on this subject, and one night when he and I were camped on the desert, we had quite a discussion over it. I told him I thought the yarns were overdrawn, but at his suggestion we promised each other that, when the time came for one of us to go, that one would try to leave for the other some actual line on the truth of the book. I promptly forgot the thing. Morg didn't. He was sensitive to the fun others might poke at such notions, so, in the last few seconds of his life, when he knew he was going, he asked me to bend close.

"'I guess you were right, Wyatt,' he whispered. 'I can't see a damn' thing.'

"That was all he said. I understood, and he knew that I did. Maybe now they'll quit writing that 'Wyatt Earp nodded grimly as he listened to Morgan's whispered demand for bloody vengeance after his death.'"

For a few seconds after Wyatt bent over him, Morgan breathed quietly. He smiled at his brothers, then for an instant held Wyatt's eyes steadily with his own. His voice was firm now and clearly heard by every man in the room.

"Take care of yourself, Wyatt," Morgan said, and died.

Wyatt went at once to tell Fred Dodge, who was ill, of Morgan's death.

"All my life, I've respected the law," Fred Dodge recalls that Wyatt said as they discussed the tragedy. "If I had been willing to go outside of it, Morgan would have been alive now. It's a pretty high price to ask a man to pay for trying to shoot square. I know the fellows who killed Morg, and I'm going after them. I've got Federal warrants for all of them in my pocket. Maybe they'll be fools enough to resist arrest."

Morgan's body was sent to Colton, California, Sunday afternoon in charge of James Earp. Wyatt rode beside the undertaker's spring wagon to the railroad, then turned back to Tombstone.

The manager of the Lingard Opera Company reported that after the Saturday night performance he had heard shooting and had seen men running along Fourth Street. Two had mounted horses which another held below the Fremont Street corner and had ridden off at a gallop, while three others had continued on foot down Fremont Street. Pete Spence's wife went to Coroner Matthews with word that just after eleven-thirty Saturday night, her husband, Frank Stilwell, and Indian Charlie had reached the Spence house, out of breath and greatly excited. Stilwell and Indian Charlie had left immediately; her husband had ridden off after threatening to kill her if she told that he, or his friends, had been in the house that night or the day before. Pete had knocked his wife down to emphasize his demand for secrecy, which may have moved her to tell what she knew.

J. B. Ayers sent word from Charleston that before daylight Sunday morning Frank Stilwell, Hank Swilling, Curly Bill, Indian Charlie, and Pete Spence had ridden into the Frank Patterson Ranch on the Babocomari. Stilwell, Swilling, and Spence had taken fresh horses to ride toward Tucson. Curly Bill and Indian Charlie had gone northeast toward the Dragoons.

Wyatt Earp went at once to Virgil's room.

"Virg," he said, "you'll have to leave Tombstone. I've got a job I can't handle if I have to worry about you. There's a coroner's hearing on Morg's death tomorrow morning, and I'll start you for California as soon as I've testified."

Wyatt was informed by telegraph on Monday morning that Frank Stilwell, Pete Spence, Hank Swilling, and Ike Clanton were together in Tucson, and ordered his Federal posse, Doc Holliday, Sherman McMasters, Texas Jack Vermillion, Turkey Creek Jack Johnson, and Warren Earp to ride with him to Contention as escort to Virgil. The coroner's jury returned a verdict that "Morgan Earp came to his death at the hands of Frank Stilwell, Pete Spence, two halfbreed Indians, and others whose names, at present, are unknown," and announced that the hearing would be continued to identify others in the murder plot. Wyatt also went before the Cochise County grand jury to testify regarding Morgan's death and left the jury room to start Virgil for the railroad. On the way out, he passed Briggs Goodrich, attorney, who had volunteered to tell what he knew of Morgan Earp's death.

At Contention, Wyatt left Warren Earp, McMasters, Johnson, and Texas Jack with the horses, while Doc Holliday and he went on to Tucson with Virgil. There was an hour's stop at Tucson for supper and Wyatt knew his enemies too well to risk the helpless Virgil at their mercy. East of the Tucson station, the train stopped for a moment and Deputy United States Marshal Joe Evans got aboard.

"Frank Stilwell, Pete Spence, Ike Clanton, and a breed I don't know are in town," Evans warned Wyatt. "Stilwell, Spence, and the breed rode in across country yesterday. Ike got in later. They've been getting telegrams all day from Tombstone and know you're on this train. You'll have to take care of yourself. Bob Paul's out of town."

Evans was crippled beyond ability to play a militant peace officer's part.

Dusk was falling as the train reached the Tucson station, Wyatt and Doc guarded Virgil and his wife while they ate supper, then helped Virgil into his car. The eastbound train which Wyatt expected to take back to Benson would leave soon, and Wyatt sent Holliday to the eating-house to order a meal which they could eat hurriedly, once Virgil was under way. A few minutes before the California train was to start, Wyatt took leave of his brother. It was almost dark now.

"Good-bye, Virg," Wyatt said, "I'll be seeing you soon."

Virgil understood the cryptic promise.

"I'll be seeing you soon," he answered. "Take care of yourself, Wyatt."

Wyatt hurried through the car. In the windowless vestibule he halted, then worked his way to peer from the platform around the corner and along the side of the car away from the station. On the adjoining track, parallel to the train, was a string of flatcars. Two cars ahead, the light from a train window glinted on two rifle barrels resting on the far edge of a flatcar, and in the shadows Wyatt made out three or four figures crouched.

Wyatt raised his sawed-off shotgun toward his shoulder. Loaded with nine buckshot to the barrel, and with the wads split, that weapon would sweep eighteen slugs across the flatcar that ought to get every man back of it. The gun would not come to firing position. Wyatt suddenly realized that he was trying to raise it to his left shoulder, necessary if he was to keep the shelter of the car corner, with his hands placed for right-shoulder shooting. In shifting his grip, the gun hit a handrail and as steel clanked against iron, the figures behind the flatcar were off on a run. Wyatt jumped from the car and ran forward along the station side of the train, figuring the men would cross the tracks toward town.

From this point on, no one who lived but Wyatt Earp could tell what happened that night in the railroad yards at Tucson. Until he gave the story to be set down here, Wyatt Earp kept his own lips sealed. Certain evidence of certain happenings was found; for the rest, all has been pure surmise.

Wyatt noted a man standing on the end of the station platform, a swarthy fellow in the ill-fitting store clothes, stiff collar, and small felt hat such as Mexican and Indian section hands affected for dress-up wear.

"Who are you?" Wyatt demanded.

The man grunted unintelligibly, and moved away.

"I took him for a laborer," Wyatt said. "I'd give ten thousand dollars, today, if I could say that I had recognized him, for I learned later that he was Hank Swilling. I'd never seen Swilling in anything but a cowboy getup; boots, chaps, flannel shirt, open vest, and big sombrero. No wonder I couldn't spot him in the dark, the dinky hat and the Tucson store clothes."

Twenty yards ahead, a man hurried across the tracks in the glare of the engine headlight. Wyatt ran after him. Two rifle shots sounded at his left and two bullets whipped through the darkness. Wyatt kept on.

"Halt," he shouted, "or you'll get it in the back."

The man stopped, and turned. This was better. If he was one of the outlaws, at least he intended to make his fight. Less than thirty feet separated the two when Wyatt recognized Sheriff Behan's deputy, Frank Stilwell.

When marshal and outlaw were about fifteen feet apart, Stilwell halted.

"His guns were in plain sight and I figured he'd jerk them," Wyatt said. "As I got closer, his right hand started down, but quit halfway and he stood as if he was paralyzed. I never said a word. About three feet from Stilwell I stopped and looked at him. Then he lunged for me.

"Stilwell caught the barrel of my Wells-Fargo gun with

both hands, his left hand uppermost, almost covering the muzzles, and the right well down. I've never forgotten the look in Frank Stilwell's eyes, or the expression that came over his face as he struggled for that gun.

"I forced the gun down until the muzzle of the right barrel was just underneath Stilwell's heart. I had not spoken to him, and did not at any time. But Stilwell found his voice. You'd guess a million times wrong, without guessing what he said. I'll tell you, and you can make what you care to out of it.

"'Morg!' he said, and then a second time, 'Morg!' I've often wondered what made him say that."

For some moments Wyatt's narrative was suspended. The interlude of retrospection was broken by the question that would not be denied.

"What happened then?" I asked.

"I let him have it," Wyatt answered simply. "The muzzle of one barrel, as I've told you, was just underneath his heart. He got the second before he hit the ground."

Additional details of Frank Stilwell's death may be found in the coroner's report, made after Stilwell's body was picked up where Wyatt left it, near the railroad crossing just west of Porter's Hotel.

"Death was instantaneous," the coroner concluded, "but the expression of fear on the face would indicate that the man was aware of his danger which he sought to avert with his left hand, as it was burned and blackened with powder."

As Stilwell fell, Doc Holliday ran from the eating-house. The California train was starting. Virgil had heard the shooting; his face was glued to his window between cupped hands. Wyatt ran alongside the moving car, a single finger thrust high.

"It's all right, Virg!" Wyatt shouted. "It's all right! One for Morg!"

25

Two and Three for Morg

For two hours after Wyatt Earp killed Frank Stilwell, Wyatt and Doc Holliday combed Tucson for Stilwell's companions, without success, then boarded a freight train for Benson, rejoined their posse at Contention, and reached Tombstone early on Tuesday morning to find fifty armed Vigilantes awaiting them. From the front rank of the reception committee, Chris Billicke shouted:

"Frank Stilwell'll never rob any more stages!"

Wyatt and his posse left their horses at the corral and walked up Allen Street. News of the plot to assassinate Virgil at Tucson and the outcome had been telegraphed to Tombstone, but no Vigilante violated the canons by asking for details. Within forty-eight hours of the time he murdered Morgan Earp, Frank Stilwell had paid for the crime as fitted the best traditions of Western justice. That his fellow murderers would make similar payment was taken for granted by these men schooled in frontier necessities.

Wyatt and Doc Holliday needed sleep At the Cosmopolitan Hotel they were told that Behan had telegraphed to

Tucson asking for notification of any charges against Wyatt Earp or Doc Holliday.

"Johnny'll get into trouble, if he keeps on," Wyatt remarked, and went to his room.

About three o'clock in the afternoon, the operator of the Tombstone telegraph office awakened Wyatt with word that a message had come for Johnny Behan from Tucson, stating that Wyatt Earp and Doc Holliday had been accused of murdering Frank Stilwell.

"Is it a telegraphed warrant from Bob Paul?" Wyatt asked.

The telegrapher said Behan's message was from Ike Clanton, announcing that Ike had sworn to such a charge as complaining witness.

"Have you delivered it?" Wyatt inquired.

"Not yet."

"Can you hold it a bit?"

"As long as you say."

"An hour'll do," Wyatt said. "Will you tell Colonel Herring I want to see him?"

When the attorney reached the hotel, Wyatt had Warren Earp, Doc Holliday, Sherman McMasters, Turkey Creek Jack Johnson, and Texas Jack Vermillion in his room. Colonel Herring suggested that Wyatt surrender to Behan, as he could readily clear himself of a murder charge. Wyatt objected; first, because his arrest would delay pursuit of the assassins still at large; second, because he believed he'd be murdered once Behan had him disarmed; and, third, because Behan had neither right nor authority to arrest him.

"I've a job in hand that I don't aim to let Johnny Behan spoil," Wyatt insisted. "You telegraph Bob Paul that I'll surrender to him any time."

Wyatt sent two men to the corral to saddle horses and replenish supplies for his posse, and with Colonel Herring drew papers which placed all property he controlled at the disposal of his father, Nicholas Earp. When the men returned from the corral, a meal was served in Wyatt's room.

"Go over and read Johnny Behan's telegram, then tell 'em to deliver it," he instructed his attorney. "We'll wait here."

As Colonel Herring returned, Chris Billicke appeared

with word that Behan was in the hotel lobby with Dave Neagle, and that eight deputy sheriffs, all heavily armed, stood in Allen Street.

"Colonel," Wyatt suggested to Herring, "you'd better wait up here until this is over."

"Not I," the attorney answered. "I want to see this."

Wyatt belted on his six-guns, jerked his black sombrero into place, and slung his Wells-Fargo gun, muzzle foremost, in the crook of his right arm. His posse was similarly armed, with the exception of Doc Holliday, who had small faith in the shotgun as a weapon and carried only his pistols. Rifles for all were in their saddle boots.

"I'll go first," Wyatt ordered. "Warren, you get behind me; then Sherm and Turkey Creek. Doc and Texas Jack bring up the rear. If you insist on coming, Colonel Herring, you can walk with me."

At the head of the stairs, Wyatt halted.

"Remember, boys," he cautioned for the twentieth time, "no gunplay."

Down the stairs they moved, two abreast. As Wyatt reached the lowest step, Dave Neagle approached him, leaving Behan by the street entrance.

"This is none of my affair, Wyatt," Neagle began; "but the sheriff's going to arrest you, and he thought maybe if I talked to you, you could save some trouble."

Wyatt spread his left hand, palm down, on top of the newel post.

"Dave," the marshal answered, looking at Behan as he spoke, "you tell the trouble-dodging sheriff that I'll let him cut off any finger on that hand if he'll only try to arrest me."

Behan beat a hasty retreat to confer with his eight deputies in the middle of Allen Street. Wyatt went to the hotel desk for a moment, then led his men to the walk. As the door swung to behind Texas Jack and Doc Holliday, Wyatt shook hands with his attorney.

"So long, Colonel," Wyatt said, ignoring Behan, who stood in the road and, back of him, the eight deputies, each with six-guns at his belt and each carrying a sawed-off shotgun. "You'll hear from me in a day or so."

"Come on, boys," Wyatt said, and started for the corral. He stopped as Johnny Behan moved toward the curb.

"Wyatt," the sheriff called, "I want to see you."

"Behan," the marshal shot back so sharply that the sheriff stopped short, "if you're not careful, you'll see me once too often."

Wyatt and his five deputy United States Marshals turned their backs contemptuously on Sheriff Behan and his eight deputies, including Woods, Breakenridge, Campbell, Perkins, and Soule among others, and walked down Allen Street.

Back by the hotel door, Colonel Herring let out a most illegal whoop.

"That's the kind of clients to have!" he yelled.

H. Solomon stood in the door of his bank.

"Good luck, Wyatt," Solomon called. Then his eye caught a shortage of armament. He darted indoors and was out again with a sawed-off shotgun and a belt of buckshot shells such as every frontier banker kept at strategic spots. He ran to the marshal's posse and thrust the weapon into Holliday's unwilling hands.

"Take it, Doc," Solomon insisted. Holliday, for a wonder, was blessed with sufficient graciousness to comply.

Inside the corral, Wyatt and his men swung into their saddles, then rode out to turn west along Allen Street. The red ball of a setting desert sun haloed the six horsemen in ominous relief as they halted momentarily to look back toward the heart of Tombstone, where the sheriff and his deputies still stood in the road. Wyatt sat his horse facing Behan's men until his posse had gone on, Texas Jack and Sherm McMasters, then Warren, Jack Johnson, and Doc Holliday. He struck a match to light a cigar, got his smoke going to suit, wheeled and brought up the rear at a slow walk.

From the corral gate to First Street crowds stood beneath the wooden awnings to watch the posse go. Between the lines from which some epithets and some good wishes were shouted, the little cavalcade rode very slowly and in silence, cool, keen eyes alert under sombrero brims. No hostile move was made. At the edge of town, Wyatt spoke, the pace was increased, and the horsemen passed over a hill.

Next day *The Nugget* told how "Wyatt Earp was run out of Tombstone," and had Sheriff Behan's deputies explain that the Earps left just as they, the deputies, "were going up the street to get some guns and arrest them."

Twenty old-timers who saw Wyatt Earp ride out of Tombstone that evening of March 21, 1882, including Fred Dodge, Jack Archer, and Al Martin, who stood less than thirty feet from Wyatt Earp and Sheriff Behan as they spoke to one another for the last time, have furnished the truth. For good measure, there is the *Star* news dispatch telegraphed from Tombstone within an hour after Wyatt Earp left:

> The sheriff made a weak attempt to arrest the Earp party, but Wyatt Earp told him he didn't want to see him. The Earp party then got their horses and rode slowly out of town. There is an uneasy feeling among the outlaw element, as Wyatt Earp is known to be on the trail of those who attempted to assassinate Virgil and who murdered Morgan in cold blood.

Wyatt Earp and his five deputy marshals camped for the night two miles out of Tombstone. Next morning, Vigilantes sent Wyatt a copy of the final verdict of the coroner's jury which found that Morgan Earp was killed by Peter Spence, Frank Stilwell, "John Doe" Fries, a halfbreed Indian known as Florentino Cruz, or Indian Charlie; and another halfbreed Indian, Hank Swilling.

"Johnny Behan's raising a posse to arrest you," the Vigilante reported, "and you'll have to arrest his posse if you want to serve your warrants. Ike and Phin Clanton are his first recruits, and John Ringo's on the way to join."

"Where's Curly Bill?" Wyatt asked.

"Curly Bill rode into Tombstone last night, had a talk with Behan, and rode out again," the Vigilante said. "Behan deputized Curly Bill and eight of his gang to arrest you or shoot you on sight for the murder of Stilwell. What's more,

Curly Bill and John Ringo were in Tombstone the night Morg was killed. They rode in about ten o'clock, hid out in the west end of town, and rode out with Swilling after the shooting."

A second messenger arrived with word that Indian Charlie was at Pete Spence's ranch, a water hole on the western slope of the Dragoons.

"I've got a warrant for him," Wyatt said. "Guess I'll serve it."

"The same way you did Stilwell's," the Vigilante suggested.

"Tell the committee I'll be back at the old powder-house before night," Wyatt instructed the messenger, then added: "If Johnny Behan gets his posse together, you can tell him where I'll be."

Wyatt and his deputies rode up to Pete Spence's ranch by a route commanding the spot where the rustlers usually camped. Two groups of men were loafing near the spring, one up the gulch, the other down. Wyatt saw Indian Charlie in the first and rode to the second, where he questioned Johnny Barnes, Ted Judah, and two or three others for whom he had warrants, while he gave the man he really wanted time to betray himself.

The halfbreed, hoping that he had not been recognized, edged toward an incline rising to scrub timber which might furnish cover for escape. Wyatt let him go until Cruz was possibly one hundred yards away.

"Stop him," he said to Sherman McMasters, a crack rifle-shot. "Don't kill him. I want him to talk."

The breed was halfway up the slope, spread-eagled against the bare rocks. McMasters pressed the trigger. Indian Charlie howled, and clapped a hand to his left thigh. McMasters spurred his pony to the foot of the incline.

"Come down here!" he ordered.

The halfbreed obeyed, and when Wyatt reached him was standing with hands in the air.

"Hardly drew blood," McMasters said. "The way he yelled, you'd think I'd killed him."

"Are you Florentino Cruz?" Wyatt asked.

"*Sí! Sí!* Me no steal horse! Me no steal horse!" the halfbreed clamored.

Wyatt dismounted and led his prisoner around a shoulder of rock, out of view of those by the water hole, but could not get beyond the halfbreed's insistence that he neither understood nor spoke English. Under McMasters's fluent Spanish, however, Indian Charlie broke down and offered to tell what he knew of the outlaw plots.

Ike Clanton, Frank Stilwell, Curly Bill, John Ringo, Billy Claiborne, Hank Swilling, and Phin Clanton had led the attempt to assassinate Mayor Clum, he said, and on two occasions Frank Stilwell and Ike Clanton had attempted to bushwhack Doc Holliday at the upper end of Allen Street in Tombstone.

The halfbreed declared that he had had no part in the attempted assassination of Virgil Earp, but knew that Ike Clanton, Hank Swilling, Frank Stilwell, and John Ringo had fired four of the five shots from ambush; the fifth man in the party he insisted he did not know.

"He's a liar," Doc Holliday cut in, but Wyatt told Indian Charlie to go on with the details of Morgan's murder.

The halfbreed said that Curly Bill, Ike Clanton, John Ringo, and Frank Stilwell, meeting, the Sunday before Morg's death, at the Clanton Ranch, had plotted to kill both Wyatt and Morgan Earp. Frank Stilwell, Pete Spence, and he had gone into Tombstone on Friday, and hidden at Spence's house. Hank Swilling had joined them on Saturday, and Pete Spence had taken him, Charlie, to Allen Street, where he had pointed out Morgan Earp, so there'd be no mistake in identities later on. He had known Wyatt by sight for some time, the halfbreed declared. Then they took their horses to a gulch at the edge of town, where Swilling stayed while the others returned to Spence's house.

When Swilling signaled about ten o'clock that night, Indian Charlie continued, they went to the rear of the courthouse, across from the theater, and met Curly Bill and John Ringo, who had their horses. Hank Swilling then went back to the gulch and got his horse, but Stilwell and Spence said to leave theirs there, as after they had finished off the two Earps there'd be no reason to run. They waited back of the courthouse for some time, Indian Charlie said, and several people whom he did not know came and went with messages. He added that when he said he thought it was foolish to have so many people know of their plan, Curly Bill told him to shut his mouth.

Some man whom Indian Charlie had not recognized reported that Wyatt Earp had gone to bed, but that Morgan was playing billiards right by Hatch's back door, and that it would be easy to shoot him through the glass and get away through the alley. Curly Bill and Stilwell decided they'd get Morgan, anyway, and the messenger said that if there was any change in the situation, a man named Fries would let them know.

As they were starting for the alley, Fries brought word that Wyatt Earp had just gone into Hatch's. Curly Bill, John Ringo, and Hank Swilling had ridden about halfway to the alley entrance, while the rest walked. Bill and Swilling dismounted, Ringo held their horses, and said he'd watch Fremont Street. Spence and he, Indian Charlie, went toward Allen Street to stand guard there. Other men were at the other end of the alley, he understood.

Curly Bill, Frank Stilwell, and Hank Swilling walked into the alley together, Indian Charlie said. A few minutes later, there was shooting, and everybody ran.

At Patterson's ranch, Indian Charlie heard Frank Stilwell claim that he killed Morgan Earp. Curly Bill and Hank Swilling said they fired at Wyatt, but the glass deflected their shots. Stilwell boasted that he'd killed one Earp and put another out of business; that it was his shot that hit Virgil Earp in the body when he was ambushed, and that he'd get the third one and Doc Holliday with him before he quit. Then, Stilwell, Spence, and Swilling rode for Tucson to fix an alibi for the night before; Curly Bill and he had ridden the other way. He had come to Spence's ranch and he didn't know where Curly Bill was. He had heard that Wyatt had killed Frank Stilwell, and the man who told him had said that the marshal had missed Swilling because he hadn't recognized him in the dark.

That was Wyatt's first intimation that the man in store clothes by the Tucson tracks had been one of Morgan's murderers.

"Who told you that?" the marshal demanded.

"A fellow from Charleston who camped here last night," the halfbreed replied. "I do not know his name."

Indian Charlie was lying now. His informant had been Hank Swilling, in person.

The halfbreed had begun his story in fear for his life, but, as McMasters translated his statements, recovered much of his nerve. The marshal's calmness possibly deceived him.

"Tell him I have told all I know," Indian Charlie said to McMasters. "Ask him if I can go."

Wyatt knew enough Spanish to catch the query. The halfbreed's information had rendered him distinct service, clarified the past and pointed the future. And Indian Charlie might prove useful. Wyatt was about to send him into Tombstone under arrest when another question occurred to him.

"Neither of my brothers nor I ever harmed you, did we?" Wyatt asked.

"No," the breed admitted.

"Then what made you help kill my brother?"

"Curly Bill, Frank Stilwell, Ike Clanton, John Ringo, they're my friends. They said we'd all make money if you were out of the way, and Curly Bill, he gave me twenty-five dollars."

"For what?" Wyatt demanded.

"For shooting anybody who interfered while he killed the Earps," the halfbreed replied on the spur of the moment.

"That twenty-five-dollar business," Wyatt told me years later, "just about burned me up."

Indian Charlie sensed the sudden change his ingenuous admission had wrought. Now, he begged for mercy, with frantic offers to tell much more that his friends had done.

"Sherm," Wyatt said evenly, "tell him in the plainest Spanish you know that he'll have his chance to earn another twenty-five from Curly Bill."

McMasters interpreted.

"Tell him to pull himself together. He's got a pair of guns on. Tell him that the rest of you will step back, that I will count three slowly, in Spanish. That when I say one, he can make his fight, can start for his guns. I will not go for mine until I have counted three. That will give him a jump on me that ought to satisfy even a halfbreed. If he gets me, you and my friends will ride away and not molest him."

Indian Charlie understood English well enough when he wished. Before McMasters translated, his eye shone with renewed hope.

"Make sure he understands," Wyatt cautioned, and McMasters repeated his instructions. The halfbreed nodded, and the interpreter stepped from possible line of fire.

"*Uno,*" Wyatt began.

Indian Charlie's right hand dropped to his gun butt, where it fumbled feverishly.

"*Dos,*" the marshal said.

Indian Charlie was no finished gunfighter. In the face of a target that could shoot back, he couldn't take his time. At last, his six-gun was coming free. But Wyatt Earp had not underestimated his man.

"*Tres!*"

The Buntline Special flashed from the holster, and roared three times. The first slug struck the halfbreed squarely in the abdomen, the second between the shoulders, the third drilled his temples, all before he hit the ground with his unfired weapon clutched at last in his right hand.

Wyatt and his posse rode back to the water hole.

"There's a dead man up near the brush," Wyatt told Johnny Barnes. "Go to Tombstone and notify Coroner Matthews."

Again, if Wyatt had known all there was to know, he might not have let Johnny Barnes go free. The minute Wyatt and his posse were out of sight, Ted Judah rode into Tombstone to report the death of Florentino Cruz to the coroner while Johnny Barnes's pony burned the wind toward the Whetstones.

From Spence's ranch, Wyatt led his posse back to the old

powder-house at the east edge of Tombstone, and sent Texas Jack into town to report his return.

Indian Charlie's body was taken to Tombstone and a coroner's inquest called. Judah and others, scared into truthfulness, testified that the halfbreed had left Pete Spence's ranch, with Spence, the day before Morgan Earp was murdered, and had returned the day after and apparently had firsthand knowledge of the crime. The jury refused to return a verdict against Wyatt in connection with Indian Charlie's death.

The report that Curly Bill and eight followers had been deputized by Sheriff Behan to arrest Wyatt and his posse was further confirmed and confidential agents in Charleston sent word that Curly Bill was somewhere on the Babocomari. Sheriff Bob Paul warned the vigilantes that Behan was proceeding against Wyatt Earp without sanction from Pima County, and that the character of Behan's posse was evidence of his purpose to use Stilwell's death as justification for killing Wyatt Earp and Doc Holliday in cold blood.

"Whenever Pima County desires the arrest of Wyatt Earp," Paul said, "I'll let Wyatt know I want him, and he'll come in. I know where Wyatt is at all times. If he is in Cochise County when I am ordered to serve a warrant, I'll ask Sheriff Behan to go with me, but he must go alone. I have told him that, but he persists in cloaking the most notorious outlaws and murderers in Arizona with the authority of the law. I will have nothing to do with such a gang, and Behan will wish he hadn't if he's with his so-called posse when it meets up with Wyatt Earp. Warrant or no warrant, there'll be a fight, which Wyatt won't lose. I have not been ordered to arrest Wyatt Earp. When I am, I shall proceed according to law."

Wyatt now decided to round up Curly Bill, and arranged to have one thousand dollars sent to him at Iron Springs, where he proposed to camp while riding the Babocomari wilderness.

Iron Springs—on later maps the designation is Mescal

Springs—was a fine water hole in the Whetstone Mountains about thirty-five miles west of Tombstone across the San Pedro Valley, a few miles from the Pima County line and about five miles north of an old Tucson–Tombstone trail, a route supplanted in popular favor by a road across an easier pass. This was the trail by which Frank Stilwell, Hank Swilling, and Pete Spence had made such fast time to Tucson after killing Morgan Earp.

Morgan Earp had been assassinated Saturday night. Within ninety-six hours two of his murderers had paid for his death with their lives. Wyatt was now taking up the trail of the chief instigator and guiding spirit of the plot.

When Wyatt and his posse reached a fork in the trail about five miles from Iron Springs on Thursday afternoon, there was no evidence of travel to the water hole within several days. Numerous horse trails led off from this point in confusing manner, so Wyatt ordered Warren Earp to wait at the fork for Charlie Smith, the Vigilante messenger. Wyatt, Doc Holliday, Sherm McMasters, Turkey Creek Jack Johnson, and Texas Jack Vermillion would ride on and make camp.

The fork to Iron Springs climbed a narrow, rocky canyon into the Whetstones, a veritable inferno beneath the desert sun, and, after two or three miles in which no sign appeared that others recently had used the trail, vigilance relaxed. Wyatt loosened the gunbelts about his waist. Horses and men were weary and hot.

About one hundred yards from the water hole, the trail rounded a rocky shoulder and cut across a flat shelf of deep sand. Ahead, Iron Springs was hidden by an eroded bank possibly fifteen feet high. Beyond the hollow, where the mountain slope resumed, was a grove of cottonwoods. Between this grove and the water hole was an abandoned shack, hidden from view by the bluff. Across the sandy stretch Wyatt rode, coat unbuttoned, six-guns sagging low, Winchester in the saddle boot, Wells-Fargo shotgun and ammunition belt looped to the saddle horn. His horse had quickened at the scent of water and Wyatt let him make the gait.

Fifty feet from the springs, intuition brought Wyatt up short. He swung out of the saddle, looped his reins in his left hand, and with his shotgun in his right hand, walked forward. Texas Jack and Sherm McMasters, still mounted, were behind him, Holliday and Johnson, much farther to the rear. In the sand their advance made no sound. Another step gave Wyatt full view of the hollow. As he took it, two men jumped to their feet less than ten yards away, one yanking a sawed-off shotgun to his shoulder, the other breaking for the cottonwoods.

"Curly Bill!" Sherman McMasters yelled in astonishment, wheeled his horse, and ran. Texas Jack followed instantaneous suit. Curly Bill's shotgun roared, and a double charge of buckshot tore through the skirt of Wyatt's coat where it flared out and hung down over the butt of the six-gun at his right hip.

The outlaw leader threw his hands above his head, hurled the weapon which he had stolen from Bartholomew in the Bisbee stage holdup against the bank almost at Wyatt's feet, screamed once in awful agony, and fell dead. Eighteen buckshot, a double load from Wyatt's Wells-Fargo gun as the marshal pressed both triggers, had struck Curly Bill squarely in the abdomen, just beneath the chest wall, well-nigh cutting his body in two.

Pony Deal, who had been Curly Bill's companion, was almost to the cottonwoods. The flimsy shack threatened to burst as seven other rustlers fought in panic to be first through the narrow door and into the timber.

"From the instant I laid eyes on Curly Bill," Wyatt Earp said in after years, "I was seeing and thinking clearly. Nothing that went on in that gully escaped me, although what happened in a very few seconds takes much longer to tell.

"I can see Curly Bill's left eye squinted shut, and his right eye sighting over that shotgun at me to this day, and I remember thinking, as I felt my coat jerk with his fire, 'He missed me; I can't miss him, but I'll give him both barrels to make sure.'

"I saw the Wells-Fargo plate on the gun Curly Bill was

using and I saw the ivory butts of Jim Hume's pet six-guns in Hume's fancy holsters at Curly Bill's waist as clearly as could be. I recognized Pony Deal, and, as seven others broke for the cottonwoods, I named each one as he ran, saying to myself, 'I've got a warrant for him.'

"Johnny Barnes, Ed and Johnny Lyle, Milt Hicks, Rattlesnake Bill Johnson, Bill Hicks, and Frank Patterson were legging it across the little clearing to join Pony Deal.

"I knew Curly Bill was cut in two and I threw the loop of my shotgun over my saddle horn and grabbed for my rifle. My horse was a high-strung fellow, and I'd started him off by shooting Curly Bill right across his nose. He reared and I missed the rifle."

Pony Deal and his friends chose this moment to open up on Wyatt from the cottonwoods. The rustlers had been too frantic to remember their rifles, were restricted to the six-guns they wore, and were highly excited. Wyatt got behind his horse, but could not calm the animal sufficiently to get his Winchester from the boot. Holding the reins in his left hand, he dropped his right to jerk his own six-shooter. The Buntline Special wasn't there. He finally located the weapon hanging well down on his leg, and at the back. The loose belt had let it slide out of place.

In the meantime Wyatt had been mystified at the absence of support from his posse, and, as he ducked back of his horse, he glanced over his shoulder. Holliday, McMasters, and Johnson were riding for the rocky shoulder at the other side of the open flat, and just about making it. Halfway between was Texas Jack, struggling to get free of his horse which had been killed by the rustlers' fire.

Wyatt turned his six-gun loose at the cottonwoods and was rewarded by yells of pain. He had scored two hits, he knew, possibly a third. In the lull he tried to swing into the saddle, but his gunbelts had slipped down on his thighs and he could not spread his legs to mount. He put two more slugs into the cottonwoods to gain a moment's time in which he managed to hitch the belts to his waistline, shove his empty six-gun into the right holster, and jerk the one from his left hip. With this in his right hand, and with that hand holding his ammunition belts in place, he snubbed the reins in his left hand with which he grasped the saddle horn and endeavored to pull himself astride.

The outlaws cut loose again.

"If you get my position," Wyatt explained, "you'll understand that my nose was almost touching the tip of the saddle horn. I thought someone had struck a match on the end of it—my nose, I mean—and I smelled a very rotten egg."

A forty-five slug from an outlaw's gun had creased the leather point of the pommel.

As his horse quieted, the marshal got astride and his right hand free to put five shots into the timber. Outlaw firing ceased abruptly, and Wyatt jerked his Winchester. His horse now backed steadily while Wyatt kept the cottonwoods covered with his rifle.

"Get out, Jack!" Wyatt shouted to Vermillion who had pried his leg free. But Texas Jack would not leave the saddle and weapons he cherished above all else. He ran around his fallen horse, ripped off the cinches, threw the saddle—rifle boot, shotgun, ammunition belt, and all—over his head and shoulders, turned and streaked it on foot. Doc Holliday spurred out from the turn in the trail and helped Texas Jack to safety.

Wyatt put two rifle shots into the grove as a silencer, wheeled his horse, and made for cover. A volley of pistol shots followed him, and his left leg went numb.

Beyond the shoulder of rock his four companions waited. Their panic had passed.

"That was a great fight you made, Wyatt," Doc Holliday said. "How bad are you hit?"

"Just my left leg, I guess."

Wyatt swung off to inspect damages.

The saddle horn had been splintered, his coat hung in shreds, there were three holes through the legs of his trousers, five holes through the crown of his sombrero, and three through the brim. Despite the numbness in his left leg, he could find no wound. He lifted his boot for closer inspection and found a bullet embedded in the high heel. As far as his body was concerned, he had come out of that hail of lead unscratched. His horse had been nicked in three spots by slugs which barely gouged out the hair.

"Let's go in and get 'em," Doc Holliday urged. Mc-Masters and Johnson seconded the idea.

"We wouldn't last ten yards across the flat," Wyatt said. "They're organized now."

"What'll we do?" McMasters inquired.

"Our horses haven't had water all day," Wyatt replied. "We'll pick up Warren and go find some, and a horse for Jack if we can. We ought to meet Charlie Smith coming in."

At the fork in the trail, Warren was waiting, with no sign of Smith. They went on with Texas Jack up behind Holliday hoping to meet the messenger before they turned off the road.

"I got Curly Bill," Wyatt told Warren, and recounted the happening at Iron Springs.

"Where were the others?" Warren naturally asked.

"I was too far ahead for them to do me any good," Wyatt replied.

Beyond that observation, neither Wyatt nor any of the men who had been with him when the shooting started ever mentioned to one another in Wyatt's hearing the fight at Iron Springs.

"They were good men, and game ones," Wyatt said in after years. "We didn't expect to find anyone at the water hole; there was no sign that the trail had been ridden in days. As we rode up, we'd have sworn there wasn't a man in miles besides ourselves. We learned afterwards that Curly Bill and his crowd had come in by an abandoned trail from the northwest.

"Riding along, half dozing in the saddle—I was the only one fully awake—to run bang into Curly Bill with a sawed-off shotgun in his hands and Pony Deal beside him was enough to startle anyone. Sherm McMasters's wild yell of surprise was the signal. Except for Texas Jack, they were all beyond the turn in the trail before they sensed what was up. Then they were ashamed, but it was too late. I didn't want to rub it in, which is all I could have done if we'd ever discussed it."

From the Whetstones, Wyatt led his posse to camp about four miles from Tombstone. Here Wyatt wrote letters to Wells, Fargo and Company and *The Epitaph,* telling of Curly Bill's death. Texas Jack took these into town and returned with a Vigilante who reported that two of Behan's deputies had watched Charlie Smith so closely that he feared to leave Tombstone. Tony Craker and Dick Wright, two substitute messengers, had started for Iron Springs with Wyatt's expense money, late, but expecting to find him at the water hole.

John Ringo and Hank Swilling had been reported at various points from the San Simon to the Huachucas. Ike Clanton had fled to New Mexico. Ranchers from all parts of Cochise County were now sending undercover information to the Safety Committee about all rustlers under observation and it was believed that once Curly Bill's death became known, the flood of information would increase in volume and value. Wherefore, it was suggested that Wyatt remain where he was for further word of Swilling and Ringo.

26

Johnny Behan's Honest Ranchmen

On Saturday, March 25, one week after Morgan Earp's death, Hank Swilling appeared in Tucson to add his affidavit to Ike Clanton's murder charge against Wyatt Earp in the killing of Frank Stilwell. That evening, Johnny Behan announced he was prepared to take Wyatt Earp "dead or alive."

The Tombstone Safety Committee suggested that Wyatt go north to intercept Swilling on his return from Tucson to the San Simon and pick up John Ringo's trail, if possible. The Vigilantes would communicate further with the marshal through Hooker's Sierra Bonita Ranch.

The Epitaph had published a full account of the battle at Iron Springs, but had purposely misstated the location as Burleigh Springs, to the southwest, to cover the marshal's actual whereabouts. Behan and his followers feared that their whole organization might disintegrate, once Curly Bill's death was established, and were denying that the marshal and the outlaw had met, let alone shot it out.

Wyatt and his posse left the Tombstone powder-house

Sunday morning for Benson, on the strength of authentic word that Hank Swilling would leave Tucson on the Sunday evening train for San Simon. Also, they were told that Sheriff Bob Paul, of Pima County, would reach Tombstone Monday with warrants for Wyatt and Doc Holliday, and had so notified Sheriff Behan.

At Dragoon Summit station, Wyatt went through the evening train in vain search for Hank Swilling. The conductor reported that two men with tickets from Tucson to San Simon station had been summoned from the train at Benson; Swilling had been tipped to the marshal's plans. The Federal posse camped that night near McKittrick's, and on Monday morning, started for Sierra Bonita.

At five o'clock that same morning, Sheriff Johnny Behan and Under-Sheriff Harry Woods left Tombstone with twenty-one men whom Behan characterized in a letter to *The Nugget* as a "brave posse of honest ranchmen," a phrase over which for half a century Tombstone old-timers roared with appreciative laughter. Ike Clanton, John Ringo, Hank Swilling, Phin Clanton, Frank Patterson, Pony Deal, Rattlesnake Bill Johnson, Jim Hughes, Ed and Johnny Lyle, rode as full-fledged deputies in the sheriff's train with ten others of like notoriety. Behan later defended his choice of deputies by explaining that the outlaws were the only persons in Cochise County who would accompany him in pursuit of the Earps. A news dispatch which reported the sheriff's departure concluded:

> Sheriff Paul, of Tucson, returned to that city. He refused to go after the Earps, because the posse selected by Behan was notoriously hostile to the Earps, and said that a meeting with them meant blood, with no probability of arrest.

Deputy Sheriff Hereford was absent from Tombstone, while Deputy Sheriff Breakenridge has recorded that he refused to accompany his chief against the Earp party because Behan would not let him ride the horse he preferred, having assigned that animal to John Ringo.

Progress of Behan's force was reported in bulletins sent to *The Nugget* by everyone who met the doughty sheriff on the trail, and supplemented by wire dispatches every time Behan passed a telegraph office. Beginning with announcement that the trail was "very hot," the bulletins had the "capture imminent," the "posse of honest ranchmen close on the heels of the Earps," the "fugitives trapped," and finally, "poor Frank Stilwell's murderers surrounded with no chance for escape. The Earps must surrender or be killed."

So much for Behan's bulletins. Now for the facts.

When Wyatt Earp and his posse reached Sierra Bonita in the afternoon of Monday, March 27, General Hooker had received confirmation of Curly Bill's death through the Cattlemen's Association; Dan Tipton, sent by the Vigilantes with the money which Tony Craker and Dick Wright had sought to deliver at Iron Springs, was at the ranch.

Craker and Wright had ridden into Iron Springs after dark Thursday, blundering into Pony Deal and his gang in the belief that the campers were Wyatt and his posse. None of the rustlers knew the messengers—one reason for their selection—and the two passed themselves off as teamsters looking for stray mules. As such, they were allowed to water and feed their horses. While the messengers were resting, a spring wagon was driven up the trail from the Babocomari by Frank Patterson, and a lifeless body lifted into it. Craker and Wright also saw that two other men were wounded, Milt Hicks in the arm, and Johnny Barnes in the upper chest or shoulder. The rustlers explained that one of their friends had been killed in a fight and two wounded. They did not say who had fought against them, nor give the name of the man killed, but Craker and Wright recognized the dead man as Curly Bill. Also, they saw a Wells-Fargo gun and a pair of ivory-handled, gold-trimmed Colt's put into the wagon beside the body.

From conversation which they overheard, Craker and Wright were certain that the rustlers were taking Curly Bill's body to Frank Patterson's ranch, but Pony Deal made them ride off before the wagon started down the trail. They had tried for two days to find Wyatt in the Whetstones and had reached Tombstone after he started north. Craker and Wright had told their story to John Thacker and he had gone to the Babocomari to verify Curly Bill's death for Wells, Fargo and Company.

Hooker then said he had been authorized to pay the Cattlemen's Association reward of one thousand dollars for Curly Bill, dead or alive, to Wyatt Earp. Wyatt answered that blood money for Morgan's murderers was one thing he did not want, but that he would like to replace the rented horse which Texas Jack was riding. Hooker had a hundred animals of thoroughbred cross run into his corral.

"Each of you take one," he urged, but Wyatt was satisfied with a fresh mount for Texas Jack.

"How about me?" Dan Tipton asked. "All I've got is that old livery plug."

"He'll get you back to Tombstone," Wyatt said.

"I'm not going back," Tipton insisted. "I'm throwing in with you. Tombstone's done, anyway."

After some argument, Tipton had his way, and picked the gaudiest pinto in Hooker's string.

"Better try again," Wyatt advised. "I never did know a paint horse that knew anything."

Tipton stuck to his choice, and his judgment of horseflesh provided Wyatt's only comment on Tipton's value to the marshal's posse.

Lou Cooley, a Wells, Fargo and Company employee, now rode into Hooker's with an additional one thousand dollars for Wyatt and word that John Thacker had returned to Tombstone with conclusive evidence that Curly Bill had been killed at Iron Springs, had been carried to Frank Patterson's ranch on the Babocomari, and buried there about dawn of Friday morning.

Thacker had seen the grave and talked with the two Mexicans who dug it. They had been put at the job by Patterson when he rode in from Iron Springs to get his wagon, and had worked while he drove back for the body. Later, the pair had filled the hole with dirt. They had seen the dead man's face, plainly, as he was lowered into the grave and recognized Curly Bill. Patterson had paid the gravediggers five dollars each, and threatened to kill them if they ever told of their midnight job. For ten dollars each, the Mexicans said, they would dig up Curly Bill's body, show it to Thacker, and bury it. Thacker also had been told of Curly Bill's death by J. B. Ayers in Charleston, who said that three rustlers who had been at Iron Springs had stopped at his place Friday morning and while drinking had talked freely of the fight and its outcome.

Hooker's foreman, Billy Whelan, interrupted Cooley to report that horsemen were approaching from the southeast. Through field glasses the cavalcade was identified as the Behan posse. Apparently the sheriff had glasses also, for he and his twenty deputies halted well beyond rifle-range.

General Hooker offered the use of his house as a fortress —it had been built to withstand Apaches—and his riders as reinforcements, but Wyatt feared that such a battle would endanger Hooker's family. Pointing to Reilly Hill, an isolated butte about three miles away, on top of which was a spring, he said:

"We'll camp there. When Behan comes up, tell him where we are."

But it was not until daylight Tuesday morning that Behan, who had seen Wyatt depart and must have noted his campfire on Reilly Hill, led his posse up to the Sierra Bonita and demanded, in the name of the law, as General Hooker afterward stated, that men and horses be fed. Hooker issued the necessary orders. While breakfast was cooking, Behan asked Hooker if he knew the whereabouts of the Earp party.

"If I did, I wouldn't tell you," the cattle king replied.

"I warn you," the sheriff replied, "that we are officers of the law and you are protecting murderers and outlaws."

"I am, am I?" General Hooker snapped. "Well, let me tell you something: I know the Earps, and I know you."

He ran his eye over the "honest ranchmen" and named them one by one in scorn.

"Except for you and Woods, there isn't a man in this outfit who hasn't rustled my cattle and horses, or stolen my payrolls. Officers of the law, are you? Well, damn such law, damn you and damn your posse! You're a set of horse thieves and murderers."

General Hooker's remarks are set down exactly as he recorded them, later. At this point, Ike Clanton, possibly remembering the incident of the head in the sack and one thousand dollars he had missed, cut in.

"Damn the son-of-a-bitch!" Ike snarled as he jerked his gun; "he knows where they are. Let's make him tell."

Billy Whelan threw a gun on Ike as he jumped to his employer's side.

"Skin that back!" Whelan ordered. "You can't come here, into a gentleman's home, and call him a son-of-a-bitch. If you're looking for a fight and talk that way, you'll get it before you find the Earps. You can get your fight here. Now, damn you, skin that back! Skin it back!"

Ike Clanton shoved his gun into the holster, with a mumbled apology. Hooker turned to Behan.

"Nice fellows you've got here; murdering horse thieves, every last one of 'em. I'll feed 'em, in the name of the law, but I wouldn't insult an honest cowhand by setting 'em at my bunkhouse table."

Behan and Woods both disclaimed intimacy with their posse.

"They're not our associates," Behan insisted. "They're only with us on this occasion."

"If that's the case," General Hooker replied, "I wouldn't ask even you and Woods to eat with them."

When the sheriff led his men to a table set in a woodshed he found that places had been fixed apart from the others for Woods and himself.

"They took 'em," Hooker commented afterward.

After a breakfast for which payment was neither offered nor asked, Behan announced that he was going to Fort Grant after Apache trailers, and left his men at Sierra Bonita while he rode to interview Colonel Biddle. Fort Grant was just across the valley, in plain view of Sierra Bonita.

But, before leaving the ranch, Behan called Billy Whelan to one side, and asked him not to say anything in Tombstone about occurrences of the morning.

"Here," said the sheriff, taking a diamond stud from his shirt-bosom and handing it to the ranch foreman, "here's a little present for you. It cost a hundred dollars. Take it and forget what you heard this morning."

The cowboy took the stud, and very carefully remembered everything that had happened, to tell about it afterward to every audience that would listen.

At Fort Grant, Behan asked for the services of the Apache scouts to hunt the Earps, and in reply to Colonel Biddle's question admitted that Hooker would not help him.

"Wyatt Earp's United States Marshal," the army officer replied, "and you're the sheriff of Cochise County. I know Wyatt Earp well, and I've heard a lot about you. I string with Hooker. You can't get any scouts here."

Behan countered with a proposition to hire the scouts as private individuals, not as a military force, and said he'd hang up a five hundred dollar reward for them, to be paid if the Earps were killed or captured.

Colonel Biddle knew as well as Johnny Behan what a hundred Apache warriors—scouts, or no scouts—might do when cloaked with a bit of the white man's authority, properly primed with white man's whiskey, and with five hundred dollars hard money, in prospect. He ordered Behan off the reservation.

Back at Hooker's, Behan reported his failure to get the scouts.

"I'll tell you where they are, since you can't find 'em," General Hooker offered. "They're over there on top of Reilly Hill. Wyatt Earp, Doc Holliday, Texas Jack, Turkey Creek Jack Johnson, Sherm McMasters, young Warren Earp, and Dan Tipton. Seven of 'em. There are twenty-one of you. Why don't you go arrest 'em?"

"We hear they're heavily armed," Behan countered.

"Just the way you are," Hooker replied. "Six-guns, rifles, and shotguns. Go on over. Wyatt told me to send you."

Behan drew off for a conference with his men, after which

he rode away from Sierra Bonita, swinging far out from Reilly Hill as he headed for Tombstone, which he reached in safety, as *The Nugget* reported. One item which Under-Sheriff and Editor Woods failed to record in his newspaper was Behan's expense account for his posse. It is of interest, inasmuch as Johnny's friend, business associate, and county treasurer promptly honored the warrant.

> Item: Posse of twenty-one men, three and one half days' ride over approximately 100 miles, three blanket camps, one breakfast at the expense of H. C. Hooker; to Johnny Behan and his honest ranchmen, Cochise County, debtor, $13,000.

After Behan's departure, Wyatt returned to Sierra Bonita and there learned of the presence in Behan's posse of John Ringo and Hank Swilling.

"If I'd known that, I'd have tackled 'em," the marshal commented.

He now moved his camp to Cottonwood Springs, hoping that Ringo and Swilling might fall into his hands when the sheriff's force disbanded.

Pete Spence went into Tombstone when he heard that the marshal was back in the Dragoons, surrendered to Behan on the old stage-robbery charge, and asked for protection in the calaboose. Behan told Spence he could occupy the jail, but would "have to take care of himself." Two nights of this was all that Pete could stand. He stole a horse, rode south to the Mexican border, back to Tucson by the Nogales Road, and was sentenced by territorial court to a long term in Yuma Penitentiary.

On April 4, Wyatt wrote to *The Epitaph* an account of his activities since the fight at Iron Springs. After telling of his camp on Reilly Hill he said:

> Our stay was long enough to notice the movements of Sheriff Behan and his posse of honest ranchers, with whom   had they possessed the trailing abilities of the average Arizona ranchman—we might have had trou

355

ble, which we are not seeking. Neither are we avoiding these honest ranchers, as we thoroughly understand their designs.

Johnny Behan now held closely within the Tombstone limits. His posse broke up. Ringo, Swilling, and Ike Clanton rode at night across the Sulphur Springs Valley toward the San Simon. Wyatt took after them.

In the meantime, *The Nugget* had offered one thousand dollars to anyone who would prove that Curly Bill was dead. *The Epitaph* replied with an offer of incontrovertible proof if *The Nugget* would place its cash in escrow so that there could be no "welshing," and placed two thousand dollars of *Epitaph* cash in escrow to be paid to anyone who could produce Curly Bill alive. Thus began a controversy which became almost a national issue, and which since has raged with undiminished interest among those who have followed the exploits and the endings of the gunmen of the old frontier.

There are as many legends concerning the survival of Curly Bill after the Iron Springs fight as have been woven about the escape of John Wilkes Booth after the death of Abraham Lincoln, and of similar worth. As has been the case with almost every notorious criminal, Curly Bill was scarcely cold in his grave when a hundred would-be heirs to his gory reputation sprang up in the Western camps, each taking his nickname in that peculiar emulation which is stock-in-trade with their kind. Some one of these impostors might have enjoyed his dubious glory throughout the course of history if Johnny Barnes had not crawled into J. B. Ayers's saloon at Charleston and begged for the comfort of a bed in which to die. The outlaw, suffering from an infection of the chest wound received at Iron Springs, said he wanted to square himself before he cashed in, and Ayers sent for Fred Dodge.

To the Wells-Fargo confidential agent, Johnny Barnes told the full story of the outlaw conspiracy, under Behan's protection, with much that neither Dodge nor Wyatt Earp had known. One revelation was that he, Barnes, had been the fifth man in the gang that tried to kill Virgil Earp. It was a charge of buckshot from Johnny Barnes's gun which tore the bone from Virgil's arm and crippled him for life. Also, Barnes verified to the smallest detail Wyatt Earp's story of the battle at Iron Springs. He said that Curly Bill had been taken to Frank Patterson's ranch and buried just at dawn, and told where to find the grave.

In writing of Barnes's confession, nearly fifty years later, Fred Dodge added:

"Later on, Ike Clanton, who was not in the fight, although his knowledge of it was as good as if he had been, told me all about the whole thing, and his account was the same as Johnny Barnes's. The men that were there, of course, were Ike Clanton's men, and *he knew*. It would take a book to explain exactly how I got all my information, but my key to the whole situation was J. B. Ayers."

For almost a month, Wyatt Earp and his posse ranged the Cochise County desert. The leaderless outlaws scattered, a majority riding out of Arizona never to return. And at about this time, Johnny-Behind-the-Deuce returned to pay off his score against the outlaws who once had tried to lynch him and in so doing to pay the debt he owed to Wyatt Earp for the marshal's lone-handed play against the Tombstone mob. Johnny-Behind-the-Deuce set up a lone camp at an isolated water hole in the Chiricahuas, from which he scouted information for Fred Dodge.

John Ringo, Hank Swilling, Pony Deal, and Ike Clanton were located at Fronteras, Sonora, twenty miles south of the Mexican boundary, where they planned to stay. Hank Swilling, however, was killed in an attempt to rob a Mexican trading post, and his three companions fled.

After a series of raids on every rendezvous from the Huachucas to the Peloncillos and the Guadalupe Range, Wyatt had scattered the rustler gang to the far corners of the frontier. Here and there some desperate individual hid out in the mountains, or camped at a little-known desert water hole, but the rule of organized outlawry in Cochise County was broken for all time.

Late in April, Wyatt Earp and his posse returned to the

Tombstone powder-house for conference with the Vigilantes. The marshal wanted the matter of Stilwell's death cleared against Holliday and himself. It was agreed that, if Wyatt and Doc surrendered to the Tucson authorities, Johnny Behan would be waiting with Cochise County warrants at the conclusion of any hearing there, and, furthermore, with certain judges in Pima County office beholden to the Behan political ring, it was possible that the two might be remanded to Behan's custody. Which meant that Wyatt Earp and Doc Holliday would be taken over the Cochise County line and killed in cold blood. Vigilante attorneys advised that Wyatt go to a neighboring state and let Governor Tritle file extradition papers under the Tucson warrant, in which case the worth of the charge could be established before an unprejudiced court. Colorado was chosen for this proceeding.

On his way out of Arizona, Wyatt made one final sweeping cleanup of the water holes, north and east through the Dragoons, across Sulphur Springs Valley, into Galeyville and Paradise through the San Simon, hoping for a chance meeting with Ike Clanton or John Ringo. During this last series of raids, columns of *The Nugget* were filled with wild and purely fictitious tales of fights in which the marshal's posse was engaged, casualties suffered by the posse being enumerated until they wound up on May 10 with publication of the statement that Wyatt Earp was dead, killed in a desperate encounter with a "vigilance committee of cowboys."

It so happened that on that date Marshal Wyatt Earp telegraphed to Sheriff Bob Paul in Tucson that he, Wyatt Earp, and Doc Holliday had reached Gunnison, Colorado, where they would await extradition for the killing of Frank Stilwell. Paul replied asking Wyatt to go to Denver. A news agency dispatch dated Tucson, May 16, reads:

Governor Tritle has placed requisitions in the hands of Sheriff Paul, who leaves for Denver tomorrow. The Tombstone "cowboys" are very indignant that the

Governor has commissioned Sheriff Paul for this business. They wanted Sheriff Behan of Tombstone to have the requisitions and bring the Earps to Cochise County in order that they might have an opportunity to murder them. The wise action of the Governor, however, has frustrated the hope of these bloodthirsty cut-throats.

After a hearing which took due cognizance of depositions from numerous Arizona officials and Tombstone businessmen, Governor Pitkin of Colorado refused to honor the extradition requests, holding that the murder charge was merely a ruse through which Behan and his friends hoped to gain custody of Wyatt Earp and Doc Holliday in defenseless state, "for purposes best known to themselves."

By this time Wyatt had decided not to return to Arizona.

There had come to Wyatt Earp, with brief respite from the red trail of vengeance, a deeper, more poignant sense of Morgan's loss than bloodshed and killing could appease. Solace was no longer to be had from strife; that he knew; for ten full years he had been a fighting man; suddenly his soul was weary and ached for peace.

Moreover, Tombstone, as a prosperous mining community, was definitely through, and once she hit the downgrade, the boom silver camp of the century dropped to obscurity more rapidly than she had shot out of the mesquite to lurid notoriety and fabulous fame. Water flooded the mines. Glory holes pinched out. The silver market slumped. Thousands of men were laid off and the rest struck when wages were cut. Incendiary fires destroyed mine workings and mills; a great conflagration swept the city. Charleston and Contention suffered like catastrophes. Some rebuilding was done, but Charleston was headed for the heap of adobe ruins, Tombstone was sinking to the status of a shadow city, such as they were destined to remain.

After his Denver hearing, Wyatt went to Trinidad, where Bat Masterson had a gambling house, and there he and the men who had accompanied him from Arizona parted company. Wyatt had about two thousand dollars in cash. He split this six ways, giving a full share to each of the others, keeping but one share for Warren and himself.

Sherm McMasters and Turkey Creek Jack Johnson went to Utah, Dan Tipton remained in Trinidad with Bat Masterson; Doc Holliday and Texas Jack went to Denver. Some years later, Doc Holliday died of tuberculosis in a Colorado sanitarium. In the last moment of life, so Wyatt was told, Doc, who often had offered odds of eight-to-five that a six-gun would get him before consumption could, asked for whiskey. His regular ration of a tumblerful was poured and Doc downed it with relish. He smiled up at the man who was caring for him.

"This is funny," Doc said, and died.

From Trinidad, Wyatt and Warren Earp returned to Gunnison, then in the throes of a mining boom, where Wyatt ran his three-hundred-dollar bankroll into a ten-thousand-dollar stake at another man's faro bank.

When it was certain that Wyatt Earp was not returning to Arizona, John Ringo, Ike Clanton, and Pony Deal rode back to Tombstone from Old Mexico. Wyatt never saw them again, but brief mention of their destinies may be of interest here, with a word of Johnny Behan's plunge from power.

In July 1882, John Ringo was found dead in a clump of oak trees in Turkey Creek Canyon, shot through the head. His death was attributed to every cause, from suicide to murder by Buckskin Frank Leslie, and as many legends were woven about his mysterious taking-off as around the supposititious survival of Curly Bill; wherefore, Ringo's death is cited customarily as one of the unsolved mysteries of the frontier. The yarn-spinners have not had access to the old Wells-Fargo reports.

Mention has been made that Johnny-Behind-the-Deuce was to pay in full the debt he owed to Wyatt Earp. The tinhorn hated John Ringo, for Ringo had been ringleader in the Charleston mob which sought amusement in lynching Johnny-Behind-the-Deuce. As Fred Dodge writes in furnishing details of Ringo's death, "Johnny was not in the same class as Ringo." So, when the tinhorn gambler chanced on John Ringo, boiled-drunk and sleeping it off under the oak trees along Turkey Creek, Johnny-Behind-the-Deuce played a sure thing, and shot John Ringo through the head.

Pony Deal and John Yoast found Ringo's body. Deal, who was running with Ringo steadily at the time, suspected Johnny-Behind-the-Deuce, ran the tinhorn down and killed him. Ranchers who buried one John O'Rourke at the edge of Sulphur Springs Valley apparently never suspected that he was Tombstone's legendary figure, Johnny-Behind-the-Deuce.

Pony Deal was killed soon afterward in a gunfight near Clifton, and in the same territory Ike and Phin Clanton were caught red-handed with a bunch of stolen stock. Ike left Phin to face the music, turned to run, and was killed with a shot in the back. Phin Clanton was sentenced to a long term in Yuma Penitentiary.

Months after Ringo's death, Billy Claiborne tangled with Buckskin Frank Leslie in a gunfight. Further line on the historic worth of folklore may be had from the generally credited yarn that Claiborne tried to kill Leslie, because he knew that Buckskin Frank had murdered John Ringo. Charles Liftchild, of the old Tombstone firm Glover and Liftchild, who saw the fight start and finish, is one of a half-dozen eyewitnesses to testify that Claiborne, who was drunk, went after a gun when Leslie put him out of the Oriental, where Claiborne was making himself obnoxious, and that Leslie killed the outlaw in self-defense.

As for Johnny Behan, the sheriff of Cochise County fulfilled completely the promise of his first and only term as a peace officer. Storm clouds, which had gathered while Wyatt Earp's extradition proceedings were under way at Denver, broke with a grand jury indictment against Behan, on May 24, 1882. Then came the deluge. For the next year and more, no inconsiderable portion of Cochise County's criminal docket for 1882–83 was devoted to the sheriff's acts while in office, and Johnny left Tombstone about two jumps ahead of his successor in office. Behan eventually returned to Tucson, where he died.

As for Arizona, it turned to building up a legendary figure of Wyatt Earp. That figure still lives, and is either accused of half the crimes ever committed in the Territory, or hailed as the outstanding exponent of law in a lawless land. On at least one point, all legends agree.

Whatever else may be said of Wyatt Earp, against or for him, and no matter what his motives, the greatest gunfighter that the Old West knew cleaned up Tombstone, the toughest camp in the world.

27

The Last Play

Colorado mining camps boomed in the early eighties, and for five years Gunnison, Trinidad, Silverton, Aspen, and Denver were Wyatt Earp's stamping grounds. He did some prospecting, but spent more time at faro bank or poker tables with greater success. In June of '83, Wyatt made his historic last visit to Dodge City, in response to Bat Masterson's urgent representation that he was the only man in the West who could walk into that cowtown and get an even break.

Luke Short was "short" in Dodge.

Some months after Bat and Luke left Tombstone in 1881, Bat's brother Jim got into difficulties which summoned Bat to Dodge. He stepped from the train into a gun battle with Jim Peacock and Al Updegraff in the Plaza. Half of the camp took a shooting interest in the fight before someone hit Updegraff and Bat and Peacock ran out of ammunition. Bat was ordered out of town under the muzzles of Ab Webster's shotgun. The next season, Dodge City boomed again and

Luke Short returned to purchase the Long Branch from Chalk Beeson.

Ab Webster, elected mayor of Dodge on a "reform ticket," owned the Alamo Saloon, and when Luke Short engaged as a piano player a strikingly attractive young woman who immediately corralled the cowboy trade, Ab had his council pass an ordinance prohibiting employment of females in Dodge City saloons. Luke Short discharged his musician. That night the girl went to work in the Alamo, and the bulk of the Long Branch business followed her.

Luke sent out of town for another pulchritudinous piano-pounder. Mayor Webster posted two deputy marshals in the Long Branch to make sure the new girl did not play. Meanwhile, in the Alamo, the first cause of dissension performed to steadily increasing patronage. Luke announced that, if he couldn't get justice any other way, he'd gun for it. Whereupon the council outlawed Luke. He was put on a westbound train and told he'd be shot if he showed in Dodge again.

Bat Masterson represented to Wyatt that all of Luke's money was in the Long Branch, and that Luke, in fairness, ought to have a chance to settle his business affairs. Knowing Dodge, Wyatt agreed.

While Luke Short and Bat waited at Kinsley, Wyatt went on to the camp. With him he had Texas Jack Vermillion, Dan Tipton, Johnny Millsap, and Johnny Green. The first person Wyatt recognized as he swung off the train at Dodge was Prairie Dog Dave Morrow, by the badge on his shirt a full-fledged officer of the law.

"Hello, Wyatt," Dave said. "I'll bet you're in here to straighten out this Luke Short mess. About time somebody did. Luke got a dirty deal, and the dirty work was wished on me."

"You a marshal now?" Wyatt asked.

When Prairie Dog Dave said that he was, Wyatt introduced his four companions and asked Dave to deputize the five visitors as Dodge City peace officers, which would give them legal right to carry weapons. Dave caught the idea and ran across to the calaboose, from which he returned with five deputy marshals' badges.

Wyatt posted his companions at strategic spots around the Plaza he knew so well, and sent word to Ab Webster that he wanted to meet the mayor and town council in executive session. Wyatt went alone to the powwow, and, after letting the officials know that he had a correct idea of the controversy, concluded:

"Luke Short is at Kinsley. I'll wire him to come on. He'll stay in Dodge as long as he wants to, to continue business, or close out. If Ab Webster has a woman piano player, Luke Short can have one. If Luke can't have one, no one else can. I have four friends in town with me. We're here to see that Luke gets an even break, and we can stay indefinitely. Does he get it?"

Over Ab Webster's protests, the council agreed that Luke did. Short and Masterson came into Dodge on the next train. Luke contended that the marshal's force was stacked against him, and that once Wyatt left, he would again be run out. This resulted in selection of what became known in frontier history as "The Dodge City Peace Commission," eight men appointed to select, in turn, a new set of peace officers for the camp.

Billy Harris, of Beeson and Harris, who had returned to Dodge from Tombstone, Luke Short, Bat Masterson, Billy Potillion, a cowcamp editor, Charlie Bassett, Frank McLean, and Neal Brown made up the Peace Commission under Wyatt Earp as chairman. They functioned for ten days, after which Wyatt returned to Silverton.

In the spring of '84, Wyatt joined the gold rush to the Coeur d'Alene, Idaho, which ended with Wyatt's money in a mining claim that petered out. Lou Rickabaugh, Wyatt's old Tombstone partner, was in El Paso, Texas, then the boom town of the Southwest, and he urged Wyatt to join him. Wyatt's El Paso trip brought his celebrated encounter with Bill Rayner, in what, it transpired, was Wyatt's farewell gesture to the gun-toters of the Old West.

It was inevitable that a man who had achieved the

reputation run up by Wyatt Earp should be thrust again and again into the public eye, no matter how he might wish for peaceable retirement, and when Wyatt reached El Paso in April 1885, it was reported at once that he had come to take the marshal's job, a post which had cost the lives of several proficient peace officers, and for which a competent man was sought. Nothing was further from Wyatt's mind, but the rumor would not down, and on the evening of April 14, a deputy United States Marshal warned Wyatt that Bill (William P.) Rayner and Buck (Charles N.) Linn were out to show him up.

Bill Rayner, on his periodical hunts for trouble, aimed to merit his sobriquet of "the best-dressed badman in Texas," and when he pushed through the swinging doors which separated the bar of Taylor and Look's Gem Saloon from Lou Rickabaugh's billiard room and gambling casino at the rear, he looked the part. He wore a black sombrero, black Prince Albert, and gray trousers pulled down over a pair of fine black boots. In his left hand he carried a pair of light gray gloves; his right hand hung to the skirt of his coat, which was unbuttoned and flaring slightly at either hip over the butt of an ivory-handled Colt's. Rayner was primed for doings reported in next morning's *Times,* under the heading:

EL PASO INDULGES IN A LITTLE PISTOL PRACTICE

Powder Is Explosive

Wyatt Earp sat at Rayner's left in a high spectator's chair near the front door. Every similar seat was occupied, a long row down each side of the room. Rayner stepped up to the first man at his right and slapped him across the mouth with his gloves. The victim was startled, but, knowing Rayner, evaded the challenge.

Wyatt Earp, in his custom, was unarmed. He sat quietly, watching Rayner's progress across the room, knowing, as everyone else in the place appeared to, that the play was aimed at him. Rayner was slapping every face as he reached it, stopping before each chair to follow the blow with some scurrilous remark. At regular intervals he swept the coat-skirts back, to display his dreaded pair of guns. No one tried to get out of Bill Rayner's way, but, as he started up the row of chairs toward Wyatt, those he had passed edged out of a possible line of fire. Wyatt sat with his attention apparently on a billiard game, but the corner of his eye caught Rayner's every move.

"I figured I could do either of two things," Wyatt said: "walk out, or wait for him. I couldn't have stayed in El Paso if I had dodged the issue, and I wasn't aiming to be run out of town. So I sat still.

"Rayner assumed that I carried a gun, and his play was to go for his gun with his right hand as he struck at me with his left. So I said to myself, 'You slap and I'll show you a trick they don't know in Texas.'

"I didn't move as Rayner came up the line, except to shift my weight to my left arm, leaving my right free. When he slapped, he'd expect to see my right hand go to my belt or my left armpit. Instead, my right fist was going to catch Mr. Rayner smack on the jaw, as hard as I could punch, and, if I was any guesser, his fight would leave him then and there."

Rayner hit the man next to Wyatt a sharp blow, paused for the resentment which he knew would not be expressed, and stepped in front of Wyatt Earp.

"Your name is Wyatt Earp, I believe," Rayner observed.

"That's right," Wyatt admitted.

"You're quite a fellow, I understand."

"I never said so."

"You've never met any Southern gentlemen, I take it?"

"Quite a few gentlemen," Wyatt replied.

Rayner drew his gloves through the groove of his right hand, and smacked them smartly against the palm.

"Then I suppose you know that when a Southern gentle-man goes hunting trouble, he likes to take his gloves along? He sometimes finds them useful."

"The kind of trouble you're heading into right now,

Rayner," Wyatt said in a cold, even voice, "can't be handled with gloves."

"Oh, you know who I am?"

"Certainly, and what you're aiming to do."

"And what are you going to do about it?"

"You slap my face and you'll learn. You'd have saved time if you'd walked right up to me instead of spreading your brag all over the place."

The best-dressed badman in Texas had another idea.

"Will you take a drink with me?" he inquired.

"Certainly," Wyatt answered, arose and went with Rayner to the bar.

Before ordering, Rayner suggested that relations would be less strained if each placed his weapons on the bar, and made some show of putting one Colt's in front of him.

"I don't carry a gun," Wyatt replied, opening his coat, and slapping his pockets to show that this was truth.

"In that case," Rayner observed, "I ought to buy wine."

Dan Tipton, Wyatt's friend of Tombstone days, now in El Paso with the United States Customs, entered and overheard enough to surmise what was in the air. The wine consumed, Rayner took his Colt's from the bar, and walked into the gambling room. Tipton sidled up to Wyatt and handed him a six-gun.

"Take this, Wyatt," he urged. "When Rayner gets this way, he's got to fight, and he'll be coming at you again."

Wyatt slipped the forty-five into his pocket, and walked with Tipton toward the faro tables.

Bob Cahill, a young fellow about twenty-one, was dealing at one of Rickabaugh's games, at which "Cowboy Bob" Rennick was a player. Rayner walked to the back of Rennick's chair and began to flip the brim of the cowman's sombrero. When Rennick asked the trouble-hunter to stop bothering him, Rayner announced, "I am going to the bar. I shall have a drink and I shall return. Then, Mr. Rennick, you may throw me out."

As Rayner strode through the room, Rennick reached across the faro layout, grabbed a six-gun from the dealer's drawer, and jumped from his seat. Bill Rayner burst back through the swinging doors, a six-gun in either hand, the right roaring as he came. Four slugs splintered the chair where Rennick had been, before Rayner discovered that the seat was unoccupied. Rennick shot twice, hitting Rayner in the left chest and the right abdomen. Rayner dropped his guns, turned and staggered to the street, dropped unconscious, and was taken home to die.

Five minutes later, Buck Linn tore up and down El Paso Street with a gun in either hand, stuck his head through the door of the Gem Saloon, fired four wild shots in the direction of the rear room, and went out again, hunting, he said, Bob Cahill, the faro dealer whom he erroneously blamed for Rayner's wounds. Bob Cahill was still dealing faro when word came that Buck Linn had left the Ranch Saloon with the announcement that he was going back to the Gem and kill Cahill.

"Someone let me take a gun," the dealer requested.

"Better get out while you can," Wyatt Earp advised.

"I'm sticking," Cahill answered. "Let me take a gun."

Tipton handed over the weapon that Wyatt had returned to him.

"What'll I do?" Cahill asked. "I never was in a gunfight in my life."

"You'd better get out," Wyatt repeated. "We can calm this fellow."

Cahill insisted that he would stick.

"All right," Wyatt said. "If you're going to make your fight take your time. He'll come shooting. Have your gun cocked, but don't pull until you're certain what you're shooting at. Aim for his belly, low. The gun'll throw up a bit, but if you hold it tight and wait until he's close enough, you can't miss. Keep cool and take your time."

Buck Linn came through the swinging doors.

Wyatt leaped back against the wall.

"Take your time, Cahill," he called. "Take your time."

Linn circled the billiard tables, shooting rapidly.

Bob Cahill took Wyatt Earp's advice and waited until Linn's third shot, when Linn was about ten feet away. He fired once, then a second time as Linn cut loose with his fourth. Cahill's first bullet tore through Linn's abdomen and splintered his spinal column; the second struck him squarely in the heart. Buck Linn was dead when he hit the floor.

Both Rennick and Cahill were acquitted in the deaths of Rayner and Linn, as having shot in self-defense.

"The victims had no one to blame but themselves," the *El Paso Herald* observed. "Their train of life collided with loaded revolvers and they have gone down forever in the smash-up. Thus endeth the first chapter of our spring fights."

Upon leaving El Paso, Wyatt Earp returned to California, where he spent the next two years in San Diego, during the realty boom which transformed that sleepy Spanish village into its first semblance of a Yankee town, and where Wyatt added considerably to his means. There was a good bit of the mining-camp atmosphere to San Diego's recreational life in those days, and at various times Wyatt owned and operated establishments which outshone Tombstone's Oriental for play and pay. In San Diego, Wyatt acquired the first of his thoroughbred racehorses, which were to occupy him at San Francisco and on Eastern tracks for the ensuing decade, and by the nineties, Wyatt was held as an outstanding authority on sporting events, as one newspaper put it, "sustained by the respect dealt to a generation of reputation for gameness, squareness, and fair play."

In 1894, Wyatt's reputation as the one man feared by all Western desperadoes called him temporarily from his stock farm near San Jose. During violent labor troubles, the Southern Pacific Railroad found it desirable to send a pay train carrying several hundred thousand dollars in cash from Oakland to El Paso with stops at numerous isolated points between. Outlaw plans to hold up the pay train were suspected and Wyatt was asked to guard the treasure. He wiped the dust from his old Wells-Fargo gun and with it climbed into the cab of the pay train locomotive. Wyatt Earp's guardianship of the huge cash shipment was widely published and the pay train went through to destination unmolested.

In the late fall of 1896 the all-absorbing topic in the boxing world was the forthcoming bout between Bob

Fitzimmons and Tom Sharkey, scheduled for December 2, at Mechanics' Pavilion in San Francisco, for a ten-thousand-dollar purse. J. J. Groom and John Gibbs, promoters of the bout, could not name a referee to meet the approval of Martin Julian, Fitzimmons's brother-in-law and manager, and it was finally decided that the National Athletic Club governing board was to pick the referee the afternoon before the fight.

Wyatt Earp, who was racing at Ingleside, was in the lobby of the Baldwin Hotel at noon of December 2, about to take a streetcar to the track. In preparing for his trip, he had stuck his old Buntline Special in a holster on his right hip. Late streetcars from Ingleside had been providing booty for a gang of highwaymen who sought the cash which racetrack men necessarily carried, and Wyatt, who usually had several thousand dollars in his pocket, did not intend to let his money go without a fight. Groom and Gibbs came into the hotel with a representative of the National Athletic Club and asked Wyatt to referee the Fitzimmons–Sharkey bout.

Wyatt demurred because of Julian's advertised attitude, but finally agreed to officiate if no more suitable person was found.

"I'll be at dinner in Goodfellow's Restaurant, across the street from the pavilion at eight o'clock," he said. "If you can't get anybody else, you can find me there."

With which preliminary, Wyatt went from his dinner table to the ringside five minutes before the main event was called.

The happenings in Mechanics' Pavilion on the evening of December 2 created more furor, possibly, than any similar event in the history of the American prize ring. So much was and has been made of it that a factual account may illuminate an otherwise endless dispute. In addition to Wyatt's own recollections, there are offered the opinions of numerous sports reporters at the ringside, and their running accounts of happenings set down at the time. Hearsay, rumor, and legend are cited, for what they may be worth.

Twenty thousand rabid prize-ring enthusiasts crowded Mechanics' Pavilion when Wyatt Earp crawled through the ropes in response to the announcement that he would referee. To quote the Associated Press reporter's ringside dispatch, "the crowd howled for Earp."

Certain individuals howled also their disapproval and Wyatt raised his hand. He intended to make his position clear with words, for him a most unusual undertaking.

"I have been asked to referee this bout," he said. "There has been so much advance scandal, with rumors of 'fixing' and crookedness, that no matter what happens, I'll be accused of dirty work. The National Athletic Club and the promoters want me to referee. I don't care how the fighters and their managers feel about it. But, if you spectators don't want me, I don't want the job. I'll call things as I see them, not as someone else may want them called. With that understood, if you people out there want me, I'll go ahead."

The howl of approval which the twenty thousand set up determined Wyatt's course, and he stripped off coat and vest for his work. Then the twenty thousand did roar.

"I had completely forgotten how I was dressed," Wyatt recalled, "and there on my right hip, the old Buntline forty-five, with its twelve-inch barrel and the walnut butt, stuck out like a cannon. I know I turned red to my heels as I unbuckled the gun and handed it to Police Captain Whitman, who sat at the ringside."

"He's a two-gun man!" someone shouted. "Get the gun inside his shirt!"

"Have you got another gun, Wyatt?" the policeman asked.

"No," Wyatt replied.

"Search him!" one of the objectors yelled.

Whitman stood up, and bellowed:

"Wyatt Earp's word is good with me!"

Again the majority voiced raucous approval and the fighters were called to the center of the ring.

Bob Fitzimmons was a finished boxer, Tom Sharkey probably the most awkward fighter who ever graced a squared circle; and Ruby Bob was perfecting that right uppercut to the solar plexus which was to win world championship. His technique called for a left to the jaw just prior to this blow, which would straighten up his opponent and leave his abdomen a shining mark. In the third round, so ringside reporting had it, Wyatt Earp would have been justified in awarding the decision to Sharkey when one of Fitz's rights hit the sailor below the belt.

"You hurt?" the referee asked.

"Not much," Tom gasped. "Don't stop it!"

Sharkey was a glutton for punishment, if one ever lived. Twice, in subsequent rounds, Wyatt warned Fitzimmons about his body blows.

In the eighth round, Fitzimmons landed a left hook squarely on the button of Sharkey's jaw and started his huge right fist from the floor to Sharkey's abdomen. Any fighter less awkward than Tom would have given way from that punch to the jaw. Sharkey could be counted on to do the unexpected and he stumbled forward instead of back Fitzimmons's right, coming up, struck the sailor in the groin. Sharkey collapsed. Wyatt waved Fitzimmons to his corner, and awarded the decision to Sharkey on a foul. But let the Associated Press ringside reporter continue·

> Sharkey was undoubtedly badly hurt. He was unable to move his legs, though he clutched spasmodically at his groin with his gloved hand. His seconds rushed into the ring and raised him up, but he fainted away and was borne from the ring unconscious. Hardly any one of the spectators saw the foul. It was apparently unintentional.

Upon receiving physicians' confirmation of the foul blow, Wyatt handed a certified check for ten thousand dollars to Lynch, Sharkey's manager. Martin Julian howled his protests, but the crowd booed him down. Next day, when Lynch tried to cash the winner's check, he learned that payment had been stopped through court injunction obtained by Julian. This touched off the fireworks.

The owner of a San Francisco newspaper, who had bet twenty thousand dollars on Fitzimmons to win the fight, devoted columns in his newspaper to support Julian's protest, with the open charge that Wyatt Earp's decision had been determined in advance, and out of a matter of no very great importance, promoted an international issue.

Reporters in their follow-up stories stressed repeatedly the irrefutable evidence that Sharkey had been fouled, but the San Francisco newspaper owner was determined to save his twenty thousand dollars even after the injunction withholding Sharkey's purse had been thrown out of court. He prosecuted Wyatt Earp for carrying a pistol without a permit, on which charge Wyatt paid a fifty-dollar fine, and dug up every episode of Wyatt's career as a peace officer which might be colored to discredit him. He charged that Wyatt had telegraphed to friends all over the country just before the fight, instructing them to bet on Sharkey, but at the showdown was unable to produce copies of any such messages filed or identify any recipients of such a tip. Next, he telegraphed to towns where Wyatt had lived, in search of opinions derogatory to the man. The reply from Wichita is typical of what he got.

"Wyatt Earp is the most fearless man I ever met," Dick Cogswell replied in behalf of his community. "He was marshal here and he was marshal of Dodge when these were cattle-shipping points, and he was a success. Wyatt Earp is an honest man. All who were associated with him here declare that he would decide in accordance with his belief in the face of an arsenal."

The San Francisco short-sport did not print this in his newspaper, but an enterprising reporter gave it to a press association, and the campaign against Wyatt Earp's general reputation ceased. Hard on the heels of this news, a committee of six physicians, two designated by the complaining newspaper, two by promoters of the bout, and two selected by the first four medical men, filed a report on their examination of Sharkey, which established conclusively that he had been fouled, and the newspaper owner quit the fight. His sole accomplishment had been to start an argument which hearsay authorities were to dispose of with their customary aplomb in every gathering of sporting men for the next quarter-century.

Some weeks after the Sharkey–Fitzimmons imbroglio,

Judge W. F. Fitzgerald, then Attorney General of California, who had been justice of the Arizona Supreme Court at Tucson during Wyatt's Tombstone days, asked Wyatt to come to his office in San Francisco.

"Wyatt," Judge Fitzgerald said, "William McKinley takes office as President next March and he has asked me to recommend the right man for United States Marshal of Arizona. The job is yours if you'll take it."

Wyatt was flabbergasted.

"Why, I couldn't," he said. "There's a murder warrant against me in Tucson, for that Stilwell business."

It was Judge Fitzgerald's turn to evidence surprise.

"Do you mean to tell me you've let that hang over you all these years?" he asked.

"Couldn't help it," Wyatt replied. "I'm still wanted in Arizona for murder, and"—he added with a grin—"as far as I know, I'm still a United States Marshal for the Southeastern District of that Territory."

"Didn't Bob Paul write you what happened?" Fitzgerald went on. "He was supposed to. After Colorado refused to honor the extradition, we found that, with Behan disposed of, there was no one to press any charge against you, and from all the evidence available, the killing of Stilwell was justifiable homicide if ever there was one. So the Supreme Court quashed the indictment. There's no reason in the world why you shouldn't go back to Arizona. Your appointment as United States Marshal will be acceptable to the Republicans of the Territory; I've already made sure of that."

"I'll think it over," Wyatt said. "I appreciate all that the offer implies, but I want some time."

When he returned to Judge Fitzgerald with his decision against accepting the Arizona appointment, Wyatt explained:

"It would give me satisfaction to return to Arizona as United States Marshal, but it would make trouble. Every braggart in the Territory would be gunning for me, simply to run up a reputation. You and I know the stripe too well to believe otherwise. I'd have to shoot, or be shot; and there are a lot of newcomers over there who wouldn't appreciate that. The old-timers will understand why I'm turning down the job."

After another season with his racehorses, Wyatt left San Francisco to join the stampede of '97 to the Alaskan goldfields. In Nome he opened and ran the Dexter, as famous for color and high play as the Oriental had been in the Tombstone boom. He returned to the States in the fall of 1901, and, after outfitting in Los Angeles, drove overland on a prospecting expedition to the boom camp of Tonopah, Nevada.

For the five years next succeeding, Wyatt Earp and his four-animal hitch of mules roamed the California and Nevada deserts, on the prospecting expeditions which kept him in the wilderness he preferred to the settlements. In San Francisco he had married Josephine Sarah Marcus, daughter of a pioneer merchant in that city, who, as Wyatt put it, "was a better prospector and camper than I ever hoped to be."

After a season in Goldfield, Wyatt and Mrs. Earp headed their mules south into the Colorado River country, through Rhyolite, Las Vegas, and the Needles to the Mojave Mountains, prospecting as they went. In the desert foothills of the Whipple Range, Wyatt discovered and staked the Happy Day group of gold and copper mines.

In the meantime, Wyatt developed Kern County oil lands which he had pioneered to lucrative production, and for the closing years of his life he and Mrs. Earp divided their time between their highly profitable oil and mining properties and their homes in Oakland and Los Angeles.

Warren Earp had returned to Arizona in 1900, and while employed as special officer for the Arizona Cattlemen's Association was killed by two cowboys. Virgil Earp, after recovery from wounds received in Tombstone, had served for some time as marshal of Colton, California—a position in which his identity often has been confused with Wyatt's. He had joined Wyatt during the Goldfield excitement and died of pneumonia in that camp in 1906. Wyatt's father, Nicholas Earp, died at Colton in 1907; his brother Jim, at

Los Angeles, in 1926; and Newton, his half-brother, at Sacramento, California, two years later.

The years of 1927 and 1928, Wyatt Earp devoted largely to providing the material upon which this narrative of his life has been based. The enterprise was against his first inclination, but no clearer statement of his subsequent attitude is possible than that of the letter which announced his eventual decision to provide the first full and accurate account of his career as a marshal of the Old West.

"I am not ashamed of anything I ever did," Wyatt wrote. "Notoriety has been the bane of my life. I detest it, and I have never put forth any effort to check the tales that have been published in recent years of the exploits in which my brothers and I are supposed to have been the principal participants. Not one of them is correct.

"My experiences as an officer of the law are incidents of history, but the modern writer does not seem willing to let it go at that.

"What actually occurred at Tombstone, for example, was only a matter of weeks; it was not my whole life. My friends have urged repeatedly that I make the truth known in print. Now, you and I shall do it, and correct many mythic tales."

On January 12, 1929, some time after we had finished the two-year series of conversations which have been transcribed into this work, Wyatt wrote me that he feared an illness of several years back was recurring, and that we might have to postpone for a few days our trip to the desert country he loved so well and during which we were to round up any loose ends to be found dangling in my end of our mutual undertaking. In the course of this letter he remarked:

"For my handling of the situation at Tombstone, I have no regrets. Were it to be done over again, I would do exactly as I did at that time. If the outlaws and their friends and allies imagined that they could intimidate or exterminate the Earps by a process of assassination, and then hide behind alibis and the technicalities of the law, they simply missed their guess.

"I want to call your particular attention again to one fact, which writers of Tombstone incidents and history apparently have overlooked: with the deaths of the McLowerys, the Clantons, Stilwell, Florentino Cruz, Curly Bill, and the rest, organized, politically protected crime and depredations in Cochise County ceased. Oh, yes, there were individual crimes committed thereafter, as there would be in any bailiwick, but organized outlawry ended with the deaths of Curly Bill and his gang.

"Let me repeat:

"For my handling of the situation at Tombstone, I have no regrets. Were it to be done over again, I would do exactly as I did at that time."

Just before daylight Sunday morning, January 13, 1929, Wyatt Earp died, quietly and peacefully at his Los Angeles home. Had he lived two months and six days longer, he would have been eighty-one years old.

Mrs. Earp survived him; there were no children.

One monument to the memory of Wyatt Earp is of a type, I think, that would please him greatly if he could know. A few weeks after his death, it became desirable to fix a permanent name for the United States post office and railroad station which serves the little desert town nearest to Wyatt's Happy Day group of mines. Some three hundred neighbors and friends—miners, ranchers, storekeepers, and other hardy souls on the edge of the last frontier—joined with the Santa Fe Railroad in petitioning the Government to acknowledge the contribution which Wyatt Earp had made to the building of the West. The Government complied, and the settlement in the heart of the Colorado Desert—almost in the shadow of the Hoover Dam that is to reclaim a barren wilderness for a softer generation—is now officially known as Earp.

Perhaps the notable feature of a thousand varying accounts of Wyatt's exploits on the old frontier which have filled newspaper columns since his death has been the unanimity with which writers have marveled that the man could have come through his long and hazardous career physically unscathed. And there is striking evidence of the place this most famous marshal of the old frontier has come to occupy in Western lore in the fact that few have thought to speculate upon the possibility of deeper hurts, the scars of wounds that never heal.

Yet, in my last talk with Wyatt, he said to me:

"The greatest consolation I have in growing old is the hope that after I'm gone they'll grant me the peaceful obscurity I haven't been able to get in life."

Not vindication, nor exculpation, it is to be noted; he asked merely to be let alone.

INDEX

Index